Cursed with a p[...] propensity to re[...] of her childhood lost in books. A degree in English Literature followed by a career in computing didn't lead directly to her perfect job—writing romance for Mills & Boon—but she has no regrets in taking the scenic route. She lives in London: a city where getting lost can be a joy.

Meredith Webber lives on the sunny Gold Coast in Queensland, Australia, but takes regular trips west into the Outback, fossicking for gold or opal. These breaks in the beautiful and sometimes cruel red earth country provide her with an escape from the writing desk and a chance for her mind to roam free—not to mention getting some much needed exercise. They also supply the kernels of so many stories that it's hard for her to stop writing!

WINNING THE SURGEON'S HEART

ANNIE CLAYDON

CONVENIENTLY WED IN PARADISE

MEREDITH WEBBER

MILLS & BOON

First Published in Great Britain 2020
by Mills & Boon, an imprint of HarperCollins*Publishers*
1 London Bridge Street, London, SE1 9GF

Winning the Surgeon's Heart © 2020 by Annie Claydon

Conveniently Wed in Paradise © 2020 by Meredith Webber

ISBN: 978-0-263-27963-4

MIX
Paper from
responsible sources
FSC® C007454

Printed and bound in Spain
by CPI, Barcelona

WINNING THE SURGEON'S HEART

ANNIE CLAYDON

MILLS & BOON

CHAPTER ONE

SILENCE FELL. FROM the thirty people who had entered the challenge, there could only be two winners, and it looked as if the judges were ready to announce who they were.

Hannah's friend, Sophie, was bent forward, clutching her knees and stretching the muscles in her back. The most challenging task in a long and challenging day had been saved until last, an obstacle course that had drained everyone. But they'd done it together. Hannah laid her hand on Sophie's shoulder and she looked up, grinning.

'I think you're in with a chance. Not so sure about me.'

'We'll find out soon enough. Are you okay?'

Sophie nodded, straightening. 'We'll all be aching tomorrow.'

This was more than just a matter of winning for herself. Hannah and Sophie had worked together for five years, crewing an ambulance that worked out of Hamblewell Hospital. When the hospital had entered Arial TV's *Hospital Challenge*, lured by a generous cash prize, they'd decided to enter together. The selection day had involved both physical and mental challenges, and was designed to whittle thirty entrants down to two, who would go on to represent the hospital in the televised challenge. Hannah had set her heart on winning with Sophie.

She caught Sophie's hand, squeezing it. A stage had

been erected on the open space behind the hospital building, and in the heat of a summer's day there was almost a carnival atmosphere amongst the spectators. The chairman of the judging panel had picked up the microphone and was tapping it to see whether it was working. A frustrated murmur travelled through the crowd that had come to watch and cheer the competitors on.

'Get on with it, mate.' Sophie whispered, and Hannah nodded. The suspense was getting to her as well.

'The judges have come to a decision—'

The microphone cut out suddenly, and Hannah rolled her eyes. If they'd wanted to keep everyone on tenterhooks for as long as possible, this couldn't have been planned any better.

There was a short pause as the microphone was inspected and pronounced fit for use, without the need for any further tapping. The judge smiled, turning once more towards the crowd.

'Sorry about that… As you all know, today's winners will go forward to represent Hamblewell Hospital in the Hertfordshire heats of *Hospital Challenge*, the first of which will be hosted here next Saturday. We hope you'll all be here to cheer our team on. We've been obliged to choose just two winners today and our task hasn't been easy…'

There was a pause. Everyone was holding their breath already, and if the guy didn't get on with it, someone was going to pass out. It was just as well that there were plenty of medical staff on hand…

'Hannah Greene!'

Hannah heard a cheer go up, somewhere far away. She felt Sophie grab her, hugging her tight. Suddenly it felt as if her legs weren't going to carry her.

'Go… Go.' Sophie had freed her now, and was pushing

her towards the stage, where the judges were all on their feet and joining in with the applause.

'Sophie…' Hannah didn't want to go alone. She'd thought that both names would be announced together, and taking this walk without her friend seemed impossible.

'You've won, Hannah. You've got to go and shake the man's hand.' Sophie gave her one last push, and a path opened up in front of her through the other competitors. She walked towards the podium in a daze.

Then it hit her. Sophie was going to be next, it was impossible that the judges hadn't seen the way they'd encouraged each other in completing the challenges. They were already a team, used to going together into every kind of situation. Hannah climbed the steps onto the stage, shook the judges' hands and then turned to the crowd, throwing her arms up. Everyone cheered wildly, and she could see Sophie jumping up and down, suddenly finding that last bit of energy.

'We've obviously made a popular choice.' The judge smiled, waiting for the cheering to die down, and there was silence again. 'And going on to join Hannah for *Hospital Challenge* is Matt Lawson…'

What?

Hannah tried to smile, but it felt as if her own achievement had suddenly turned to dust. She didn't even *know* Matt Lawson. She looked for Sophie, and she was cheering along with everyone else, seeming not to notice that it was her name that should have been called.

The crowd parted, and a man began to walk towards the stage, stopping to shake a few hands as he went. Hannah *did* know him, although not by name. He had a reputation as being an excellent surgeon, but many of the female staff ignored that and concentrated on his looks. Hannah herself had been guilty of a little objectification on that score…

His sun-coloured hair and the tan gave him the look of someone who spent more time outdoors than inside. Probably blue eyes. Hannah had imagined the blue eyes and then consigned the whole image to the *look-don't-touch* category.

She felt herself blush as he shook the judges' hands, and then grinned at her. Blue. They were blue, the shade more intoxicating than she'd imagined. Dark, like a Mediterranean sea.

That was where he belonged. On a holiday she had no intention of taking. Not here, not in her real life. He congratulated her, and then turned to wave to the crowd. This was *not* happening.

She stood, trying to smile, for what seemed like an age, until they were allowed to climb down from the stage. Sophie was the first to get to Hannah and hug her.

'I'm so excited… And you've got the dreamboat as a partner!'

Hannah felt tears of exhaustion and disappointment in her eyes. 'I don't want him. Why didn't they pick you?'

Sophie puffed out a breath. Hannah was about to get one of her friend's reality checks.

'Look, I'm not going to pretend that I'm not disappointed. But you did a lot better than me, and so did he. Did you see the way he got over that climbing wall?'

Yes. Hannah had looked, just as Sophie had. Matt Lawson had been in the second group around the obstacle course, and they'd both seen the way he'd negotiated the steep wall. And she'd dared to notice that he looked just as good—better actually—in action than he did when she'd seen him walking along the corridors of the hospital.

'I can't do it on my own, Sophie. We're a team.'

'Well, you're just going to have to get used to being in a new team, aren't you? I'll be cheering you on all the way.'

'But…' This sounded a lot like self-pity. She should be thinking about how Sophie must be feeling, not having been chosen after all the effort they'd put in. 'I'm so sorry…'

'Nonsense. We said that we'd be happy if just one of us was chosen, didn't we? This is *my* achievement as well, we did it together. Give me a break, will you?'

They'd said it would be enough if just one of them won. Hannah hadn't actually meant it. But Sophie was glowing with joy, and it would be unfair if she didn't feel it too.

'You'll stick with me, won't you? I can't do this without you.'

'Are you kidding? I'll be with you all the way. You'll be there for both of us, eh?'

Matt hadn't seriously expected to win this thing. As the only member of the surgical team who'd had any chance of being able to negotiate a climbing wall, he'd been strong-armed into signing up for the challenge by his colleagues, who had all been keen to have someone represent them. He'd stepped up his gym routine a bit for the last three weeks, and that had been about it.

He'd seen Hannah and her partner, making their way around the obstacle course. They were both fit, and both up for the challenge, but Hannah was clearly the stronger of the two. Although the tasks they'd encountered today were meant to be done individually, he'd seen Hannah slow a little once or twice, waiting for her partner to follow so that they could pace each other around the course.

They were a team. They wore matching T-shirts, emblazoned with the logo of the ambulance service. He knew that the nature of their job meant that they had to rely on each other, and that the ambulance crews had a fierce sense of pride. He wondered how Hannah felt about being teamed up with a complete stranger.

She'd seemed less than enthused about the judges' decision when he'd been called up to the stage. But as she walked towards him across the grass, she was smiling. Matt had to admit that it was a very nice smile, at that.

'Congratulations.'

'That was a surprise…' He felt strangely at a loss for words. 'For me, I mean. You were a dead cert to win.'

She blushed a little. It was a fine accompaniment to her smile. 'You made it over the climbing wall in one go. I took two.'

Matt was privately of the opinion that she could have done it in one. His automatic assessment of her mobility and strength told him that the wall shouldn't have been a problem for her and that her partner was the one who'd taken two goes. The judges had clearly seen that as well, and Matt decided not to mention it.

'I'm looking forward to the next round.'

Hannah nodded. 'Me too. Would you like to meet up? To train?'

That sounded rather more enticing than Matt had supposed it might. Hannah's was the kind of beauty that was enhanced by the application of a little grime and sweat. This morning, he'd noticed her chestnut hair tied back in a shining plait at the back of her head. And, of course, her smile. But as the day had gone on, he'd started to appreciate her fearlessness and tenacity. She was messy and exhausted, but she still shone.

'I'm afraid I can't this week, I have a pretty full schedule at work. I imagine they're going to be throwing the unexpected at us next Saturday, so I guess the best we can do is just keep up the fitness training and get a good night's sleep on Friday.'

That obviously wasn't the answer that Hannah was looking for. It was too bad, because he couldn't just put off a few operations because it happened to suit him. She should understand that.

'Okay. Well… I'll keep training with Sophie. As long as you don't mind.' She motioned towards her partner, who was walking towards them.

'Why should I? If it works, don't mess with it.'

She and Sophie had the kind of partnership that Matt had observed in others, and had never really experienced for himself. He was part of a team at work, in just the same way that she was, but he confined that to knowing the strengths and weaknesses of his colleagues and what they could reasonably be called on to do during working hours. Hannah and Sophie were obviously friends, and he almost envied it.

'Hi. I'm Sophie. Congratulations. You did a great job and you really deserved to win.' Sophie held out her hand and Matt took it. Her manner was a little more open than Hannah's and her grin a little easier, but somehow it didn't reach into the corners of his soul the way that Hannah's did. But then no one had any business with his soul, that was his to contend with.

'Thanks. You and Hannah are a great team…'

Sophie threw her arm around Hannah's shoulder, laughing. 'I think I've hit my limit today. You and Hannah can go on and win this thing.'

That was obviously important to both of them. Matt hadn't really thought much about it, he'd reckoned on giving a reasonable account of himself and then going home. But suddenly he wanted to be a winner. And he wanted Hannah at his side, winning with him.

'The hospital could do with the money.'

'We're all relying on you two.' Sophie laughed. 'No pressure, obviously.'

'Pressure? What's pressure?' Hannah murmured the words quietly.

Sophie chuckled, nudging her friend in the ribs. 'Don't listen to her, Matt. Hannah's very focussed at times.'

He could see that already. And he liked Sophie immediately, she was the kind of woman that he usually chose to spend his free time with. Conventionally pretty, with blonde hair and blue eyes, she seemed easygoing and uncomplicated. Hannah, on the other hand…

Hannah was compelling. Beautiful. Almost certainly not the right kind of woman to get involved with, because bonds made with Hannah might not be easy to break. Matt dismissed the idea. No one was going to get involved with anyone, he should relax and look at this as an extension of his work. Money for the hospital *was* an extension of his work.

'We'd better get going…' Hannah was scanning the crowd intently, obviously looking for someone. 'I'll see you next Saturday, then?'

A whole week suddenly seemed a very long time to wait. But Matt hadn't planned on winning today, and he was going to have to fit his training sessions in whenever the opportunity presented itself.

'You know where to find me if you want me?'

Hannah nodded quietly, and it was Sophie who answered. 'Yes, we know. We'll leave a message with the surgical unit…'

Matt watched as the two women walked away from him. Sophie was obviously reliving one or other of the obstacles, tracing shapes in the air in front of her to illustrate the point. Hannah was listening intently. He wondered if she ever gave herself a break and loosened up a bit.

'Mum…!'

A small boy, of about six, was running across the grass towards them, followed by an older woman. Even if he hadn't called to her, Matt would have guessed this was Hannah's son, his tawny eyes and red-brown hair matched hers almost exactly. Hannah stretched out her arms in an expression of joy, falling to her knees, as the boy ran straight into her arms.

If she'd employed half the exuberance that she'd shown just now, she would have floated over the obstacle course, instead of battling her way through it. Sophie and the older woman were chatting and laughing together, and Hannah was doing a little victory dance with her son. The thought that he wanted to do a very different kind of victory dance with her was enticing and entirely inappropriate, but it was the kind of image that was difficult to erase from his memory.

It would fade. Memories *did* fade when you were a stranger, always on the move. Matt had learned to travel light, making no lasting personal attachments to hold him back.

He'd been travelling light since he was eight years old. Always running, always trying to leave behind the bad memories. But they were the ones that had caught up with him now, crowding in and obscuring the sun. As clear as if it had all happened yesterday, and blocking the view of Hannah and her family.

Matt had known that his father had an uncertain temper and that he'd sometimes hurt his mother and made her cry, but he knew now that his mother had protected him from the worst of it, locking him in his bedroom or sending him to a friend's house to spend the night. Afterwards he'd seen his mother wince in pain as she'd bent or reached for something. There had never been any bruises on her face, but as he'd got older Matt had begun to understand that was the one place his father had never hit his mother.

His father had hurt him once. Just once, but Matt still remembered the pain and the terror of being unable to escape the hand clamped firmly around his arm. Now he thought of it as a good thing, because it had been the final straw that had made his mother pack their bags and leave.

At first it had been exciting, a taste of the kind of freedom that Matt hadn't even realised existed. They'd changed their names, using his mother's surname instead of his father's, and had embarked on a new life, in a new town. And then his father had found them and they'd run again. Another new life in another new town. Matt had forgotten how many there had been. In the end he hadn't bothered to make new friends, because he'd known that he and his mother would be moving on again.

Matt watched as Hannah played with her son in the late afternoon sunshine. They seemed happy, carefree. No looking over their shoulders…

Until Hannah *did* look over her shoulder, straight at him, and caught him staring. Matt raised his hand, giving a smile, and she returned the gesture. Then he turned and walked away. He had no business wanting Hannah's warmth. He needed her as a teammate, and that was just for the next few weeks. After that, he'd be moving on again.

CHAPTER TWO

LIGHTS, NO SIRENS. There was no lack of urgency in getting their patient to the hospital, but Hannah needed to be able to hear his laboured breathing. And Sophie needed to be able to hear if Hannah called out to her to stop.

The ambulance swayed a little as it turned into the hospital. Sophie specialised in giving their patients a smooth ride, but speed was of the essence. She'd radioed through to the hospital, asking for immediate assistance, then put her foot down.

They drew up outside A and E, and Hannah concentrated on monitoring their patient, a middle-aged man who'd been hit by a bus. Sophie climbed down from the driver's seat, opening the back doors of the ambulance, and Hannah saw a tall figure in surgical scrubs waiting outside.

'What are you doing here?' As usual, Sophie voiced the question that was on Hannah's mind. Matt Lawson should be in the operating theatre, not A and E.

'Just helping out.' Matt was smiling and relaxed, but when Sophie and Hannah manoeuvred the stretcher out of the ambulance he moved quickly, his eyes on their patient as he guided them through the melee of people in A and E to an empty cubicle. It wasn't unusual for the doctors in A and E to place a call for specialist help from other departments when they were busy, and Matt must have been the one to answer.

Matt had clearly been told about her provisional diagnosis, and everything necessary to confirm it was laid out ready. He pulled on a pair of gloves, listening as she relayed Ben's name and what she'd already observed about his condition. Taken together, his symptoms indicated that Ben might be in the early stages of a tension pneumothorax, and if it went unchecked the progressive build-up of air in his pleural cavity could prove fatal.

'I'll need you to help me lift him. I appear to be flying solo.' Matt murmured the words to Hannah quietly, so that Ben couldn't hear.

'I'll stay. Sophie and I are on our lunch break now.' It looked as if everyone was busy with other patients, and Matt would need her help.

'Thank you.'

The warmth in his smile prompted an inappropriate thrill in Hannah's chest as her heart beat a little faster. She pulled on a disposable apron and gloves, trying not to think about how Matt's assessment of her actions seemed suddenly all-important.

They lifted Ben onto the bed, and Sophie folded the ambulance stretcher, ready to take it back out to the vehicle. Matt was talking to Ben as he quickly examined him, and Hannah readied the ultrasound machine, handing the probe to Matt as soon as he turned around to look for it.

'Great, thanks.' Even that small approbation meant more than it should. Matt was studying the screen on the ultrasound carefully, his brow furrowing for a split second before he made his decision. 'You were right, this is a tension pneumothorax. I'm going to do a thoracostomy—can you assist?'

Hannah nodded. Ben was conscious and Matt had undoubtedly left out the word *emergency* in describing the thoracostomy for his benefit. But they had no time to lose now. Hannah had taken Ben's shirt off in the ambulance, and now she raised his arm, smiling at him as she placed it behind his head.

'What's…happening…?' Ben began to move restively. Breathlessness and agitation were two of the symptoms that Hannah had already noted.

'The doctor's going to do a small procedure that'll help you to breathe more easily. We need to you stay as still as you can.' Hannah tried to reassure Ben and hold him still without getting in Matt's way. She'd never before felt so conscious of the touch of another body, working next to her.

Ben flinched as Matt swabbed the area at the side of his chest, moving again so that he could see what Matt was doing. Hannah couldn't blame him, but he had to keep still.

'Ben, this will be over soon. I'm going to inject an anaesthetic now. Look at Hannah, not me.'

Matt's voice was relaxed and calm. The kind of voice that you needed to hear when you were afraid and in pain. Ben quietened, his gaze fixed on Hannah, and she gave him a reassuring smile.

'Very still now.' She heard Matt's voice behind her and leaned forward, preparing for the inevitable reaction when the needle went into Ben's chest. Matt was working quickly and deftly, but no amount of skill could render the procedure painless.

Ben groaned, gripping her hand tightly, and Hannah heard a tell-tale hiss of air as the tension in the pleural cavity was relieved. Matt withdrew the needle carefully, taping a plastic cannula in place.

'All done. You did really well.' Matt smiled at Ben as he started to examine him again, to check that the procedure had relieved his symptoms. 'Hannah and I are a team, you know. We're entering a competition to win money for the hospital.'

This wasn't just idle talk. Matt was assessing Ben's ability to understand and reply.

'Yeah? You're lucky to have her.' Ben's face was less ashen now.

'Don't I know it.' Matt smiled, and tingles ran down Hannah's spine. She reminded herself that Matt's sudden impulse to chat was for Ben's benefit, not hers. 'I'm rather hoping that she'll keep me in line.'

Keeping Matt in line felt like a delicious and yet difficult prospect. Hannah shot a smile in Ben's direction. 'It looks as if I'm going to have my work cut out for me.'

'Just let me know if he gives you any trouble.' Ben's hand found hers again and Hannah gave it a squeeze. 'I'll sort him out for you.'

'Thanks. I might take you up on that.'

Matt chuckled, and his glance of approval told Hannah that he'd seen exactly what she had. Ben was much less breathless now, and he was more alert. As Matt set about checking Ben's blood pressure, one of the A and E doctors arrived with a nurse, ready to take over from them.

Matt briefed the doctor, while Hannah said goodbye to Ben. When she left the cubicle, she saw that Matt was already at the far end of the busy space outside but he'd stopped by the door and was waiting for her. Hannah stripped off her apron and gloves, and went to join him.

'Spotting the early signs of a tension pneumothorax isn't easy in the best of circumstances, let alone in the back of an ambulance.'

Hannah nodded. Matt's easygoing humour had given her no clues about what he thought about the course of action she'd taken, but she was pleased that he approved.

'We were close to the hospital, and the symptoms were inconclusive. Doing a thoracostomy in the back of an ambulance isn't ideal, and I decided it was better to keep going so that Ben's condition could be properly confirmed…' She bit her lip. Matt's gaze was making her feel very nervous.

'You don't need me to tell you that you made the right decision, do you?'

'No, I don't.' She really wanted him to, but that had more to do with his blue eyes and his smile than it did with any medical considerations.

Those eyes, and the thought of how it had felt working next to him, were playing havoc with her senses. And Ben wasn't here to concentrate her mind on other things. Suddenly it felt as if she was standing too close to Matt, but stepping back now was only going to betray her embarrassment.

'I should be getting along now. Sophie's probably waiting for me, with some lunch.'

Matt nodded amiably. 'I'll see you on Saturday.'

'Yes. Saturday.' Hannah tried to think of something friendly and encouraging to say, and came up empty.

As he walked away, she couldn't resist watching him, telling herself that assessing the width of his shoulders was something to do with deciding on Matt's ability to handle whatever they were confronted with on Saturday. She jumped, as Sophie seemed to appear out of nowhere and caught her staring.

'I'd say you don't have too much to worry about on the teamwork front.'

Hannah shrugged. 'It's different. We both knew what had to be done…'

'Yeah. Keep telling yourself that. You two looked as if you were reading each other's minds.' Sophie grinned at her. 'Come on. Let's take our break while we can. I could murder a cup of tea.'

Hannah nodded. There was a lot to do before Saturday rolled around, and she could begin to feel nervous about that later.

The four teams had started to gather on the open space behind the hospital building at seven thirty, for the first of four Saturdays that were intended to single out one team to represent Hertfordshire in the finals of *Hospital Challenge*. Many of Hannah's friends and workmates were there to watch, and the other teams had brought carloads of their own supporters.

Hannah had been issued with three red T-shirts, with the name of her hospital emblazoned on the back, and she was wearing one. The other teams were wearing blue, green and yellow, so that they could be picked out easily by the cameras. There was a large marquee that no one was allowed access to, and everyone was eyeing it with a mixture of curiosity and apprehension.

Matt was nowhere to be seen. Hannah had greeted the other teams, shaking hands with them and keeping her eye out for the splash of red that she hoped might announce his arrival.

Finally she saw him. Strolling across the grass towards her, wearing the same red T-shirt, with a pair of cargo pants and trainers. They hadn't been told what to expect, other than that anything might be thrown at them today, and Hannah had made the same decision.

'Hello.' She wanted to ask where the hell he'd been, but that might not be the best start to this new partnership.

'Hi. Sorry I'm late.' He looked at his watch. Matt wasn't late, it was just that everyone else had been half an hour early. 'I stopped by my office…'

'Doing *real* work, then.' Hannah tried to smile.

Matt shrugged. 'This feels surprisingly real at the moment.'

One hint that he wasn't as laid-back about all of this as he made out. 'I'm a bit nervous, too.'

He laughed suddenly. 'Did you get the pep talk from Human Resources?'

'The one about how everyone's going to be watching, and the good name of the hospital is on our shoulders? And how much the hospital can do with the cash prize, if we win?' Hannah quirked her lips down. 'Yes, I got it.'

'And of course we both feel a great deal better after that.' There was a twinkle in his eye, and Hannah felt herself relax.

'So much better. Nothing like the weight of expectation to give us wings. I wonder what the other teams have up their sleeves.'

He nodded, motioning quietly away from the groups of people that surrounded them. Hannah followed him to a quiet spot in the shadow of the hospital building.

'My office window is just up there.'

Hannah followed the line of his finger. The windows of the second-floor surgical suite looked out over the people milling around the marquee. It occurred to her that Matt hadn't been up there, working.

'What have you seen?'

'I reckoned that the first thing we needed to do was assess the competition. We're not the only team who don't know each other all that well. Look at the blues and the greens.'

Hannah looked. The two green T-shirts were giving each other a high five, which she'd seen them do before, and it was obviously for the benefit of the people around them.

'I'd agree with you about the greens. Too demonstrative.'

He nodded. 'And the blues have their backs to each other most of the time.'

'The yellows seem pretty tight.'

'Yes, they are, I know them. Jack and Laura crew an ambulance, working out of Cravenhurst Hospital.'

Matt looked suddenly uncomfortable. Hannah had tried to hide her feelings but he must know that she'd wanted to be partnered with Sophie.

'So we reckon that two of the other teams are like us, and don't know each other too well. But the yellows are already very used to working together...' Matt's brow puckered in thought. 'Maybe we just pretend we have a tension pneumothorax to contend with. We did pretty well there.'

Looking beyond the personal, and functioning as a team. A self-contained unit, relying on each other and seamlessly compensating for each other's weaknesses. That was so easy to do with Sophie, and so very challenging with Matt. Relying too much on him seemed like stepping into a vortex, which would claw her down into the kind of relationship that she'd promised herself she'd never have with a man again.

So don't look at him as if he's a man. He's a person, a fellow competitor.

As soon as the idea occurred to her, Hannah dismissed it as ridiculous. Matt was all man, and every nerve ending was urging her to be all woman in response.

'Perhaps for a start we should tell each other our greatest weakness.' Hannah puffed out a breath. You couldn't just ask that of someone without being willing to go first. 'I'll start—'

He shook his head, laying his hand on her arm, and suddenly her greatest weakness wasn't her tendency to plan everything down to the smallest detail. Her greatest weakness was Matt's touch…

'Why don't you tell me what *my* greatest weakness is? When you find it. In return, I'll tell you yours.'

That was a great deal more challenging. But this was supposed to be a challenge after all.

'Okay. That could work.'

'And in the meantime, concentrate on our strengths. We'll need those if we're going to win.' He gave her a gorgeous smile. 'And we *are* going to win, aren't we?'

'Yes, we are. Do you want a high five?' Hannah had just seen the greens do it again, and this time it seemed a little less confident than it had before.

'Is that your thing?' He turned his gaze on her, and she shivered as the vortex seemed to beckon her once more.

'No, not really.'

'Right, then. Let's disappoint Human Resources and dispense with that.'

She liked his quiet humour. The way he looked for real answers, and didn't just follow what everyone else did.

Then she saw it, glistening in his eyes. Despite all of his outward unconcern, Matt wanted to win too. He wanted to make them into a team that could win together. She'd been too quick to jump to conclusions about him.

'How long do you suppose we'll have to wait?' There was obvious activity going on amongst the production crew, but no one seemed very interested in rounding up the contestants yet.

Matt chuckled. 'Probably until our nerves are just hovering around fever pitch.'

He didn't seem to be anywhere near fever pitch at the moment. If Hannah hadn't known better it would have infuriated her, but Matt was obviously working things through in his own way. Maybe they'd just taken the first step in their team-building exercise.

Matt was used to waiting. The quiet, measured activity of the operating theatre, where lives hung in the balance and the slightest slip could make a world of difference to a patient, had taught him that being ready wasn't a matter of straining at the leash.

The competitors had been called to a roped-off area to one side of the tent, but it didn't look as if anything else was going to happen any time soon. Matt sat down on one of the benches that had been provided and Hannah sat next to him, fidgeting. He could almost feel the tension radiating out of her.

'The little boy you were with last week. He's your son?' Maybe talking would calm her a little.

'Yes.' She smiled suddenly, that wide open, joyful smile that he'd seen last week. 'His name's Sam.'

'How old is he?'

'Six.'

That got the basics over. 'Where is he today? With his father?'

Hannah's smile slid from her face. That clearly hadn't been the right thing to say, and Matt wondered why on earth he'd made the assumption. He should have just come out and asked if Hannah had a partner, if he'd wanted to know so much.

'No, with my mum. She's going to bring him along here later to hear the results announced. It's just me and Sam. His father isn't on the scene.'

'I'm sorry... I didn't mean to pry.'

'That's all right.' Mischief kindled suddenly in her eyes. 'If we're going to be a team we should get to know each other.'

Matt laughed. 'Okay. Matthew Robin Lawson. Thirty-six years old, born in Newcastle, single. I've been here for a year, and before that I was working in Glasgow.'

'You've moved around a bit?' Matt shot Hannah a questioning look and she smiled. 'You don't have a Newcastle accent.'

'Yeah. The only family I'm in touch with is my mother, and she lives in Devon. I go wherever there's a great job that will challenge me.'

It sounded suddenly as if the life he'd made for himself was missing something. The vital ingredient that Hannah seemed to possess, a family and good friends. But this was what he knew. He'd grown up as an outsider, and that was how he felt comfortable now.

'And you watch people.' It came unerringly out of the blue, and combined with the warmth in Hannah's eyes it carried a momentum that almost knocked him backwards.

'I guess so. We used to move around a lot, and I found it pays to sit and watch for a while when you're the new kid in school.'

She seemed to see more in that then he'd said. It felt good to be accepted, but Matt knew that being accepted wasn't everything. Being safe was everything, and he didn't want Hannah to know about that.

'And you?'

'Ah. Hannah... Do I *have* to tell you my middle name?'

'You do now. How bad can it be?'

She grinned. 'Hannah Eloise Greene.'

'What's wrong with Eloise?' It suited her softer side perfectly.

'It's...well it's a bit girly, isn't it? I'd prefer something a bit more...' She waved her hand, as if she were groping for the right word. 'Adventurous, maybe.'

'Flash? Jet?'

Hannah laughed, and Matt warmed to his theme. 'How about Olympia, if you want to go classical? Or Juno?'

'No! Olympia and Juno are far too elegant for me. And one of my friends called her little boy Jet.'

Matt chuckled. 'Flash it is, then.'

'Okay. Hannah Flash Greene…it's got a ring to it. Twenty-six years old, born right here in this hospital. My father died six years ago, and Sam's father and I split up before he was born. My mum and I bought a house together, and she looks after Sam when I'm at work. I'm lucky, because it's a good arrangement for both of us.'

'I imagine it's great for her to be able to spend time with her grandson.' Matt hadn't had too much contact with his family. Staying below the radar had meant that his mother had considered it unwise to visit either set of grandparents, and his aunts and uncles had been just names to him.

'Yes. She didn't know what to do with herself when Dad died. I was away, and…' Hannah shrugged. There was something she didn't want to say, and Matt didn't intend to press her. This had just been something to talk about, he hadn't meant to share any secrets.

'Contestants! This way, please.' One of the production assistants called out suddenly and they both jumped.

They'd been told that there would be cameras in the tent, and that they should do their best to ignore them. Inside, there were four sections, each screened off from the others. A smiling woman handed Matt an envelope.

'Everything you need is in here. Follow the red markers.' She gestured towards the canvas door that bore a red flash. 'You can go now.'

Hannah unzipped the doorway, and Matt saw trestle tables, piled high with medical equipment. He watched as another canvas door at the far end of the tent was opened, revealing a carport with a small red car parked in it. They

stepped inside and someone zipped the doorway closed behind them. It was an odd feeling, being completely alone
with Hannah, but knowing that they were being watched
by cameras. He opened the envelope, sorting through its
contents.

'Car keys and a map… Phone… Ah. Instructions.' He
handed the sheets of paper to Hannah, craning over her
shoulder to see.

'Okay…' She scanned the paper quickly. 'We've got to
take the things we think we might need, and wait for the
phone to ring. The red car's ours, and we'll use it to get to
a medical emergency that's happening somewhere inside
the red ring on the map. We don't know where yet, or what
kind of emergency…'

'Sounds like a normal day for you.' Matt grinned at her,
spreading the map out on top of one the boxes that were
heaped on the trestles.

Hannah studied the map, frowning. 'The red ring's a
good thirty miles from here.'

'Which means we have to make a decision. We can't
get everything here into the car, so we either take what we
think we'll need and make a start, or we wait here for the
phone call and risk being delayed in traffic.'

Hannah nodded, looking up at him. Perhaps she was
waiting for him to make the call.

'What do you say, then, Flash? This is your area of expertise, not mine.'

She grinned suddenly. 'I say we go. We can open up
the boxes and take just the amount we might need from
them.' She pointed at the large box of dressings. 'Even if
we need all that, there are only two of us and two people
can't apply that many dressings.'

'Agreed. Why don't you make a selection and I'll put
everything into the car.'

She raised an eyebrow. 'You're sure about that?'

'Positive. I'm used to having whatever I could possibly need within reach. I'll go with your best guess over mine.'

'All right, Robin…' He raised his eyebrows and Hannah chuckled. 'You asked for that. You can start with the defibrillator and the oxygen kit—we should definitely take those.'

Fifteen minutes' concentrated work, and they were ready to go. Hannah had used plastic bags and torn wrappers to contain reasonable amounts of as many different things as possible, repacking boxes and labelling them with a marker pen. She'd added a couple of large zipped bags to their provisions, commenting that they were obviously there for a reason, and picked up the bag of sandwiches and the six-pack of water bottles, stowing them in the footwell of the car.

'Can you see what the others are doing?' Matt drove out of the carport, and he caught an enticing trace of her scent as she craned round in the passenger seat, trying to see what was going on behind them.

'Yep. Yellows have gone already. Since they're an ambulance crew I wouldn't be surprised if they haven't done the same as us. Blues and greens look as if they might be staying put.' She twisted back round in her seat, surveying the road in front of them. 'I hope we've done the right thing.'

'We've done it now. We look forward, not back.' Matt could feel a tightening excitement in his chest. This wasn't just about winning, not even just about bringing home the cash prize for their hospital. Suddenly, it was Flash and Robin, on the road together. Ready to face whatever was thrown at them.

CHAPTER THREE

HANNAH HAD PICKED a spot that gave easy access to main roads in all directions, and was approximately at the centre of the circle. They got out of the car, stretching their legs, and even though it was only ten thirty, she broke open one of the packets of sandwiches. Who knew when they'd get a chance to eat later on? After ten minutes, the phone rang. Matt answered it, listening carefully and scribbling notes on the back of the map.

'It's at Lloyd Court. Apparently there's someone who's collapsed. No further details at the moment.'

Hannah rolled her eyes, spinning the crust of her sandwich into a nearby waste bin. 'What, like where he is or what might be wrong with him?'

'I suppose they think that's far too easy. They'll pass further information through to us in the next half-hour. Do you know Lloyd Court?'

She nodded. 'Yes, it's a country park. And it's huge, it'll take us all day to find someone there.'

Matt handed her the car keys. 'We'd better get a start, then.'

As Hannah turned into the wide avenue that led to the heart of the country park, he got another call. He listened carefully and then turned to her.

'Apparently our patient's had a heart attack. There was

one phone call from him, he couldn't give his exact location but he said he'd been walking on the estate here for around half an hour, and that he was surrounded by trees. His name's Justin Travers and they've given me a phone number for him, but apparently he's not answering.'

The spike of adrenalin made a clear summer's day move into even sharper focus. 'Why give it to us, then?'

'That's what I'm wondering...' Matt was fiddling with the phone as she drove, and Hannah concentrated on the road ahead, turning into the car park that sprawled to one side of the visitors' centre. She got out of the car, opening the hatchback.

'What are you doing?' She started to unload the boxes, sorting out what they would need for the walk ahead of them.

'Just looking...ah! Got him!'

'What?' Matt didn't seem to appreciate that this was an emergency situation. Okay, so it was a fake emergency situation, but they had to pretend it was real.

'I did an internet search for the number. There's a business connections page for a Justin Travers and he's obviously a walker. Look...' Matt held out the phone and Hannah glanced at it, then went back to unloading the boxes from the car. She grabbed the two rucksacks and started to fill them with the things they might need.

'He's a made-up person, Matt. He's not going to have social media.'

'Or they're testing us. What would you do if you were in this situation for real? You'd try to find out who he was if you could.' He handed her the phone and Hannah scrolled through the page that was displayed. The guy was a self-employed computer consultant, and his hobby was walking. He'd been on a recent expedition to Mount Kilimanjaro, and his contact number was clearly shown.

When she scrolled down a little, his other hobby was listed as '*Watching* Hospital Challenge'. That couldn't be a co-incidence.

'I was wrong...' She suddenly felt very small. Matt hadn't underestimated the complexity of the challenge the way she had. He hadn't dismissed her experience either. She hadn't shown him that respect.

He shook his head. 'No, we were both right. We need to get moving now and expand our search area, because someone like this is going to be able to walk further in half an hour than most people could.'

'What do you suggest?'

'Serious walkers tend to travel in a straight line and if that's what he did, then there's just one area of woodland that's approximately two and a half miles from here.' Matt indicated an area to the west.

'And we go there first?' There was woodland to the east as well, but that was only a mile away. Further on was an area of grassland.

'It's a risk. Under normal circumstances there would be search parties out, going in every direction, but we have to choose. We can't split up, the instructions say that we both have to be at the scene together.'

Think. Think!

Hannah turned, staring at the hill that led away to the west. This was the challenge that any experienced walker would set themselves. When she faced Matt again, he was regarding her steadily.

'Okay. I agree, we go west.'

Matt shouldered the heavier of the two bags, and added two bottles of water to its weight. He set off at a fast walk, and Hannah wondered if she should remind him that they needed to pace themselves. He probably was pacing himself. She watched his back, gritting her teeth. It was a matter of pride that she could keep up.

But after a mile her head started to swim, and the muscles in her legs and shoulders were screaming. She stopped, letting her bag fall to the ground. Matt turned.

'Perhaps we should have some water…' Just a few minutes' rest, and she'd be ready to go again. He nodded, handing her one of the water bottles.

He was waiting for her. Matt made a show of consulting the map, but they both knew exactly which way they were going as the woodland at the top of the hill stood starkly on the horizon. One minute. Just one minute and she'd be ready to pick up the bag and go again.

'Drink a little more.' He picked up the half-empty water bottle that she'd put down on the grass, handing it to her. Then he caught the strap of her bag, shouldering it with his.

'No… Matt, I'll be okay…'

'We have to get there together. If I get tired, you can take the bag back.'

His tone was quiet. Gentle, even. Not like the shouted exhortations to keep going that she'd trained with.

'Don't give me permission to give up…'

He grinned suddenly. 'You don't have my permission to do anything other than keep walking. I'm going to need you when we get there, so let's go.' He turned, obviously slowed by the extra weight but still able to keep going.

It was a lot easier without the bag. Hannah caught up with him, walking beside him.

'You don't believe in a little encouragement?'

'What, you mean bullying you until you pick the bag up again and start walking? No, I don't believe in that.' He was suddenly tight-lipped.

'Sometimes a bit of a push is what's needed.'

He nodded. 'Yeah. But don't ask me to do it.'

Matt wasn't wasting any words, and it wasn't just the extra weight he was carrying. This was a line that he didn't cross. His relaxed attitude to everything wasn't a matter of *laissez faire*. It was more like a decision about how he was going to interact with the world.

'I get it. If I need any shouting to get me back on my feet, I'll do it myself.'

'I'd appreciate that.' He gave her one of his sudden smiles. Those deep blue eyes were enough to drag anyone to their feet, heart pumping faster and legs suddenly strong.

'I'll take my bag back in a little while.'

He nodded. 'All right. I can't make it all the way like this.'

He had his strengths, just as she did. And finding them, using them, was a challenge that was both daunting and delicious.

Matt knew what Hannah had been asking of him. He knew that getting her to her feet wouldn't be a matter of real aggression, and more one of channelling her thoughts and reactions towards one clear aim. But he still couldn't do it.

It had been more than twenty-five years since he'd cowered before his father's wrath. Everything he'd done and said had been calculated to please, because when his father had got angry it had been over the smallest things. This wasn't the same, and pressuring Hannah back to her feet wouldn't have been the same kind of aggression that his father had dispensed so freely, but he still couldn't bring himself to do it. It wasn't who he was. What he'd made himself be.

When she took her bag back, he caught the scent of her sweat. Not stale or pungent, but an exciting sweetness, which spoke to his body on a level that he'd learned to ignore. He should ignore her touch, too. Something about the way that she snatched her hand away from his when he gave her the bag told Matt that she felt something too, and he couldn't help but smile.

'We split up?' They'd reached the edge of the woodland, and Hannah took the map from him, spreading it out on the ground. The trees formed a wide band that stretched out ahead of them.

'I think so. I'll walk along the ridge, there, and you take the path.' Matt chose the more uneven, sloping terrain. Physical effort might take his mind off her auburn hair, glinting in the sunlight, and the way that her sweat-dampened T-shirt didn't hide her curves as well as it had.

'Giving me the easier route again?' For a moment her expression told him that she might well argue with that.

'Don't worry. I reckon there are enough challenges ahead of us to go round.'

Hannah grinned suddenly. 'Probably. Thanks, I could do without climbing to the top of that ridge.'

They walked more slowly now, keeping each other within sight and scanning carefully for any signs of the man they were looking for. Matt caught a glimpse of blue, between the trees on the other side of the ridge, but when he scrambled down towards it, he saw that it was an abandoned plastic carrier bag, fluttering in the breeze.

'Anything…?' He heard Hannah's voice, calling to him.

'No. Nothing.' Matt shouted back, and she started walking again. As the woodland area started to narrow, the ridge wound down to meet the path.

'Where *is* he? Suppose we're wrong, Matt.' She seemed suddenly exhausted from the effort it had taken to get here.

'Suppose we're right?'

Hannah nodded, straightening suddenly. 'We'll walk through to the end of these trees, and then double back for a second look, shall we? When we're sure he's not here, we can think again.'

They walked for another ten minutes and then he saw it. Deep amongst the trees, in a patch of bright sunshine, the body of a man propped up against a tree stump. They forced their way through the undergrowth and Matt felt a bramble tear at his arm, catching at the supple branch before it hit Hannah straight in the face. She ducked ahead of him, jogging towards the man and falling to her knees beside him.

Matt wasn't sure what to expect right now. Surely they weren't supposed to carry out resuscitation procedures on what was presumably a perfectly healthy volunteer? Then the man opened his eyes, grinning up at Hannah.

'Hi, there. You made it, then.' He jerked his thumb behind him. 'Go over there.'

Hannah didn't move. 'Are you all right?'

The man snorted with laughter. 'Yes, of course I am. We try to make everything as authentic as possible, but I draw the line at having a real heart attack.'

She frowned suddenly. 'Have you got some water?'

Matt felt for the water bottle in his bag. They'd both been caught up in the illusion, but Hannah had stepped out of it for a moment and seen a real issue. The man had been sitting in full sunlight, and it was a hot day. His face was already a little red.

'Actually, I could do with some. Looks as if I'll be here for a while.' He took the bottle from Matt. 'Thanks. Now go on, will you? Five minutes in that direction.'

Hannah got to her feet, staring ahead of them. She turned questioningly to Matt and he shrugged. He couldn't see anything either.

They walked downhill through the brush, and he saw something amongst the trees. The shape of an expertly camouflaged tent. They approached it, and Matt ducked around the tent flap, seeing a busy crew and four tables, each bearing one of the team colours. He turned to Hannah, holding the flap aside for her.

'Great.' A young woman approached them, beaming. 'Go over to your table…'

'In a minute.' Hannah's grim determination to get the job in hand completed seemed to have deserted her. 'I'd like to speak to whoever's in charge.'

'You're still being timed.' The young woman frowned.

'Then I'd like to speak to them straight away, please.' She shot an apologetic look at Matt and he nodded. He knew now what was on her mind, and he wasn't about to tell her to forget it and hurry her over to the table.

A man responded to the woman's beckoning hand, and hurried over. 'Is there a problem?'

'Yes, there is. The man lying out there is in direct sunlight, and he's got no water, we gave him some of ours. He's already looking a little red in the face, and I'm hoping he doesn't get sunstroke.'

Matt grinned. Go, Flash.

'Um…' The man scratched his head. 'Did he say he felt ill?'

'No. But prevention's always better than cure, and I was sure you'd want to know.' Hannah shrugged. 'Health and safety, and all that…'

She was being nice about it, but there was a hint of firmness beneath her smile. Matt never had to explain what he wanted, he just made a decision and everyone went with it. Hannah must face this kind of situation every day, and she was clearly practised at getting her own way with the minimum of confrontation and fuss.

'Yes, of course. Thanks for letting me know, I'll get straight on it. If we sit him in the shade a little closer to the path, and make sure he has plenty of water, would that be okay with you?'

'That's fabulous. Thanks.' Hannah flashed him a smile, and turned to make her way across to the red table.

'That's very sportsmanlike of you.' Matt shot her a smile, so that Hannah would be in no doubt that he approved. 'The other teams will be able to see him more easily if he's closer to the path.'

She shot him a querulous look. 'You think I should have done anything different?'

'No. I'm just pleased to see that I have a teammate who *won't* stop at nothing to win.'

Hannah flushed a little, then leaned towards him. 'You just wait and see what I'll do if you don't get over to that table. Right now.'

That was almost an incentive to stay put. Hannah could do anything she wanted with him, the more up close and personal the better. The sentiment must have shown on his face, because she raised her eyebrows.

'Since you asked so nicely…' Matt turned and walked over to the table.

CHAPTER FOUR

THEY'D SPENT ALMOST an hour going through what they'd brought in their bags, and how they would have treated their patient, with two of the judges. About halfway through, the yellow team had turned up, but there was no sign of the blues or the greens. Finally they were allowed to go, walking with one of the production assistants along a path that led to the perimeter of the park, and then being ferried back to the visitors' centre by car.

Matt got into the red car, feeling his back pull as he did so. He reached for the ignition, and Hannah stopped him.

'Your arm's bleeding.' She reached under her T-shirt and into the pocket of her jeans, pulling out a packet of antiseptic wipes that she must have saved from the medical bag she'd been carrying.

Matt was vaguely aware that thorns had ripped through both the fabric of his T-shirt and his flesh at some point, and that his shoulder was stinging. Now that he looked, he could see a trickle of partly coagulated blood.

'It's okay.'

She gave him the look that she probably saved for any of her patients who proved intractable. Half smiling, half determined.

'Okay, so you want to be a man about it. I won't tell anyone. I find that it's in my own interest to keep you as healthy as possible over the next four weeks, so you'll just have to take a hit for the team.'

The stinging felt a little too close for comfort to the scar on his shoulder, which he kept hidden from everyone. But he did what he imagined everyone else doing in the face of Hannah's charm. He pulled the sleeve of his T-shirt up, gratified to find that if he held it in place the dark red mark wasn't visible.

'Oh. Nasty.' Hannah squinted at the gash on his arm. 'Hold on a minute. Sharp scratch.'

'Ow! That's not a sharp scratch. What did you do?' If he was going to forgo being a man about it, then he may as well go the whole hog.

'You had a thorn still in there.' Hannah held up a vicious-looking spike. 'I think there's another one. That might be a slightly sharper scratch...'

It was. But this time it didn't take Matt so much by surprise, and he kept quiet about it. Hannah wiped the wound carefully, and then applied a plaster from her pocket. 'That should hold it. Although—'

'Give it a good wash when I get back? I've got that part...' Matt pulled the sleeve of his T-shirt back down again.

'Yes, of course. Sorry, force of habit.'

She leaned back in her seat, staring out at the sun-dappled grass in front of them. Suddenly Matt didn't want to start driving again. He was used to knowing people in terms of the way they did their jobs, and it didn't usually occur to him to make small-talk about his colleagues' lives. But Hannah was different.

'You know this place pretty well?'

She nodded. 'Yes. We used to come here on Sunday afternoons when I was little. My dad taught me how to fly a kite here.'

It must be nice to have those memories. To be able to access them whenever you wanted and smile.

'You've never thought of moving away?' He was interested. It was an experience that was so very different from his.

'Not really. After my dad died my mum was just…lost. I was away for a while, and by the time I managed to get back, my dad was already gone. I couldn't leave her again.'

'I'm sorry. That must have been very difficult.'

'It was for Mum.' Hannah shrugged off whatever regrets she had of her own. 'He knew that I was coming back for him, he just couldn't wait.'

A tear trickled down her cheek, and she wiped it away impatiently. Matt wanted very badly to comfort her, but wasn't sure whether she'd accept it.

'I imagine that there isn't much you can tell people that you love that they don't already know.'

She nodded. 'That's what I think as well. I hope so, anyway. My biggest regret is that I never got to tell Dad that he wasn't to worry about Mum, because I'd look after her.'

'I dare say that you know what your son's capable of, even better than he does, at times.' Matt really wasn't qualified to give advice on families. But maybe all that time when he was a kid, spent watching other people's families, studying them carefully from the outside, gave him a slightly different perspective.

Hannah laughed suddenly. 'Yes, you've got that right. It's just as well that I can out-think him a bit, or I'd never manage to keep up with him.'

'I guess that having a child puts things into perspective. You get to understand your own parents a little better.'

'Yes, it puts a lot of things into perspective. I wish that Sam could have known my dad, he would have adored him.'

'You've taught him how to fly a kite?'

Hannah laughed. 'No, actually, I haven't. That's a very good idea, though. Maybe I'll wait for a windy day and bring him up here.'

The question was on the tip of his tongue. Whether Hannah might wait for that windy day, and call him to see if he might come along. He had no idea how to fly a kite and it seemed suddenly as if it was something he'd be interested in learning about.

He didn't ask. Hannah's was one of those families that had fascinated him as a child, stable and loving, the exact opposite of his own. But they were unknown territory and he'd kept his distance. And anyway, Hannah was really just an acquaintance. One who he felt suddenly very close to, after working through the challenges they'd been set for today, but still just an acquaintance.

He jumped as someone rapped on the car window, and Hannah pressed the control to wind it down. The yellow team had been dropped off in the car park now, and were making their way to their car.

'Guys, we need you back at the hospital. We're doing a few interviews there, and when the other teams get back we'll be announcing the winners.'

'I don't suppose you know where the other teams are, do you?' Hannah's competitive spirit emerged suddenly and the young woman shook her head.

'Sorry…'

'Okay, thanks.' Hannah wound the window back up. 'Can't say or won't say, I wonder.'

Matt chuckled, reaching for the ignition. 'We'll find out soon enough.'

Hannah had stepped over the line a little. She usually gave the sanitised version of what had happened when her father had died, just that she'd been out of the country and got back as soon as she could.

She didn't tell anyone about the clawing guilt. About how she'd left, accompanying her boyfriend on travels that were his dream, not hers. John had been her dream, and she'd followed him.

Her father had asked her what she really wanted, and she'd told him it was this. She wanted to see the world. He hadn't believed her, and he and her mother had obviously been worried for her, but they'd let her go without any more argument, waving her off at the airport with fixed smiles on their faces.

And that was the last time she'd seen him. When the telegram had got through, routed through various different post offices, she'd called her mother and found that her father was dying. John had waved her off at the airport rather more cheerfully than her parents had, and she hadn't seen him again either. By the time she'd arrived home, her father had died, and she'd never had the chance to tell him that she was sorry.

The car turned into the road that ran through to the back of the hospital and she saw her mother with Sam. He was standing right at the front of the spectator area, waving the red flag that she'd helped him make. Matt stopped the car, right in front of him.

'Mum… Mum!' Sam was hallooing at the top of his voice. Hannah shot Matt a smile and got out of the car.

'Mum… Did you win?'

'We'll have to wait for the judges to say.' Hannah stroked her son's cheek as his face fell. 'But we did the best we could, and that's what matters.'

What seemed to matter now was winning, but Sam accepted the thought without question, jumping up and down and waving his flag. Hannah gave him a hug and

Sam craned around as Matt got out of the car. He gave Sam a wave and the little boy pretended not to notice, suddenly shy.

Hannah beckoned Matt over, and he walked towards them. 'Sam, this is Matt.'

'Hi, Sam.' Matt squatted down on his heels in front of the boy, giving him his space and smiling quietly as he waited for Sam to get over his attack of nerves. 'That's a great flag.'

'I made it.' Sam gave the flag another wave, and Matt nodded solemnly.

'I can see that. It's better than all the others.' He grinned when Sam waved the flag more vigorously. 'It was the first thing we saw when we got to the hospital.'

Sam liked that. He began to chatter excitedly as Matt got to his feet and introduced himself to Hannah's mum. His quiet manner, and the way he held his hand out to shake hers, elicited a glance in Hannah's direction from her mother. No doubt about the meaning—Mum liked the strong silent type, and good manners always impressed her.

The home crowd had seen them, and people were beginning to cheer, the banner with the name of the hospital lifted aloft after what must have been a long wait to greet them. Hannah lifted Sam over the barrier, feeling her fatigued muscles protest at his weight, and he waved his flag wildly.

Anxious to get as good a view as possible, Sam reached for Matt's taller frame. Hannah saw Matt hesitate, and then he smiled. As she delivered Sam into his arms, the brush of Matt's skin against hers was suddenly all she could feel. He hoisted the boy onto his shoulders, holding him carefully so that he didn't fall, and Sam howled with delight.

'He's not too heavy for you, is he?' Matt grinned a no,

and Hannah tapped Sam's knee to get his attention. 'Don't wriggle so much. Matt won't be able to hold you.'

'I won't let him go.'

This. *This* was what it would be like if Sam had a father. If John had responded to the news that she was pregnant by wanting anything to do with his child. But he hadn't. He had been too busy with his own life to bother with hers or the one they'd unwittingly created together. Hannah felt a lump rise in her throat, and realised that her mother was staring at her.

'Do you mind staying here with Sam for a moment? I'll go and park the car up…' She wanted to get away from here before the picture of a complete family formed too clearly in her mind.

'Um… Yeah. Sure.' Matt clearly wasn't used to being around kids, and he was taking the responsibility seriously, but he was grinning from ear to ear. If he wanted to let Sam down, then her mum was there to take him.

'Keys…?'

'In my pocket.' Matt didn't seem at all disposed to let go of Sam, although one hand was probably quite enough to keep him from falling from his perch. Hannah saw the outline of the keys under the heavy material of his trousers, and felt her mouth go dry.

She was even thinking twice about this? She should be pleased that Matt was so careful, and that he was taking extra care that Sam didn't fall.

'Okay. Sharp…um…scratch.' The joke dried in her throat. It wasn't really necessary to warn Matt every time she went near him.

His momentary, heavy-lidded look told Hannah that he noticed her touch as much as she did his. She reached forward, fishing the keys from his pocket with two fingers, stepping back as soon as she had them, feeling the metal dig into her hand as she held them a little too tightly.

'I'm just going to park the car, Sam. You'll stay here with Matt and Grandma?' Sam gave her a cursory nod, concentrating on waving his flag.

Sophie caught up with her in the car park, flinging her arm around her shoulders as they walked back together.

'I see he's made friends with Sam. How was he?'

Beautiful. Challenging. 'Um…he's got good stamina.'

'I like a man with good stamina.' Sophie laughed and Hannah dug her elbow into her ribs.

'I meant for climbing hills. He's a good problem-solver as well.'

'Yeah? I *love* a good problem-solver…'

'Shush. If you're so keen on stamina and problem-solving, why don't you try him out for yourself?' Now she'd said it, Hannah wished she hadn't. Sophie had better *not* try Matt out for herself.

'Nah. He's all yours…' Sophie ended the conversation abruptly, jogging forward to greet Sam. 'Hey, there, Sam. You're very tall all of a sudden!'

Sam leaned over, tapping the top of Sophie's head, and she laughed.

'We'd better go and sign in. Are you going to join us, Sophie?'

Recognising that Sophie had played a part in their efforts today, and wanting her to share in the credit, was a nice gesture on Matt's part. The walk between here and the awning that covered the reception area was lined with people and they were all cheering.

'No, that's okay.' Sophie grinned conspiratorially at Hannah's mother. 'You take Sam.'

As they started to walk, she heard Sophie's voice behind her. Then the people lining their way started a Mexican wave, cheering and shouting. She heard Matt chuckle as Sam screamed with glee.

'Oh! She didn't…'

'I think she did.' Matt's voice seemed very close all of a sudden. 'One last push and we're home…'

The embarrassment, and the thought that there were so many expectations on her shoulders, made this walk seem harder, and longer than all the rest put together. Sam waved his flag, as people ducked and straightened in a new ripple that followed them all the way to the reception area. Matt lifted Sam down, and Hannah hugged him.

'Run straight back to Sophie and Grandma now, sweetie. Matt and I have to do some things, but I'll see you later.' Hannah gestured to her mother, making sure that she saw that Sam was on his way back.

'I can take him. Sign me in…' A worried look crossed Matt's face, and Hannah shook her head.

'It's okay. He can do that by himself.' Hannah watched as Sam scampered back, making sure that he didn't get distracted. Sophie took his hand, bending down to say something to him, and Sam turned, giving her a wave.

'He's great.' Matt was watching too. 'I'll bet he's a bit of a handful…'

'He's more than just a bit of a handful. But all the best kids are.'

Matt nodded thoughtfully. Then he turned suddenly, as if tearing himself away from the boy, and walked towards the signing-in table.

They'd responded to the interview questions, giving all the expected answers. They'd enjoyed the challenge, and were feeling good, and hoping they'd done well. Now that they were alone, Hannah's optimism seemed to have subsided into a worried determination. They'd reached their pretend patient first, but there was still the matter of how they'd answered the judges' questions. Matt was confident that they'd outlined the right course of action clinically speaking, but maybe they'd missed something that the other teams had seen.

Hannah was getting more and more nervous, and he tried to think of something he might say to her. There was nothing. He was nervous, too.

Taking Sam onto his shoulders had been the most challenging part of the day. Being responsible for a child, even if it was only for a few minutes and his grandmother was close by. Sam hadn't been taught to be afraid, and the way he'd clung to Matt, confident that he'd keep him safe, had been a new experience.

He shouldn't read too much into it. Hannah's mother and Sophie both looked after Sam as naturally as Hannah did. The boy was a happy, normal kid. The thought that he could be a part of what Hannah had was entirely inappropriate. And the more urgent desire to touch her was equally inappropriate.

Finally, the four teams were gathered, cameras pointing at them to record their reactions. One of the judging panel stood up and started to talk into the microphone, giving an overview of each team's performance. Hannah was standing next to Matt, looking very nervous.

'I'm taking bets on how long he's going to drag this out…' He bent, whispering into her ear behind his hand, so that the camera couldn't record his words. Even now there was a freshness about her scent that worked its way into his consciousness.

She looked up at him, smiling suddenly. 'Two minutes.'

'Okay. I'll say thirty seconds. Loser buys coffee next time round.' Matt reckoned it would be closer to three minutes. But at the moment, buying coffee for Hannah was his idea of being a winner.

She threw him a sceptical look. Matt fixed his eyes on the clock and Hannah followed suit. The second hand ticked around, and he felt her nudge him when it had signalled that two minutes had passed. He looked down at her and found that her smile was worth the price of a thousand cups of coffee.

'You win.' He murmured the words to her just as the judge's voice crashed into his consciousness.

'And the winners are... Matt and Hannah, for Hamblewell Hospital.'

Cheers erupted from the crowd, and Matt could see Sam jumping up and down, doing the victory dance he'd done with Hannah last week. Hannah seemed paralysed by the news, and he took the lead, shaking the hands of the other competitors. Matt waited until she'd followed suit, and then propelled her towards the judge.

She shook his hand, smiling and holding aloft the medal that he'd draped around her neck. Matt received his, standing next to Hannah, as everyone cheered. It was a dizzying, almost surreal experience. Winning this with Hannah was a more potent achievement than he'd thought.

An endless round of handshakes and congratulations. And then suddenly they were alone.

'Well done, Flash.'

'You too, Robin...' She frowned suddenly. 'Don't you want to be Flash? Robin sounds as if you're my sidekick...'

'Hey. You stick with your own middle name, and I'll stick with mine. I've become attached to it over the years.' He wasn't particularly attached to either of his first names, because he guessed they'd been his father's choices. But on Hannah's lips the name had acquired new and better associations.

He pulled the medal ribbon over his head. 'Would Sam like this?'

'You earned it. He can have mine.'

Matt put the medal into her hand. 'Give him this one. Then you can both wear one.' He reckoned that Sam might like that.

'Are you sure…?' Hannah looked up at him and he nodded. 'Why don't you come and give it to him yourself, so he can say thank you? We'll probably have to go for a drink somewhere before I get to go home and lie on the sofa—you're welcome to join us.'

There was nothing that Matt would like more. Being with Hannah for just a while longer. Seeing that softer side of her, which seemed to retreat behind a determined shell when she was competing. But it wasn't a good idea. He was already becoming too aware of her, and it was an uneasy path to take.

'Thanks, but I'd like to get home. I've got a few things to do.' The lie sounded hollow on his lips. 'Actually, lying on the sofa sounds like a good idea.'

Her gaze searched his face for a moment. Then she nodded. 'I'll let you go, then. Thanks for today. And the medal, Sam will love it.'

Matt watched her walk away. She knelt down in front of Sam, putting the medal around his neck, and Matt's heart began to swell as the little boy picked it up gravely, examining it. Then Hannah pointed behind her in his direction and started to turn…

He turned away quickly. It wouldn't do for her to know that he was watching, greedy for every detail of the scene. Matt walked away, starting to feel the heaviness of his limbs and the sting of the wound on his shoulder. He should go home, take a long shower, and forget all about Hannah until next week.

CHAPTER FIVE

HANNAH WAS TRYING not to think about Matt. That wasn't easy, because Sam hadn't stopped talking about him, and her mother had mentioned that he seemed nice and wondered innocently whether he had a family. Sophie didn't have such reservations.

'I asked. He's definitely single.'

Hannah leaned back in the front seat of the ambulance, closing her eyes. 'And they know this how?'

'I spoke to one of the nurses in Orthopaedics. He comes into the ward quite a lot on account of operating on quite a few of their patients.'

'Oh, and they've compiled a dossier?'

'Yeah, pretty much. He lives just around the corner from the hospital. Been here a year, isn't married and doesn't have a girlfriend, despite being a complete and utter god in the looks department.' Sophie frowned. 'That sounds a bit too good to be true actually. I wonder if he's got a dark secret.'

Hannah had wondered that too.

'Maybe he just likes to keep his personal life to himself.'

'So you know something? That you're not telling me?'

'No. We don't all have your dating stamina, I haven't had a partner in years either. I suppose that doesn't count, though, I'm not a complete and utter goddess...'

'Don't be ridiculous. You're a super-goddess.' Sophie pulled a face. 'You just can't believe that there's someone out there who won't let you down, the way John did.'

'And I've got a six-year-old, and a job. It doesn't give me a lot of time for dating.' Hannah was sure that she could have made time if she'd really wanted to, her Mum was always telling her she should go out more. But guilt stopped her. She'd let her father down, and she wouldn't break the promise she'd never had the chance to make to him. She'd never get carried away, thinking that she was in love, and let down the people she really cared about. Her place was with Sam and her mother.

'Sure you couldn't squeeze him in?' Sophie grinned, and then puffed out a breath as the radio hissed into life.

Good. Something else to think about for a while. Something that didn't involve Matt's broad shoulders, or what might happen if a girl should accidentally-on-purpose cut through that gentle veneer of his. She'd seen the fire and the determination beneath it, and it had made her shiver.

'Here we go…' Sophie glanced at Hannah, starting the engine of the ambulance.

The second part of the competition was being held at the blue team's hospital. Matt had texted Hannah, saying that he'd be there at seven thirty, and since she'd won the bet, he would be bringing coffee. Hannah had texted him back, saying she looked forward to a latte with no sugar and her phone had pinged almost immediately with a smiley face.

Matt stood out in the crowd, and she didn't have to look for his blond hair and red T-shirt. He was next to the blue team's contingent of supporters, chatting to a girl of around thirteen in a wheelchair, who'd obviously been brought down from one of the wards to watch. Hannah walked over to him, reaching out to tap him on the shoulder, but he seemed to sense she was there before she even touched him.

'Ah, there you are.' He was holding two large cardboard beakers and he handed one to Hannah. 'Latte, no sugar. Mia, this is Hannah.'

'Hi, Mia.' Hannah grinned down at the girl. 'You're here to cheer for the blues, are you?'

'I'm cheering for Dr Matt as well. He's my doctor.'

Matt grinned. 'Well, that's very kind of you. I'll run even faster knowing that you're watching me.' He gestured to a large screen that had been set up to one side of them. Clearly whatever they were going to be doing today would involve another location, and the cameras would be relaying what was happening.

'He'd better run if he's going to keep up with me.' Hannah shared the information with Mia and she grinned.

'That sounds a lot like a challenge.' Matt was smiling too. 'Hannah's an ambulance paramedic, Mia.'

Mia's face lit up. 'That's what I want to be...'

'It's a hard job, but I love it. I wouldn't do anything else.' Hannah wondered what was wrong with Mia and whether it would prevent her from dealing with the physical demands of the job.

'When you're better, you'll be able to do anything you want.' Matt came to her rescue. 'The ambulance service will be lucky to have you.'

'You've played a big part in making that possible.' The woman standing next to Mia was obviously her mother.

'It's been my pleasure. I'm glad to see Mia doing so well.' Matt bent down again. 'Will you come back later today?'

'You bet. I'll be cheering you and Hannah.'

Hannah grinned at her. 'Thanks. Ambulance crews have to stick together.'

They took their leave of Mia and her mother, strolling across the grass towards the reception tent. 'I didn't realise you worked here as well.'

'I operate here from time to time. Mia had severe scoliosis, which is my specialty.'

'She obviously thinks a lot of you.' In Hannah's experience you could generally judge a doctor by what their patients thought of them.

'She's a brave girl, and very determined. The first time I met her, she gave me a list—she'd written down all of the things she wanted to be able to do after her surgery.'

Hannah laughed. 'And how are you doing with that?'

'It's looking good. Mia's already working with the physiotherapists, and she's doing well. She'll tick everything off her list, given a little time.'

'It must be nice, being able to follow through with your patients. I don't always get that opportunity.'

'Some of them I don't get to know too well, on account of their being under anaesthetic. But I try to make time to see how they're doing, especially the kids. Giving them a decent start in life is...' Matt shrugged. 'It's what it's all about, really.'

Hannah nodded. She'd been lucky and had had the best start in life; whatever mistakes she'd made had been hers alone. Something about Matt told her that maybe his life had been shaped by other people's mistakes.

This time the teams were called one by one. They waited for what seemed like an age after the red team had been summoned, and finally they were kitted out with heavy boots, along with work gloves, jackets and hard hats. Then one of the production assistants ferried them by car to a row of old warehouses, empty and due for demolition. She drove away without another word, leaving them alone.

'What do we do now?' Hannah looked around. The site seemed deserted, although it was fair to assume that there must be cameras somewhere, trained on them.

'I'll walk that way a bit.' Matt gestured to his left. 'Maybe you go the other way, and see if you can see anything.'

'Okay. Stay within hollering distance.'

He nodded, walking away from her. Hannah started to walk, scanning the crumbling brick fascia of the warehouses. If the hard hat was anything to go by, they were expected to go inside one of them, but which one…?

'Hannah… This way…' She heard Matt's call, and turned, running towards him. His trajectory was more determined now, and she guessed he must have heard or seen something.

'I thought I heard someone calling out…' He was suddenly silent and Hannah heard it too. A woman's voice, shouting for help.

'I think it's coming from over there. Must be on the other side.' The voice was too faint to be coming from any of the doorways that they could see.

Matt nodded and they jogged together across the rubble-strewn ground towards the end of the row of buildings. Hannah felt her foot turn, and pain shot through her knee. Then she yelped in surprise as her downward trajectory suddenly reversed itself.

Matt had caught her, and she was pinioned against him. One arm wrapped firmly around her waist and the other hand… He moved it quickly away from the curve of her hip but it was too late. She'd already felt the pressure of his fingers.

'Um… Sorry. Are you okay?'

Maybe. Hannah wasn't quite sure. Maybe it was the sudden close-up of his blue eyes that had turned her legs to jelly, or maybe the shock of almost falling face first onto the sharp stones. Maybe that fleeting touch, but she could hardly blame him for that. Matt hadn't had the time to check exactly where he was putting his hands, and he was clearly a little embarrassed about it.

'Yes. Fine. Thanks.' He could let go of her now. Even if every fibre of her body was clamouring for his.

He nodded, hesitating for just one moment before he stepped away from her. In that moment, Hannah could have sworn that he felt it too. The heat of an attraction that stubbornly failed to respond to reason. Matt turned to retrieve her hard hat, which had spun out of her hand, landing some feet away.

Her knee hurt. But she could keep going. 'You go on ahead, I'll catch you up.'

'I'll wait.' There was no trace of impatience in his tone.

He was right, they should stay together, and Sophie would have done the exact same thing in these circumstances. But when Matt did it, all Hannah could think about was that she'd had no more than a taste of his strong arms, and she wanted more. She tried to concentrate on her knee, flexing her leg, and the pain subsided a little. When she took a couple of steps it felt better still.

'I'm good.' She started to walk again, and Matt fell into step beside her, still watching her. When they reached the other side of the warehouses, which faced the road, the voice became louder and clearer.

'Up there.' Matt was the first to see it. A flash of red at one of the upper windows. As they ran closer they could see it was a woman waving a red scarf.

'Are you okay?' Hannah shouted up to her. The woman was making a great job of appearing panicked and distressed.

'I'm all right. My boyfriend… He's hurt…' The woman seemed about to climb out of the window.

'Stay there. Don't try to climb down, we'll come to you. What's your name?' Matt was already on his way towards the door, leaving Hannah to deal with the woman.

'Isobel. You can't get up here…'

'Okay, Isobel. Leave that to us. Are you safe where you are right now?'

'Yes.'

'Can you see your boyfriend?' Hannah knew that when dealing with someone who was panicking and probably in shock, she had to give clear, step-by-step instructions.

'Yes…'

'Listen to me carefully, Isobel. Put your hand on the windowsill.' Isobel hesitated, but she did it. 'Good. Now turn and look at him. Tell me what you see.'

'He fell… There's blood and I think he's broken his leg.'

'Is he breathing?'

'Yes…'

'What does his breathing sound like, can you hear a rasping sound?'

'No, he's breathing easily.'

Hopefully so. 'That's good, Isobel. Have you got a phone on you?'

Hannah waited while Isobel did as she was bidden. Where was Matt? He should be up there by now, but she suspected that was going to be far too easy a solution. He appeared again at the door, running towards her.

'The way up there is blocked with rubble. We're going to have to dig our way through.' He glanced up at the window, where Isobel was watching them. 'Do you have an idea of the situation?'

'I've got pictures. Or I will have…' Hannah's phone beeped, and she opened the texts that Isobel had sent. The pictures showed a large open space, and a lifelike dummy with a good representation of a broken leg. There must be a wound as well, because blood was pooling on the floor. Isobel had obviously been well drilled in giving answers that matched the scenario, and this felt chillingly real.

Matt scrolled through the pictures. 'We need to get up there as fast as we can. We're going to have to hope that Isobel doesn't decide to start panicking again. I'll need your help to clear the debris.' The scenario obviously felt real to him as well.

'Maybe we can improvise. Perhaps there's something we can use as a tool, rather than digging with our hands.' Hannah looked around.

They were near the perimeter of the site, where the warehouses were separated from the pavement by a chain-link fence. On the other side of the road was a row of shops, and a group of men was fixing a new fascia sign to one of them. Their aerial work platform, mounted on the back of a truck, caught Hannah's attention.

'Do you think we could reach the window with that?'

Matt studied the vehicle for a moment and then, before Hannah could stop him, he made for the fence and began to scale it. It bent a little under his weight as he hauled himself over the top, twanging back into shape when he jumped down on the other side.

'Hey...!' A little discussion might have been nice.

'What?' Matt spread his hands in a querying gesture. 'It's a great idea.'

'What if they're nothing to do with the challenge? Are we allowed to ask for their help?'

'Wouldn't you and Sophie, if this were real?'

He had a point. Hannah sighed, turning back to Isobel and calling up to her to stay where she was until they could reach her. When she glanced behind her she saw that Matt was talking to the men, and they were retracting the aerial lift work platform. Matt got into the passenger seat of the truck and it drove away.

Five minutes later, the truck bumped across the service road at the back of the warehouses. The driver parked under the window, and Matt and Hannah climbed onto the aerial platform, donning their helmets.

'What did you tell them?' Hannah whispered the words as the platform began to rise towards the window.

'I said this was a challenge, which was being filmed for TV, and that we were competing for Hamblewell Hospital. They were more than happy to give it a go.'

Fair enough. Matt had turned his attention to directing the driver exactly where to place the platform. As soon as it was level with the window, he helped Hannah inside the building, making straight for the figure lying on the floor, while Hannah took a moment to calm Isobel.

The exercise hadn't been just an exercise. It had made Matt think. Would he be a better surgeon now, having faced the kind of situations that ambulance crews had to contend with?

They'd rigged up a makeshift splint and bandages, and ferried Isobel and their patient back down to the ground. As soon as she stepped off the platform, Isobel broke character, smilingly telling them that the challenge was now finished, and a couple of cars appeared to ferry them back to the hospital.

It would be at least two hours before they were needed again. That was good, because Matt had something urgent on his mind.

'What's the matter with your leg? You're limping...'

'Am I?' Hannah turned her mouth down, as if he hadn't been meant to notice.

'Yeah. I'll take a look...' There was no point in going

through the toing and froing of Hannah denying there was anything wrong, and him telling her that he knew there was. It was only the long route to an outcome that he'd already decided on.

'It's nothing. I just twisted it a bit when I fell. Don't make a fuss, Matt.'

Making a fuss was a tempting prospect at the moment. But his childhood had taught him that conflict was no way to reconcile a disagreement. Matt swallowed his annoyance and tried logic instead.

'You're my teammate. I need you in full working order for next week.'

That silenced her. She followed him into the hospital building, and Matt ignored her frown as he took the lift up to the orthopaedic department. A quick enquiry of one of the doctors that he knew elicited access to one of the treatment rooms, and he ushered Hannah inside.

'This is entirely unnecessary. Do you think I can't do this for myself?'

'I'm sure you can. Since you haven't yet, I'll do it for you. Like I said, I need you to keep up with me…'

That did it. She sat down on the couch, unlacing her boots and letting them fall to the floor with a clunk. Red socks. Matt studiously ignored the fact that they seemed somehow special and delightful when worn by Hannah. When she swung her legs up onto the couch, he quickly snatched up a pillow and placed it at the other end for her head.

'Comfortable?'

'No.' She glowered at him. Clearly she'd prefer to be somewhere else right now. 'I'm not your patient, Matt.'

So that was what was bothering her. Hannah was far more comfortable with being invincible, and just taking him along with her for the ride. Irritation started to prickle his skin, and he took a step back, putting his hands into his pockets. The one thing that he could never be, with Hannah, was indifferent. He had to own that, and ignore the impulse to provoke an equal reaction from her. He was a doctor, and acting that way would be good right now.

'All right.' He gave her his best doctor-patient smile. 'Point one. You *have* hurt yourself and someone needs to take a look at it. Getting yourself in the right position to examine your own knee properly isn't easy, I've tried it.'

She stared at him. Clearly Hannah took the point, and Matt decided to move on.

'Point two, I'm an orthopaedic surgeon. Which means I'm qualified.'

'Over-qualified, I'd say.' Hannah still wasn't going to give up. Neither was Matt.

'Point three. I'm your teammate. When are you going to start trusting me?'

He'd hit a nerve. Hannah sat up on the couch, grimacing at him.

'Are you telling me that our partnership isn't working for you?'

It worked just fine. He was aware of Hannah watching him carefully from time to time—most of the time actually—but it still worked. 'It *could* work a little better.'

He knew that look. It was the wary, thoughtful look of someone who had been hurt.

'And you think that's *my* fault?'

He shook his head. His father had blamed everyone else for his own shortcomings and that was something that Matt didn't want to emulate.

'No, it's *our* fault. Mine as well. I think that we're both people who like to manage things on our own, and that we both have difficulty in trusting others. That usually works pretty well for both of us, but the whole point of this competition is to take us out of our comfort zones.'

She was thinking about it. Hannah was either going to roll her trouser leg up and let him take a look at her knee, or she was going to get off the couch, grab her boots and limp off down the corridor.

Her lip curled, and she reached for the leg of her trousers, folding the material carefully as she pulled it up.

'You'll be wanting to see the other knee. To compare.' She reached for the other trouser leg, rolling that up too. Matt wondered if he should congratulate her on anticipating his next move, and decided that she might not take that too well.

'Thank you.' He stepped forward, looking at both knees carefully.

'I don't see any swelling, I'm going to check the movement... Tell me when it hurts.'

She nodded, and Matt carefully bent her leg, watching her face intently. Maybe he should trust Hannah enough to just tell him when there was any pain...

Or not. He saw it in her face but she said nothing.

'That hurts?'

'A little.'

'Okay, how about that?' He moved the leg again, checking the ligaments on the other side of her knee.

'No, that's fine.'

'And this...?' He dug his thumb into the side of her knee, and she shook her head. That was good. Matt moved on to the spot that ought to hurt, and she winced.

'Yeah. That's a little tender.'

He nodded. 'And what's your diagnosis?'

Hannah smirked. 'You're the expert. You tell me.'

Matt gave her a small smile. 'I'd say it's an injury to

the medial collateral ligament. Grade One so it shouldn't give you too much trouble. Treatment?'

She gave him an argumentative look. 'Don't patronise me. I may not be a doctor, but I'm fully aware that rest, ice, compression and support should sort it. I'll be okay by next week.'

He rose to the challenge. 'It should be improved. It'll be a few weeks before the knee is back up to full strength.'

'Right. I stand corrected, Mr Lawson.'

'And I'll know that I need to compensate for you a bit.'

She didn't like that one bit. Hannah flashed him a look that left him in no doubt that she was contemplating jumping off the couch and strangling him.

'Just as you might like to compensate for me,' Matt added, quickly.

'Compensate how?' Hannah had obviously decided to put the strangling on hold for a moment.

'Getting help from those men with the aerial lift truck was a great idea. But I got the distinct impression that you thought I was jumping the gun…'

She looked at him steadily. 'And were you?'

He may as well admit it. 'Yes, I was. I reckoned I'd climb the fence before you had a chance to try it. You were already limping and I'm not sure you would have made it with that knee.'

Hannah grinned suddenly. 'You're probably right. But a bit more communication would have been nice.'

'Point taken. Can I trust you to remind me if I forget that?'

'Oh, yes, I'll remind you.' Hannah thought for a moment. 'Can I trust you to pick me up if I fall over again?'

Matt chuckled. 'Yeah. Any time.'

Trust wasn't something he usually shared with people he didn't know well. But he and Hannah had to become a team if they were going to win the prize for their hospital. *Hannah's* hospital. He might be moving on soon.

Matt dismissed the thought of the job application forms, lying on his desk at home. That was the future, and as ever he was uncertain about where he'd be a few months from now. This was now.

'Would you like to come back and have dinner with us afterwards?' Hannah's question broke his reverie. 'Sophie's bringing Sam along to see the results announced, and Mum's making burgers, she always makes a few extra and puts them in the freezer so there's plenty to go round. We could talk tactics for next week.'

It wasn't the kind of invitation he usually accepted. But getting to know Hannah better was the obvious precursor to building trust and teamwork.

'Thanks. That would be great. I'll go and see if I can rustle up some ice and a light knee support. Why don't you stay here?'

She nodded. Then she smiled suddenly. 'Did you miss something?'

Matt chuckled. 'You mean did I miss telling you that your knee is just fine, and apart from a slight injury you have good movement and excellent muscle tone? Or the part about the small ganglion cyst on the side of your knee?'

'So you *did* find it? What were you thinking, that you wouldn't mention it?'

'I didn't want to sound like a know-all. I reckoned you must be aware of it, and I'm sure you also know that it might well disappear on its own, without any treatment. I don't imagine it hurts.'

'No, it doesn't. It's nice to know that you caught it, though.' Hannah gave him a brilliant smile, and Matt smirked back.

'Now that we have that cleared up, I'll go and get the ice. Stay put.'

He'd wanted to protect her. Matt had wanted to be nice to Hannah, and not make her feel that he was criticising or second-guessing her, the way his father had with his mother. But he'd been doing it all wrong. A woman like Hannah, and maybe a man like him, thrived on straight-forwardness and honesty.

'All right. Hurry up, we don't have all day.'

CHAPTER SIX

THE CHEMISTRY BETWEEN Hannah and her new teammate had undeniably been growing, and even though she'd tried to ignore it, Hannah had to admit to herself that she enjoyed it. Maybe that, along with a fierce desire to keep up with whatever pace Matt set, was why she'd fought so hard when he'd suggested he examine her knee.

But as soon as he'd walked into the consulting room, he'd changed. No less confronting, but he was cool and professional. Hannah let Matt place the ice on her knee, and sat patiently until he told her that would do for the time being. Then he wrapped a soft support around her leg, checking that it didn't hamper her movement but that it was tight enough to aid the healing process.

'I thought I'd go along to the orthopaedic ward and see Mia. You want to come?'

'Yes. They won't mind that we're not their team?'

'We're on their team, in every way that counts. There are a lot of ambitions in that ward, and we're the ones who are working to help them achieve those ambitions.'

It was a nice way of putting it. 'That's what makes you want to win?'

'One of the things.'

He led the way to the ward, and when he and Hannah entered there was a small murmur of excitement. She saw

Mia waving from the far end, and when the ward sister nodded in response to Matt's request that they might spend some time here, she walked over to her.

'How did you do?'

'Hmm. Not sure. We did our best.'

'That's all you can do.' Mia spoke with a wisdom beyond her years and Hannah suspected that it was what Matt and the rehab specialists had told her.

'Would you like to hear about it? We had a rescue situation, a bit like the ones that you can come across, working as ambulance crew. We had to deal with it on our own, though usually an ambulance crew has back-up from the other rescue services.'

'You bet I want to hear about it.' Mia's eyes were shining.

Hannah heard Matt's quiet chuckle behind her. 'I'll leave you to it. Would you ladies like some juice?'

Mia nodded, and Hannah grinned at him. 'Hey, we're not ladies. What are we, Mia?' She turned to Mia, mouthing the answer.

'We're ambos!'

'My mistake. I'll get you two ambos some juice.'

Matt had left her with Mia while he worked his way around the ward, talking to the other kids. He had a nice way with them, and they were obviously relaxed and confident in his company. Hannah reckoned he must spend a lot more time here on the ward than his job required.

She ended up talking to Mia for over an hour, answering her questions, without being too blunt about the distressing parts of her job. It was clear that this was part of the dream that kept Mia going through all of the pain and the distress of her condition.

'We have to get going now. Sorry, Mia.' Matt returned, shooting Mia an apologetic look.

'That's okay. Thanks, Hannah.'

'My pleasure. I'll pop in again, and let you know what other scrapes Dr Matt has got himself into.'

'Oh, really?' Matt feigned outrage and Mia giggled. 'Next time Hannah gets herself into a scrape, I'll make sure to take a picture and send it to you…'

They walked out of the ward together, and back down to the area where the outside broadcast trucks were parked. It felt as if it would have been almost natural to take Matt's hand. As if they were close, in a way they hadn't been when they'd arrived back here. That wasn't appropriate, though, or wise. The alternate reality, where she and Matt could be *that* close, didn't exist. There was only this world, and in this world Hannah didn't take chances.

They waited, and Hannah went across to greet Sam when he arrived with Sophie. The crowd grew, along with the obvious tension amongst the contestants, all waiting to see who was going to be the winner.

'I reckon they dug their way through…' Matt nudged her, nodding towards the green team, whose T-shirts were covered in grime.

'Maybe that's what we were all supposed to do.' Hannah turned the corners of her mouth down. They'd solved the problem, making use of the resources at their disposal. In the real world you didn't question your luck, or the presence of the right person at the right time.

'We'll see.' Matt took a deep breath as they were all gestured up onto the podium.

There was the inevitable wait as microphones were tested and the judges got ready to announce their decision. Hannah saw Sam in the crowd and waved to him.

Mia was amongst the home supporters, with her mother, talking excitedly.

Then a judge stepped forward. She congratulated all of the teams, going through what had caught the judges' eyes about each of them. The truck *had* been put there by the TV company to see if any of the contestants would spot it and ask for help. Hannah waited, trying to keep her face from betraying her thoughts.

'And now for the winners. For the second time—it's Matt and Hannah…'

A roar went up from the crowd, drowning out the rest of what she was saying. And suddenly, without thinking, all the pent-up emotion burst through and she was in Matt's arms.

There was nothing else. Just his arms around her, and the feeling that she wanted to get closer, to touch his skin. Hannah couldn't help letting out a sigh, as she felt herself melt against him.

'Way to go, Robin.' She felt his lips brush her cheek, a thrilling second that should have lasted longer.

'You too, Flash.'

Then he let her go. They shook hands with the other contestants, and Matt took her hand, leading her up to the judge to receive her medal. Hannah waved to the cheering crowd, unable to look at him but powerless to stop thinking about the feel of his strong body.

Hannah was still limping slightly as she hurried across the grass towards Sophie and Sam, but her knee was clearly less painful than it had been. Matt watched as she hugged Sam, and they did their victory dance. He wanted her so much he could hardly breathe.

Hannah was in conversation with Sam, and it seemed to be about something important. Sam was nodding, and

Hannah hugged him, and then stood up as Sophie took his hand to walk towards the ice-cream van that was parked in the car park behind them. Then Hannah began to walk along the line of spectators, looking for someone.

He knew what she was about to do, just as surely as if she'd shouted her intentions over her shoulder at him. Hannah walked along the line of kids who had been brought down from the wards to watch, and Matt jogged across the grass towards her. He wanted to see this.

She knelt down opposite Mia, who was talking excitedly. Then Hannah took off her medal, hanging it carefully around Mia's neck.

'Hannah, are you sure…?' Mia's mother spoke up.

'Of course. Mia deserves this.' She grinned down at Mia, who was clutching the medal to her chest, just in case her mother decided to try and take it away from her. 'What you're doing now is hard, Mia. But if you can do all that Dr Matt and the physiotherapist tell you, then you can do anything.'

Matt wanted to hug her again. He wanted to feel her body against his, and this time it wasn't just a heat of the moment thing. He'd thought about it and he *needed* to hug her. Instead he smiled at Mia's mother.

'What about a photograph?'

'Oh, yes, of course.' Mia's mother began to rummage in her handbag, and Mia produced her own phone from her pocket. 'Give it to me, darling, and we can take one with Hannah and Dr Matt.'

The photos were taken, and then Matt saw one of the nurses beckoning him over. 'Will Sam mind if we stay a minute for some more photos?'

'No, Sophie's promised him an ice cream and from the looks of the queue they'll be a little while.' She smiled. 'I asked him if he'd mind me giving my medal to a girl who was sick and had been very brave, and he told me that was the right thing to do.'

Matt chuckled. 'That was kind of him.'

'He has his moments. He surprises me all the time, though, he's starting to think about things. I found him tipping the contents of the bin out on the kitchen floor the other day. They'd given them all a talk about recycling at school, and he told me that Grandma wasn't doing it properly.'

'Good for him. It's his future.' Matt felt a lump form in his throat. Sam didn't just know what was right, Hannah had taught him. He knew only love, and he understood that other kids weren't as lucky as he was.

'Let's take some photos, then…' She smiled up at him, striding across to a little boy who was waving to them, telling the child next to him to be patient and he'd get a photo too. Matt joined her, kneeling down next to the boy's wheelchair and smiling for the camera.

The other teams had seen what they were doing and had joined in, posing for photographs with the children. Hannah was chatting to the last little girl when Matt saw Sophie walking towards them, balancing two ice-cream cones in one hand. Sam was dawdling along next to her, intent on demolishing his own ice cream as quickly as possible before it melted.

'Hi, Matt. You and Hannah did a great job today. Four points ahead on the leader board.'

'Thanks. It was mainly Hannah…' He might have helped things along, but it was Hannah who had inspired him. Who'd made him want to win more than anything.

'Well, you deserve an ice cream at least.' Sophie proffered one of the cones she was carrying and when he hesitated she gave an impatient nod. 'Take it. I'll share with Hannah.'

The ice cream was cool in his mouth and welcome on

a hot summer's day like today. Matt bent down, squatting on his heels in front of Sam.

'Hey, little man. I have something for you.' He took the medal from around his neck, and put it around Sam's. The little boy regarded it steadily.

'Look at that! I think Matt deserves a thank-you, don't you, Sam?' Sophie nudged Sam's shoulder.

'Thank you.' Sam took Matt by surprise, suddenly flinging his arms around his neck, depositing the last of the ice cream from his cone on the back of Matt's T-shirt. Then he ran over to Hannah, showing her the medal, and she turned, her eyes bright. Matt would have given anything to receive that one look.

She mouthed a thank-you, and Matt nodded.

'I think that warrants a photograph.' Sophie gave the last ice-cream cone to Hannah and took her phone from her pocket. Hannah came to stand next to him, her shoulder touching his, and Sam stood in front, leaning against Matt's legs. They could almost have been a happy family. Matt longed to put his arm around Hannah.

The moment was captured, but didn't last long enough. He'd watched Hannah and Sam together, and seen her ice-queen mask slip when she was with her son. And now, for just a little while, he was a part of it all. Matt had told himself that it was impossible to miss what you'd never had, and for the most part he believed it. Right now, the ache of knowing that they were just posing for the camera was almost unbearable.

'Are we ready to go?' Hannah bent down towards Sam. 'It's burgers tonight, your favourite. Aunt Sophie and Matt are coming with us as well.'

'Hooray!' Sam careened around in a circle, and Hannah smiled.

'Right, then. Hungry mouths to feed...'

* * *

Matt followed Sophie's car to one of the small villages that bordered Hamblewell. The house was set a little way back from the road and surrounded by a neat garden, the russet-coloured bricks blending in with the flowers and climbing plants around the doorway.

There were already two cars parked in the driveway, but Sophie manoeuvred in beside them with only inches to spare, leaving the space outside in the road clear for Matt to park. He saw Hannah lean back, undoing Sam's seat belt, and he tumbled out of the car, running towards the front door.

'Grandma... Grandma!' He shouted through the letter box. 'Mum and Matt won! They're ahead of everyone else!'

Hannah's mother opened the door, and Sam tumbled inside. She greeted Matt, and hugged Hannah, obviously enjoying the sudden influx of noise and laughter. Hannah showed Matt through a large, comfortable sitting room to a shaded patio at the back of the house.

'Sit down. I'll go and get some drinks.' Hannah disappeared through the open door of the kitchen, and the sound of voices erupted. She backed out of the kitchen, holding her hands up in a gesture of surrender, and Matt heard Sam's voice.

'Go away, Mum. We're cooking!'

'Okay, sweetheart. I'll leave you to it. I love you,' Hannah called in through the open door, and turned back towards Matt. 'Apparently drinks will be brought out to us. The kitchen's out of bounds.'

Matt sank into the cushions of the wooden patio chairs. 'That's nice. I could do with a rest.'

'Me too.' Hannah grinned, sitting down and unlacing

her boots. She stripped off her socks, wiggling her toes as she stretched her legs out in front of her.

Sophie appeared with two glasses and a jug of iced lemonade, setting them down beside Hannah on the table and producing an ice pack from under her arm. 'Which one of you needs this?'

'Me. Thanks.' Hannah reached up, taking the ice pack and applying it to her knee. 'It's okay.'

'You're sure? I've heard your version of *okay* before.'

'Matt took a look at it. Grade One MCL injury.' Hannah pulled her trouser leg up, unwrapping the knee support. 'See I've even got this…'

Sophie nodded her approval, pulling one of the other chairs around so that Hannah could prop her leg up on it. 'Don't let her move, Matt.'

'Right you are.' Matt grinned as Sophie disappeared back into the kitchen. This was nice. The rough and tumble of a loving family home.

Hannah leaned forward, pouring the lemonade and handing Matt a glass. She took a couple of mouthfuls of her own drink and then settled back into her seat, obviously tired out.

'Have you always lived here?' The sitting room had the quiet air of an established home.

Hannah shook her head. 'No, my parents lived right out in the sticks. I'd moved into a flat in town to be closer to the hospital while I was training, and then I took a year out to travel. When my dad died, my mum decided that she wanted to move into town so that she was less isolated. I was pregnant, and we decided to get this place together. It suited us both.'

'It must be great for Sam. To have his grandmother so close.'

'It's great for me, too. Sophie and I work the early shift, so Mum gets Sam up and takes him to school and then I'm there to pick him up.' She smiled lazily. 'Mum's joined a book club *and* the local women's guild. She's a busy women these days.'

'Not so much at first, then? After your father died?'

'No. My dad was her whole world. It took a while before she was able to pick herself up again when he died.'

Supporting her mother through her grief, *and* looking after a child on her own. It can't have been easy for Hannah. Maybe her fierce determination had been forged in that fire. 'It must have been difficult for you, too.'

Her finger started to tap on the side of her glass, the rhythm suggesting stress. 'I made my mistakes. Not being there when my dad died. Getting pregnant with someone who didn't want to know.'

'You were just…living your life, weren't you?'

Hannah gave a dry laugh. 'I'd feel better about it if I had been. I'm not sure that I actually *was* living my life, my ambitions were always to go into medicine. I was just blindly following someone who turned out to be the wrong guy.'

Matt knew he was the wrong guy, too. He had a lot in common with Sam's father, he couldn't stay in one place for too long, and he didn't know how to take on the responsibility of being a father. A concerned and dedicated doctor was about as much commitment as he could manage.

He had no answer for Hannah. But she smiled suddenly, providing her own.

'We live and learn, though. I know that I belong here.'

'It's a good place to belong.' A great place. Hannah had attained her ambitions work-wise and she was raising a happy little boy who wasn't afraid of the world.

Sam ran out of the kitchen, wearing a super-hero apron.

He flung himself across Hannah's legs, dislodging the ice-pack which slithered onto the decking.

'Aunt Sophie says I've got to come and see if you're moving.'

'Well, you can tell her I'm staying absolutely still.' Hannah smiled, stroking her son's hair.

'I mixed the burgers.' Sam decided that he should report on his own progress.

'Did you? I can't wait to taste them.'

Sam nodded sagely. 'Aunt Sophie's got to cook them first or they'll make you ill. You'll have to wait.'

'Yes, I dare say I will. Did you wash your hands?'

'Yes.' Sam held out his hands, and Hannah went through the motions of inspecting them. Then he scooted back into the kitchen, clearly not wanting to miss anything that was going on in there.

'So… Are we good for next week?' Sam had broken the train of thought that had been carrying Matt to the inevitable conclusion that he would never be able to touch Hannah in the way he wanted to. That was just as well, it was better not to even consider the prospect.

'We're good.' She flashed him a mischievous smile. 'Since I'm not supposed to move, I can't pick that ice-pack up, can I?'

Matt went to stand, then leaned back in his seat, realising that Hannah was teasing him. 'It's a therapeutic measure. I'll give you a special dispensation.'

She snorted with laughter, leaning forward and grabbing the ice-pack from the ground, gesturing towards him with it as if she were about to lay it on his skin, and Matt chuckled. Hannah was enchanting, and he couldn't help wanting to know her better. Wanting to feel her again, hugging him as they won another victory together. If he had to wait another week for that, then patience was his new best friend.

CHAPTER SEVEN

THERE WAS A subtle difference in the way that Hannah greeted him the following Saturday. Something had changed.

They were both still nervously anticipating what the day might hold. But they were a team now. Ready to push each other to the limit, instead of just pushing themselves. The competitors were sent to separate rooms on the ground floor of the yellow team's hospital, and after a few minutes a production assistant entered.

'One of you is to come with me.'

Which one? Before Matt could volunteer to go, Hannah spoke.

'I'll go.'

He swallowed down the questions about whether her knee was all right now, and if he shouldn't be the one to pave the way. Hannah was fearless, and she wanted to be first.

'Okay.' He smiled at her. 'Good luck with it. Whatever it is.'

He felt a sinking feeling as he watched her walk out of the room, and the door closed behind her. Up till now, he'd wanted to face the odds and succeed. Today he wanted to face the odds with Hannah at his side. Matt sat down, leaning forward to plant his elbows on his knees and staring at the floor. Waiting, keeping his focus, was a part of his job. He knew how to do that.

Ten minutes later the door opened again, and he jumped to his feet. Hannah appeared, and he scanned her quickly for any signs of what she'd been doing. She was holding two safety helmets in her hand.

'It's an obstacle course. We have to do it together.'

'Okay.' They'd both done an obstacle course before, that shouldn't be too much of a problem.

'Only I have to guide you.' She gave him one of the helmets and Matt inspected it. There was an earpiece, which he assumed was linked to the microphone on Hannah's helmet. And his also incorporated a pair of black-out goggles, which would render him completely sightless. Matt swallowed hard.

'All right. Anything you want to say to me while I can still see you?' Perhaps they could quickly work out some kind of code—anything that might help them.

She smiled suddenly. 'Good luck, Robin. I'll be there with you every step of the way.'

Matt decided that the best thing he could take with him was Hannah's smile. He took one last, long look, and put the goggles over his eyes, rendering himself completely blind. He felt Hannah carefully checking that everything was in place, and then her fingers brushed his cheek.

'I can't touch you either. Not after we get out of this room. We both have to get across six obstacles.'

'Both of us?' That meant that Hannah was going to have to do the course, and guide him as well.

'Yes. It's going to be tricky. If I tell you to freeze, just stay where you are. I'll be working out our next move. But I'll be there, all the time.'

'I know…' He suddenly felt helpless, totally reliant on Hannah. It was both terrifying and exciting.

'Let's give it a go. Can you hear me okay through the earpiece?'

'Yep.'

'Good. Turn thirty degrees right, and then take three paces. The door will be right in front of you.'

Even that small obstacle was difficult, and he took two goes to get it right. Hannah was quiet and patient, and he began to rely on her voice. The soft scent of her body became suddenly more prominent, and he tried to resist it. But sinking into it, allowing it to reassure him, gave him confidence. As she guided him carefully around the room he began to move more steadily.

The sound of the door opening, followed by a woman's voice. 'Ready…?'

'Yes, we're ready.' He felt Hannah's fingers curling around his in one last touch that was overwhelming in its intensity. 'Stick with me, eh?'

'Like glue.' Someone checked his helmet and then took his arm and led him slowly out of the building. He felt the caress of a breeze on his cheek and grass under his feet, and heard a cheer from the red team's supporters. Then a loudspeaker called for silence, and he was turned around a couple of times, leaving him dizzy and disorientated. Then Hannah's voice. The only thing he had to cling onto.

'Ready to go?'

'Give me a minute.' Matt took a deep breath, steadying himself. He imagined Hannah's smile in front of him, and the world began to stop its frantic whirl. 'I'm ready.'

An almost eerie silence had fallen across the supporters, as four teams started to make their way towards the four identical sets of obstacles that faced them. Matt needed all of her attention and all of her concentration.

'There are six obstacles. The first is stepping stones. Six paces ahead of us…'

He followed her instructions. Hannah put her foot on the first stepping stone, feeling it spring slightly. 'There's a bit of movement in the stones. When you put your weight on it, it sinks down.'

That was bound to disorient him. But Matt was letting her guide him, and they cleared the stones without any mishaps. When she glanced across at the blue team, she saw that one of them had fallen, and they were back at the start again.

'How are the others doing?' Matt muttered quietly to her.

'Forget about them. It's just us…' Just them and a couple of hundred other people, all standing silently so that the teams could hear each other. But Matt had to concentrate, and she had to be his only reality at the moment. The thought elicited a quiver, deep in her stomach.

She saw his lips curve and he nodded. 'How many steps to the next one?'

'I'd say about ten. Keep going until I tell you to stop…'

They made their way carefully across the hanging loops, Matt's strength allowing him to go slowly and let Hannah tell him where the next hand-hold was. The water slide was easier, and Matt did it almost without any guidance, just a reassurance when they got to the top that he could allow himself to slide down the other side. A tangle of elastic ropes proved unexpectedly difficult and Matt got snagged up in them, but Hannah talked him through. They were ahead of the other teams, and she wondered whether he could hear the excitement in her voice.

Then she put a foot wrong. She was keeping her eye on

Matt and landed awkwardly as she jumped down from the climbing net. Pain shot through her knee and she gasped.

'Hannah…?' He was standing quite still, his hand moving to the strap of his helmet. He knew she was in trouble, and any moment now he was going to take it off so that he could come to her aid.

'Don't… Keep the helmet on…' Hannah resisted the temptation to tell him that she was all right. She'd done that last time, and he'd known it was a lie. 'My knee hurt a bit when I jumped down. It's not too bad, I can finish. You can look at it then.'

'Tell me if it gets worse…'

'Sure…' He didn't move. 'I promise. Now get going…'

She took a couple of steps and found that the pain was subsiding, her knee strengthened by the support that she wore. The last, and most challenging, of the obstacles was still ahead of them.

The climbing wall had to be fifteen feet high, and was surrounded by air-filled cushions. It seemed almost impossible, towering above them.

'This is the last one.'

He must have heard the tremor in her voice. Matt nodded, his lips forming a thin line. 'Let's do it.'

She managed to guide him up the first ten feet, climbing by his side. Then, concentrating on where Matt should reach, she missed one of her own footholds, slithering back down before she could grab on again.

'Hannah!'

'I'm okay. Wait…'

He waited, stock still, while she climbed back up again. By the time she reached him, she felt as if she were nearing the brick wall that all athletes slammed into at one time or another.

'Stop a minute. Catch your breath.' He must have heard

her ragged breaths through the earpiece, and that wasn't a request, it was a command. Hannah settled herself firmly on two good footholds, clinging to the wall and laying her head against its surface. The short climb to the top seemed suddenly impossible.

He was skimming his fingers across the wall, finding his next handhold. Slowly, he hauled himself up, his foot searching for a secure support. He was climbing blind, and Hannah could only watch, wishing that she had his strength.

'How much further?'

'Five feet.' It seemed like five miles.

'One step at a time, then.'

That sounded great. In principle. 'I don't think I can…'

'Don't think about it, just do it. Move!'

This was so different from the way he'd wordlessly picked up her bag, refusing to goad her into trying harder. But Matt was right there, with exactly what she needed right now.

Suddenly she was strong again. 'Damn you, Robin!' She reached for the next handhold and found it.

'Get a move on, Flash…'

He was grinning now, and Hannah couldn't help a grim smile. Together they climbed to the top of the wall.

'It's a shallow slide back down. Then about fifty metres to the finishing line.'

'Got it. You go first.'

Hannah struggled to pull herself over the top of the wall, sliding gratefully down the shallow incline on the other side. Matt was still at the top, automatically looking around in an instinctive attempt to orientate himself.

'Matt… Follow my voice.' She called up to him and he turned his head towards her, then pointed directly at her. 'That's right. You're facing in the right direction, just climb over the top and slide down.'

They stumbled across the finishing line together. Matt fell to his knees, and Hannah reached for him, unbuckling the chin strap of his helmet so that he could take it off. As he blinked in the sunlight, she finally allowed herself to sink down onto the grass.

'Is your knee okay?' He sat down on the grass next to her.

'It's throbbing a bit. It only hurts as much as the rest of me.'

Matt chuckled, seeming content to take her word for it. 'How did we do?'

'We were neck and neck with the blues, I wouldn't like to make the call. We were well in the lead, but I slowed us up a bit on the last obstacle.'

'You did a great job. That wasn't as easy as it seemed.' He grinned at her.

'You too.' Hannah held out her hand to give him a high five. It wasn't the empty gesture that it might have been at the start of this competition. When their palms touched, he laced his fingers together with hers, gripping her hand in an expression of triumph. Something else as well. There was tenderness in his face, and when his gaze met hers it held her breathless in its thrall. One moment of exquisite closeness.

A cry sounded behind them, and they both looked round. Laura, the blindfolded partner for the yellow team, had fallen from the slide on the other side of the climbing wall. Her partner Jack had waved the first-aid team away, bending down beside her and talking intently. Then she got up slowly, and started to walk uncertainly towards the finish line.

The greens were trailing behind, but beginning to catch

up now. A murmur ran around the crowd and the production assistants standing in front of them all motioned for quiet. Matt stood up, holding out his hand, and Hannah felt his strength boost her onto her feet.

The greens were closing, but Laura made it across the finishing line first, collapsing into Jack's arms. There was a moment of silence as he lowered her to the ground and took her helmet off, obviously concerned about her. Then he gave a thumbs-up to the crowd. Matt started to clap, and the other teams joined in. The applause caught in the breeze, spreading through the audience.

The yellows waved, and a cheer went up. The director was hurrying over to them, obviously concerned, and after a brief conversation he picked up a microphone.

'Laura's okay…' He paused as a ripple of applause ran around the crowd. 'We're going to break now until after lunch, and we'll have the second challenge ready at two o'clock.'

'There's *another* one?' Hannah grimaced up at Matt.

'So it seems. I hope it involves sitting down.' He grinned, stretching his limbs, and started to walk towards where Hannah's mum was standing with Sam.

Her mum had apparently been texting Matt, and had already elicited an agreement from him to join them for lunch. They found a shaded spot at the edge of the area that had been set aside for today's event, and her mother unpacked the sandwiches, while Matt went to his car to fetch the drinks. There was a chilled bottle of sparkling, non-alcoholic cordial, so that Sam could share their toast to a continued run of success.

'Where on earth does he get the energy?' Matt had talked with her mother about the book that she was currently reading with her book club, and they'd found a shared enthusiasm for a couple of writers. Now he was playing with Sam on the grass, the two of them engaged in a game of tag.

'Maybe he's got some to spare, not having a child to look after.'

'Hannah…' Her mother shot her a reproving look. 'You know I'll always look after Sam whenever you want.'

'I know. I didn't mean it like that, Mum. My time with Sam's the best part of my day, I wouldn't give it up for anything.'

'You could. If you wanted to go out sometimes.' Her mother looked pointedly across at Matt. 'Matt seems very nice, maybe he'd take you somewhere.'

Hannah rolled her eyes, trying to make out that the idea hadn't occurred to her already, and been rejected. 'Don't you start. I've only just managed to get Sophie to shut up about it.'

'Yes, she said.' Clearly her mum and Sophie had been comparing notes. 'I dare say Sophie's been suggesting something a little more…intimate than a visit to the cinema.'

Hannah chuckled. Mum knew that Sophie didn't mince her words. 'Yes, she has.'

'You don't need to jump in with both feet.' Her mother glanced across at Matt. 'Although…I wouldn't blame you if you did.'

'Mum!'

'What, I'm not supposed to think about things like sex? He's very attractive. And where do you suppose you and your sisters came from? Your father and I—'

'Mum, stop!' Hannah rolled over onto her back, closing her eyes. 'As far as I'm concerned, you found us under a gooseberry bush. I'm not going to even consider any alternatives.'

'Whatever.' Her mother gave a sigh. 'But I've got some experience of this, Hannah. When your father died, I thought that it was the end of my world too. Don't get me wrong, I miss him every day, and I'll always be grateful to you for helping me through that time. But I have a few more things I want to accomplish now, and you should too.'

'You think that Sam and my job aren't enough for me?'

'You always say they are. It doesn't mean that you can't have more.'

Thankfully, her mother didn't press the point. She called Sam back over, and Matt followed, throwing himself down onto the grass.

'Sam, have something to drink, it's very hot.' Her mother produced one of Sam's favourite toys from her bag. 'And you can show Matt your spaceship if you like. He doesn't want to go running around too much, he's got another challenge to do this afternoon.'

Matt shot her mother a grateful look, and turned his attention to Sam's demonstration of the spaceship's various features. He was nice with him, always including him in his conversation and listening to his opinions, giving them as much weight as if he were an adult. Sam was unable to put Matt's respect for him into words, but he felt it and liked Matt.

After half an hour, the contestants were called back and escorted to the same rooms they'd been in that morning. There was no wait this time, and Matt was taken straight out again, leaving Hannah to wonder what was in store for them. He reappeared ten minutes later, holding the same helmets they'd been wearing that morning.

'No! Not another one?'

'Well, thankfully this one *is* sitting down.' He handed Hannah's helmet to her, and she saw that it was fitted out with the same goggles that he'd had earlier. 'You get to drive an electric buggy.'

'Blindfold… They want me to operate a vehicle blindfold.'

Matt shrugged. 'That's okay, isn't it? You've got me to tell you which way to go. The course is laid out in the park, next to the hospital. I drive you over there, and then you take over.'

She wondered if he'd felt this way this morning. Blind and reliant on him. Matt was allowed to steer her out of the building and across the grass, and every touch was electric. All that stood between her and the ground.

He helped her into the buggy and they made the short trip over to the park. It was announced that the contestants would have ten minutes to familiarise themselves with the vehicles, and Hannah slid across into the driving seat. His hands guided hers to the steering wheel and once she was confident about being able to find the forward and reverse gears without too much fumbling around, he bent down, guiding her feet to the accelerator and footbrake pedals.

'I've got it. How do I start this thing?'

She felt his fingertips touch her hand, guiding it towards the starter keys. She twisted them, hearing a muted whine as the electric engine started up. A few tentative moves forward and then backwards again, and then she heard someone shouting an instruction.

'We're going to start in a minute.' She heard Matt's voice in the speaker fitted to her helmet. 'I can't touch you now…'

Hannah shivered. It sounded like an erotic promise, just his voice in the darkness and a shared purpose…

'What are the others doing?' This was a race, and Hannah tried to keep her mind off anything that she and Matt might do together in the darkness. 'I can't hear their buggies.'

'No, everyone has their own separate course. Ours goes to the left of the ornamental pond and it looks as if the others go to the right.'

'Right. So when in doubt steer left, or we both end up in the water.'

His deep, low chuckle sounded in her ear. 'Yep. If we do, just hold onto the buggy and I'll fish you out. There's a slalom for starters, so go slowly. After that there's a straight run and you can speed up a bit.'

'Okay. Got it.' The fantasy of Matt in the darkness was replaced with one of Matt in the water, saving her. Hannah gripped the steering wheel tightly, waiting for the starting buzzer.

They made it through the slalom, Matt's voice in her ear encouraging her and telling her which way to steer. Then he told her to put her foot down and go a little faster.

'Stop!' His voice sounded in the microphone, suddenly tense. 'Hannah take the helmet off!'

That meant instant disqualification, they'd been told that. But Matt could see what was happening around them and she couldn't. Hannah pulled the helmet off, blinking in the sunlight. Matt already had the door of the buggy open, and he glanced back at her.

'This is real…'

CHAPTER EIGHT

THE SPECTATORS WERE ahead of them, in an area where the four courses converged at the finish line. Matt concentrated hard on directing Hannah, looking out for any obstacles in their path that the vehicle couldn't manage. He'd seen the young man fiddling with the bundle of power cables that ran beside the white lines on the grass that marked their route.

Something about the way he was yanking the cables, not seeming to know quite what he was doing, seemed wrong, and at odds with the usual professionalism of the camera crews. A sixth sense made Matt glance at the man a second time, and it was then that it happened. A spark, a cry and the man was thrown backwards. They were far enough away from the finish line and the other three teams that no one seemed to notice.

In the flood of adrenalin it didn't occur to him that this might be some carefully constructed feint to test them. This had all the awkward unpredictability of reality, and he was out of the vehicle before it had properly stopped, calling to Hannah. He ran across the grass, kneeling down beside the man.

He was pale, his lips blue. A burn on his arm where he'd touched the cable, and when Matt tore his shirt open and bent down to listen for a heartbeat, there was nothing.

Hannah was behind him somewhere and when he turned he saw her running towards them.

'Stay away from those cables! One of them may be damaged.' She swerved suddenly, giving the dark coil snaking through the grass a wide berth.

'Okay, I'll get them to switch the power off before anyone else gets hurt.' The van that held the camera crew, who'd been filming their progress, had stopped and Hannah hurried towards them.

Matt quickly checked the man's pulse again. A few thready irregular beats, which stopped again under his fingers. He positioned his hands carefully on the man's chest.

He'd done this many times before. Not here, under the heat of the afternoon sun, with a hundred different variables, one of which was a live electric cable, situated right behind him. Hannah was dealing with that... Matt forgot everything else, and started CPR.

Death could happen so quickly. And life equally quickly. As Hannah reached him, kneeling down on the other side of the man's prone body, Matt heard a rasping breath. He checked the man's pulse, and felt the regular beat of a heart that had responded to the rhythm of the chest compressions.

'Got him...' He murmured the words and Hannah nodded. The man's lips were rapidly regaining their pink colour, and his eyelids were fluttering, as if struggling to open.

She nodded. 'The camera crew have radioed down for a crash team from the hospital. They'll be here soon.'

People were running towards them now, and he heard someone shout at them to stay back. As the man's eyes opened, Hannah was there, taking hold of his hand, positioning herself so that her shadow fell across his face.

'You took a bit of a jolt there.' She smiled down at him.

'Just be still for a moment. The doctor has everything under control.'

The man nodded weakly. He still needed care, he had burns and the CPR would undoubtedly have bruised his ribs badly. But his pulse was beating under Matt's fingers. Hannah was checking the burns on his hand, and then she carefully took off his trainers, inspecting his feet.

'Not too bad. He must have been thrown clear.'

Matt realised suddenly that she hadn't seen what had happened. Hannah had reacted so quickly to the situation that he'd forgotten that.

'Yes, he was.'

By the time the medical team arrived, they'd ascertained all of the young man's injuries. Minor burns that were immediately wrapped with cool packs. There was a bump on the back of his head, and Matt borrowed a penlight to check his responses before he was loaded onto a stretcher to be ferried down to the hospital.

Hannah sat back on her heels, watching them go. Matt recognised her smile. It was the one that someone who knew they'd made a difference wore.

Then she turned, shading her eyes as she gazed towards the finish line. The yellows had already completed the course, and were celebrating their win, while the blues and greens fought it out for second place.

'I'm glad Laura and Jack made it this time. They had bad luck this morning.' Hannah turned the corners of her mouth down.

'Yeah. They deserve it.' Matt had made the only decision possible, but all decisions had a price. 'I'm...sorry.'

'What, that you forgot all about a stupid game and decided to go and save a man's life?' She shot him a reproving look.

She must feel it. Winning meant so much to Hannah.

But she was the same as him, first and foremost a healer. Matt sighed, trying to make sense of his own feelings.

'We got to him quickly, and I think he'll be okay. That's more important than anything, but I think it's okay to wish that it hadn't happened. I imagine he does too.'

She nodded, tears suddenly forming in her eyes. 'Yeah. Let's not talk about that right now, eh?'

They sat for a moment in the sunshine. The generator had been turned off, and technicians were checking cables and coiling the damaged one. The director of the unit walked towards them.

'Nasty business.' He sat down on the grass. 'I'm glad you were there.'

'Me too.' Hannah was making an effort to smile.

'I…um…don't know what we can do about this. In terms of the competition… We want to make this fair.' The director seemed intent on catching Hannah's gaze, and she seemed intent on not looking at him.

'Give us a minute, will you?' Matt spoke firmly. 'Hannah needs to go and see her son, he'll be wondering what happened. I'd like to check on the man who was hurt, and make sure that he's all right before we do anything else.'

'Yes. Yes, of course. Thank you for what you did just now.'

Hannah smiled suddenly and got to her feet. 'It's all in a day's work.'

Matt had seen Hannah jogging over to where Sam and her mother were standing. No victory dance this time, but there was a hug. *That* was what really mattered.

He walked out of the park and onto the hospital grounds, finding his way to A and E. One of the doctors there told him that Joe, the young man who had been injured, was doing well and he allowed Matt to spend a few minutes with him.

Deep in thought as he left A and E and walked back towards the park, he almost bumped into Hannah.

'Hey! What's up, everything all right?' She looked a little down in the mouth.

'Yes, fine. How is he?'

'He's okay, recovering nicely. The burns aren't too bad, and he's conscious and talking.'

'That's great.'

'So what *is* up?' Hannah shrugged and Matt shook his head.

'Don't tell me nothing…'

She puffed out a breath. 'Everyone's being so nice. Jack and Laura came to find me, and said we should take first place. But they really deserve it, they came back after what happened this morning and they're set to win today. The director said that we could do the course again but…'

'That wouldn't be fair either. You've seen it now, and you're bound to do better.'

'Yes. Exactly.' She looked up at him, her expression troubled. 'I… This just doesn't feel right, Matt. We did what we did, and that's its own reward.'

Matt thought for a moment. 'I guess we've both given up a bit to do the jobs we do. You and Sophie catch an extra shift, and you can't get back home in time to put Sam to bed.' He couldn't think of anything that he was missing by working long hours. He'd made a point of not having any home life. But Hannah smiled, and nodded.

'So what do you say we let this result stand. We're disqualified because I made a decision to tell you to take your helmet off. We made the same decision that we've had to make all of our working lives. Let's stick by that, and be proud of it.'

'That's exactly how I feel about it. But… It's not just us. What will the hospital board say if we pass up the chance of winning the money?' Hannah frowned.

'It's a matter of principle. If they have anything to say about it, then we have our answer. We can still win if we make a good showing on the final day.'

He wanted to tell her that if they didn't win, he'd help her raise the money for the hospital anyway. But he might not even be here in a couple of months. His application for the job in London was under consideration, and he'd been called for an interview.

They'd come a long way in the last three weeks. Complete strangers, who'd treated each other with prickly courtesy but didn't really trust each other. But now Matt knew her. And he knew what Hannah would choose to do.

She looked up at him, the sunlight catching flecks of gold in her eyes. 'You're right. I say we disqualify ourselves from the race. We did the right thing, and we don't need any rewards for that. Thank you, Matt.'

Suddenly he needed her close. Winning together was nothing if they couldn't lose together as well. Matt reached for her, and Hannah smiled up at him.

'I'm okay…'

'Not sure that I am.'

She wrinkled her nose. 'Maybe I spoke too soon.'

She put her arms around him, and Matt held her close. None of the people milling around seemed to notice, they were just teammates hugging each other. But this was different. It was everything. Sharing the disasters along with the triumphs, and knowing that Hannah was there with him.

'We should go.' She didn't move.

'Yeah, we should. In a moment.'

He felt her move against him, snuggling into his arms. Matt held his breath, wanting this to last. 'Yeah. In a moment…'

The announcement of the winners took place a little later than expected, but most of the spectators were still there. Pretty much everyone knew what had happened, and wanted to know how things would be resolved.

Matt had had a lengthy conversation with the head judge, and when she approached the microphone, she held a piece of paper in her hand. Clearly what she was about to say had been carefully scripted.

She started by giving the news that the young man who had been injured was doing well. Then she praised each of the teams for their performances today. Suddenly she looked up from her notes, staring straight into the camera.

'I've mentored medical staff in training for many years, and today I saw a fine example of the values that we teach. Hannah and Matt have asked that the results of this afternoon's heat stand, as a tribute to the many medical professionals around the country who put their own interests second and respond to a higher calling on a daily basis. So, after a brave comeback, I'm happy to award the medals to Laura and Jack of the yellow team. Ladies and gentlemen, you are all winners.'

There was a moment's silence. Then a piercing whistle sounded from the crowd. 'Go, Laura and Jack… Go, Hannah and Matt.' Sophie was shouting at the top of her voice, and as everyone else took up the chant, she and Sam performed the victory dance.

'Your words?' Hannah nudged Matt, whispering up to him.

'I just explained how we felt. I thought she put it very well...'

Before they could say any more, Laura and Jack had come over to shake their hands. Then the others, and before Hannah knew what was happening, she was being propelled forward. Laura and Jack beckoned to the others, and all eight of the competitors stood at the front of the stage together, waving at the crowd.

Hannah felt tears tumbling down her cheeks. She wanted to share this with Matt, but he was further down the line of competitors. She waved at Sam, and he waved back, obviously shouting at the top of his voice, although the sound was lost in all the cheering.

By the time she managed to escape and walk down the steps of the stage, Hannah's legs were shaking. She wanted to cling to Matt and hear him tell her that they were in this together, Flash and Robin, teammates...and maybe more? She shook the thought out of her head as the chairman of the hospital board hurried across to her.

'I know you're disappointed, Hannah. But you showed a very fine example today.' He took her hand, shaking it vigorously.

'Thank you.' This was the first time that Dr Gregson had even spoken to her, and she couldn't think of anything else to say.

'This is your little boy...?' Dr Gregson gestured towards where Sophie and Sam were hovering, Sophie holding onto Sam's hand to stop him running forward.

'Yes. Sam... And my ambulance partner, Sophie Turner.'

'Sam...' Dr Gregson bent down, smiling, and Sam looked up at him with the clear-eyed look of someone who had no inkling of hospital hierarchies. 'You must be very proud of your mum.'

'She's the best. Do you want to see our victory dance?' Sam flung his arms above his head, ready to start doing the victory dance again, and Sophie grabbed hold of him. Dr Gregson laughed.

'I'll leave you to your celebrations.' He glanced down at Sam again. 'Keep doing that victory dance, young man.' Dr Gregson turned, making a beeline for Matt and shaking his hand.

'That went well.' Sophie was staring after him.

'Yes, I'm glad he understood.'

Sophie nodded. Matt had extricated himself from Dr Gregson's grip and was walking towards them, smiling.

'Hey, Sam. How's your day been?'

'We won!' Sam probably didn't understand quite how or why they'd won, just that they had.

'That's right. Go, reds…'

Sam reached up towards Matt in an unmistakable gesture. Matt hesitated for a moment and then picked the boy up, settling him onto his shoulders. His obvious affection for her son was always accompanied by a slight awkwardness.

'I've got to go in a minute.' Sophie looked at her watch. 'Got a date with the new A and E doctor. He's intrigued by my parking.'

Matt chuckled. 'Obviously a man of great insight.'

'So what about you two losers?' Sophie grinned. 'Off to celebrate?'

'Enough of the losers. We can still win.' Hannah saw Matt's jaw set in a determined line.

'It would be very close…' She shrugged.

'If we win outright next week, we'll be one point ahead of the others. So that's exactly what we're going to do.' A hint of steel showed in his blue eyes. Suddenly Hannah didn't want his comfort any more. *This* was exactly what she wanted from Matt.

'Okay, then. That's what we'll do.'

Sophie chuckled. 'That's the spirit. I'll leave you to plot your strategies, I've got to run…'

She grinned up at Sam, pointing towards her cheek in a signal that this was where she wanted a goodbye kiss. Sam leaned down towards her, and Sophie stood on her toes, hanging onto Matt as she did so. So easy, so natural. Hannah supposed that it was because Sophie didn't feel the way that she did about him. Sophie could touch Matt without feeling any melting desire to fall into his arms.

'What do you have planned for tonight?' Matt started to walk towards the car park, and Hannah fell into step beside him.

'Mum's out for dinner with her book club, so it's going to be just the two of us and a cartoon marathon.'

He frowned. 'Shame. I was hoping that you might let me return last week's favour and buy you dinner. But a cartoon marathon's a tough thing to compete with.'

He could come home with them… The offer hovered on the tip of her tongue, but Hannah's courage failed her. If Sam could be persuaded to go to bed on time, then she'd be alone with Matt.

'There's a great place on the river. Family friendly…'

This was why she shouldn't be alone with him. He was just too tempting for words. But what could happen under the watchful eye of a six-year-old boy?

'Thank you. We'd really like that, wouldn't we, Sam?'

'Yes, okay.' Sam hardly glanced at her, obviously bound up in his own thoughts and oblivious of what he'd just agreed to.

'Great. I'll come and pick you up at six.'

* * *

'You look bee-yoo-tiful!' Sam elongated the word to give it particular emphasis.

Hannah had only washed her hair and grabbed a dress from the wardrobe. And applied a little make-up. And found her favourite sandals, which matched the blue of her dress perfectly.

There was no point in protesting to Sam, he hadn't developed the skill of discernment yet. 'Well, you look beautiful too.' Sam frowned and Hannah laughed. 'Okay, you don't look beautiful at all. You look handsome and *very* cool.'

'Thank you.' Sam was wearing his best jeans and trainers, with a stripy polo shirt and a hoodie. When Hannah had tried to comb his hair he'd wriggled and protested, running his hands through it so that it stood on end. Hannah had relented, wetting the comb and making the spikes a little more regular.

Her beautiful boy. She was so proud of him, and if she wanted to admire anyone tonight, Sam was a good choice. That resolution flew straight out of the window as soon as the doorbell rang and she opened the door.

Matt was wearing an off-white linen suit, just creased enough to appear relaxed. A crisp, dark blue shirt completed the look. No... *Matt* completed the look. Blond and tanned, his eyes seeming very blue and his shoulders very broad. He was simply mouth-watering.

'You look nice.' The curve of his lips told her that he considered this an understatement.

'She looks bee-yoo-tiful,' Sam corrected him, and Matt nodded solemnly in agreement.

Hannah laughed, trying to cover her embarrassment. 'Sam's gone for cool tonight.'

'Hmm.' Matt pressed his lips together. 'So did I but I think you've managed it a lot better than I did, Sam.'

'You look okay. Are we going in *your* car?' Sam craned around him, obviously interested in the sleek, dark blue car parked outside. Hannah had to admit that it was far more likely to appeal to Sam than her own red run-around.

'If your mum doesn't mind me borrowing your car seat.' Matt shot a querying glance at Hannah and she shook her head.

'No, that's fine. Mine's easy to swap over into different cars, Sophie doesn't have one either so we're always switching it.'

She transferred the car seat into Matt's car, careful not to scratch the leather upholstery, and Sam sat quietly as they drove, transfixed by the dashboard display. They meandered through country lanes, drawing up next to a quiet, tree-lined stretch of the River Colne.

'A boat!' Sam was wide-eyed with excitement, and Matt smiled.

They walked down the gangplank onto a red and white painted barge, which had been fitted out with bench seats and tables. The evening sun sparkled on the water, and they sat under the shade of a canvas awning.

Matt was the perfect host, making sure that they both had whatever they wanted. The waiters were attentive and friendly, bringing a glass of wine for Hannah and sparkling water for Matt and Sam. Sam responded to being treated like an adult by acting like one, and her little boy suddenly seemed very grown up.

'Mum, look. Swans…' Sam knelt on his seat, hanging over the side of the boat, and Hannah grabbed hold of him before he fell overboard. He twisted round, taking a bread roll from the basket on the table.

'No, we mustn't give them bread, Sam. It's not what they're meant to eat, and it isn't good for them.'

Sam slid back into his seat and Matt pushed his plate towards him. 'You can give them some lettuce.' He started to separate the shredded lettuce from his mixed salad with his fork.

'Lettuce?' Hannah raised her eyebrows. 'Really?'

'Yes, swans like lettuce, and it doesn't do them any harm. A bit like pondweed, I suppose.'

Sam picked up the lettuce, and Hannah grabbed hold of him again as he climbed up, leaning over the side of the boat. When he scattered the lettuce on the water, the swans dipped their long necks, gobbling it up.

'They're making a funny noise...' Sam shivered with laughter, and Hannah saw Matt gesture to one of the waiters. He disappeared, coming back with a small bowl of shredded lettuce. Matt was grinning broadly, enjoying this as much as Sam was.

This was so relaxing. So nice. Taking the world as it came, on a lazy river, as the sun began to go down. If she'd been with Sam's father...

There wouldn't have been times like these. Sam was John's son, but Matt was the one who had time for him. And whatever she'd seen in John felt like a pale counterfeit of the way she was beginning to feel about Matt. She knew that Sam would benefit from having a father figure in his life, but this was the first time she'd wanted someone for herself in a very long time.

They lingered over coffee, talking. The lights that were threaded around the canvas awning began to brighten in the gathering dusk, and Matt signalled to the waiter to bring the bill.

'Thank you so much for tonight, Matt.' Hannah turned

to him as they stepped off the gangplank and onto the path that led up to the car. 'It was just what I needed after today.'

'Me too. Thank you for coming.' He reached out suddenly, brushing her arm with his fingertips. The world around her began to melt away, shrivelling in the heat of his gaze, as somehow the impossible didn't seem quite so impossible after all. Unspoken words hung in the air between them, waiting impatiently for the chance to be turned into reality.

Then, from somewhere behind her, Hannah heard Sam's thin wail of distress. He'd found his way down to the water's edge, and one of the swans that he'd been feeding had left the water and was waddling towards him. Sam was standing quite still, transfixed by the lumbering creature that was more than twice his size.

Before she could move, Matt was there. He gathered Sam up in his arms, shooing the swan away from him. When he turned back towards Hannah, his jaw was set hard in a mask of distress.

'Hey, little man. You're all right...' He was trying to smile for Sam's sake, and not making a very good job of it. Sam was crying now, and the agony on Matt's face as he strode back to where Hannah was standing was obvious.

They'd been close by, and Hannah had only taken her eyes off Sam for one moment. That moment had been enough, though, and the unforgivable part of it all was that Hannah's eyes had been on Matt. All of her attention had been on Matt, and she'd let Sam wander off.

She swallowed hard, trying to control her panic. This wasn't the same as leaving her family and following John halfway around the world. She hadn't abandoned Sam in favour of Matt. All the same, when Matt delivered Sam into her arms, she hugged her son as tightly as she could.

'Mum... Mum, you're squeezing me.' Sam's tears had

disappeared as abruptly as they'd appeared, and he was wiping his nose on the shoulder of her best dress. Still holding onto her son, Hannah managed to swipe her own tears away before either Matt or Sam could notice them.

'I'm sorry, sweetie. The swans are pretty big close up, aren't they?'

Sam nodded. 'I think it *might* have eaten me. But it didn't.'

'No, of course it didn't. Swans don't eat little boys, they eat lettuce. We just have to make sure that we stay away from them when they get out of the water. If they get frightened and flap their wings, they could hurt us.' Hannah managed a smile and Sam cheered up immediately, eyeing the swan as it drifted serenely at the water's edge.

'How *big* are they when they flap their wings?' Now that he was safe in her arms, he was clearly thinking about the logistics of the matter. 'Not as big as Matt.'

'No, not as big as Matt.'

'That's all right, then.' Sam had assessed the situation with a child's logic, and decided that Matt's presence made everything all right. It was a very tempting conclusion to make, and Hannah resisted it.

Sam's assertion didn't seem to be convincing Matt either. He still seemed distressed about the incident. But he smiled, taking his car keys from his pocket.

'Would you like to try out the computer in my car?' He'd obviously seen Sam's interest in the dashboard, and seemed to be trying his best to make things up to Sam. The little boy slithered down from her arms, running to Matt.

'Yes!'

'You've done it now. We'll be here all evening while he switches things on and off.'

Matt didn't seem to mind that. He didn't mind finger-marks on the high-tech touchscreen controls either. In the end, Hannah called a halt to the endless questions, and Sam was strapped firmly into his car seat for the drive home.

The house was still dark, and Hannah let Sam run past her into the sitting room. 'Would you like to come in for some coffee?' The words flew recklessly from her lips, and when he shook his head it was almost a relief.

'Thanks, but you probably need to get Sam to bed now.'

'Yes, any minute now he's going to realise that he's tired and keel over.'

Matt nodded. 'I'd best get going. I'll see you next week.'

She couldn't turn away from him. She needed him to touch her, just once, before she let him go. Hannah reprimanded herself. Had she forgotten already what had happened the last time she'd gazed at Matt, her attention only on him and not on what Sam had been doing?

A thump from the sitting room settled the question.

'I'd better go and see what he's up to. Goodnight, Matt. And thank you.'

'Thank *you*. I really enjoyed tonight.' For one moment, the heat of his gaze seemed like the touch of a lover. Then he turned quickly, walking to his car.

CHAPTER NINE

MATT HAD BEEN thinking about the swan all week. He'd rationalised it. The beautiful creature, gliding over the water with barely a ripple in its wake, had turned so quickly into a lumbering, terrifying threat. It was all about his internal child, and how his father's moods had turned on a whisper into something dark and dangerous.

But he still couldn't get the picture of Sam, standing paralysed by fear, out of his head. The boy had recovered quickly, but it had shaken Matt to the core.

He wanted so much to love Hannah. He was rapidly beginning to care for Sam as well, and Matt wanted to protect the boy. But he'd been taught a valuable lesson, which he should heed. Love had its responsibilities, and it would be better never to love than to fail the people he cared about.

But today he didn't need to fall in love with her. He just needed to win. *They* needed to tap into the connection they'd made and win.

His senses had become attuned to the sight of the red T-shirt. It was a precursor of all the other delights, her scent and her smile, and when he caught sight of it he couldn't help a thrill of anticipation.

'Hey, Flash...' He walked up behind her, murmuring the words, as she stood alone looking at the large marquee that had been erected in the grounds of the fourth hospital.

She whirled around, reddening a little, as if he'd caught her thinking something she shouldn't.

'Hey. Are you ready, Robin?'

'One hundred percent.' More, if that were possible. If wanting to do anything for your partner counted, then they'd win by a mile.

'Sorry. I've only got ninety-nine…'

He grinned. 'That'll do.'

'I hope so.' She turned the corners of her mouth down. 'I'm still having a little trouble with my knee. Not so you'd notice, but I get a few twinges when I run.'

That was new. Hannah wasn't just admitting a weakness, she was asking for his help and encouragement. It was a surprising start to the day.

If he needed to, he'd pick her up and carry her across whatever finish line lay ahead of them. The thought was unexpectedly sweet. But if wanting your teammate so badly that he thought it would crush him at times was an unorthodox incentive, he'd take it. Whatever it took to win.

'I can run for both of us. Anyway, they'll have to ring the changes at some point and concentrate on our medical skills, so hopefully there won't *be* too much running.'

'Yeah. We'll be okay.' She gave him a smile that reverberated through his whole being.

For the first time, all of the contestants were gathered together to hear their challenge for the day. A succession of medical problems that had been devised to test their skills under pressure. The marquee was divided up into four consulting areas, each with a camera and a judge in attendance.

'Thank goodness.' Hannah walked towards the red team's compartment, and Matt saw a little stiffness in the way that she moved. Ninety-nine percent had been an exaggeration—he calculated that she was only eighty percent fit.

They had ten minutes to arrange their workspace. A temporary floor was laid, and the cubicle was furnished with an examination couch and a desk, two chairs on either side of it.

'What do you say we get rid of this?' Matt gestured towards the desk.

'Good idea.'

He pulled the desk back, grouping the four chairs in front of it. Hannah nodded her approval.

'That's better. Nothing to separate us from our patients.'

'Right. Are we all set?'

'Just about.' Hannah pulled the phone over to the other side of the desk, so that it was in reach, and picked up the thick pad of paper. 'You talk and I'll write?'

She was deferring to his status as a senior doctor. Matt didn't have a lot of time for that, Hannah's experience was different but no less valuable. 'We'll take turns.'

The challenge started in earnest, and their patients came thick and fast. In the few moments he could spare to think about anything other than the problem before him, Matt was impressed with the way that their obviously healthy patients had been schooled in exactly what symptoms they should be showing, and made up to give all of the appearance of having various complaints. There were a few very minor injuries, one of which concealed a greater problem. Hannah had a way of quickly spotting the difference between a teenager who just required a plaster on his finger and a woman whose black eye was as a result of difficulties with her balance.

Matt found a case of unregulated diabetes, and called for emergency support. When a man appeared with a well-designed glove over his hand and arm, made of practice suture skin, which had been slashed to imitate a deep cut, Hannah smilingly moved to one side while he stitched it. As the man left, a bell rang and the judge, who had been sitting silently in the corner, told them that they had a thirty-minute break.

'Good thing we have a surgeon on the team. I learned something.' Hannah was making for the exit of the marquee and Matt followed her.

'Where are we going?'

'Canteen. That's my area of expertise, I know where the canteen and the washrooms are in every hospital in the district. Sophie and I sometimes end up here with patients for the specialist burns unit.'

'I think I must be getting soft…' It was a long time since he'd seen so many different people in just three hours, and it looked as if there would be more this afternoon.

Hannah's assessing glance almost made him blush. Matt hadn't realised he'd retained that ability. Today was turning into a walk down memory lane, in more ways than one.

'No. You're not getting soft.'

Coffee, protein and calories. Matt hadn't lost the knack of pacing himself, and eating for staying power. He added two bottles of water and a couple of energy bars to his tray, and they took them with them when they hurried back to the marquee.

He was a delight to watch. Confident and yet always on the lookout to make sure there was nothing he'd missed. Hannah had learned a few things from him during the course of the morning, and yet he was always happy to stand back and let her work when her own knowledge and skills were most useful to them.

They were a dream team. Very different but able to work together. If they didn't win today, it wouldn't be for want of trying, and certainly not through any lack of expertise. Matt's specialty might be surgery, but he had an encyclopaedic knowledge of many other aspects of medicine.

Whatever happened, they could hold their heads high in the knowledge that they'd given this their best shot. They could go back to their jobs on Monday...

Hannah tried to ignore the sinking feeling in the pit of her stomach. She loved her job, but it didn't bring her into contact with Matt on a daily basis. Losing him seemed suddenly worse than losing their chance at the prize for their hospital.

They worked until they were both exhausted. Another three hours, and then a half-hour break before a final three hours. When the judge told them that they were finished, she flopped into her chair, puffing out a sigh.

'Whatever happens...' Matt sat down, catching her gaze. Those blue eyes were always like a sensual tide, washing over her.

'Whatever happens, we gave it our best shot. Thank you so much, Matt.'

'It's been a privilege.'

The feeling of wanting to reach for him was tearing her apart and he seemed to understand that. He glanced up at the cameras mounted around the edges of the compartment, quirking his lips down. The touch of his long fingers, moving slightly on the arm of his seat, seemed designed only for her.

That was all there was. Something unspoken. The heat of his gaze and the sudden and certain knowledge that he felt something too. Something that neither of them could act upon.

'How long do you think it'll be?' Two minutes of this

was delicious. Any more and the longing for what she couldn't have would turn to torture.

'She said half an hour. And I know just how to spend it…'

Here? In front of the cameras? Hannah dragged her imagination away from the only thing that she could think of right now, the caress of his lips on hers. He couldn't possibly mean that…

'How's that?'

'Get on the couch.' Her eyebrows shot up and Matt grinned, as if he knew exactly what she'd been thinking. 'I'd like to take a look at your knee. Assuming it's not okay, that is.'

Hannah grinned. 'Of course it's okay, what else did you expect? I'll humour you, though.'

'Thank you. I'd appreciate it.'

She sat on the edge of the couch, swinging her feet. Matt nodded towards the leg of her sweatpants, and Hannah rolled it up, taking off the support he'd given her last week.

He flexed her leg up and down, his fingers resting lightly on the side of her knee, on just the spot that it hurt. 'There's still some inflammation there.'

'I haven't had much chance to rest it. But even if we do win, it's two weeks before the finals.'

'Yeah. You know what to do, keep going with the ice, and try to stay off it as much as you can. If it gets any worse then you might need a short course of anti-inflammatories.'

Hannah nodded, wrapping the support back around her knee and getting to her feet. A sharp stab of pain told her that she'd got it wrong and the support needed some adjustment.

'Let me…' He bent down and suddenly his gaze met

hers. The now familiar chemistry started to fizzle between them, and Hannah jerked backwards.

'No, I'll do it.' She willed him to understand what she didn't say.

Not in front of the cameras.

He nodded. Neither of them could deny it any more, but that was between the two of them. They could hide it from everyone else.

They walked companionably out of the tent, wandering down to greet Sam and her mother. Everything as it should be. The light in his eyes had been quenched, and Matt was just a teammate again.

The wait wasn't so bad. Hannah concentrated on Sam, and going to get ice cream for everyone took up a few minutes. Then they were called to the stage to hear the judges' verdict.

If Matt felt anything, then he was hiding it well. He smiled at the other competitors, seeming more relaxed than anyone as they chatted together. The challenges had brought all eight of them together, and whoever went on to the finals would do so with the blessing of the others.

There was the usual preamble…thanking everyone for being here, praising each of the teams and giving everyone a special mention. Then the verdict.

'This has been more than just a competition. We've seen all our teams hold true to their values and exhibit bravery and determination. Our winners today will be going forward to represent Hertfordshire in the finals, and we wish them well in the challenges to come. Ladies and gentlemen… Matt and Hannah!'

There was a roar of applause that seemed to come from somewhere very far away. Hannah hardly heard the congratulations from the other teams, and barely felt the hands that shook hers.

'Matt...?'

He was there. The only thing that was real. Matt grinned at her, hugging her in the kind of bear hug that a teammate might give. They'd done it. Despite everything, they'd really done it.

She received her medal, and then turned back, beckoning to the others to come forward. This moment was for everyone. The roar of the crowd increased as all eight of the competitors joined them, waving to the crowd.

It was surreal. She had what she'd wanted, and now she couldn't see any way forward from here. She *had* to talk to Matt, somewhere alone.

Something was up. Matt could see it in Hannah's demeanour, and feel it, nagging away in his own chest. There were issues, ones of their own making, and they both knew it.

It wouldn't have mattered so much if they'd lost. They could have bowed out gracefully, congratulating the winners and knowing they'd given it their best shot. Hannah would have disappeared back into her world, and he could have gone back to his. Whether or not he got the job down in London, he'd be gone soon. Matt knew that there would be other opportunities, and that his decision that it was about time he moved on was the driving factor in making those opportunities into a reality.

'Would you like to pop back to mine for a quick coffee? It's on your way home, and maybe we can plan our next move.' His offer was deliberately casual, as if this was just a matter of teammates sitting down together for half an hour to talk. But those moments alone with her in the tent had persuaded him that they *did* need to talk and that the conversation might not be an easy one.

'That's a good idea.' She glanced back towards Sam

and her mother. 'I'll just let Mum know that I'll be back home later.'

He nodded. He knew what would come next. Watching while Sam and Hannah performed the victory dance, and Hannah draped her medal around her son's neck. He'd seen them do it before, but it never ceased to delight him, and he stared at them, hungry for every moment of the little ceremony.

He gave her the address, and saw her car following his through the Saturday evening traffic, back to the flat close to the hospital that he'd occupied for the last year. When Hannah parked behind him, and he led the way upstairs to his front door, it seemed that he'd merely occupied it. It wasn't a home, the way her house was.

'This is nice.' She looked around when he ushered her into the sitting room. Tidy and impersonal, all of the furniture selected by the landlord. It was pretty much the same as the day he'd walked in here, apart from the clothes in the wardrobe and the two boxes of his most valued possessions that were stored in the cupboard in the hallway.

'It's…close to the hospital.' The large windows gave a great view of the centre of the town, and the hospital was within walking distance.

'It has loads of potential.'

Yeah. Potential. There wasn't much point in realising that potential, because he'd always known that he'd be moving on. Having to tear yourself away from a place that he'd made into a home wasn't something that Matt ever reckoned on doing.

'I just wanted to talk.' Now that they were here, he didn't know how to put it into words. The situation was clear enough, the irresistible attraction that they'd found together was real, but it wasn't something that he could act on. Putting that tactfully and yet clearly was his problem.

'Yes, I know.' She turned her gaze on him and he was trapped again. In one of those delicious moments that he fought to ignore, but didn't know how. 'Where's that coffee you promised me?'

That was a much easier prospect. She followed him into the kitchen, looking around at the shiny white cupboard doors, and sleek stainless-steel fittings.

'Wow. Do you ever cook in here, or just make coffee.'

'I cook.' He opened the refrigerator door, and the contents betrayed him. Two pints of milk, four large cartons of juice and a ready meal. He grabbed some milk, and closed the door again quickly. This had suddenly turned into an exercise in questioning his lifestyle, and Matt was happy with the way he lived. No ties that could turn into bonds. No strings to cut.

She leaned back against the worktop, watching him, as he filled the machine with water and ground coffee. Then Hannah spoke.

'Matt, this has been hard for us both. Making the kind of relationship that allows us to push our own boundaries, and win.'

That was a good start. Matt wished he'd thought of it himself. 'I think we've done pretty well.'

'Yes, we have. This next phase is going to be even more challenging.' She gave him a knowing look.

Coffee had dripped into the two cups, and he added milk to Hannah's, leaving his black. He could do with the bite, to concentrate his thoughts. She walked across the room, picking up her cup, and then retreated back to the other side of the kitchen.

'Hannah, over the last four weeks I've come to really respect you. You're an amazing person.' An amazing *woman*. But it was best not to think of their partnership as that of a man and a woman.

She took a sip from her cup, as if allowing his words to sink in. 'That's nice. Thank you.'

'If I were anyone else, I'd… I wouldn't be hesitating. Last week, I wouldn't have let you turn away from me on the doorstep, without asking if I might kiss you.' He gave a smiling shrug. 'I would have followed up with roses, of course.'

'It sounds as if I've been missing out.' She was tracing the rim of her cup with her finger. 'You're not… I don't know. You don't have a secret wife or girlfriend some-where, do you?'

'No, I've never been married, and I don't have a sig-nificant other either. It's nothing like that.'

'Then you could be in witness protection.' She was re-garding him steadily. 'Or you could have a dark past…'

'No.' She was getting warmer, and Matt would prefer that Hannah stop there. 'Nothing like that either. Just… baggage.'

She narrowed her eyes in thought. 'I know about bag-gage. So what kind of baggage makes you ask me out for a meal and then change your mind when you get to my doorstep? Don't get me wrong, I'm not blaming you for it, I haven't been all that consistent either.'

Hannah was refreshingly honest. And she made it sound as if she'd hear pretty much anything that he could say, and understand. He liked that about her.

'I didn't have much of a childhood. My work is every-thing and settling down with someone—anyone—just isn't for me. But I do care about you, and that's why I've been giving you the kind of mixed signals that don't produce very good teamwork.'

She nodded. 'If I hadn't waited for you to ask, and kissed you…?'

The thought made him tremble. Locked in Hannah's

gaze, he couldn't dismiss it as just something that would have rounded the evening off nicely.

'I would have loved every minute of it.'

'Every *minute*?'

It was useless to suppose that if Hannah had kissed him, it wouldn't have lasted minutes. The flush of her cheeks showed Matt that she knew that as well as he did. He could have kissed her for hours without quenching the impulse to kiss her again.

He had to think rationally, though. Matt tore his thoughts from all that their kisses might have meant to him.

'Can we just accept this, Hannah? That there's something between us, but neither of us wants to take it any further. Just let it be.'

She smiled. 'I guess…yes. I'd like that.'

'So we're good? Ready to face whatever's thrown at us next, and win this thing?'

'Yes, we're good. I really want to win too, and we needed to clear the air a little.'

The air between them didn't feel at all clear. It felt full of all the same heavy anticipation and frustrated longing that had built up over the last month. But they'd acknowledged what they both wanted out of this, and that would stand them in good stead for London, and the finals of *Hospital Challenge*.

Hannah drained her cup, putting it into the sink. 'I'd better be going. I think that Sam wants to do the victory dance. Yet again…'

That was his cue to let her go. Matt had every intention of letting her go, but he couldn't, not just yet. It wasn't helping that Hannah was suddenly still, her gaze locked with his. Matt had thought that acknowledging this would make it easier to set it aside…

Hannah took one step towards him. 'Since we both know exactly where we stand now, I'm just wondering whether our own victory dance would be out of the question?'

Actually… No, it wouldn't. There could be no harm in stepping across the boundaries now, since they both knew exactly what the boundaries were. It gave them permission for a little flirting.

'Not sure I can manage the wiggle…not the way you do it, anyway.' Matt allowed himself a step. They were standing close now.

'We could go for something a little more sensual.'

Matt reached for her, laying his hand lightly on her back. She curled her fingers into his other hand, and he felt her body against his. The effect was electrifying. He took a few slow dance steps, feeling her follow his movements.

'Like this?'

'It's a great start.' He felt Hannah's hand on his arm, and as the muscles flexed involuntarily under her touch, she smiled.

Breathless moments, locked in each other's arms. Matt knew that anyone with any sense of caution would move away now, but he couldn't. He ached for just one step further.

'I can't help wondering…' She laid her head against his shoulder. Matt knew exactly what she was wondering because he was wondering too.

But before he kissed her he had to hear her say it. Out loud and in words of one syllable. 'May I—'

'Yes, you may.' Suddenly, he was too impatient to let her even finish. Matt raised an eyebrow and she laughed. 'Kiss me. Then I can kiss you back…'

Maybe that would be an end to it. But he wanted this, even if he couldn't take any more from Hannah. He wanted to show her that if things had been different then he could have loved her.

She stood on her toes, and he bent, kissing her lips. Just as soft and sweet tasting as he'd imagined, but he hadn't bargained on the searing jolt of feeling that ran down his spine. Hannah's hand gripped his shoulder and she gasped as he lifted her up, turning round to sit her on the kitchen counter.

'Too much…?'

She grinned. 'Not enough.'

The more he let hunger percolate into his kiss, the better Hannah liked it. He planted his hands on the counter top, on either side of her, leaning forward as she wrapped her arms around his neck. It was sweet and arousing, and he was going to have to stop soon… Not just yet, though.

When he drew back, he found he was still caught in her gaze, and there wasn't one thing he could do about it. Hannah had to be the one to set him free.

'I really do have to go.'

'I know.' He stole one last kiss from her lips and then lifted her down onto her feet. Keeping his arms around her, he began a long, slow dance that took them out of the kitchen and into the hallway.

'I like this…' Hannah laughed and he performed a dip, holding her securely in his arms. His lips almost touched hers in another kiss but not quite. This had to end soon, but while it lasted he'd squeeze every ounce of delight from it.

He managed to get the front door open without breaking the swaying motion, and then Hannah spun away from him. He raised her fingers to his lips, in one last gesture.

'Goodnight, Hannah.' Her real name suited the moment a little better than the joking nicknames.

'Goodnight, Matt.' She gave him one last smile, and then she was gone. He heard her footsteps on the stairs that led down to the lobby and he closed the door, leaning back against it.

That should have been a big mistake. Something that led to an embarrassed goodbye and the need to make things right afterwards. But it wasn't. They'd struggled against this, but it was what they both wanted. Maybe making it clear that it was just for this moment, and it would lead nowhere, had made it all the sweeter.

And somehow it had made things easier. No more wondering what might happen if he kissed her. They had a way forward, and that way was clear. In two weeks' time it would lead to the greatest test they'd faced.

CHAPTER TEN

HE'D BEEN PERFECT. Kissing her as if she wasn't just the most beautiful woman in the world, she was the *only* woman. Dancing her slowly towards the door, and in a gesture of old-fashioned charm kissing her hand. Every time she thought about it, she was back in that moment, feeling everything she'd felt then.

The idea that any man could make her want him so badly should have been terrifying. But Matt understood that this would go nowhere, and so did she. They'd allowed it in because they both wanted it, but it wouldn't divert them from their purpose.

Texting him had been a lot easier than it had before. Hannah had asked herself none of the agonised questions about whether this was too soon, or not soon enough. When she'd received the email, giving details of their trip to London, she'd just picked up her phone and suggested they meet to discuss it.

Their arrangements to meet up for coffee, at the end of Hannah's shift, had been put off for a day. A major accident on the bypass around the town had left ten people, travelling on a coach, with serious injuries, and they were both busy. The next day, Hannah was waiting for him in the hospital canteen.

Matt sat down in the chair she'd saved for him, and

Hannah pushed towards him the black coffee she'd bought for him.

'You got this for me? Thanks.'

'I'm guessing you must be tired.' She could voice those concerns now that they'd come to an understanding. It was okay to feel something, and okay to notice him.

'Yeah. We were operating pretty late into the night last night.' He smiled suddenly. 'We didn't lose anyone.'

'Thanks. I was wondering, and Sophie and I haven't had a chance to find out yet.'

'There were a number of injuries that were as a result of passengers being thrown around in the coach that was hit. The driver was badly hurt, and he'll probably need more surgery, but he's stable and doing better than I'd expected.'

Hannah nodded. She didn't often get the opportunity to discuss the patients she brought in with the surgeon in charge of their case, and this was the kind of good news that both she and Sophie always hoped for.

'I was worried about him. He'd lost a lot of blood from his stomach wound.'

Matt nodded. 'You were right to be. There was a lot of damage, and we had to remove his spleen. But if my stitches hold, then he should be okay, given time.'

'They'll hold.' Hannah grinned at him. It was okay to recognise that Matt was a talented surgeon as well.

'I'm grateful for your confidence in me.' His gaze met hers, and Hannah didn't try to fight it. They'd acknowledged this, and set their boundaries.

'So. What about the email, then…?' She reached into her pocket for the paper copy she'd made, and found that Matt had a similar copy in his hand. They both smiled at the synchronicity.

'It seems pretty straightforward. Nothing about what we'll be doing, just that we need to turn up on Thursday evening, and we'll have no contact with the outside world until the winners are announced the following Monday evening.'

Hannah nodded. She hadn't explained yet to Sam that she wouldn't be calling him every day. 'That's the first hurdle...'

'I...um...took the liberty of calling them. I asked whether contestants might be allowed one call to their families every day, and they said yes. Supervised, of course, so that you don't get to chat about the competition. But you can call Sam and tell him goodnight.'

He'd done that for her. Matt clearly wasn't too worried about calling his family.

'Thank you. It didn't occur to me to do that, I just hated the idea of not being able to talk to him.'

'Yeah, I didn't much like the idea either.' He scanned the paper in front of him again. 'How are you getting down to London?'

'I thought the train?'

'I was going to take my car. The hotel has parking for guests, and you never know, we might need it.'

'Won't they provide us with cars if we need them?'

He shrugged. 'Who knows? It can't hurt to prepare for every eventuality. Would you like a lift down there?'

'Yes, okay. Thanks. What are you taking in the way of...anything else?'

'A full range of clothes. From a smart suit to sweats and trainers.'

That sounded a bit over the top. They weren't going for a whole month. But Matt seemed serious about the idea.

'I was thinking...' She'd hardly thought about it at all, actually. 'Probably just a couple of pairs of trousers and a few tops?'

Matt grinned. 'Think about it this way. They've told us nothing so I reckon we should be prepared for anything.'

He had a point. 'I'll bring a dress and high heels, then. And whatever else I might need for any situation.'

He grinned suddenly. 'If you don't get to wear the dress, I'll take you to dinner. And don't forget your swimsuit either, the hotel has a really nice pool in the basement.'

Dressing up for dinner with Matt. Hannah was going to have to put in a little more thinking time over her packing.

'You know this place, then?'

'I was there a long time ago. It's a little off the beaten track, but very exclusive. A well-kept secret.'

'One that you know about.' She grinned at him and Matt shrugged.

'Someone's got to. Or they'd never have any guests.'

'All right. Play the man of mystery if you must. I hope your car boot is bigger than it looks, because my luggage expectations have just tripled.'

Matt grinned, taking a sip of his coffee. 'We'll manage.'

They strolled together back to the ambulance parking bays, and Matt took his leave of her. He'd pick her up at two o'clock on Thursday afternoon, along with all the luggage she could manage to wheel down her driveway.

'You two are looking very cosy.' Sophie was waiting for her in the front seat of the ambulance.

'We're teammates.' Hannah felt herself redden. Sophie couldn't possibly understand this. How it was okay to touch Matt's arm and smile when they parted.

'And I thought that *I* was your teammate.' Sophie turned the corners of her mouth down.

'You're my *real* teammate. Matt's just temporary...' Hannah shook her head as Sophie laughed.

'That's okay. I know when I'm beaten. I don't have his outstanding set of attractions.'

'No, you don't.' Hannah decided to play Sophie at her own game.

'Ah, so you admit it. You *are* attracted to him.'

'Who wouldn't be, Sophie?'

Sophie stared at her. 'Then it's one of two things. You're either sleeping with him already, and not telling anyone, or there's a massive deal breaker in there somewhere. He's not gay, is he?'

'He's not gay, and I'm not sleeping with him.'

Sophie leant back in her seat puffing out a breath. 'So you're not going to tell me, then.'

Hannah laughed. 'There's nothing to tell. We're attracted to each other and I kissed him. But neither of us wants to take things any further, we're just… Neither of us are in the right place for that.'

'You *kissed* him? How was it?'

'It was…fine. Nice.' Beyond describing. 'I'm not going to give you a blow by blow account of it. We like each other, but that's it.'

'That's very adult of you.' Sophie's tone told Hannah that she didn't believe it for a moment. When Hannah thought about it, she'd probably have exactly the same reaction. But that was the way things were with Matt, and she had to make it work.

'I've got Sam to think about…'

'Yeah, yeah. I know. There's nothing like having kids to bring out the adult in you…' The radio on the dashboard burst into life suddenly, signifying the end of their break, and Sophie grabbed it, taking a note of an address and then manoeuvring the ambulance out of its parking space.

'You can't do it, Hannah. You can't fancy the pants off him, and then kiss him, and then just decide that's enough and you're going to stop there. I know you like things neat and tidy, and I'm the last person to blame you for it after what happened with John. But relationships are untidy things.'

It was a piece of wisdom that Hannah didn't need right now. 'Well, maybe this is the way this particular relationship has worked its way through. It's for the best anyway. We need to work together.'

'Right. You just go ahead and believe that.' Sophie flashed her a grin as she turned out of the entrance to the hospital. 'If it turns untidy, then you know who to call. I promise not to tell you that I told you so.'

Sophie wouldn't need to say *I told you so* because none of this was anything that Hannah hadn't been saying to herself. But when Matt picked her up at two o'clock on Thursday afternoon, his relaxed and cheerful mood was infectious. Sam flung himself at him, and Matt took the time to play with him for a while. Her mother made tea and then Matt took her bags to the car while she hugged Sam, telling him that she'd call him.

'That's okay, Mum. I can go to bed on my own.' Sam sounded as if he had this all worked out. He was testing out his own independence, still needing her but wanting to do things on his own as well.

'Well, I can't. I want to speak to you before I go to sleep.'

'All right, then. I'll be here.' Sam wriggled out of her arms, and ran over to where Matt was putting her bags into the car. 'Bye, Matt.'

Matt straightened up. 'Bye, Sam. Got your victory dance ready for your mum when she gets back?'

The vision of a completely different victory dance floated

into Hannah's mind, and she told herself for the hundredth time that it was okay. She and Matt had an understanding.

'Yes.' Sam thought for a moment, obviously bothered by something. 'What happens if you don't win?'

Matt squatted down on his heels. 'We don't need to win, Sam. We just need to do our best. You think your mum will do her best?'

'Yes.' Sam pointed towards the bags in the boot. 'She's taking *all* her clothes with her.'

'Then I'd say she deserves a victory dance when she gets back.' Matt waited while Sam considered the matter. There would be no rushing him now, he always made time to listen to Sam.

'Yes.' Sam leaned towards Matt, covering his mouth with his hand as he whispered something in his ear. Matt laughed and gave him a nod.

'I think so too.'

There was a bit of rearranging, and squashing of corners, and finally the boot closed with all their luggage inside. Sam and her mother stood in the driveway waving, and when Matt flashed all of the car's lights in response, Sam hallooed. Hannah craned around in her seat, watching until she couldn't see her son any more.

'First time you've been away from him for so long?'

'Yes. I know he'll be fine, but I can't help missing him already.' Hannah settled back into her seat, staring at the road ahead. 'What did he say to you?'

Matt chuckled. 'He told me that he thinks the victory dance makes you happy.'

Hannah couldn't help smiling, and wanting to hug her little boy. 'He sees more than I think he does sometimes.'

'Kids do.' Matt quirked the corners of his mouth down. 'But you're a great mother, Hannah. He sees good things.'

'I hope so.' The better she knew Matt, the more it felt

that at some time he'd been made to feel that the world wasn't a good place at all. That he'd had to build his own confidence and sense of security, rather than inheriting it, and that he was always afraid of it slipping away.

But they were Matt's secrets. He had his reasons for keeping them, and he'd told her what she needed to know. She should respect that.

And there was a road ahead. Beckoning them both into something that was both exciting and terrifyingly unknown.

Matt knew this hotel. When his mother had left his father, she'd fled to London. Afraid of staying with any of her family here, in case his father should discover them, they'd stayed here for two weeks. Then moved on to another hotel and then another, until his mother could find a more permanent place to live. Permanent had turned out to be six months.

But this place was special. His mother had explained carefully that they'd needed to leave, but Matt hadn't needed any explanations. His arm had still been in a sling from what his father had done to him, and he knew full well that they were fleeing from fear and pain, and that this was the start of a new life. While his mother had been engaged in meetings with solicitors and those members of her family that she felt she could trust enough to share the secret of their whereabouts, he'd explored every inch of this new world.

He drove past the unassuming entrance, and took a sharp right into the garage, below the building. They unloaded their bags from the car, and took the lift up to the lobby, where a porter immediately stepped forward to take their luggage, seeming almost offended that they'd dared to bring it this far themselves.

It was quiet here. No shouting, no screaming. It felt just the way it had then, like an oasis of calm in the busy heart of the city.

'Hannah… Matt…' A young woman that he'd seen before amongst the TV crew stepped forward. 'You made it. How was your journey?'

She made it sound as if they'd braved hell and high water to get here. This time it had only been fifty miles of motorway and a few traffic lights.

'Good. Thank you.' Hannah smiled at her. 'We're looking forward to the weekend.'

Matt felt her elbow in his ribs, and realised that he should be a part of this conversation. 'Yes. Looking forward to it.'

They were whisked over to the reception desk to sign the register, and then ushered upstairs. The top-floor suite comprised two bedrooms, on either side of a comfortable sitting room.

'We've booked the whole place out for the weekend, and we have full use of all of the facilities, so make yourselves at home. This suite is your bolthole…' The woman smiled at her own joke and Matt allowed himself a grim smile. The idea of the hotel as a bolthole was more appropriate than she knew.

'There are no cameras here, we've set up a few rooms downstairs with static mounted cameras, and of course the outside broadcast team may be following you at times. But we'll try to keep that as unobtrusive as possible. Dinner's at six, and then there's a meeting, where we'll outline your challenge for the weekend.' The woman smiled apologetically. 'I'm going to need your phones.'

Matt took his from his pocket, handing it over. 'Any last-minute texts, Hannah?'

'Oh. Yes, of course.' She'd been looking around at her

new surroundings, and had momentarily forgotten that she'd promised to text her mother when they arrived. 'I just have one more to send.'

'Yes, of course.'

The woman smiled, waiting as Hannah typed furiously. She obviously had a little more to say than just a quick notification of their arrival and Matt reckoned that there would be hugs and kisses for Sam in there somewhere. Finally she gave up her phone, her momentary grimace showing that this might just be the hardest thing she did this weekend.

Their luggage arrived, and was placed in their rooms. And then they were alone. Standing on opposite edges of the large rug that filled the space between the two comfortable sofas.

'What do we do now?' Hannah looked at her watch. 'We have two whole hours...'

'Unpack?' Matt shrugged. 'Relax.'

She rolled her eyes. 'Do you feel as if you could relax? And it'll only take ten minutes to unpack...'

Gold medal for unpacking, then. Hannah had brought four bags with her, and ten minutes sounded like a record-breaking sprint.

'So...let's unpack first. And then decide on a relaxation strategy.'

Hannah was as good as her word. It was nine and a half minutes from when he closed his bedroom door to hearing her knock.

'Aren't you done yet?' Hannah's voice drifted through from the sitting room.

'Uh...nearly.' Matt decided to work out the intricacies of the shirt press later, and stuffed everything that was left in his case into the wardrobe. That would have to do for the time being.

Hannah was bright-eyed and restless. Staying in their suite would be like trying to contain an inquisitive tiger, and he suggested they take a walk around the hotel. They explored the ground floor, finding that the lobby was full now of new arrivals, and slipping away to peer into the dining room and bar, and check out the conference room at the back of the building.

'The pool's that way. And a steam room!' Hannah had caught sight of a sign that pointed towards the staircase that led down to the basement. 'I brought my swimming suit.'

Matt had too, reckoning that a few early morning laps might prepare him for the days ahead. He followed Hannah downstairs.

'Oh, and a gym.' Hannah peered through the glass doors and turned away. 'What a shame. It looks great, but I doubt we'll have enough energy to spare for it.'

A young man in sweatpants and a polo shirt, emblazoned with the name of the hotel, approached them. Hannah smiled, asking him to show them the pool, and he led the way.

'This is gorgeous!' The long narrow pool shimmered under green and blue lights, with Roman-style columns supporting wide beams that ran across the ceiling. The theme continued along the far wall, which was decorated with a mosaic that ran the full length of the pool, and depicted scenes of nymphs, dressed in classical costumes.

'The Pamper Room is open all day, and you can make an appointment for a full session…' The man broke off as Hannah waved her hand dismissively.

'No pampering. But you have a steam room?'

They were shown the steam room, which was tiled in blue and green to match the pool, and big enough to accommodate eight or ten people. Hannah turned to Matt.

'What do you think?'

He thought…that there were many good reasons why he shouldn't spend time with Hannah clad only in a towel. But they had boundaries now. Ground rules. Before he could change his mind again, Matt nodded.

'Yeah. It would be good to relax.'

By the time he left the small dressing room, anchoring the thick white towel securely around his waist, Matt was having second thoughts about this. But leaving Hannah to sit alone, while he made an escape back to his bedroom, was unthinkable. He opened the door of the steam room, finding that she was already there, swathed in a similar towel to his.

He sat down on the tiled bench, opposite hers, leaving plenty of space between them. Keeping his gaze on the floor seemed like a good option, although he could still see her feet, which were already a little pink, presumably along with the rest of her. Matt swallowed down the lump in his throat.

Steam rose between them, and he felt beads of sweat begin to form on his forehead. He should break the silence, but couldn't for the life of him think of anything to say. Then Hannah started to tap her foot…

'All right, I'm going to look. Only you have to look too.'

That was one way of breaking the ice. Suddenly this didn't seem so hard after all.

'Okay. Do you want to go first?'

'No. I think we should do it together.'

Sweat trickled down his spine. He looked up at her, and found that she was unashamedly looking him up and down. Relief washed over him as he realised that Hannah liked what she saw.

He liked what he saw, too. The curve of her shoulders, and her pale skin, flushed with the heat. Her hair was pulled up in a messy bun, but a few strands had escaped and were sticking to her brow. The place where her towel was tucked over itself, between her breasts, was endlessly fascinating.

And this was okay. They'd given each other permission, and he felt no embarrassment. Even the dark scar on the back of his shoulder didn't bother him. Matt was always conscious of it, although few people ever asked about it and those who did accepted his excuses without question. Hannah couldn't see it from where she was sitting, and it suddenly seemed too unimportant to waste any more time on.

'That's got that over with.' He grinned at her and she grinned back. Hannah's chuckle was infectious, and laughing together drove away the last remnants of awkwardness.

'Could I just say—'

'No, you couldn't just say anything.' Matt saw the mischief dancing in her eyes and decided he probably didn't want to hear it.

'All right.' She mouthed the words instead. *Nice shoulders.*

Okay, so he'd been wrong. He did want to hear it.

Fabulous knees, he mouthed back at her, and she laughed.

Hannah leaned back, closing her eyes. Matt took one last look at her, and did the same, feeling the cool of the tiles against his skin. The image of her smile stayed with him, curling through his thoughts like the subtle scent of pleasure.

CHAPTER ELEVEN

MATT HAD BEEN congratulating himself on not only surviving the steam room but enjoying the chance to relax and laugh a little with Hannah. But when she appeared from her room, dressed for dinner, he found the juxtaposition of two separate images was far more arousing than he'd bargained for.

She wore a slim patterned skirt, with high heels and a wraparound blouse. Hannah looked both elegant and seductive, and when the image jostled in his head with that of one tiny bead of sweat running past the curve of her neck, and down towards her breasts, it was almost unbearably erotic.

This had to stop. It would, as soon as they got started on the challenge. It was just the effect of having too much time on his hands.

They made their way downstairs to the dining room, chatting awkwardly in the lift with two of the other contestants. Dinner was a matter of mostly surveying the room and picking at their food in between times.

'They look...ready for anything.' Hannah nodded towards a table where two men were laughing loudly together.

Matt shook his head. 'Too confident, I reckon.'

'What about them, then?'

He followed her gaze towards two women, who were talking intently, oblivious of everything that was going on around them. Matt could see the tension in their movements.

'Too nervous.'

She rolled her eyes. 'So what are we, then?'

He leaned towards her. 'We're the dream team. Flash and Robin.'

That made her laugh. Maybe Flash and Robin could achieve what Matt felt unequal to at the moment and confine their intimacy to that of friends and teammates.

They were shepherded into a large sitting room, and the director of the project stood up. The silence was so sudden and complete that a pin dropping would have made everyone jump. Matt reckoned that you'd even hear the swish of it on its way down.

'Ladies and gentlemen. Welcome, and I hope you've all made yourselves comfortable here. We'd like to thank the Elsynge Hotel for allowing us to set up shop here for the weekend.' He nodded towards a man wearing a blue jacket with the logo of the hotel on the breast pocket, who returned a benign smile, gauged to imply that nothing was too much trouble.

'You'll be wondering what your task is for the weekend. It's very simple. You all know that the winners will be taking back a cheque for their hospital. We want you to produce a presentation of how that money might be spent, by eight o'clock on Sunday evening.'

There was a hum of whispered conversation, and one of the nervous women raised her hand. 'What kind of presentation are you looking for?'

The director smiled. 'That's up to you to decide. Show us what you think we need to see.'

The two confident men were talking animatedly. Hannah turned to him, frowning. 'How are we going to do that? It's up to the hospital board to say how the money's spent.'

'I don't know. It's a good question, you should ask.'

She raised her hand hesitantly, and Matt jolted her elbow, pushing it up so that she caught the director's eye.

'I've got a good idea of how I'd like to see the money spent, but it's not my decision. The board of our hospital would be in charge of that.' A hum of agreement went around the room. Matt supposed that all of the other contestants were in much the same position.

'We understand that the final decision belongs to the spending committees of your various hospitals, but this is your chance to influence that. You'll be submitting your presentations on Sunday evening, and on Monday you'll have a chance to talk to the judges. We've invited representatives from each of your hospitals to attend, and see your ideas. This is your chance to speak directly to them, as well as us.'

Hannah flashed a look at Matt. This was real. And it was a responsibility that neither of them had expected.

One of the over-confident guys put up his hand, and stood to ask his question, so that everyone could see him. 'Can we leave the hotel if we want?'

'Yes, you can go anywhere at any time. The only thing we ask of you is that you sign yourselves out, and take along the production assistant who'll be assigned to you. There may also be a camera crew, but they won't accompany you anywhere without specific permission, we don't want to cramp your style. The one thing we need from you is that you don't use your time away from the hotel to contact anyone other than the specific person you're going to see. This is a project that you have to complete alone.'

There were more questions, but Hannah seemed not to

hear them, sitting deep in thought. As soon as the meeting broke up, she wound her way through the groups of people still talking in the conference room, and Matt followed her as she hurried back to their suite.

Hannah felt sick. She'd determined to win the money, and had been happy to leave it to others to decide how it was best spent. But now there were a hundred different areas of need, all jostling for position in her head. It was an impossible decision.

'This is above my pay grade, Matt.' She flopped down onto the sofa.

'Yeah. Mine too.' He sat down, his brow furrowed.

'Maybe we should make a list of all the various departments. Then we could pinpoint their specific areas of need…' Hannah shook her head. That was a terrible idea. 'That alone would take us all weekend. We don't have the time.'

'And I'm not sure it'll get us any further—every department needs something. How would we choose?'

'Pick names from a hat?' She sighed. 'I just can't think of any one thing that's more important than everything else…'

'We should pick something that we love. Something we'd go that extra mile to achieve, because that'll show through in our presentation.'

'Yes, that's good.' Hannah thought hard. 'I wish my head weren't so full of all the different options. I can't stop thinking for long enough to know…'

'Me too.' Matt stared at the ceiling. 'I suppose we could always get drunk.'

Hannah chuckled. 'Yeah. If I'm drunk enough to unclutter my head, then I'll have a twenty-four-hour hangover. That's not going to help much.'

'Exercise?'

Sex.

Happily she hadn't voiced the first thing that flew to mind. But the general principle was a good one, they couldn't plan their way through this. They had to find something that took them out of the mire of pros and cons.

'Exercise sounds good. I'd say running, but my knee's still a bit shaky.'

'What about swimming?' He grinned suddenly. 'Although you might not be able to keep up…'

They'd effortlessly leap-frogged their way to a conclusion, each relying on the other's ideas. This was a good way forward. Hannah got to her feet, making for her bedroom.

'Don't bank on it Matt, if I have to cheat to get ahead of you then I'll have no hesitation in doing so. I'll see you down there.'

Matt was already in the pool when she entered the large, tranquil space. They were alone here, and the empty corridors had attested to the fact that the other contestants were probably in their rooms, busy hammering out ideas. Maybe they should be too, but they'd always relied on each other rather than follow the crowd.

Hannah slipped off her fluffy hotel robe, and got into the pool. Maybe he was watching her, but she felt no self-consciousness. She wanted him to.

'Ready?' He was treading water, ripples splashing over his shoulders. He really did have great shoulders. His skin seemed almost golden under the overhead lights. Maybe exercise would quench the urgent need to touch him, although Hannah doubted it.

'Yes. Ten laps?'

He shook his head, motioning towards the clock above

the door to the changing rooms. 'What about ten minutes? No competing, just push at our own personal best.'

Because he knew he'd win. Hannah decided to see his suggestion as generous, rather than patronising, because that was certainly the way he meant it.

'Okay, ten minutes.'

It was ten minutes of hard work. Hannah swam regularly, and it was obvious that Matt did too. When their time was up, he waited for her, bobbing up and down in the water.

'Any ideas yet?'

'Nope. You?'

'Nothing. Another five minutes?'

She nodded pushing off from the side of the pool.

This time she waited for him, because Matt had not only passed her but managed to squeeze extra laps in as well. 'Anything?'

He grinned at her. 'Another five?'

'You're on.'

They were both slowing now. After five more minutes of concentrated swimming, Hannah was tiring and her knee was beginning to throb a little.

'That's enough, Matt. I can't do another five...'

'Me neither.' He swam to the side of the pool, boosting himself up out of the water. It was an exercise in perfection, and Hannah watched as he grabbed the towelling robe from the seat where he'd left it. Then he sat down, waiting for her to collect her robe and join him.

'What have you got?' He picked up a towel, rubbing it vigorously across his head, and Hannah peeled off her bathing cap.

'I've got... Nothing. I'm still out of breath...'

'You've got something. I know you have.' Matt's smile, and the look in his eyes was as intoxicating as when he'd kissed her. Taking her away from everything she thought she knew…

Suddenly a thought shot into her head. 'Sam was born with a cleft lip and palate. You've noticed the scar?'

'Only because I'm a surgeon. Someone did a very good job.'

'Yes, they did. His was relatively minor, but it's more common than a lot of people realise, about one in seven hundred babies. He had feeding difficulties, though, and it was a struggle for a while. A lot of kids have much more severe problems, ear infections and speech difficulties.'

Matt nodded. 'What kind of project would have helped him?'

'I don't know… The surgery and care Sam had was marvellous. A lot of kids are hesitant about taking solid food, and they and their parents have problems with the way that people treat children with any disfiguring condition.'

'So we concentrate on support, rather than medical treatment. You think that's the best way to spend the money?'

'Yes, I do. We can make more of a difference there, the money will go further.'

'I agree. So we'll go for that?'

He hadn't suggested anything himself. If it were up to Hannah to spend the money, that would be her choice, but this team was made up of two people.

'No. I'll hear your ideas first.'

He shrugged. 'Sam's important…'

'Yes, he is. Come on, Matt, what's important to you?'

'I guess…' Matt thought for a moment. 'Young people like Mia. We have all the facilities to give them the best medical care, but it's difficult for them to stay positive. They have to really stick at the exercises.'

'It would be really good to help them.'

'It would be really good to help kids like Sam, too.'

They were at an impasse. Neither wanted to let go of the projects that were so close to their hearts, but neither could deny the other's. Hannah stared out over the water, the overhead lights reflecting on its surface. It was restful. A luxury that wasn't always available in the busy wards of the hospital...

'A sensory room?' Matt suddenly voiced the idea that had been forming in her head.

'Yes! We could create an area that can be changed to meet different needs. Anyone benefits from being relaxed and happy, babies like Sam and youngsters like Mia.'

'Maybe a pool...' Matt was grinning now.

'Earth to Matt. That's far too expensive.'

'So what if we build a capacity for expansion into the plan? Raising extra money is a possibility, isn't it?'

'I guess so.' Hannah was almost breathless from excitement. 'I want to start *now*, Matt. I mean this very minute...'

'Me too.' He jumped to his feet. 'You reckon we have our idea?'

'Yes, I do.' A thought occurred to Hannah. 'What do you think the hospital board will say?'

'We can't worry about that. We're both medical professionals, and we understand what's needed and what can and can't be done. We have to just make the decision the best we can.'

'Yes. You're right.'

They'd done it. Together. His ideas and hers, twined together in something that felt like an embrace. Hannah slipped on her canvas shoes, and together they hurried away from the pool and up the stairs.

The media room was locked and she rattled the door handle impatiently. The unit director appeared from the adjoining room, where cameras and microphones were being set up, in readiness for tomorrow.

'Sorry. It's closed until tomorrow.' He was eyeing their robes and grinning.

'We've been swimming. And we need the internet.' Matt returned his stare.

'Like I said. No internet until tomorrow at ten o'clock, we'd like you to spend this evening deciding on your projects. After that you'll have twenty-four-hour access.'

'But we've already decided.' Hannah tried to reason with him and he shook his head.

'Okay. Thanks anyway.' She heard Matt's voice behind her and felt him tug lightly at her sleeve. He was right, no one was going to be allowed into the media room tonight, and they should go back to their suite.

Hannah followed him into the lift, looking up at him dejectedly. 'So what are we going to do now? It's fourteen hours until the media centre opens and we can't start researching.'

Matt chuckled softly. 'How about we just dream a little more, then?'

CHAPTER TWELVE

THE HEAT WAS oppressive tonight, and when Hannah had showered off the chlorine from the pool, she slipped on a pair of shorts and a T-shirt. When she walked into their shared sitting room, Matt was on the house phone, just ending a call.

'You managed to get a line out?'

He laughed. 'No, I was just ordering some drinks.'

He was wearing a faded pair of jeans that had been washed and worn until they were like a second skin. She'd seen him work his body so many times now, and there was always something new to like. His strong arms, slicing through the water in the pool, or straining to support his weight when he tackled the climbing wall. Those long legs that seemed to eat up the miles. She'd seen him talking to people and the way that his quiet manner put them at ease, had watched him and Sam discussing the world, nodding solemnly to each other as they came to a conclusion. But her favourite version of Matt was this one. Relaxed and smiling, his eyes seeming very blue against his tan, and sparkling with ideas. She fetched a pad, and started to make a list.

'What do you think about building?' The drinks had arrived and he was swirling his thoughtfully, allowing the ice to clink against the sides of the glass.

Hannah put down her pen. Aspirations were one thing, but this was way beyond their budget. 'Building. You're serious?'

'I'm not sure yet. But prefabs are low cost and very configurable. We could make a space that was exactly as we wanted it.'

'Prefabs?' Hannah shot him a pained look. 'The only thing I know about prefabs are that my old school had a few of them tacked on to the main building. They were far too hot in the summer and freezing cold in the winter.'

'They've come a long way since then. I worked at a hospital in Glasgow that had some prefabricated wards and they were great. Clean and modern and very comfortable.'

'But…they're too expensive for us, aren't they?'

'Yeah. But what if we could approach a manufacturer, and ask if they'd like to donate to a high-profile charitable project—' Hannah started to laugh and he gave her a reproachful look. 'Hey…this is being filmed for TV, it doesn't get more high profile than that. And lots of manufacturers use donations to gain publicity. It's tax-efficient…'

'You make it sound almost do-able.'

'*Almost* can be stretched a little, can't it? What do you say to phoning round a few suppliers tomorrow and just testing the water. I could do that while you investigate some of the cascade lights you were talking about.'

'Okay. I'll put it on the list.' Hannah scanned the paper in front of her. 'So we have exercise and therapy equipment, different kinds of lights and a sound system, along with a new building and… What about an outside area, where kids can play in the summertime? We could have a play fountain, Sam loves the one in the park near us.' They were moving in the realms of the impossible, and somehow it all seemed possible.

'Sounds good. Anything else?'

'That's enough for the time being. We'll be lucky to get half those things into our budget.'

'Then we have to prepare the presentation. In three days.' Matt chuckled.

'Oh, yes. I forgot the part about the three days.' Hannah grinned at him. 'Maybe we'll have to forgo sleeping.'

'In which case we should probably get an early night. Although I think it's going to be too hot to sleep tonight.'

Dreams and hot nights. And Matt. The man she couldn't have, because they'd both agreed that romance wasn't on their agenda. But maybe fantasy was.

She'd never made the first move before. But the look in Matt's eyes told her that he wouldn't push her away. Even if he couldn't stay with her tonight, he'd make his regret into something delicious, as he had when he'd slow-danced her to his front door. Hannah stood up, walked over to the sofa and sat down next to him.

For a moment they didn't touch. And then he curled his arm around her shoulders, and she snuggled against him.

'This is nice.' She felt him drop a kiss onto her brow. '*Really* nice.'

If she had any doubts, she should stop now. She could stop, and Matt would understand. That very fact chased the what-ifs away. They couldn't change each other's lives, but that didn't mean that the next few hours had to be spent apart. She reached for him, and he was there. When she kissed him, he was so deliciously there that everything else melted away.

'Hannah…' He broke away from her, his eyes dark with desire. 'Are you sure? This can't change anything between us…'

'But do you want it?'

'Can you doubt that?'

She moved closer to him, feeling the strong beat of his heart under her hand. 'Then I'll be plain, Matt.'

'Please. I like it when you speak your mind.'

She leaned forward, whispering in his ear. Words for him alone that made him almost choke with surprise.

'All that? In just one night?'

'If you can't stand the pace…'

'Just try me, Hannah. Only you'll be coming first…' The world tipped as he got to his feet and gathered her up in his arms, carrying her across the room and into her bedroom. There was no stopping him now and…

'Wait! Matt do you have condoms?'

'No.' He hesitated for a split second, and then put her down onto the bed, kneeling in front of her. 'I don't want to wait, Hannah. But I *can* improvise… Trust me, we'll be safe.'

'I trust you Matt.' She reached for the lamp beside the bed, flipping it off. 'We've done this before. Led each other in the darkness.'

He smiled. 'Yes, we have.'

The bedroom gave a stunning view of the city through floor-to-ceiling windows. Matt closed the heavy drapes, shutting out the lights that stretched across the horizon. He was just a shadow now, caught in the gleam of the lamps from the sitting room, and when he shut the door she could see nothing. But he was there. She could feel his fingers caressing her cheek and his lips on hers. He pulled her T-shirt over her head, and Hannah tugged at his jeans and heard the sharp sound of the zipper.

He laid her down on the cool sheets, and she felt his skin, warm and firm beneath her fingers. And then everything seemed to focus on his touch, and the darkness and exquisite pleasure.

Just Matt. Only his hands, and his mouth, finding each

and every place that made her shiver. He was guided by each catch of her breath, each whimpering cry that tore itself from her lips. Precise and careful, his fingers showed no hesitation, no mercy as they travelled across her stomach and down between her legs…

Fireworks in the night. Losing herself in the loud clamour of desire, and then finding him there, still holding her, his body warm and strong next to hers.

'Nice one, Flash…' His lips touched her ear, as he whispered the words and Hannah shivered, aftershocks still running through her body. Her mind was a blank, just pleasure and satisfaction and the warm presence of the man who had given her these gifts.

She could feel his erection, impressively hard against her leg. And then one thought came rushing into the vacuum, urgent and complete.

When she pushed him over onto his back, he let out a groan of relief. Maybe he'd thought she might just curl up in his arms and go to sleep, but that wasn't what teammates did. As her fingers explored, she felt the urgency of his desire, and she whispered in his ear.

'I'm not leaving you behind, Robin.'

Matt liked sex. It was straightforward and uncomplicated, because he always made it that way. But this was different.

Complex, multifaceted, and more satisfying than he'd ever realised. When Hannah had come, it had been a dizzying triumph, marked by her cries in the darkness and the feel of her skin, suddenly burning against his. When she'd tipped him over, making it very clear that she was about to take him where she'd just been, he'd felt profound thankfulness and sudden, unrelenting need.

They hadn't even gone all the way, but it seemed further than he'd ever been before, venturing into unknown territory. If he'd been able to think, that might have worried him, but thinking was out of the question at the moment. He was helpless in Hannah's hands, his body responding to her and only her. He came hard and fast, and in the sudden agony of desire he could hear her low purr of pleasure.

And then came the new pleasure of seeing her. It seemed like another first time, as uniquely pleasurable as the last, standing under the shower together, letting it cool their bodies. He wanted another first time now, more than he'd wanted it before.

'I'll go downstairs…' He kissed her, feeling her hands caress his back, along with the cascade of water. 'I'm sure I saw a condom machine in the cloakroom downstairs.'

'Mmm. We can go all the way next time.'

The thought that there was more propelled him out of the shower and he scrubbed his hair dry, finding his jeans and T-shirt on the floor by the bed where they'd been discarded. Hannah followed him, wrapped in a white bath towel, and the only thing that could slow his haste was stopping to kiss her.

'Hurry up.' She looked up at him, and he found himself transfixed in the warmth of her golden-brown eyes. 'Go…!'

'Then let me go.'

She knew the ties that bound him. Her eyelids fluttered downwards and he was free. Matt threw an exhortation over his shoulder, telling her not to move one inch, and hit the corridor, making for the lift at a run.

When he got back, she was sitting on the bed, still wrapped in the towel. Waiting. He took the packets of condoms out of his pocket, laying them on the side table, and she nodded, smiling. The light from the lamp by the bedside caressed her face.

'Get undressed.' Hannah didn't move. This time she wanted to watch.

As he pulled his T-shirt over his head, she gave a smiling nod, as if she liked what she saw. He was ready for her now, and Matt hoped it wasn't too soon. But as he stripped his jeans off her smile broadened. Hannah stood, letting the towel fall to the floor, watching his reaction. That pleased her too.

Sliding carefully, slowly inside her was a new pleasure, because he could see her face. Moving until they were both lost in the moment. A thin sheen of perspiration began to form on her brow, and he felt sweat trickle down his back.

This time he felt her orgasm. Saw her face, and the way her hair spread across the pillow. It tipped him over the edge as surely as her voice in the darkness had done. Afterwards, they lay for a long time, curled up on the bed, the heat of the night too fierce for anything other than a sheet to cover them.

Finally Hannah moved. 'I'm thirsty. Would you like something?'

'I'll go.' Matt tore himself away from her, putting on his jeans and walking through to the sitting room, where there was a small refrigerator, stacked with drinks. Picking up two glasses, he put them down on the bedside table, leaning over to touch her cheek with the can from the fridge.

'Ow!' She yelped, sitting up and then caught the can from his hand, pressing it against her cheek again. 'That's really nice.'

Heat and cold. Two more opposites to explore maybe. Next time. Matt usually didn't make any promises to himself about a next time, but it was impossible that there shouldn't be one. They had a long, long way to go before tonight was finished.

He sat down on the bed, pouring the drinks, aware that

Hannah was watching him. Being watched usually bothered him, but for the moment he couldn't remember why. She took the glass, pulling the sheet up around her.

'I see your shoulder.' She was sipping her drink, looking at him steadily.

Now he remembered. Being with Hannah was like drawing a line between now and then—before Hannah, and after Hannah. But suddenly the past broke through, snapping ferociously at his heels.

Most people didn't even notice the dark mark on the back of his shoulder, and if they did he lied about the cause. The scar was so old now, hidden from his view when he faced himself in the mirror, that he could afford to ignore it. But Hannah had seen more in the way of injuries than most, and anyway telling her anything but the absolute truth would be a betrayal so outrageous that he couldn't even think about it.

'I'm not asking you to talk about it, Matt. But I want you to know that I see it and that…whatever happened to you, I wish it hadn't.'

Her eyes filled with tears suddenly. She knew. But even now, Matt couldn't let go of the secret he'd kept from everyone.

'What do you think happened?' It wasn't fair to ask her to take all the risks, but Matt couldn't go there unless Hannah led him. Maybe she wouldn't. Maybe she'd want to believe that he'd fallen out of a tree when he was a kid…

She moved, pushing the pillows behind her so that she could sit up a little straighter.

'You carry your shoulder a little differently…lower than the other one. That's probably the result of it having been dislocated. It's not that obvious…'

'And…?' It was poor encouragement to go on, but it was all that Matt could give.

'The mark on your shoulder...'

'When did you see that?' Suddenly it was important, and Matt didn't know why.

'Just now. I didn't see it when we were swimming.' She leaned towards him, planting a kiss on his cheek. 'I was enjoying the rest of the view too much.'

That was what he wanted to hear. That Hannah had only just seen this, and that her reaction had been to ask almost immediately. That she'd cared enough to want to know.

'What do you think the mark is?'

'It's a burn, and it looks as if it happened some time ago, probably when you were a child.' She hesitated and Matt nodded her on. 'I saw a mark once that was exactly that shape, when someone accidentally burned themselves with the tip of an iron. I may be wrong...'

'You're not wrong. And it wasn't accidental.'

Her eyes filled with tears. 'I'm so sorry, Matt. I know you don't want to talk about it.'

Suddenly that was all he wanted to do. Hannah had reached in and found his secret, and she'd had the courage to tell him that she knew. The heart to cry for him. Matt curled up on the bed, laying his head in her lap.

'I want to tell you about it...'

She held him, giving him the strength to haltingly begin the story. His father's rage and his mother's tears. The more he talked, safe in Hannah's arms, the easier it became.

'My mother took it all. Until I was eight years old.'

'What happened then?'

'He came home early from work one day. I was in the kitchen with my mother, she was doing the ironing. When she heard the front door slam, she told me to go and play in the garden, and went out into the sitting room. But I didn't. I listened at the door, and heard him shouting at her, about something that had happened at work. I knew what it sounded like when he hit her, I'd heard that often enough before…'

He couldn't go on. Hannah waited, holding him. It would be quite okay if he stopped here, she'd understand. The knowledge gave him the strength to continue.

'For the first time, I didn't try to hide. I ran into the sitting room and attacked him, but of course he was far too strong for me. He picked me up, and took me into the kitchen, locking the door behind us. I could hear my mother, begging him to let me go and promising she'd do anything he wanted if he didn't hurt me. He told me he'd give me something to help me remember that I was never to do that again…'

'He burned you. With the iron.'

'He branded me. It hurt so badly that I struggled and screamed and he yanked me up by my arm and threw me across the room, that's when my shoulder dislocated. Then I heard the sound of glass breaking. My mother had smashed the kitchen door, and she was standing over me, with a spade from the garden in her hands. She told him she'd kill him if he ever laid a finger on me again. She was so different, like…'

He felt Hannah's arms tighten around him. 'Like a mother protecting her child.'

'Yes.' He could imagine Hannah like that if anything or anyone ever threatened Sam. Flaming with rage, like a lioness defending her cub. The thought that what had happened to him would never happen to Sam comforted him.

'That was the last time I saw my father. He walked out of the house, and my mother picked me up and took me straight to the hospital. She was bleeding from the broken glass, and she told them some story and they patched us both up. Then she took me back out to the car, and told me that we were never going back. She left me with a neighbour while she went back to pack a few things, and then we left.'

'It must have been…' Another tear escaped from Hannah's eye. 'I can't imagine how you must have felt.'

'I felt as if we'd escaped. We drove for hours, all the way to London. We came to this hotel, she had family here but she was too afraid to go to them in case my father found us. We stayed here for two weeks, and I thought that this would be the beginning of a new life for us. I'd have friends, and a nice school. Everything was going to be all right.'

It had been just like now. Everything would be all right, if he just stayed here in Hannah's arms. Matt knew he couldn't, that they had serious work to do tomorrow, but he could still believe it for a while.

'It wasn't, of course. My mother's family helped her out, and we weren't short of money. We moved from hotel to hotel, until we got a little house, and then after a few months we heard that my father had found us. We ran, and then he found us again, in the cottage in Wales. After that, we just kept running, never really knowing if he was following or not, but never staying in one place for more than six months.'

'Where is she now?'

'When I went to medical school, she decided to go to France for a year. She loved Paris, and settled there for a while. She wrote a book, loosely based on her own experiences, and to her surprise it sold. That gave her a lot of confidence, and she came back to England and started to get involved with a charity that helps battered women. She got a job as a columnist for a newspaper and… I don't know if she'll ever really mend. But she has a good life now, and she's happy.'

'That's wonderful. I wish you'd tell me what the book's

called, I'd love to read it.' Hannah paused, as if she wanted to ask a question but wasn't sure how.

'What?' Matt moved, taking her in his arms. Now that he'd told her everything, she was the one who needed his comfort.

'Will *you* ever mend? You seem to still be moving around.'

'I'm not all that sure how else to live. I've mended my own life with my work.'

'But you won't stay, will you?'

He knew what she was asking. Matt's departure might be soon, if the job in London came through. But that wasn't certain yet, and this wasn't the time for uncertainties.

'No. I won't stay.'

She smiled, reaching up to caress his cheek. 'That's okay. You know that permanence isn't my thing either. Just as long as we'll be friends.'

The thought that wherever he was, he could always just pick up the phone and talk to Hannah warmed him. One thread, to anchor him to the past.

'Always, Hannah. I may walk away, but I'll never forget you.'

A sudden crash above their heads startled them. Then Hannah grinned. 'Thank goodness. Do you think the storm's coming our way?'

'Let's hope so.' The oppressive heat that had been building up for days now seemed to have loosened its grip a little. Matt got up, drawing the drapes back and opening the sliding doors that were cut into the expanse of glass. There was no balcony outside, just a safety rail, but it allowed cool air to filter into the room. It felt as if the temperature had just dropped by ten degrees.

'Oh! That's lovely.' She ran to his side, throwing up her arms so that the breeze could bathe her body. Then suddenly a sheet of rain started to fall, blowing in through open doors. Hannah squealed, and Matt caught her in his arms, kissing her.

'Matt! Again?' She'd felt his erection harden against her.

It came as a surprise to him as well. Just the thought of his father was usually enough to slake any thought of being close to anyone. But his thirst for Hannah was stronger than that. He felt her move against him, turning desire into blind longing. She wanted more too.

'It's not me. It's you... I can't get enough of you, Hannah.' A thought crossed his mind. 'Ever made love in a storm before?'

'If I have I don't remember it.' She wound her arms around his neck, lifting herself to coil her legs around his hips, in an invitation to *make* her remember it this time.

Thunder still rolled over their heads, feeling as if it was shaking the whole building. Then lightning, bathing the whole room in sudden brilliance. Hannah's kiss was like the touch of a hurricane, dragging him irresistibly into its force.

'Now... Before it goes, Matt.'

He wanted that too. He wanted to hear her scream, carried away with the force of the storm. Everything else was blotted out, and *now* was the only thing that seemed real...

Hannah woke, shivering in the chill of the breeze from the open doors. The storm had left clear skies in its wake, and sunshine was filtering in through the windows. She pulled the duvet up around her shoulders, snuggling against Matt.

Last night had been life-changing. The force of the storm had been nothing in comparison to the journey they'd made together, and now he was sleeping soundly, his arm slung possessively around her waist. He really had possessed her last night, in every way possible. Head and heart, along with her body.

But there was no time for that today. No time to think about how this couldn't last. They had things to do. She leaned towards him, riffling her fingers through his hair and kissing his cheek as his eyes fluttered open.

'Hey, sleepyhead.' Hannah had hoped for that smile, and it was everything that she wanted it to be.

'Hey, yourself.' He closed his eyes, drawing her close, and then opened them again suddenly. 'What's the time? Did we miss the alarm?'

Hannah twisted around so that she could see the clock. 'Six o'clock. We didn't miss the alarm.'

'That's good.' He closed his eyes again. 'We can take our time. Get up and have breakfast. Maybe review our list, before the media centre opens at ten.'

'Yes. We could.' Hannah snuggled against him, holding him tight, and she saw his lips curve into a smile.

'Or... I think you haven't quite made me your very own creature yet. You might want to seal the deal, so that I do everything you tell me today.'

'You're not my creature, Matt.' He could be easygoing when he wanted to be, and that was most of the time. But last night he'd shown a controlled mastery, which had driven her beyond anything she'd thought she knew about sex, and had taken her breath away.

'What am I then?'

Right now he was sleepy and smiling. Hannah knew that could change in an instant.

'You're my...teammate with benefits.'

He chuckled. 'High five...?'

Matt held up his hand, and she grabbed it, kissing his fingers. Finally...finally he opened his eyes again.

'You're thinking we should do this for the team?' He grinned lazily at her.

'No. Just because we want to.'

'My sentiments exactly.' He pulled the duvet back, throwing it onto the other side of the bed in one strong motion. The heat of their bodies would soon counteract the morning chill in the air.

CHAPTER THIRTEEN

EVERYTHING WENT BETTER and faster today. A good appetite for breakfast made it taste delicious and they stayed at the table, ordering more coffee, while they divided up the things they needed to do today. As soon as they were allowed into the media room, they sat together in their cubicle, concentrating on the screens of the laptops in front of them.

'I think the lights are sorted. I've found a place that does them really cheaply, and they're sending me through a quote that's good for sixty days.' Hannah wrinkled her nose. 'Do you reckon sixty days will be enough?'

Matt shrugged. 'We have to win this thing first. Then we can worry about the sixty days.'

'True. How are you doing with the prefabs?'

His lip curled into a teasing smile. 'Not too badly.'

'What? Tell me, Matt!'

He chuckled. 'I spoke to a few companies, and they offered to send me their best quotes. One offered ten per cent off the list price, which was still far too expensive for us. So I decided that I needed to go to the top. I called the managing director's secretary at Laurence Construction.'

'And she spoke to you?'

'I said I was a surgeon with an interesting proposition. I thought that a bit of mystery might help.'

Hannah laughed. 'Yeah, okay. Go on.'

'I told her what we were doing, and what we wanted. She said that she'd make some enquiries and get back to me, and I reckoned it was just a polite brush-off. But she called back after twenty minutes, and Sir James Laurence wants to see us. He's not in the office today, but he'd like us to drive down to his home in Sussex tomorrow morning.'

'Really? That's amazing. But do we have the time?'

'It's a risk, but I don't see that we can afford not to take it. I told her that we were being filmed but that I'd tell the production company that we wanted to speak privately, and she said that he'd welcome the cameras as long as there were no microphones.'

'That sounds promising. Surely he won't want us to drive all that way just to say no to us in front of the cameras.' Hannah thought for a moment. 'What do you say we get all our computer work and phone calls done today, then plan a round trip tomorrow to pick up the samples we need and go and see Sir James?'

'Yep. And we can start writing up the budget and the proposal tonight.'

'Sounds good. I suppose we'd better get on with it then.'

They worked until six, eating lunch in their cubicle. Hannah disappeared to make her evening phone call to Sam, and when she didn't appear in the dining room, Matt went to find her. She wasn't in their shared sitting room, but when he went to her bedroom door, he could hear what sounded like crying. Matt knocked, and there was no answer.

'Hannah…?'

'I'll be down in a minute.' Her voice had a brittle, cracked edge to it.

'Can I come in?'

'I'm just combing my hair. I'll see you downstairs.'

Right. After last night, wanting privacy to comb her hair was the worst excuse he'd heard in a long time. Matt walked over to the sofa, sat down and waited.

It took Hannah ten minutes to comb her hair, or whatever else it was she was doing. When she did appear she rushed towards the main door of the suite, obviously bound up in her own thoughts, and she didn't even see him.

'Hannah.'

'Oh!' She gave a yelp of surprise, and whirled around. Matt could see that her eyes and the tip of her nose were a little pink, which would have been enchanting if they weren't sure signs she'd been crying.

'I didn't see you there.'

'I was waiting for you.'

'Okay, well…are you coming?' She opened the door, giving him a puzzled look when he didn't move.

'No. What's the matter?'

'Nothing.'

Matt rolled his eyes. 'Now I *know* it's something. If it really is nothing you'd tell me about it.'

She frowned at him but closed the door, walking over to sit down on the sofa. 'It's not like my knee, Matt. It doesn't affect the competition.'

'So I'm not allowed to care about it? You've been crying, Hannah. What's the matter?'

'It's Sam.' She capitulated suddenly. 'He left his school project out on the patio last night and it got ruined in the storm. Mum explained to his teacher, but he still got nought out of ten, and he'd worked so hard on it. He was really upset.'

'I'm sorry.' Matt reached for her hand, but she didn't move any closer to him.

'It's one of those things. I dare say he'll have forgotten

all about it by tomorrow morning, but he sounded so miserable on the phone. I just wish I'd been there.'

Something else was bugging her, something that she wasn't admitting to. The thought of the storm last night brought with it the vision of their embrace, and Matt knew suddenly that Hannah would never admit this to him. He had to voice it, the way she'd voiced what he couldn't.

'And you were here, having sex. The fact that it was really great sex probably makes it a lot worse.'

She laughed, a tear rolling down her cheek. 'Yes, it does actually. Sorry…'

'Don't be. I know you promised to always be there for him.' That promise meant a lot to Hannah, after what had happened with her father.

'I'm learning that I can't. He's growing up and he wants to make his own way in the world. When I pick him up from school now, I have to wait at the far end of the playground, I'm not allowed to go right up to the classroom door. He says that's just for little kids.'

'It sounds hard. I wouldn't be able to do it. But he knows you're there when he needs you Hannah, and that you'd do anything for him. That's what really matters.'

'Unless I have something else I have to do.' She turned the corners of her mouth down.

'That's just not true. I might not know how to raise a child, the way you do, but I have first-hand experience of this. Kids understand exactly who loves them.'

'Thank you.' She heaved a sigh. 'I'm sorry Matt, after what happened to you this must seem so trivial and stupid.'

'It seems loving. And after what happened to me, it's a joy to see it. Sam's got a happy, stable home and he doesn't know anything about the kind of fear that I felt. That's really important.'

Hannah took his hand, squeezing it. 'I think it might

be really important that you can say that, Matt. Thanks for talking.'

She seemed about to stand, and Matt pulled her towards him in a hug. First things first. Dinner could wait for another few minutes. 'If you really want to see him we can go now. I'll drive you home.'

She laughed. 'Don't be crazy. We'll be disqualified.'

'It's like we said before, if we can't keep our values, then all of this is meaningless. If you really need Sam, or he needs you, then we'll go, whatever the consequences.'

He felt her lips brush his cheek. 'Thank you for saying that. I know you'd do it as well. But Sam wouldn't like it one bit, he's as keen for us to win as anyone.'

'Then we won't disappoint him?'

'I won't disappoint *you* either. Come down to dinner now, and then we can get on with what we have to do this evening.'

They worked late into the night, and Matt wondered whether he'd be going to his bedroom alone tonight. Maybe after her call with Sam, Hannah would feel too guilty. But when they finally decided that they needed sleep, she took his hand, pulling him towards her bedroom with a whispered promise that sleep wasn't the only thing she intended.

They were up early, and Matt had gone to his room to dress, his lips still tingling from her kisses. He rescued his shirt from the press, and put on the suit and tie he'd brought. Hannah emerged from her bedroom wearing a slimline sleeveless dress, buttoned at the front, with high heels. She was carrying a matching jacket, and her hair was caught behind her head in a neat, shining fold.

'I really wish you hadn't worn that…'

Dismay registered on her face. 'Why? Do you think I should wear tights? They're so hot in this weather...'

'You look beautiful, and very businesslike. I just want to muss you up a bit again, and those buttons...' Matt leaned in, his hand hovering over the top button on her dress. 'Far too much of a temptation.'

'Ow!' She was clearly pleased with his assessment. 'Keep your hands off my buttons, Matt. You can do whatever you like with them later.'

They had a quick breakfast, drawing enquiring looks from some of the other contestants, who were mostly wearing jeans or sweatpants. The production assistant who was going with them to ensure they didn't do anything that broke the rules bundled into the back of Matt's car, her phone in her hand, and an outside broadcast van followed them out of the underground car park.

'Thank goodness for air-conditioning.' Hannah stretched her legs out in front of her, looking at the sun beating down on the pavements. 'Our first stop is Streatham. They supply specialist lights, and they're only open in the morning, so we'll have to pop in there on our way.'

It took fifteen minutes for Hannah to look at the lights she wanted, and they left with an armful of brochures and some photographs. Then they drove out of London, picking up the motorway before turning off into winding country lanes. Sir James Laurence's home was nestled in four acres of sunlit garden just outside a pretty village, and they drew up outside the large country house at just before ten thirty.

Matt took their jackets from the hanger inside the car, pulling his on despite the heat. The house was spectacular, a grand entrance at the front and topped by a couple of round turrets and a flag.

'Here goes nothing...' Hannah murmured the words,

putting on her jacket and walking uncertainly across the gravelled driveway in her high heels. Matt caught her arm to steady her in pretty much the same way that he would have done if they were scaling a climbing wall, but when she tucked her hand into the crook of his elbow, it felt like something very different. The kind of thing a woman might do after the kind of night last night had been.

A woman in a designer suit, not a hair out of place, was waiting in the large, cool hallway. Hannah stepped inside, smiling. It occurred to Matt that she was so used to walking into different homes and different situations that even this didn't faze her.

'I'm Helena, Sir James's secretary.' Matt recognised the well-modulated tones from when they'd spoken on the phone yesterday. 'You have a film crew with you?'

'They couldn't keep up.' Hannah grinned at her. 'I dare say they'll be here in a minute. This is the production assistant, Cecile.'

'I'll show you where you can set the cameras up, Cecile. Sir James will be on the terrace, so there's no need for extra lighting.' Helena was clearly used to dealing with everything and anything.

An older woman, dressed in sneakers, jeans and a flowery shirt, hurried towards them. Her blonde hair was perfectly styled, and she carried a pair of gardening gloves, which she laid on the hall table.

'Hannah and Matt!' The woman exclaimed, grabbing Hannah's hand. 'I'm so pleased you could come.'

If Hannah was taken aback by the greeting she didn't show it. She beamed at the woman, giving her hand a friendly squeeze.

'I'm Patti Laurence. I just *love Hospital Challenge*!'

'You've been watching?'

'Oh, yes. Every episode. That little victory dance you do, is that with your son? He's very cute.'

'Thank you. Sam's six—I'd show you the proud mother photos, but they've confiscated my phone for the duration.'

'Oh, really.' Patti shot Cecile a stern look, which she didn't deserve. 'I hardly think you'd cheat. Not after giving up your chance to win to help that man.'

'I'd be tempted to. I really miss Sam, I'd be calling him ten times a day to find out what he's doing if I could.'

'Yes, I can understand that. I was exactly the same with my two when they were Sam's age.' Patti turned to Helena. 'I'll make the tea, dear, the tray's ready in the kitchen. Why don't you deal with the cameras?'

'Yes, of course.' Helena smiled, shepherding Cecile away.

'And, Matt…' Patti smiled at him, shaking his hand vigorously, and then turned back to Hannah, taking her arm. 'This way, dear.'

Hannah had clearly made an impression. That was okay, Matt was happy to take a back seat and watch her. His love of watching Hannah wasn't confined to watching her dress or undress, pretty much everything she did fascinated him.

Patti led them out onto a large terrace, chattering to Hannah all the way about *Hospital Challenge*. She showed them to a set of comfortable wicker seats arranged around a glass-topped table and shaded from the sun.

'I'll just get the tea tray. I won't be a minute.' Patti turned towards the garden, yelling at the top of her voice. 'Jamie! Coo-ee! They're here!'

'Let me help you with the tea, Patti.' Hannah took off her jacket, hanging it on the back of one of the chairs, and followed Patti into the house.

Matt sat down, surveying the garden for any sign of Sir James. Just as Patti and Hannah reappeared, Hannah carrying a large tray stacked with what looked like very fine china indeed, he saw a man in a check shirt and corduroy trousers walking towards him across the lawn.

'There he is.' Patti walked down to the edge of the lawn, waiting for her husband, and Hannah deposited the tray on the table.

'Glad I didn't drop this. It would have been my pay cheque for at least three months.' She sat down on the edge of one of the chairs, her nervousness suddenly visible. 'Patti just happened to mention that Sir James likes it when people get to the point. We don't need to try to persuade him, just show him what we have.'

Matt nodded, taking off his jacket and draping it over the back of his seat, feeling the cool breeze with a sense of relief. This heat wasn't conducive to formality. Hannah looked cool and calm as she rose to shake Sir James's hand. White haired, his face lined and tanned, he seemed kindly and welcoming, but his piercing blue eyes were that of a canny businessman.

Patti poured the tea and pushed the plate of biscuits towards them. Helena appeared with a leather portfolio, handing it silently to Sir James, and he smiled and thanked her, glancing towards the camera crew who were standing at the other end of the terrace, waiting for something to happen. Helena turned and signalled to Cecile that they could start filming now. This all seemed effortless but it was organised down to the last detail.

'Are you staying, dear?' Sir James turned to his wife.

'Of course I am. This is *Hospital Challenge*...' Patti shot him an outraged look.

'Yes. Of course.' Sir James turned to them and his smile faded, replaced by an air of businesslike efficiency. 'Tell me what you have so far. And what you need.'

Hannah glanced at Matt and he nodded her on. She was

doing just fine so far, and he didn't see any point in messing with perfection.

Hannah started to talk. She pitched straight in, telling him a little about her own experience with Sam, and saying how much she would have appreciated a facility like this. Then she widened it out, speaking about how a sensory room might benefit all kinds of children, and outlining briefly the kinds of activities and therapies that could be carried out there. Her enthusiasm shone through, and somehow she managed to ignore the fact that Sir James was clearly weighing and calculating the worth of each word she said.

'We have a very preliminary plan…' She turned to Matt, and he handed her the folder they'd brought, containing the pages they'd printed out at midnight last night.

Sir James studied the sheets carefully. Patti smiled and offered them both a biscuit.

'It's taken you under two days to do this much?' Sir James put the folder back onto the table.

'I'm a mother, and I've been an ambulance paramedic for six years. Matt's been working as a surgeon for ten. That's how long this has taken us.'

Great answer. Sir James obviously liked it a lot too, as he allowed himself a brief smile before he turned, looking around him. Helena appeared suddenly at his side.

'The microphones are off, they're just filming a few long shots of the meeting.' She anticipated his question and Sir James nodded.

'Thank you, Helena. Will you arrange for them to have some tea, please?'

'Of course, Sir James.' Helena hurried away and Sir James picked up the leather portfolio from the table, unzipping it.

'This is what I can offer you. It's our newest design, and

I'm very proud of it. It's built with a close to zero carbon footprint, and it's a configurable space that includes underfloor heating and air-conditioning for days like these.' He handed a glossy brochure to Matt. 'Page six for the plan and an artist's impression.'

Matt flipped thankfully past the building specifications, which meant very little to him. When he got to page six, he saw Hannah's eyes widen. The L-shaped, timber-framed building looked stunning, and there were diagrams showing how the space could be converted to suit practically any requirement.

'We're exhibiting this at a show in a couple of weeks' time. After that it'll be taken down and we'll have no use for it. It would be a shame to consign it to a skip.'

'This is…beyond anything we'd imagined.' Matt spoke first, because Hannah was still staring, lost for words.

'Too big? If you can't fill the space, then…' Sir James shrugged, the steel in his eyes glinting. Matt saw Hannah sit a little straighter in response to the challenge.

'We can fill it. And there's plenty of room for a facility like this, the hospital has a large open space at the back. I suppose we'd need planning permission, but…'

'I can help you with that.' Sir James smiled suddenly. 'Our planning department nurtures an excellent relationship with local authorities around the country, and our building specifications are tailored to exceed the requirements of planning regulations. With any luck, it shouldn't be a problem.'

Matt doubted that Sir James left anything to good luck. Hannah glanced at him and he nodded.

'Sir James, this is incredibly generous of you. All we can do is thank you, and say yes. We'd very much like to take you up on your offer.' Hannah hesitated, staring down at the brochure, and then her back straightened. Matt sensed that something amazing was coming and waited to hear what it was.

'If we don't win, then we won't get the money to fit this building out. But I can raise the money for a less ambitious scheme, and I'll approach the hospital board and persuade them to accept it. Would it be too presumptuous of me to ask if you'd consider donating this building anyway? Even if we don't win?'

Matt could have hugged her. Hannah had come a long way in the last six weeks, and had gained the confidence to make her ambitions work. Sir James laughed suddenly, flashing a glance at his wife.

'I like your plan very much. What do you think, Matt?'

'I…' Matt spread his hands in a shrug. 'I've learned one thing over the last six weeks. If Hannah says she'll do something, she'll find a way to do it.'

'That's agreed, then. Although I'm sure we're both looking forward to seeing you win, eh, Patti?'

Patti rolled her eyes, smiling at her husband. 'Of course we are. I'm so thrilled we can be a part of it.'

Sir James threw off the persona of a hardheaded businessman, becoming an avuncular host. Patti called towards the kitchen, asking for more tea, and Hannah drank hers thankfully, sitting quietly as Matt answered Sir James's questions about how the building should be configured to best suit their purposes. Patti joined in with the conversation, obviously keen for them to stay as long as possible, and Matt listened carefully to her suggestions.

'You've both been very generous with your time and hospitality. We should be on our way.' Finally he drew the conversation to a close, and Patti grimaced in disappointment.

'Of course you must.' Sir James squeezed his wife's

hand. 'We can go and see the project when it gets underway, darling.'

'Yes, we'd love you to come and see us. I'll bring Sam along and we'll show you around.' Patti brightened visibly at Hannah's words.

'I'd love that. Wouldn't you love it, Jamie?'

Sir James chuckled. 'Yes, I would.'

There was an unobtrusive movement, from the other side of the terrace, as the camera crew started to pack up their equipment in response to Helena's chivvying. Sir James walked through to the front door with them, and shook Matt's hand.

'Thank you so much. This is an incredible gift, and it'll help a lot of people.' Hannah held her hand out, and their host grasped it between his.

'I should thank you, Hannah. Patti had a heart attack three years ago, in the middle of the night. An ambulance came, and the two young men were…' He shook his head, as if words failed him.

Hannah nodded. 'They made a difference.'

'They were wonderful. So kind and good humoured. They whisked me off to the hospital, and I had a couple of stents put in.' Patti confided the information to Matt, plainly considering stents as part of his territory.

'And you're fully recovered?'

'Oh, yes! I've got more energy than I had before!' Patti beamed at him.

Sir James was hanging on to Hannah's hand, and she leaned forward a little, putting her free hand onto his. Matt knew that look, and the silent invitation to say exactly how he felt. If Sir James could resist it he had more steel in his heart than Matt did.

'I shook their hands. I didn't have the words to thank them properly, I was so worried about Patti. I've always regretted that omission.' Sir James's words were directed at Hannah.

'Trust me, they knew. Seeing a loved one suffer a heart attack is frightening and distressing, and when someone manages to overcome that to shake my hand, it means everything to me. That, and Patti's recovery is all the thanks that they could want.'

Sir James nodded, letting go of Hannah's hand. He was a man of few words, but he felt this deeply. He put his arm around his wife, and the couple bade them a cheery goodbye.

'I'm going to hug you. Just as soon as we have a moment alone.' Matt murmured the words as he offered Hannah his arm across the gravel.

'I'm going to hug you back.' She turned to give a final wave to their hosts as Matt opened the car door for her. 'What nice people.'

'You gave Sir James a reason to be generous. I'm proud of you.' He settled himself into the driver's seat, waiting for Cecile to come running across from the outside broadcast van and get into the back seat of the car. 'Where now?'

'Fulham. There's a shop there that does all the different kinds of specialist seating that we might need and I'd like to try some of them out. Then back to the hotel. I think we can specify the rest of the specialist equipment from the internet.'

Matt pulled out of the driveway. The stakes were higher now. Hannah had worked so hard for this, and she'd stepped out of her comfort zone when she'd come here. They had to win.

CHAPTER FOURTEEN

BY THE TIME Sunday evening rolled around, Matt and Hannah had been working flat out since the media centre had opened on Friday morning and they were both exhausted. Hannah had made the presentation boards, and Matt had worked through the spreadsheet, making sure they were within their budget. They'd printed off the requisite fifteen copies of their detailed presentation and bound them, and they were ready by seven o'clock. She'd called Sam and then joined Matt up in their suite.

'How's he doing?' He was sprawled on the sofa, and Hannah moved his leg so that she could sit down, leaning against his knee.

'He's good. Mum took him to the zoo today, and he had a great time.'

'That's nice.' Matt's eyes were almost closed, and Hannah's were sore and prickling from lack of sleep as well. 'Is it too early to go to bed?'

'No. Considering we had two hours' sleep last night, I think it's acceptable. I think I feel worse than if I'd worked straight through.' Hannah yawned.

'Nah. A few hours is better than nothing. Will you take it the wrong way if I take you into the bedroom, rip all of your clothes off and then go to sleep?'

'You've got the energy to rip my clothes off?' Hannah teased him.

'No, not really. On second thoughts you might have to do that yourself. Finishing the presentation is about as much gratification as I can take tonight.' Matt gave her a lazy smile. 'I may well feel differently in the morning.'

Sleep and then Matt's embrace. It sounded like heaven. 'Thank you, Robin. For everything. I wouldn't be here without you.'

'Thank *you*, Flash. I wouldn't be here without you.'

Monday had been set aside for the judges to talk to the competitors about their projects, and there was also time to see the other teams' proposals. Their phones had been returned, and Hannah couldn't wait for Sam to get home from school so that they could video call and she'd be able to show him what she'd been doing, and where she was staying.

The hospitals that were competing had sent representatives to discuss the proposed projects with the judges, so that they could assess their viability. Hannah saw Matt with Dr Gregson, the chairman of the hospital board, the two men chatting affably as they made their way across the room towards her.

'Hannah.' Dr Gregson held his hand out to her. 'You and Matt have made the most wonderful effort for the hospital. We're all enormously grateful to you both. Win or lose.'

'Thank you.' Hannah took his hand, feeling her ears burn.

'Hannah's come to an arrangement with Sir James Laurence.' Matt was grinning.

'You have?'

She would have preferred a little more time to decide how to put this to Dr Gregson, but he was here now, and obviously pleased with what they'd done. Matt was right, she should strike while the iron was hot.

'I asked him whether he'd be willing to donate the pre-fab if we didn't win the contest. We wouldn't be able to afford to do everything we'd planned, but I told him that I'd raise the money for the sensory rooms myself. If you and the board will agree to it, that is.'

'That's very enterprising of you.' Dr Gregson thought for a moment. 'You have my full support, Hannah. I'm sure the other members of the board won't need a great deal of persuasion either, I've already spoken with some of them on the phone and they're delighted with your ideas for the project.'

'Thank you.' Hannah heaved a sigh of relief.

'Of course it may not be necessary.' Dr Gregson smiled. 'I may be biased, but your project is the best I've seen. We'll speak again when we find out whether you've won.'

Dr Gregson took his leave of them, and Matt turned to her, smirking. 'That wasn't so bad, was it?'

'It was horrible, Matt! I could kick you.'

He assumed a look of innocence. 'Why? You didn't have time to get nervous about what you were going to say. And you were perfect, just as you were when you charmed Sir James into giving you a prefab.'

'He didn't give it to me, he gave it to the hospital. And anyway *I* didn't charm him. Our project speaks for itself.'

'It speaks with your voice.' Matt's confidence in her always made Hannah smile. 'I'm going to go and check my email. Will Sam be home from school yet?'

Hannah looked at her watch. 'Oh, yes. I'd better call him now, before it's time for the results to be announced...'

Matt's email had obviously contained something that had soured his mood. When Hannah took her phone upstairs so that Sam could say hello to him, he was sitting, staring at the wall. He cheered up a little to talk to Sam, but Hannah was sure that his smile wouldn't last for long after she left him to give Sam a guided tour of the swimming pool and the gym in the basement.

When she arrived back in the conference room, he seemed cheerful enough. They sat and waited as the final preparations were made, and he curled his fingers around hers. They were both nervous, but being nervous together somehow made it all right.

Finally the chairman of the judging panel picked up the microphone, and a heavy silence fell. Hannah could feel a bead of sweat running uncomfortably down her back.

'I'm going to keep this short, because everyone wants to know who the winners are. But I want to thank everyone here. The projects you've created in a very short time have all shown imagination and flair, and a sound understanding of what your various hospitals need. I gather that a number of your projects will be going ahead, win or lose, and I can only applaud the determination and resourcefulness of all the contestants here this afternoon...'

Get on with it. *Get on with it.* Hannah shot Matt an agonised look and he squeezed her hand.

'And now our winners. Hannah and Matt from Hamblewell Hospital.'

She couldn't breathe. She was going to have to stand up and walk to the podium, but her legs wouldn't carry her. Applause started to ripple through the room, and it swelled into a cacophony of sound in her ears.

'One last push, Flash...' She heard Matt's voice in her ear, and it gave her strength. He rose, following her to the end of the row of chairs and walking beside her to where the judges were waiting to greet them.

She lost count of the number of hands that she shook.

The chairman of the judges handed her a large, golden envelope, and she didn't dare look inside to make sure that this was real. Matt took the microphone, thanking everyone, and then turned to her.

'I'm not going to ask Hannah to say anything, because I'm not sure that she can…' He grinned at her as a rumble of laughter spread around the room, and Hannah mouthed a silent, *Thank you.* She'd only make a fool of herself if she took the microphone now.

'I do want to say one thing, though. This last six weeks has been challenging and the person who's challenged me most is my teammate. Thank you, Hannah, for being my partner, my guide and my inspiration.'

She could feel tears rolling down her cheeks. Matt put his arm around her shoulders and she clung onto him. There were more hands to shake, and when Dr Gregson came to congratulate them she pressed the envelope into Matt's hand for safekeeping. Drinks were passed around, and she took a sip of champagne, feeling too dizzy to drink the rest of it.

Finally the gathering began to break up. The contestants who came from further afield were going to be staying on at the hotel tonight, but those whose journeys home were shorter were already leaving. She saw Matt signal to her, and followed him out of the room and up to their suite.

'We did it, Matt!' As soon as the door closed behind them she flung her arms around him. 'I can't believe it, I'm so happy.'

'Yeah. We did it.' He'd been smiling and relaxed downstairs, but suddenly he seemed more tense. Maybe he was thinking about the drive home.

Or maybe he was thinking about *being* home. Back to reality. The last four days had been a fantasy, and neither of them had had time to think ahead. But now they had to, because the bubble was about to burst, and when it did they'd have to face all of the issues that threatened to tear them apart.

But they'd won. That had seemed impossible but they'd done it together. They could do this too, if they wanted to. She could show Matt that his father hadn't irrevocably soured his life.

'Would you like to go home?' He was smiling but his eyes had lost their fire.

'Yes, I would. Thank you.'

He nodded, turning away from her. 'I'll finish packing my things. Will you be ready in half an hour?'

They took their leave of everyone, thanking the production team once again and shaking the hands of the contestants who hadn't left yet. Matt drove in silence, all of his concentration on the road ahead.

Hannah would wait. They could talk when they got back, and she'd tell him. She could be there for him, if only he'd be there for her. As they turned off the motorway into familiar roads, she began to feel more calm, more certain of what she wanted. This couldn't be an ending for her and Matt.

He drew up outside her house, looking at the front door, seemingly deep in thought. Hannah turned to him.

'Should we talk?'

'Don't you want to go and see Sam?'

'He'll be in bed, asleep. I didn't know what time we'd be back, so I told him that I'd be late and that I'd see him tomorrow. He'd only try to stay awake otherwise.'

Matt nodded. 'We should talk. Soon.'

'Why don't I take my bags inside, and we can go for a walk?' The evening was still warm, even though the light would be fading soon.

'Yeah. That sounds good.'

He took her bags from the boot, carrying them to the door. Hannah's mother was waiting for them, and she whispered that Sam had decided that the sooner he went to sleep, the sooner tomorrow would come, and had gone to bed as soon as he was told. Matt waited in the hall while Hannah crept upstairs to see Sam and to blow a kiss to her sleeping boy.

Her mother hugged her, telling her how proud she was of her, and then let her go. Hannah led Matt along the path that meandered past the houses and down towards the stream that ran along the border between the village and the open countryside.

'Matt, I know we said there would be no strings, and that suited us both. But that doesn't mean we have to be strangers...' That was a good start. If they could agree on that, then they could agree to be lovers, too.

She heard him catch his breath and didn't dare look at him.

'Hannah, I'm leaving.'

'What!' This *had* to be a joke. But when she turned to him, his face was deadly serious. 'Leaving...where? Where are you going?'

'I've been offered a job in London.'

Hannah took a breath. That didn't help. 'And you didn't tell me? Matt, you slept with me, and you didn't say anything?'

'I didn't know. The offer was there when I picked up my email this afternoon.'

'What, and someone just offered you a job out of the blue? You must have known it was a possibility.'

'I didn't know whether I'd get it or not. But, yes, it was a possibility. I've been thinking of moving on for a while now.'

'And you said nothing? You said a lot of things, but you didn't tell me that.'

'You knew I couldn't make a commitment, Hannah. You can't either. We both said it. No strings.'

'Yes, we said no strings. We didn't *do* no strings, though, did we...?' Hannah was almost breathless with anger.

'No. We didn't.' He shoved his hands into his pockets, looking at the ground. 'I'm sorry.'

'Well, *sorry* just won't do it, Matt. You know I can't just pick up sticks and follow you...' Hannah felt tears prick at the corners of her eyes. No one had said anything about her following him. She'd betrayed what she really wanted to do, at just the time when she should have kept quiet about it.

'I know. You have Sam and your mother to think about. I'd never ask you to come with me, it's not fair.'

'Then why do you have to go?'

'Because... You know why, Hannah. I didn't believe that I could love you, but I do. And I'm no good at loving anyone...'

'That's no excuse, Matt. If you loved me, then you wouldn't have to worry about whether you were good at it or not, you'd just *be* good at it.'

He looked up at her, and suddenly Hannah saw the unfairness of it all. She was blaming him for something that wasn't his fault. Matt was struggling with a terrible legacy of pain, and he couldn't break free of it. And all she could do was harangue him for it.

'Then maybe I don't love you after all.'

His quiet words cut deep. Shaking with the shock of them, Hannah turned, running away from him. Running away from the man that she'd loved who'd hurt her so very badly.

Maybe he'd follow. She reached her front door, turning to look behind her, and cruel hope tore at her as she saw his shadow, moving towards her. But he was just walking back to his car, and Hannah watched as he opened the door and got inside. After a pause, the lights flipped on and he drove away.

She couldn't go inside, not yet. Hannah wiped the tears from her face, trying to compose herself, but it was no use. She walked around the side of the house, sitting down on the steps that led up to the patio, allowing herself to cry in the darkness.

'You're putting a brave face on something.' Sophie was resting her arms on the steering wheel of the ambulance, tapping her fingers fitfully. Hannah really wished she'd stop it, her nerves were already on edge. 'You can do that with Sam, I guess that probably goes with the job. You can do it with your mum if you want to, but you can't with me.'

Hannah rolled her eyes, unwrapping her sandwiches. 'Why not?'

'Because I have to put up with you all day. And I'm your friend. What happened, Hannah?'

'I'm just a bit tired. It was a tough weekend.'

'Yes, and you've had three nights to sleep it off. And you won, doesn't that make you happy?'

She'd won nothing. The whole hospital seemed to be celebrating, and it seemed like something that had to be endured.

'It doesn't make you happy, does it?' Sophie clearly wasn't going to give up.

'No.' Hannah sighed. Sophie was going to find out sooner or later. 'Matt's leaving. He's got a job in London.'

'What?' Sophie stared at her.

'Yeah. That was my reaction. We had a…thing. And then when we got back, he told me that he was leaving.'

'Just like that?'

'Pretty much.'

'He had sex with you. Then he told you he was leaving.' Sophie's lip curled. 'Just give me ten minutes with him, Hannah. I'm going to hurt that guy.'

'No. You're *not* going to hurt him.' Matt had been hurt enough, and the urge to defend him was stronger than any of the pain that Hannah was feeling. 'He has his reasons. He's never stayed in one place for very long, he just can't do it, and I knew that.'

'What reasons?'

'Good ones.' Hannah turned the corners of her mouth down. She wanted to tell Sophie, but that would be a betrayal. She raised the sandwich to her lips and her stomach began to lurch. She'd been going through the motions of eating and sleeping for the last three days, and doing little of either.

'Does he think that you'll follow him?'

'He knows all about John. If I go with him, then I'd feel that I was putting Sam and my mum second, and he knows I can't do that again.'

Sophie considered the idea for a moment. 'Your mum just wants the best for you, you know that. And if you wanted to move to London, then…lots of people move and their kids don't fall to pieces over it. Sam would probably really like it there, and it's only thirty miles. It's practically a commute, lots of people live around here and work in London.'

'That's not the point, Soph. I'd hate myself, and no relationship can survive that.'

'You've thought about it, though, haven't you?'

'I've thought about nothing else. And I can't do it.'

Sophie puffed out a breath. 'Maybe we should go for a long run. Sweat him out of your system. Or we could go out and get very drunk.'

Hannah laughed. 'Or stay in and get very drunk.'

'That'd work.' Sophie turned to face her. 'You love him, don't you?'

'Yes, I love him. Are you going to say *I told you so*?'

'No, that's a fat lot of use. I'm just here to cheer you on, Hannah. Whatever you decide to do.'

'Thanks, Sophie. That means a lot.' Hannah leaned over, hugging her friend, and Sophie squeezed her so tight that she could hardly breathe.

She had everything, right here. Sam, her mother. Good friends like Sophie. She could work on forgetting Matt and everything would be the way it was before.

It sounded easy. Just as long as she left out the part about Matt having changed her for ever.

Did any of the old rules still apply? Hadn't Matt shown her that life wasn't all about what she couldn't do? It was about what she *could* do.

CHAPTER FIFTEEN

'*Maybe I don't love you after all.*'

As soon as the words had left his lips, Matt had known that they were a stupid, cruel lie. He'd walked away because he'd been convinced that a clean break would somehow be easier. That if Hannah hated him, then perhaps she wouldn't be hurting as badly as he was.

All the same, he couldn't let it go. He couldn't leave without saying goodbye to her and Sam. And somewhere, deep in his consciousness, it occurred to him that if he and Hannah could win *Hospital Challenge*, they could find a way to make this right and be together.

Maybe he should start with flowers. But none of the bright blooms in the florist's shop were good enough for Hannah. And anyway, a gift carried with it the expectation of forgiveness, and the very most that he could ask of her was that she hear him out.

After a week of trying to think of the right things to say, he decided that there was no right thing. He just had to apologise to her, and find out whether there was any chance that they could move forward from that. Friends, lovers. Exes who didn't hold a grudge. He'd take anything that Hannah felt able to give.

He drew up outside her house just as it was getting dark. It was Hannah's mother's book club evening, and

Hannah's car stood alone in the driveway. Sam must be going to bed about now, so he'd get a chance to speak with Hannah alone. It took a couple of minutes to screw up his courage, and his heart was pounding as he got out of the car, walking towards the front door.

Then he saw it. The lights flipped on in the sitting room, and Hannah appeared with Sam, who was in his pyjamas and ready for bed. Sitting down in one of the armchairs, she took him on her lap and opened a storybook.

Matt could almost feel the warmth between them, radiating out into the cool of the evening. He stopped, stock still, watching. It was all he'd ever wanted, and yet...

If by some miracle he did manage to make things right with Hannah, what would happen next? His father had hurt his mother, and then made things right, in a cycle that had turned into years of agony. One of the things his mother had always impressed on Matt was that apologies weren't enough, and that a person had to be truly committed to change.

He wanted to change. But what if he couldn't?

Standing in the darkness, he suddenly saw it all very clearly. Hannah had all she needed, and he should go. He should let her live her life, and find someone who loved her in the way that she deserved.

Thinking of Hannah with someone else brought a bitter taste to his mouth. Matt turned, shaken by the knowledge that however much he wanted to see Hannah again, the best thing he could do for her was to leave. He hurried back to his car, fumbling with the keys and dropping them in the footwell.

A few more moments. Just to be near her. He stared at the light in the window, like a moth drawn to a flame.

He didn't know how long he sat there, but when he saw her tiny figure move, and then the light upstairs flip on, he knew that he had to go before he was tempted by the knowledge that Sam would be in bed and Hannah was alone. Picking up his keys, he started the car and drove away.

It had been four weeks. Matt had confined himself to the surgical suite while he'd worked out his notice at the hospital, and hadn't seen Hannah. Clearly she didn't want to see him, and there was nothing else to do now but pack the last of his things and leave. Matt was going to be house-sitting for a friend for a couple of months, which would give him time to find a place of his own, and he'd already boxed up one car load of his possessions for storage. The rest would fit in the boot of his car. Matt travelled light.

The thought had always made him feel free. But freedom didn't mean a great deal any more without Hannah.

The doorbell rang and he ignored it. In his head he was already gone, and there would be no one stopping by to bid him farewell. If someone wanted to sell something, they'd have to find another, more receptive customer.

He busied himself, collecting up the last of his possessions from the sitting room, ready to be wrapped and packed into a cardboard box. The sound of a car alarm came from the street. *His* car alarm.

Matt grabbed his keys and looked out of the window. Hannah was leaning against his car, her arms folded, looking up at him. She had that determined look about her that he loved so much.

She gave him a wave and walked towards the front door of the block of flats. Matt swallowed down the temptation to lean out of the window, and shout down to her to ask what on earth she thought she was doing. Hannah had obviously made up her mind that she wanted to see him, and if he didn't let her in he guessed that she'd only go back to his car and set the alarm off again. He almost wanted her to…

The doorbell sounded, and he pressed the Entryphone. He heard the front door slam shut, and counted the beats of his heart until he reckoned she'd reached the top of the stairs. When he opened the door of his flat, he saw her walking towards him.

'What are you doing, Hannah?'

'All of your windows are open and your car's outside.' She smiled at him, and Matt's stomach lurched. 'I guessed you were in.'

'I was busy. And I wasn't expecting anyone.'

'Good. So we won't be interrupted.' She didn't wait for him to ask her in, brushing past him and walking straight through to the sitting room. Matt closed the door and followed, and she swiped a piece of packing material off the sofa so that she could sit down.

'You owe me an apology, Matt.'

She was giving him a chance. Suddenly it wasn't so very hard to apologise, because this was nothing like the way his father had used his apologies to manipulate his mother. Hannah was in control, and asking for something that was rightfully hers.

'I didn't tell you that I had plans to leave. It was wrong of me, and I apologise.'

She nodded. 'Accepted. Although I was at fault too, you told me that leaving was on your agenda and I didn't take you at your word. Is there anything else?'

He knew what she wanted to hear. It was the thing he most wanted to say.

'I told you that I didn't love you. I thought it might make things easier, but…' Matt shook his head, moving a cardboard box from the armchair, and sat down. 'It wasn't true and I'm sorry. I know I hurt you and I don't expect you to forgive me.'

'Thank you. I needed to hear that.' Somehow Hannah didn't seem hurt. She didn't seem beaten. She had that light in her eyes that ignited when she faced a challenge.

'Thank you for the opportunity of saying it.'

Nothing had changed. *Everything* had changed. The fear of seeming like his father had dissolved suddenly and Matt was his own man. His head began to swim.

'I've come to tell you something, Matt. Just so you know.'

He'd listen. Whatever it was that Hannah wanted to get off her chest, he'd take it. Matt nodded her on.

'I've thought about this a lot, and when I heard that yesterday was your last day at the hospital, I had to make a decision.' She took a deep breath, as if there was no going back now. 'I promised myself I'd never follow any-one again, but that was before I fell in love with you. So wherever you go, I'll follow. Whenever you want me, I'll be there.'

Bright, blinding light. Suddenly everything was in sharp focus and the world seemed full of colour. Maybe he'd died and gone to heaven. Matt pulled himself together.

'Hannah, you can't.'

'Try me.'

He shook his head, trying to clear it. 'What about Sam? And your mother…?'

'Mum and Sam are staying here, and so am I. But my heart will always go with you. It'll wait, and if you ever want me…' Her face crumpled suddenly and she clasped her hands together. 'If you *do* want me, then you should call.'

He wanted to hold her. Matt wanted to forget all of the reasons that they couldn't be together and plunge into the fantasy of being with Hannah. But this was real. She was serious about this, and there were real obstacles.

'I want you every day. I love you…' Matt shook his head. 'But this isn't the smart thing to do, Hannah, you and Sam deserve more than I know how to give.'

'We both know how to change. It's just a matter of whether we want to enough.'

Matt's world crashed down around him. Everything that he'd thought he knew, everything that had made it so impossible for them to be together. Hannah had done the impossible, and smashed through it all. He got to his feet, kneeling in front of her.

'Hannah, you're the bravest, most beautiful woman…' She started to cry suddenly, and he reached to brush away her tears.

'You said that I should call you when I was ready. I'm calling you now. I don't know how I can ever begin to deserve you, but I'm going to find a way. I want to be the one that loves and protects you, and Sam, for the rest of my life.'

She threw her arms around his neck. 'Neither of us has to do it alone, Matt. If we stick together we can do all the things we thought we'd never do.'

'Flash and Robin. Ready to take on anything.' He kissed her, holding her as if he was never going to let her go. There was no *as if* about it. He never was going to let Hannah go.

EPILOGUE

Six months later

IT HADN'T BEEN EASY. But that had never stopped them before.

Love had carried them through it all. The therapy, where Matt had begun to shake off the burden of his childhood trauma. His long commute between Hamblewell and London, and the lonely nights when Matt had stayed over at the hospital.

Hannah's fears for Sam and her mother had turned out to be unfounded. Sam loved Matt, and had begun to wonder aloud whether marrying his mum might make Matt his father. Hannah's mother had dismissed the suggestion that she might like to live with them, saying that she had a life of her own now. Wherever Matt and Hannah decided to make their home, she'd visit regularly. Sophie had promised to do so as well, when she wasn't busy with her A and E doctor. Hannah had confided to Matt that she thought that Sophie's days of serial dating were over.

Wanting to know more about Matt's childhood, Hannah had read Matt's mother's book from cover to cover and been moved to tears by it. The two women had liked each other immediately when Matt had taken Hannah and Sam down to Devon to visit, and the warmth of his mother's welcome had left them in no doubt that she was delighted to see her son finally settling down.

The weekend in Tuscany, when Matt had proposed to her, had been wonderful. They'd stayed on a secluded beach, eating, swimming and making love for two days, and when they'd arrived back home, Matt had asked Sam if he could be his dad.

And it had all led them here. To the doorstep of a house in a leafy suburb of London, which backed onto a park. There was a great school, just down the road, and Sam had already visited and begun to get to know the teachers and the other children. The outside of the house had been newly decorated, and the front garden planted with shrubs, but the inside still needed some work.

Matt took the key from his pocket, handing it to Sam and lifting him up so that he could reach the lock.

'Is this *our* house now?'

Matt chuckled. 'Yes, it is. I've got something to show you when we get inside.'

'What?' Sam pushed the door open and Matt set him back on his feet. He rushed inside, looking around the sitting room and then running into the kitchen.

Hannah took Matt's arm, and they crossed the threshold of their new home. The sitting room had been painted, but the floorboards were bare and there was no furniture yet. The kitchen was old, but it would do until they could afford to replace it. The minute they'd seen the large, Victorian house, Matt and Hannah had known that this was the place where they wanted to raise a family and grow old together.

'Have the painters finished in Sam's room?' Hannah knew how much it meant to Matt to be a good father, and when she'd suggested he should be the one to decorate Sam's room, he'd jumped at the chance.

'You'll see.' Matt grinned at her, calling to Sam. 'Why don't you try upstairs?'

Sam clattered upstairs, running into the master bedroom, which was flooded with winter sunshine. Hannah followed him.

'Oh! Matt you bought a bed! It's beautiful...' It was the one she'd wanted, but had decided they couldn't afford. The snowy white quilt and pillows suited it perfectly.

'Have I got a bed too?' Sam asked.

'Go and see.' Matt was standing in the doorway, grinning.

Sam ran into the room he'd chosen as his bedroom. Hannah expected to hear some reaction, but there was a sudden silence. Matt caught her hand, and she followed him.

The room had been painted and the carpet laid. In one corner, a whole constellation of stars covered the ceiling, and models of each of the planets in the solar system were suspended on fine wires. There were bookshelves, some squashy beanbag seats, and a long low bench with a child's chair. On the other side of the room was a bunk bed with moon and stars bedding.

'Do you like it?' Matt seemed suddenly nervous, but when Sam turned around he was grinning from ear to ear.

'Can I sleep here? Tonight?'

'Oh, sweetie.' Hannah turned the corners of her mouth down. 'I want to sleep here too, but we can't. All our things are at home.'

'But I live *here* now.'

Matt chuckled. 'I packed a bag for us. We'll have to go back home tomorrow, Sam, the decorators will be working here again next week. But we can stay tonight and we'll bring the rest of your things here next weekend.'

'Yes! Thanks, Dad!'

Sam started to explore his room, and Hannah crooked her finger, indicating that they could leave him to it. Outside, in the hallway, Matt caught her in a sudden embrace, his eyes bright with emotion.

'I think I just got promoted.'

Sam had readily accepted that Matt was his dad now, but this was the first time he'd called him Dad.

'You've definitely earned it. I love you, Robin.'

He chuckled. 'And I love you, Flash.'

* * * * *

CONVENIENTLY
WED IN PARADISE

MEREDITH WEBBER

MILLS & BOON

Thanks to all my family, who've suffered along the way, and to the writing friends I've made in the angst-ridden, neurotic, wonderful world of writing.

And special thanks to Elizabeth Johnson, who accepted my first book and gave me the strength and encouragement to write another, and another, and…

CHAPTER ONE

ALEXANDER MONROE McLEOD paced the small balcony outside his grandmother's room at the, to him, ridiculously named Palace of Peace and Contentment. The view from the balcony was breathtaking—the brilliant, shining blue-green sea of the Gulf of Thailand, small dark-sailed fishing vessels slowly going about their work, the bright sails of windsurfers from the resort across on the mainland flitting back and forth, and to the right infinite shades of green as thick rainforest ran riot over the sides of the mountain on which the palace was built.

In spite of the colourful and effusive brochures he'd read about the place, the marbled floors and silk-lined walls, he was reasonably sure it had never been a palace, let alone the summer home of long-dead kings of Siam. But it *had* been a very luxurious hotel, built when the village had been nothing more than a few shacks and some fishing boats. Built with its own generator for power and a permanent water supply from the spring further up the mountains.

The palace also explained his presence here. Bored out of his skull, but needing to stay—

His attention was momentarily diverted from his irritation with his situation by a woman. She was tall, long-limbed and straight-backed, with a mop of dark hair unhindered by a hat—foolish creature—and she was striding down the paved drive that ran through the perfectly kept gardens fragrant with frangipani and manicured lawns he'd swear were clipped each morning with scissors—

To an assignation she had to keep, a destination she wished to reach, or was she simply escaping the place?

Not that he could blame her.

But what lingered in his mind as she disappeared from view, where the drive curved slightly, was his first thought on seeing her—the totally absurd thought that she'd look good on a horse.

Look good on a horse?

He kicked the potted palm in one corner of the balcony and swore quietly to himself. Prolonged inactivity was obviously driving him insane. Or at least turning his brain to mush. He *had* to find something to do—something he could do without moving too far from the luxurious suite of rooms where his grandmother was dying—the same suite of rooms in which she had honeymooned with his late grandfather.

Returning here to die had been her one wish—her last wish, she'd said, probably to get him here—and although the extensive research he'd done on the place had shown him it was now actually a luxury convalescent home, he'd been doubtful. While a panel of specialists on the mainland advised on medical matters, top-class residential housekeeping, therapeutic and nursing staff made sure the guests—definitely not patients—were well cared for. His grandmother had three cheerful and gentle Thai nurses who attended to her personal needs—bathing, dressing, feeding her—with reverence and concern.

Pampered, more like! he thought with a derisive snort.

The place was a luxurious convalescent facility for anyone wealthy enough to afford its exorbitant daily tariff.

Not that the money had been a problem when his grandmother had dropped her bombshell and demanded to die in the place where she had been so happy on her honeymoon. Her side of the family had always been wealthy, but a little app he'd fiddled around with during his student years had eventually been developed and sold. DocSays had brought him wealth beyond imagining in spite of the fact that the most important of the answers it gave anyone using it was, if in doubt, to see a doctor.

Could he update it?

Think of something new?

Or had that questing part of his brain atrophied as he'd practised the medicine for which he'd been training at the time?

But it was worth a try—anything to ease the boredom of waiting around.

If there'd been something he could do for his grandmother on a daily basis—if she'd been well enough to be wheeled out into the beautiful gardens, even taken for a ride in a little tuk-tuk—he'd have been more content.

It was the helplessness he felt—the fact that he, a doctor, could do nothing more to help the woman he loved so dearly—that was getting to him.

And that thought was also annoying—the one about loving her so dearly. She'd brought him up from the age of twelve, and her answer to any upset in his young life had always been, 'Monroes don't do emotion!'

Yet, if he gave himself time to think—and at the moment he had plenty—he had to accept that what he had always felt for her was love and that perhaps the stricture should have been, 'Monroes don't *show* emotion.'

His argument against it had been that he was a McLeod but she'd blown 'such nonsense' away with an airy wave.

'For all your name, you're a Monroe through and through, and don't you ever forget it,' she'd told him in a steely voice.

But seeing her now, turned from a strong, determined woman into frail bones and fine, lined, pale skin, he realised the pain he felt when he looked at her *had* to be emotion.

Love.

A love so deep it was as if part of himself was dying.

And repeating her words to himself—Monroes don't do emotion—did little to stop the pain…

He returned to his pacing, and caught the movement out of the corner of his eye. It was the woman who'd look good on horseback returning.

On a horse?

Hilary McKenzie Steele wasn't entirely sure she should be riding up the raked gravel drive of the Palace of Peace and Contentment, but Muriel Walker, her assigned 'guest', had told her about the stables.

'Beautiful horses, Kenzie dear,' she'd said. 'There for all of us to ride, but how many do? Do the horses get the exercise they need, do you think?'

'I'm sure they do,' Kenzie replied, aware of her position as a sounding board.

Not that Muriel was sick or in need of special nursing care, she was simply bored, moving from one luxurious home or hotel to another.

This luxury convalescent hotel had been on her itinerary for a few years, though why she always insisted on a nurse as a companion, Kenzie had yet to fathom.

Anything different to give her life a little meaning, Kenzie supposed.

Which explained the horse.

Muriel, for all her die-away airs and imaginary ill-nesses, was only in her early sixties, and, Kenzie was sure, could learn to ride a horse. Surely that would give her something to do.

Kenzie rode to the side entrance. She'd left Muriel in the little sitting room just off the side lobby—Muriel dressed in jeans and a light polo top, a deceptively simple outfit that had possibly cost as much as the horse.

Tethering Bob—Kenzie smiled again at the unlikely name for a Thai horse—she went inside to fetch Muriel.

'Come on,' she told the older woman. 'It's time you learned to ride.'

Muriel, who'd been resistant to the idea from the beginning, looked at Kenzie and must have read something in her face that told her argument would be futile.

She stood and then smiled.

'If I fall off I'll sack you,' she warned, and Kenzie, al-though not entirely sure her boss turned friend was jok-ing, laughed.

Kenzie had given a lot of thought to getting Muriel onto the horse, and had come up with this side entrance as the ideal place. Not only would no one see them—she wasn't going to have anyone laughing at Muriel—but the urns that flanked the shallow steps were on a stepped platform. It had been simple enough to remove one of the urns, giv-ing Muriel steps to get up and a flat area to stand on as she swung herself into the saddle.

Or perhaps clambered into the saddle…

She was helping Muriel with the transfer from the plat-form to the horse when a man appeared, turning the cor-ner from the drive and stopping to watch the operation.

'Need a hand?'

Rich, deep, English tones made the three simple words ring through the air, hitting Kenzie's ears and somehow reverberating through her body in a way that brought heat to her cheeks.

Embarrassment at being caught?

She hoped that's all it was.

And cursed the colour that rose so easily. Honestly, you'd think by now she'd have outgrown blushing...

'We'll manage,' she said, but far too late, because now he was at the horse, steadying Muriel from the other side, putting her foot into the stirrup Kenzie had shortened earlier.

'First time?' he said, smiling up at Muriel.

The smile caused Kenzie more problems than the voice. She shook her head, trying to clear the sudden confusion. *Muriel.* She had to concentrate on Muriel, not some stranger with a beautiful voice.

Strange *man* at that and she was here to get over men...

For ever, if she had her way—but that was another problem altogether...

'Now you take the reins, and hold them so you just feel the horse's mouth at the end of them,' she told her charge.

'Just the left hand,' the stranger said, releasing Muriel's right hand from the folded reins. 'That's so you can carry the whip in your right and smack him if he's naughty.'

'Oh, I couldn't hit him,' Muriel protested, and the man laughed.

'Who are you?'

Kenzie was aware that the question came out far more forcibly—rudely?—than she'd intended, but the laughter had brought back her confusion.

He made a sweeping bow—to Muriel, not to her—and

said, 'Alexander Monroe McLeod, prisoner in this palace, and happy to be of assistance.'

Another worker, Kenzie decided, although she certainly hadn't set eyes on him in the ten days she'd been here.

'Your grandmother?' Muriel asked him softly, and he nodded, and although some things fell into place—the talk of a woman who'd come here to die, her doctor grandson with her—something else was niggling at Kenzie.

She studied the man across the horse and frowned. She knew the face, and the name had rung a bell—several bells—but what...?

And shouldn't she introduce herself?

Some instinct pushed that thought away, though why, she couldn't tell.

'So,' he said, still speaking to Muriel. 'Where are we off to on this adventure?'

'Not very far,' Muriel assured him. 'In fact, I think getting on is enough for one day.'

'Nonsense,' the man—Alexander Monroe McLeod, how grand—said. 'You need to get the feel of the animal. So, if your friend leads and I stay right beside you on this side, will you feel safe enough?'

Muriel nodded tentatively and Kenzie flicked the lead rein very gently and clicked a 'Get up,' at the horse, who moved obediently and sedately along the path.

The man with the beautiful voice and grand name was talking quietly to Muriel, distracting her from the first-time rider's usual thoughts of how precarious her perch was and how very far away the ground!

Which gave Kenzie the time to sneak glances at him across the horse's neck.

She was sure she knew the name but definitely hadn't met him. Tall, dark-haired, distinguished-looking some-how, with the kind of profile you could put on a coin.

It was such a fanciful thought she had to give herself a stern reminder that she was here to forget a man, not to be fancying a new one, no matter how attractive he was.

Yet he wasn't the kind of man you'd forget!

Perhaps she'd seen a photograph?

Lightbulb moment!

'I know who you are,' she said, unable to keep a note of triumph from her voice. 'You're the bloke who developed the DocSays app!'

'What did you say?' Muriel was obviously mystified.

'Do you know it?' he asked, the question a trifle stiff.

Kenzie laughed.

'I doubt there's a nurse in the world who doesn't. Working in a hospital can be a bit humdrum at times, so we often see what you'd say about our patients' symptoms. Harmless fun, and as you always say see a doctor, that's actually what's happening with our patients, if you see what I mean.'

Alex stared at the woman in total disbelief.

'You compare your actual hospital doctor's diagnosis with the app?'

'It's fun!' she had the hide to say, before adding, 'They're usually the same.'

As if *that* made a difference! Nurses comparing his opinions to those of other doctors as if it was a game...

'Who are *you*?' he demanded, thrown off balance by this whole situation—the horse, his earlier, and definitely weird, thoughts about the woman, and a laughing face with blue eyes that were rather startling against her lightly tanned skin.

'I'm Hilary McKenzie Steele,' she announced, undoubtedly mimicking his own introduction. 'Known to one and all as Kenzie! My mother died in childbirth and Dad gave me her whole name, so that's my excuse for its length.'

She was making fun of him, he knew, but he *had* introduced himself with his full name when Alex McLeod would have done. And all he could offer by way of explanation for its length were hundreds of years of tradition—rather feeble compared to a dead mother.

'Are you still ready to catch me if I fall?' Muriel asked, breaking into his senseless thoughts.

'I most certainly am,' he said. 'But tell me how you feel. Comfortable—'

'Or terrified?' the woman called Kenzie asked, with a smile in her voice that made it a gentle tease.

'Well, it *is* a long way up, but it feels just fine,' Muriel assured them. 'Can we go on down the drive—maybe right to the stables?'

'Of course,' Kenzie replied, although Alex felt a slight unease about this decision. He hadn't even known—or if he had he'd forgotten—there were stables and horses, but how far away were they?

'Um, Kenzie,' he said, tentatively trying the name on his lips and finding he quite liked it. 'I'm not sure I can stay much longer.'

'Oh, that's okay,' she answered cheerfully. 'You can see Muriel has her balance now and there's a dismounting block at the stables. Do you ride yourself? There are some lovely horses in the stables, and apparently there are trails up through the rainforest towards the top of the mountain.'

'And you've been here how long?' he demanded, aggrieved that the blue-eyed woman apparently knew so much about the place.

'Ten days! But I guess us menials mix with locals more than you guests do. This place is very upstairs downstairs, isn't it?'

'Oh, Kenzie,' Muriel murmured. 'I don't make you feel like that, do I?'

Kenzie laughed.

'Of course not, you silly goose. I was just teasing.'

'Teasing *me*,' Alex muttered, before looking up at Muriel.

'Are you sure you feel safe with just Kenzie here beside you?'

Muriel smiled down at him.

'Of course,' she said. 'Hasn't Kenzie already proven her worth, showing me how nice it is to be on a horse? Maybe one day, when I can ride by myself—Kenzie's going to teach me—we can all ride up into the mountains.'

She paused, still looking at him.

'That's if you can ride, of course.'

He wanted to snort. He'd practically been born on a horse! But he confined himself to a polite goodbye to both women, and hurried back into the hotel. Even when his grandmother was awake, she was barely conscious and a lot of that time had no idea who he was.

Which, of course, made him very reluctant to miss any moments with her when she did! He thought of the times he *hadn't* spent with her. Breaking a lunch or dinner arrangement because he was held up at the hospital, or, worse, out on a date, such ordinary things, but all time he had already missed with her.

And now there was no time to make it up to her—no more time…

But as he went up in the lift, he couldn't help picturing his first glimpse of the woman with the improbable name—long legs striding easily, back straight, and the cloud of dark hair—black, he thought now, or perhaps a very dark brown.

And the explanation for these thoughts?

He had absolutely no idea and the sooner he got them out of his head the better. Since the farcical end of his engagement and marriage plans he'd remained aloof to the charms of women, throwing himself into work as an alternative—and far easier—passion.

He shook his head in a futile attempt to remove the wayward meanderings of his mind. It was because he was stressed. He couldn't do anything for Gran, and doing nothing left him with too much time on his hands to dwell on life without her...

But, then, she *had* looked good on the horse... Kenzie...

The rest of Muriel's ride was uneventful, but Kenzie was glad to see a little tuk-tuk waiting to take her and her charge back to the hotel.

'You should have a hot shower, and I'll arrange a massage for you,' she said to Muriel as they climbed into the little rickshaw. 'You might need another one tomorrow, too, because your muscles have been doing something new.'

'Then I'll have to have a massage every day,' Muriel announced, 'because I'm going to conquer this horse-riding thing!'

'You're a Trojan, Muriel!' Kenzie told her, 'But you might be sore tomorrow so we'll take it easy.'

She saw Muriel safely back to her room and into the shower, arranged the massage, and ordered tea and scones for after it.

Only then did she pull out her phone and open the Doc-Says app on it. She had to smile at the pixelated image of Alexander Monroe McLeod, which looked, of course, nothing like him. The photos she'd seen occasionally— usually on the financial pages of serious papers—was how she'd recognised him.

Imagine meeting the man!

Her friends would never believe it!

Especially the ones who'd told her she was crazy to take a short contract job at a luxury convalescent home off the coast of Thailand.

'You'll be bored to death,' they'd warned her, and secretly she'd believed them, but at the time she'd have taken a job on Mars to get away from her far too small home town!

Small town, new doctor, whirlwind romance that had the entire town speculating whether Kenzie would finally get married, then the new doc's wife had arrived...

Kenzie had expected pain—and hurt pride and humiliation had certainly brought that in its train. But in many ways it had been a relief. Much as she wanted to marry and have children—and urgent as that need was becoming—she'd known all along there was something not quite right about Mark...

Something that had, thankfully, held her back from a physical relationship with him...

'Now, Kenzie,' Muriel announced, appearing from the bathroom in a cloud of steam and a luxurious peignoir, 'I will have no argument about it this time. You are to eat with me this evening. We need to plan out my riding lessons.'

'It might be best to leave any plans until morning. See how you feel then.'

'We can discuss it over dinner,' Muriel said forcefully.

So much for diversion!

'I thought the Sapphire Dining Room tonight. It's smaller and for all they tell me the same chef oversees both kitchens, I'm sure the food is better there.'

They *had* argued before about Kenzie dining with her guest, as a cleverly worded sentence in the rules and regulations for ancillary staff seemed to suggest it wasn't a good idea.

And certainly not on any regular basis!

Feeling obliged to protest, Kenzie offered her usual excuse.

'But it's formal, Muriel, you know that, and you also know that I packed for a job on a tropical island, not a luxury escape.'

A light tap on the door interrupted the argument.

'That'll be the masseuse. Let her in, and put out my medication, then go and find something to wear. Shall we say my room, at seven? We can have a drink before we go down.'

As the masseuse was already setting up her table, Kenzie dealt out the evening tablets—blood-pressure medication, statins for her high cholesterol, and tonight a weekly tablet to maintain her bone density. She put them all into a small medicine cup, set a glass of water beside it, and left the room.

Idly, as the elevator descended to the ground floor, she wondered if DocSays ate in one of the dining rooms— specifically, the Sapphire?

She pushed the thought away—she was off men—and concentrated on clothes.

If she could find a tuk-tuk outside the palace, she'd have time to get down to the markets in the little village. Not that formal wear was a common feature on any of the stalls, but if she could find a pretty sarong that went with one of her tank tops, she could tie it around her waist and look at least presentable.

The sarong was a light, gauzy cotton in swirling shades of blue, green and purple. With a silky, black tank top and her good black sandals, it would do at a push, but the idea of eating in a formal dining room with the wealthy guests of the palace was daunting to a girl from the bush, where formal meant wearing something on your feet.

Muriel was delighted to see her, admiring her outfit and her nous in achieving it. She poured a small glass of champagne for each of them and toasted the success of her first riding 'lesson'.

They went down to dinner arm in arm, Muriel sweeping Kenzie into the dining room as if she were a close friend.

And Kenzie found herself pleased to have Muriel with her, for the grandeur of the place—the *smaller* dining room at that—was almost overwhelming. She'd grown used to the beautiful grand entrance with its gold-streaked black marble floors, the potted orchids peeping from behind soft ferns, but this was something else.

It lived up to its name of sapphire, for it was decorated, almost entirely, in blue. Pale eggshell-blue walls that looked as if they were lined with velvet, darker blue upholstered chairs that made the white napery look so much more vivid. And the crystal glassware on the table sparkled, refracting light from the elegant chandelier into thousands of bright, winking, stars.

Hadn't Muriel read the line about ancillary staff knowing their place? This was definitely not Kenzie's place…

But of course Muriel wouldn't have read it! As if she would read something as insignificant as a brochure.

But the maître d' was probably word perfect in it. He raised one perfectly trimmed eyebrow, and would have led them to a table in the far corner had Muriel not protested and insisted she sit by the window.

'Oh, and there's that nice man!' she cried in delight. 'Let's ask him to join us.'

The eyebrow rose again, and Kenzie managed to mumble, 'Dr McLeod,' to prevent further strain to the small arc of hair.

And for all she'd hoped the invitation would be refused, as she slipped into her seat she saw him rise and cross the room towards them.

He smiled down at Muriel and raised the glass of red wine he held in one hand in a silent toast.

'So, how was the rest of your ride?' he asked.

'Wonderful! Great fun! I'm doing it again and next time Kenzie will ride beside me and still hold the leading rein, but that's just for safety.'

Kenzie opened her mouth to protest that they might be taking things a little too fast, but Muriel's raised hand stopped any protest.

'I haven't got time to be footling around in a paddock for days on end,' she said. 'I want to be a rider, which means I need to hurry things along.'

Alex took the chair a waiter had pulled to the table for him, and smiled at the two women. He had a feeling the younger of them wished he'd declined the invitation, yet it was she he'd been drawn towards—wanting to see her again, speak to her.

Was it a symptom of his boredom that the young woman intrigued him so much? Laughing at the nurses' use of his app, introducing herself in an echo of his stuffy announcement of his own name?

Or was it that she was just so attractive?

Naturally attractive, just herself, with no apparent effort to attract—

Well, maybe a little lipstick on beautifully shaped lips, a touch of eyeliner accentuating the smiling blue eyes, but none of the studied and worked-at perfection of most of the women he knew.

Whatever it was, she'd somehow awoken something inside him—something he'd always doubted existed...

There was certainly something about her...

But Muriel was his hostess.

'I'm called Alex,' he said to her. 'I don't think I ever did that proper introduction, and I know you're Muriel. Are you here convalescing?'

She smiled her sunny smile.

'You could say that. I did have a small operation—just the smallest of tucks, you know—but really it's a break from my usual life, which, until I got up close and personal with a horse today, had become very boring, and sometimes seemed totally pointless.'

'And the horse has changed all that?' Alex teased gently, and the woman virtually glowed with delight.

'But of course it has!' she said. 'Kenzie tells me there are horses I can hire to ride in Central Park in New York, and even Hyde Park in London. I can ride just about anywhere!'

'Have you ridden in these places?' Alex asked, turning to bring the woman for whom he'd changed tables into the conversation.

She smiled at him, curving pink lips to reveal perfect teeth, a smile dancing in the blue eyes.

'Not yet,' she said, 'but it's definitely waiting for me in the future.'

'Bucket list?'

'I don't think people my age are too worried about bucket lists,' she said, a little frown turning the words serious. 'I'm more into planning my immediate future right now.'

'Which is?'

He wasn't sure why he'd asked.

Politeness?

Not that she gave him time to ponder such things, coming out with, 'Getting married and having children,' with such alacrity he was taken aback.

'It's not *my* ambition,' Kenzie continued, trying to explain the unexpected response she'd given to his question, partly because it had shocked her as much as her dinner companions.

'My *ambition* was to become a surgical nurse, not that that could ever happen when I also wanted to work as close as possible to my home, and small country hospitals don't have surgeons.'

She paused before adding, 'Well, we do have the flying surgeon come in every six weeks, but he brings his own nurse. Anyway, now my family situation has changed I've got to do something about producing a couple of children, and my father would prefer it if they were legitimate, hence the marriage part.'

She shrugged, as if her explanation needed no further trimmings.

'I quite understand your father's feelings,' Muriel said, breaking the silence this far too personal statement had produced, but as Alex could find no follow-up it wasn't broken for long.

A waiter saved the day, arriving to collect the menus and take orders, but as the menus were still unopened on the table, Muriel waved him away.

She also took charge, telling them both to decide what they were eating so they could get back to Kenzie's problem.

'It's hardly a problem,' Kenzie retorted, then blushed and looked down at her menu, adding, in a very small voice, 'Well, I suppose it is in a way.'

She looked positively woebegone, but before he could assure her she'd have no trouble finding any number of men to marry, Muriel interrupted with a stern, 'Decide what you want to eat!'

Having been raised by his grandmother, obedience to older women was second nature to Alex, so he perused the menu and decided on a *meen molee*—fish curry, delicately simmered in coconut milk, according to the menu.

'I'm not that adventurous,' Kenzie said, 'but the green chicken curry sounds delicious.'

Muriel opted for the yellow vegetarian curry and when the waiter appeared asked him for enough rice for all three of them.

'And wine, of course—no, make it champagne. Kenzie and I had a little toast earlier, but we need a full bottle with you here, Alex.'

Alex smiled to himself. It could have been his grandmother talking, never thinking to ask his preference—never imagining, he sometimes thought—that it could possibly differ from hers, bless her.

But he felt a twinge of sadness at the thought. His mother had died far too young, leaving him to be brought up by his grandmother. She'd been strict about his keeping to the values of his name—the Monroe name, of course—but always fair, and ready to support him whatever path he took in life.

She hadn't been a physically demonstrative woman—not a hugger, and only rarely did he get a kiss, but he'd always known she loved him deeply, as, indeed, he'd loved her.

And now she was going too, and a large part of his life would go with her.

He shook away the sadness his thoughts produced. Monroes didn't do emotion!

'And are you here to further your father's ambition?'

He'd been lost in thoughts of his maternal relative, so wasn't sure if Muriel's question had been thrown at him.

Fortunately, Kenzie was quicker on the uptake.

'No!' she said firmly. 'This is just a short break to re-charge and regroup. I'll get on to it when I get home.'

'You make it sound like a military operation,' he teased, hoping to see the smile again.

'Well, not exactly,' she said earnestly. 'But I've learned you do have to be careful. People are marrying later, and while an older man—say, in his thirties—would be fine, most of them have regular girlfriends by then.'

'Thirties is old?' Alex asked, thinking he'd always con-sidered his own age—thirty-five—as still young, not yet middle-aged, let alone old.

'How old are you?' he asked, and now she did smile.

'Twenty-six, but that's not the point. I know it probably sounds ridiculous to you, but my mother died when I was born, and for years I've just kept hoping that my father would marry again and have more children. And now he's finally fallen in love again but with an older woman—so no children—which leaves it up to me to keep the family business going.'

She paused, studying him as if to make sure he was following.

'It's the property, you see,' she said. 'It's been in the family for six generations—through drought and fires and floods—and was built with the blood and sweat and tears of my ancestors. It's in our lifeblood, and my father des-perately wants it to keep going. We have a resident man-ager, and I'll run it with him if something happens to my father, but it's the next generation. I really need to produce them while my father can pass on all his knowledge and the history of the place.'

'Which a manager couldn't do,' Muriel put in. 'They'd never feel for things the way the family would."

Kenzie nodded.

'Or care for it the way the family would,' she said. 'We run fifteen thousand head of cattle—Brahmans—up the gulf. They're a lot of work—we breed them ourselves, castrate them when they're young, then shift them around according to where the feed is. And then there's the breeding stock—we turn off about eight thousand a year so you need to replace them—and then there are decisions for the future—drought-proofing, seeking out new markets when prices slump.'

As she'd rattled off all this information, Alex had tried desperately to keep up. The 'property' he'd envisaged had been a large house, or maybe a business of some sort—but fifteen thousand cattle plus enough breeders to 'turn off'—presumably to sell—eight thousand a year?

'I see!' he said, rather vaguely as he had no idea how to relate to all this information.

Fortunately, Muriel took up the conversational ball.

'My second husband had Brahmans—ugly big things they were, too. That dreadful hump. He bred them, took them to shows, won ribbons, which was nice because when he died they put the ribbons on his coffin instead of flowers, which just die anyway.'

By the time Alex had digested this bit of conversation, he was wondering why on earth he'd agreed to join the table. He'd been eating on his own quite happily for two weeks.

He could excuse himself, say he had to check on his grandmother and he'd have his meal sent up, but he knew it would be a lie as her coma-like sleep had deepened late this afternoon and he knew she wouldn't wake before morning.

Beside which, meeting this slim, upright young woman

with the sparkling smile and laughing blue eyes, who'd apparently grown up with fifteen thousand cattle, had certainly banished his boredom. The frank way she spoke of her home and her need to have children to carry on a family tradition not only intrigued him, but it touched on something deep inside him.

The concept of family, he supposed—a concept his grandmother considered of the utmost importance.

So instead of reading stories by solemn Scottish writers to Gran in the morning, he could entertain her with stories of cattle farms.

Cattle properties?

CHAPTER TWO

KENZIE WASN'T SURE exactly when it was that she'd realised she was enjoying herself, but the first courses had arrived and as they ate, Muriel regaled them with tales of her husbands, Alex demanded more information on cattle with humps, and she'd forgotten the humiliation that had sent her scurrying over here.

But the fling had taught her an important lesson. When she returned to her quest, it wasn't enough to take up with a good-looking man who could charm the socks—and probably other bits of apparel—off a woman, she had to be sure he had a serious side, and hadn't crossed marriage off his to-do list.

Or been already married…

For her, getting married had to be a business decision! Nothing more, nothing less!

Too much attraction just got in the way of seeing a person for who he was—or wasn't, as it had happened…

And who's to say they wouldn't grow to love each other? Friendship grew from small beginnings, so couldn't love?

'Oh, this is the famous soprano who's staying here.'

Muriel's comment roused Kenzie from her thoughts, and she turned to see a rather magnificent woman take the small stage.

'She's here for a rest, and was going to sing earlier in

the week but had a cold. I've heard her sing in Milan—she's really superb.'

Glad to be diverted from thoughts of seriously suitable men, Kenzie sat back in her chair and lifted her glass to sip her champagne.

The pianist provided an introduction and then the woman's beautiful voice soared around the room, filling it with both sound and emotion.

Kenzie checked that both her companions were absorbed and took a moment to have another look at the genius behind DocSays.

Not considering him as a potential partner—tech billionaires were way out of her league—she could barely handle her internet banking!

Although he *was* attractive! Attractive to her certainly—that strange spark she'd felt when they'd first met over the horse...

But hadn't she just decided she wasn't looking for attraction? Attraction could mask other more important things, like a man's being married, or not wanting to be married, and you ended up wasting time on the wrong man.

Besides which, he'd hardly want to move to a place in the middle of nowhere, with its endless sky and red soil plains and—

She cut off the thought before she got too nostalgic—better to think about the genius behind DocSays!

He was a good-looking man—a Scot, from his names, but very English-looking to her, maybe because he was wearing a suit to dinner on a tropical island...

But looking around the room, other men were similarly attired and they didn't look particularly English. More American, she decided, although the man in a dinner jacket might be Greek.

She'd returned her attention to their dinner companion—purely a research thing—so saw the moment he moved, standing up so suddenly he knocked his chair over, and strode to the front of the room.

Where the soprano had stopped singing and was now lying crumpled on the stage.

Training had Kenzie following, arriving by the fallen woman to hear Alex mutter, 'Not breathing—epiglottitis,' then yell, 'Call an ambulance, and someone get a sharp thin-tipped knife from the kitchen and some tubing—straws, anything.'

As a waiter dashed off to the kitchen, Kenzie looked quickly around, aware the woman's neck would need to be supported.

The pianist had a cushion on his chair!

She dashed across and practically snatched it from under him, leaving the shocked man staring at the drama.

'Thank you,' Alex muttered at her as she helped him roll the woman onto her back.

She slid the cushion under the singer's neck, stretching it so Alex could more easily feel for the position for the first vertical cut he would need to make beneath the Adam's apple, and the second transverse cut through the cricothyroid membrane.

His fingers moved with such certainty she knew he was good and the woman had been extremely lucky he'd been in the audience.

The waiter returned with a razor-sharp knife in one hand and a piece of plastic tubing dangling in the other. Kenzie wondered just what it might be used for in the kitchen.

As Alex took the knife, he gestured for Kenzie to take the tube.

'About five centimetres,' he told her, and she grabbed

the tube and a clean knife off a table and cut off a long enough piece for Alex to insert into the wound he was making.

She held it as she squatted on the other side of the singer, ready to hand it to him when the cuts were made.

'Just hold her steady,' he said to Kenzie, and she moved to the woman's head and held it gently but firmly while Alex inserted the tube. He blew briefly into it, watching to make sure the chest rose and fell.

Tension thickened the air.

The tube was in place, but would the woman breathe?

Alex had moved his hands ready to do chest compressions when a slight whistling sound told them she was breathing on her own.

'Well done,' Kenzie said to him. 'But what happened?'

Alex's eyes didn't move from his patient.

'According to Muriel, she's had a cold. Possibly a throat infection, and her epiglottis was swollen enough to close right up when she sang. Silly thing to do—she should have continued to rest.'

Kenzie nodded.

'But you still picked up on it very quickly. Do you still do hands-on medicine?'

He smiled at the surprise in her voice. It wasn't the first time he'd heard it.

'Of course I do! I can hardly just sit around counting the money my app made. I worked hard for a long time to finish my degree and I certainly wouldn't let it go to waste. I work in an A and E department. To tell you the truth, I'm probably addicted to emergency medicine. For me, it's the ultimate job—the pace of it—the rush!'

'Tell me about it,' Kenzie muttered. 'My rotations

through the ED when I was training were the stuff of nightmares.'

'Ah, but your pet hate is probably not boredom. For me there's nothing worse.'

An ambulance arrived, and although the paramedics accompanying the stretcher had efficiently replaced the kitchen tubing with a tracheostomy tube, inflated the cuff and secured it before moving the patient onto the stretcher, he was caught in a dilemma.

Should he go with her to the hospital? Make sure someone there knew what they were doing?

He glanced at his watch and must have been frowning for the young woman, Kenzie, touched him lightly on the shoulder.

'I'll go to the hospital and make sure she's in good hands,' she said. 'If you could explain to Muriel, she'll understand. I'm actually supposed to be off duty, but somehow we don't seem to do hours or set timetables, just hang out together. Tell her if I'm late getting back I'll see her in the morning. She's perfectly healthy but pays for a nurse—I think to keep her company.'

The blue eyes lifted to his.

'How terrible is that?'

The words were little more than a sigh, but Alex understood what she meant. Muriel, for all her money—and there must be plenty for her to be staying here—was lonely.

As are you, an inner voice whispered deep inside him. He didn't bother denying it—he'd had plenty of time to think these last couple of weeks—and for all he had friends and colleagues back in the ED where he worked, he had slowly come to realise that he'd made his work his life.

Relationships had broken down because of it.

Or because they hadn't been strong enough in the first place?

Because Monroes didn't do emotion?

Or, as one departing woman had told him, he was obsessed, but unfortunately not with her.

It was the boredom thing again! He'd tried other medical fields, thinking at first that surgery would give him the rush he needed, but it had lacked that immediacy—that often-fine line between life and death.

And a psychologist would probably tell him it was because he'd virtually witnessed that line as a child— waving goodbye to his parents who had been, within minutes, dead...

Pushing these memories aside, he slipped into the organised chaos of the kitchen to safely dispose of the knife and wash his hands, then stopped at Muriel's table.

'Kenzie's going to the hospital, but I'll be back to eat with you as soon as I've checked on my grandmother.'

Muriel shook her head.

'I really don't need someone dancing attendance on me all day, every day,' she said. 'I just enjoy the company of young people and with no children or grandchildren I'm quite happy to pay for the pleasure of their company.'

She paused, then added, 'And if I ask for a nurse I know she'll at least be university educated, so intelligent and easy to talk to, because that's part of being a nurse, wouldn't you say?'

Never having considered it before, Alex thought for a moment, then nodded. It was certainly true of hospital nurses who had to do the greater part of the communication with the patients. Doctors might come by, but were usually too rushed to explain things in any depth.

And in the ED it was the nurses who kept everything running, if not always smoothly, at least with some attempt at order.

His grandmother remained stubbornly asleep, but he sat beside her anyway, as he did at this time every evening, and read a few pages of the latest book to her. At the moment, it was Robert Louis Stevenson's *Kidnapped*, and as he spoke the words his mind went back to when she'd read to him. All the books she'd read had been by her beloved Scottish authors, although he'd by far have preferred a scary story!

After a brief stay with no response, he returned to eat his meal with Muriel. He'd read again later, if only to stop himself thinking of the woman with the laughing blue eyes.

And fifteen thousand head of cattle.

He could understand that it would have taken…was it five generations of her family to build up such a massive property holding? His own McLeod family—closely related to the clan chief at Skye—went back about twenty generations but, apart from a few enterprising adventurers, most of them had idled away their fortunes rather than amassing wealth.

But he *was* titular head of his other Scottish clan—of the Monroes, not the McLeods—and Kenzie's words about marriage and children had prodded his conscience. His responsibility as an only child was to continue the line, a fact that had been drummed into his head at an early age.

'It's up to you!' and 'Only you can do it!' were frequent refrains early on from his mother, and later his grandmother—the women in his family being familiar with the power of subtle blackmail.

And then, on his twelfth birthday, he'd actually promised. He'd been given his first grown-up kilt and a spor-ran with the Monroe crest on it.

The fact that he was actually a McLeod carried no weight with either of them, and in his best, grown-up voice, he'd promised.

He thought of the woman with the laughing blue eyes—the woman looking for a husband and two children.

Kill two birds with one stone?

Marriages of convenience were hardly uncommon in the history of his family, keen to keep as much inherited wealth as possible—even better if they could add to it.

He shook his head, smiling to himself, imagining Ken-zie at a McLeod clan dinner in Dunvegan Castle, chatting on about breeding stock and castrating the young steers. He could almost feel the wince that would go around the family gathered at the chief's table!

No, there were plenty of suitable, marriageable women back home, even if the one he'd planned to marry had married someone else when he'd brought his grandmother out here. And kept the engagement ring, *and* worn the wed-ding dress intended for their wedding when she'd wed a friend of his.

'Well, it would only have gone to waste, wouldn't it, darling?'

He winced himself at the remembered conversation, possibly because, for all the talk of how suitable the match had been, he'd been silly enough to believe she'd loved him.

Even fancied himself in love with her for a while, al-though somehow he'd always known there was something missing between them.

Guessed it was to do with him and the difficulty he had in showing emotion.

'Are you married?'

Muriel's conversational opening threw him for a moment. Had the woman been reading his thoughts?

'No, no ring, see!' he said, holding up both hands.

'Not all men wear rings,' Muriel told him. 'While some take them off when it's convenient.'

'Well, I don't have a white mark,' Alex pointed out, holding his left hand across the table for her inspection.

'Something wrong with your hand?'

Kenzie had returned, slipping into her seat as she spoke.

'The staff at the hospital weren't exactly hostile, but I think they thought I was trying to tell them their jobs so I made a quick exit. It's a small place but seems very efficient and apparently has a helicopter available on the roof if a patient needs to be transferred to the mainland.'

The explanation had been offered to both of them, but Muriel ignored it.

'I was checking he wasn't married,' she told Kenzie—about as subtle as a brick. 'He's not!'

'Well, good for him!' Kenzie said, although Alex saw the quick colour rise in her cheeks and guessed only ingrained politeness had held her temper in check.

Fortunately, their main course arrived, Muriel explaining she'd asked the kitchen to hold the dishes back.

'Because you do both have to eat, don't you?'

They ate, conversation limited for a while to comments on their meals, until Muriel managed to twist the talk back to Alex's single status.

'Well, what do you think?' Muriel demanded of Kenzie. 'Here he is, a single man, just what you're looking for.'

'Really, Muriel, you're embarrassing both of us,' Kenzie protested although she knew the colour in her cheeks would already have revealed her embarrassment—*and* the wretched man was smirking! 'I don't intend to throw myself at every single man that comes along—that's not how things work.'

'Well, it's worked for me,' Muriel said, with a mischievous smile, 'but if you've got some other plan, I'm sure we'd both like to hear it.'

Kenzie felt the heat burning now in her cheeks.

She did have a kind of plan and it would probably be helpful to talk about it, but—

'Come on, I know you want to talk about it!'

She pressed her palms to her scarlet cheeks and plunged right in.

'Okay, you'll both probably laugh at this but I thought I'd try internet dating,' she said. 'Everyone seems to be doing it these days. You get matched up with people who might be suitable and you get the chance to talk to them on the net for a while, then if you think you'd like to meet up, you start with meeting for a coffee and take it from there.'

Her voice trailed off as she finished because she had no idea about the 'take it from there' part.

'Do you hope for a spark of some kind to take it from there?' Alex asked, and Kenzie had to smile.

'I always get stuck at that part! Actually, I usually get stuck at the meeting for coffee part because it's unlikely I'll be matched up with anyone from my own town, so I'd have to arrange to meet in a regional centre, and once I've driven a couple of hundred kilometres to the coffee shop, I'm likely to be very narky if he's a dud.'

'If you have to travel that far, you could arrange to have a few that you could meet on the same day so it wasn't all wasted,' Alex suggested, definitely hiding a smirk!

'Oh, right! So, I'd flit from one coffee shop to the next— it all feels a bit like trying on clothes, doesn't it?'

'Nonsense!' Muriel declared. 'I've heard it's a very common and successful way for people to meet these days.'

Which could have ended the conversation had not Alex joined in.

'You could get started while you're here. Get your name into the system, so you can start being matched up. You can even do the internet chatting part from here and leave the actual meetings until you get home,' he said, every helpful suggestion a tease to see her squirm.

He was alleviating his boredom at her expense—that's what it was!

'I was only thinking about it,' Kenzie muttered as the subject veered out of her control.

'Nonsense!'

This was Muriel now, obviously caught up in the idea.

'We'll get on with it tomorrow after my riding lesson. Write your profile—isn't that what they ask for? Oh, this will be such fun!'

'Won't it just!' Alex put in.

'And you can help,' Muriel said to him. 'It will be very good to have a male perspective on it, won't it, Kenzie?'

As the ground beneath her failed to open up and swallow her whole to hide her embarrassment, Kenzie fought back.

'Alex won't want to be away from his grandmother for that long,' she said firmly, looking him in the eyes and daring him to argue.

Some dare!

The wretched man actually smiled—no doubt at her still scarlet cheeks—and said, oh, so casually, 'Oh, I'm sure something could be arranged. I'm often on the computer while I sit with her, and I have a pager so I can always be called back.'

He then added a devastating smile that reduced Kenzie to a boneless lump of ectoplasm, and left the room.

Ridiculous! It was embarrassment causing the consternation inside her—nothing more.

Kenzie glared at the door through which he'd vanished, then stood up.

'Come along, Muriel, it's time we left, too.'

She moved to Muriel's side, taking the older woman's elbow to steady her as they walked towards the door, although she knew that Muriel didn't need support.

Kenzie lay in the comfortable bed in the smaller bedroom of Muriel's suite. At times like this she'd have been happier staying in the staff quarters where she took her meals if Muriel didn't require her. At least there she'd have had company—other young people to talk to, a bit of light-hearted chat, nothing more.

But no! It hadn't taken her long to realise that the hotel had hired her as a companion for Muriel, rather than a nurse, although many of the guests did bring their own nurses.

But a companion's role was very different. Hadn't Muriel emphasised that point with the evening's very personal conversation about her, Kenzie's, future?

Once *that* idea, which had still been in its infancy in Kenzie's head, was out in the open, Muriel had leapt on it like another new challenge. Horse riding was all well and good, but couldn't go on all day, so sorting out Kenzie's life would appeal to Muriel as a very pleasant diversion.

But dragging Alex into it?

That was just sheer embarrassment.

He probably wouldn't join them!

Why on earth would he?

She shifted to ease the swirly feeling in her stomach and settled into sleep.

* * *

Muriel's second lesson was a great success. Probably, as far as Kenzie was concerned, because Alex hadn't appeared!

The man made her nervous—or maybe unsettled was a better description of the sensations she'd been feeling in his presence.

Because he was attractive?

Or because she found him so?

She shut her mind against all thoughts of him. She was here to take a break from men…

They'd decided to hold the lesson in the enclosed paddock behind the stables, which was basically for children and beginner riders. After a couple of rounds of the paddock, Muriel insisted Kenzie relinquish the leading rein, and around she rode, ramrod straight, her face radiant with joy at her achievement.

'I'll ride back up to the hotel to show Alex,' she announced after these successful solo efforts, but Kenzie had visions of a car or a little noisy tuk-tuk coming up the drive and spooking the horse, for all the animal was very docile.

'Not on your second lesson,' Kenzie told her. 'Perhaps, if you feel like a ride this afternoon, he might find time to accompany you on one of the short trails.'

'With you, too, Kenzie,' Muriel insisted.

Kenzie smiled at her.

'I think you might find I'm due a bit of time off,' she said. 'Not that anyone working with you really needs time off as you're so generous about sharing your adventures. But I need to email my dad and do some washing—just little things.'

Best not to mention she'd given some thought to Muriel's suggestion—or had it been Alex's?—that she might as well begin her sortie into the world of internet dating while she was here. First she had to see what the different sites offered, and the kind of profiles people supplied.

What on earth could *she* put on a profile?

Nurse, handy with cattle—

They took a tuk-tuk back to the hotel, where Kenzie once again arranged a massage for Muriel, then left to have some 'you time', as Muriel called it.

'But be back at six for a chat and a drink,' Muriel insisted. 'I know you're uncomfortable about eating with me, but we can still have a drink before dinner.'

Kenzie restrained a groan. In spite of the previous day's champagne, Muriel's aperitif of choice was a very dry martini, sent up to the room already mixed in an elaborate silver shaker, olives on sticks in a little bowl.

As far as Kenzie was concerned, it was a very old-fashioned drink, but Muriel had her particular likes and dislikes and she stuck by them.

Hating the taste but unwilling to spoil Muriel's fun, Kenzie had become adept at sharing them with the nearest flower arrangement. She was surreptitiously disposing of half a glass when there was a tap on the door and in walked Alex.

'Be a dear and phone room service,' Muriel said to him. 'We want another shaker of these. I've already had them send up a glass for you.'

So Kenzie didn't like martinis, Alex thought as he obediently picked up the phone to order more. From the doorway, it had been easy to see her tipping some into the flowers, but where would she get rid of the next one if he sat between her and the flowers?

It had to be boredom that his mind had even suggested such a ploy, but that wouldn't make it less fun.

The new cocktails arrived, the room-service waiter filling all three glasses.

'You don't like olives?' he teased as Kenzie waved the plate away.

'Spoils the gin,' she said quickly, but he knew her mind was elsewhere, her eyes searching the room for a likely hiding spot for the refreshed drink.

'Have you had any ideas?'

Muriel's question took his mind off Kenzie, which was probably a very good thing as she was dressed in a soft blue shirt with two pockets that seemed to emphasise shapely breasts, and some of her night-dark hair—shining as if newly washed—hung almost to the pockets, while those blue eyes were shielded by her fringe—

'Well?'

Maybe Muriel's first question hadn't quite worked.

'Don't know much about it,' he said, fixing his attention on Muriel so he wouldn't be distracted again. 'But I did read up about it on the net and it seems you should write something a bit quirky and fun, and ask a question to encourage the reader to get back to you.'

'What kind of question?' Kenzie demanded, and he looked back to see her glass half-empty.

Had she actually drunk it?

He peered around—no handbag she could have tipped it into, not that she would, surely. Think of the mess!

And the carpet near her feet seemed dry enough.

But the feet were slim and shapely, *and* in sandals—

'The question,' the feet's owner prompted.

He looked up, met her eyes, wondered momentarily why his mouth felt dry, and smiled to cover the fact that he'd completely lost the conversational thread.

Muriel caught on first.

'What kind of questions should Kenzie ask?'

Valiantly pulling his head back on track, although the disappearance of the martini still intrigued him, he said, 'Well, say you put in that you like classical music, then you might ask what music they like.'

Kenzie smiled—a smile so sweetly innocent he knew he was in trouble.

'And if I say I like horses do I add, "What horses do you like?"'

'You know exactly what I mean!' Alex said crossly, unable to believe he was letting this woman he barely knew get under his skin.

Or, for that matter, that he was sitting here discussing what a woman—a total stranger—should put in her internet dating profile.

Internet dating—the whole idea was ridiculous. She could end up with anyone! Who knew what lies men would tell to get set up with a woman—especially a woman as attractive as Kenzie? Presumably she'd have to put up a photo of herself…

He shook his head to clear it of his meandering—and disquieting—thoughts. He'd obviously been even more bored than he'd realised!

'Come on, you two, it will be time for dinner soon, and we've got nothing done.' Muriel handed Kenzie a pen and notepad. 'Now, start writing. Name, age, profession—I think people like to know that.'

Muriel paused and looked hopefully at them.

'What next?'

'Interests!' Alex told her. 'Although I'd steer clear of ones like "walks in the fresh air". Reading through some of them, you'd swear most of the women in the world were out walking in the fresh air.'

'Walking in the rain, perhaps?' Kenzie said, pen poised.

'Do you actually *like* walking in the rain?'

'I might if it was rain you see in English pictures, that just drifts mistily down and settles in shakeable drops on your coat, but our rain is like a deluge, taking all in its path. We don't call it the wet season for nothing, you know.'

He grinned at her and her bones did the melting thing again. This really was most peculiar. It wasn't as if she was attracted to the man! Not like she'd been to the dastardly Mark.

But even then, she was reasonably sure she hadn't felt internal agitation, neither had her wretched face flared like a beacon every time he'd teased her.

Maybe he hadn't ever teased her!

And even if she *was* attracted to Alex, she didn't want to be dilly-dallying around with a passing fling—not that she could imagine Alex as a 'fling' type of person—when she had to be concentrating on the marriage and children scenario.

'There must be some "how to" stuff about it on the internet. I'll check it on my phone,' Alex said.

'What's he doing?' Muriel asked, a little plaintively.

'Looking up how to write a good profile for a dating site. Not that he'll find anything, I'm sure.'

'Which just shows how much you know!' Alex said smugly. 'Look, there are dozens of sites about it, and even a template for writing your profile.'

'Ooh, I like the sound of a template. Then we just fill stuff in.'

Muriel was getting even more excited while Kenzie wondered why she'd ever mentioned the 'married and two children' business to these virtual strangers. They'd pushed her into it, though, with their talk about a bucket list.

And it *was* what she wanted—quite badly—so the words had just come out.

'What does it say?'

Muriel again, carried away by something new!

'Lists,' Alex replied. 'List of things you like. What do you like—something that might lead to a question.'

'You mean something along the lines of "I like walking in the rain. What's the rainiest walk you've ever had?" I'd be likely to land someone telling me about their stroll up Mount Everest only the rain turned to hail and then snow, and they'd been caught in an avalanche.'

'You're not taking this seriously,' Alex said severely. 'And here we are trying to help! What *do* you like?'

Kenzie gave up. They *were* trying to help her. At least Muriel was. She suspected for Dr A. McLeod it was just an amusing way to pass some time.

'Reading,' she said.

'That's good,' Muriel said warmly. 'Then you say what book it is you're reading now, and ask if he's read it.'

'The Iliad? I'd probably end up with some Greek scholar who wants to discuss the finer points of the Trojan Wars and I really don't know them. I'm only reading it because I'd read a book about the Trojan Wars written from the women's point of view—the women who became prizes of war and wives or slaves to the Greeks who conquered their cities.'

'You're reading the Iliad to get the male side of the war?' Alex asked, in rather faint tones.

'Well, really to find out what happened from the male perspective but it was so mixed up with gods and legends that it didn't help. So I don't think I'd get on with someone who puts it down as his favourite book.'

'As if anyone is likely to!' Alex said. 'Did you really read it?'

She looked at him and grinned.

'Truthfully, no, not all of it. I just dipped in and out.'

His answering smile started the strangeness inside her again. She battled to think of other men she'd dated—not that she was dating Alex—but as far as she could remember, what there were of them had all been normal, sensible relationships with attraction there, certainly—but squirmy insides?

And hadn't she just decided that whatever he made her feel, it wasn't something she wanted to pursue? Neither did she need the distraction of these bizarre reactions to the wretched man.

Squirmy insides indeed!

From a smile?

'Wake up, Kenzie!'

Muriel snapped her out of her memories.

'Let's go down and eat,' she said. 'Alex, you might want to check on your grandmother first, and, Kenzie, I've found a skirt that would fit you. You can wear it with your black tank top. Shall we meet in the dining room?'

Kenzie opened her mouth to protest but realised it was futile, especially as Alex had left the room as soon as Muriel had suggested it. They were puppets on her string, but as it was giving her a great deal of pleasure, Kenzie went along with it.

The skirt was gorgeous, black silky material, with a riot of flowers like a garden around the bottom of it.

And being such a showpiece in itself, she felt she had to let it shine, pulling her hair severely back off her face and twisting it into a knot at the back of her head.

Damned if she wasn't beautiful!

That was Alex's first thought when he met them in the dining room—a little late as his grandmother had not only been awake but quite rational. They'd talked for ten minutes before she'd drifted off to sleep with a smile on her face after hearing stories of Muriel's horse-riding feats.

But seeing Kenzie!

It was a wonder the *Wow!* he'd thought hadn't burst from his lips.

He'd accepted she was attractive the first time he'd seen her, and the frank openness of her blue eyes when she'd spoken to him had certainly stirred something inside him.

But beautiful?

And now, right there in front of him, at the table by the window, was the woman he'd first associated with horses, looking so regally serene *and* so startlingly beautiful his breath caught in his throat and he had to pause to gather his senses.

And she was searching for love on the internet?

What was wrong with the men in her part of the world? And as for the fellow who'd led her on had hurt her...

He wasn't a violent man, but he wouldn't mind meeting *him* in a dark alley one night.

Because whoever it was *had* hurt her.

She might make light of it, saying this was nothing more than a little break to regroup, but he knew enough about gossip—he imagined small towns were like hospitals in that regard—to know how painful and humiliating that could be.

He pulled out his chair a little more forcibly than necessary and slid into his seat, careful not to look at Kenzie lest he have that breathing problem again.

She and Muriel were discussing the menu, Muriel encouraging Kenzie to try the little grilled octopi that were a specialty of the area, and Kenzie flatly refusing.

'I don't really like seafood, and I particularly don't like seafood with eyes. I'm having the steak because I happen to know it's the highest quality, imported from Australia.'

'Cattle have eyes,' Alex teased, because her cheeks had flushed as she'd argued with Muriel and he wanted to see that colour rise again.

'But not in the part I eat,' she said bluntly, glaring at him across the table, although that telltale colour *was* there again. 'Now, shall we talk about something else? Muriel would like to do one of the shorter mountain treks on her horse tomorrow, would you like to join us?'

The talk turned to horses and whether Muriel was really ready to be let off a leading rein—which she wasn't in his opinion but he doubted Muriel would listen to him, so determined was she to become a rider.

He would like to join them, very much so! If only to see Kenzie back in her jeans and T-shirt so he could get this evening's Kenzie out of his head.

'I'll have to see,' he said. 'My grandmother was more alert this evening than she's been for over a week and if she's like that tomorrow, I wouldn't want to leave her.'

'Of course not!' Kenzie said. 'But if you do come, you have a pager, I think you said, and could get back quite quickly to her room. We really won't go far.'

The waiter arrived at that moment to take their orders, which gave Alex time to consider whether he actually wanted to go on a short ride in the rainforest with Kenzie and Muriel.

Maybe not so much with Muriel…

Though having Muriel around was good because, much as he was attracted to Kenzie, he didn't want to get too involved with her. His life was on hold at the moment, so he could offer little more than a brief flirtation. And considering she'd just come out of a bad relationship, he certainly didn't want her to be hurt again.

He picked up his wine glass to taste the wine he must have ordered from another waiter who'd appeared by his chair, nodded his head and watched the waiter pour the women a glass each before adding more to his.

It was a very good shiraz, and the mellow liquid slid easily down his throat.

Giving him the courage to have another look at Kenzie, as she sat, head cocked, listening to Muriel tell her about some riding gear she'd ordered through the boutique in the palace foyer.

Better by far that he leave the women on their own tomorrow, whether his grandmother was alert or not. It had been the talk of internet dating that had made him look at Kenzie in a different way.

Had to have been…

CHAPTER THREE

'ALEX'S GRANDMOTHER MUST be feeling well today,' Kenzie said, as she and Muriel climbed into a tuk-tuk to go down to the stables next morning.

What she didn't mention to Muriel was the relief she'd felt when he'd failed to appear at the arranged time.

Neatly be-suited for dinner in the formal dining room, he'd looked no different from the man they'd dined with the previous evening, yet something *had* been different about him. Something that was in the air between them—that had been there since he'd first appeared on the other side of the horse.

Or had she been imagining it?

Imagining that his teasing meant more than it did?

Imagining an attraction?

She shook her head. A practical, country-reared young woman, she'd had no time for the love-sick talk of the girls at boarding school. The 'Did you see how he looked at me?', 'Do you think he might like me?', Should I ask him to the dance?' conversations that were regularly heard after lights out in the dorms.

So, to be imagining there'd been something different in the air between them was completely foreign to her—a whole new concept.

Was it? she wondered. Hadn't she felt a tug of attraction to Mark when they'd first met?

She tried to remember, knew she'd liked him from the start, but more than that?

She shook her head.

He'd been amusing, fun to be with, and most of his attraction, she'd worked out later, had been his confidence in himself—his confidence that he could win any woman he wanted, although that hadn't led her far enough to go to bed with him.

Thank heavens!

But Mark was in the past and Alex was a very different man, unlike anyone she'd ever met.

Was it his difference that stirred something inside her?

Or maybe it was just the talk of internet dating and her nervous reaction to dipping her toe into that possibly murky water.

Whatever! She was glad he hadn't come. Glad because of the distraction he was causing her.

Kinda glad…

The trek into the fringe of the rainforest was highly successful, Muriel declaring she was ready to go further the following day, but Kenzie knew that, as a new rider, Muriel should rest the new muscles she'd been using.

'But the riding,' Muriel protested.

'You won't forget what you've learned in just one day off and it will be good for you to do something different.

'Now a shower and a massage for you,' Kenzie told her, when they returned to her room at the hotel.

'And you, what do you do now?' a deep voice asked, and Kenzie spun around to see a serious-faced Alex standing just outside.

'Oh, Kenzie's free until late afternoon, when she joins

me for a drink,' Muriel volunteered. 'Do come in. Is there something she could do for you?'

The question was asked with the expectation of an immediate answer, and Alex said politely, 'I thought we could have a chat.'

'Oh, yes?'

Kenzie hid an inward groan—no way was Alex going to get away with such a vague reply.

He looked from Muriel to Kenzie then back to Muriel and shrugged, holding out his arms in a helpless gesture.

Hesitating...

Pausing...

Not the cool, composed, tech-brilliant Alex they both knew.

'You're dithering!' Kenzie said to him, aware the words had a very accusatory tone.

He half smiled.

'So would you be!' he muttered, then he took a deep breath and they discovered what it was all about—the words blurted out as if he was afraid he might not get them finished if he lingered too long on them!

'You'll find out anyway,' he said, by way of a beginning. 'But my grandmother is conscious and quite alert and she's declared that her dying wish is to see me married. I've pointed out it's virtually impossible—small matters like a lack of a bride and international rules and regulations, but she's waved all that away.'

He paused, his face now tight with strain.

'She's spoken of it before—this wanting to see me married before she dies, and foolishly, I suppose, I've always assured her she'll still be around when I take the plunge.'

He looked away, through the window and out over the blue-green sea, thinking that he would have been married by now had his grandmother's health not deteriorated to the point where she hadn't long to live.

Not that he had any regrets about bringing her out here, which made him realise his relationship with Melanie had been wrong from the beginning. Something they had simply drifted into…

'And now she won't be—alive, that is—if I don't go along with her.'

He sounded so down-hearted Kenzie wanted to pat his hand, or put her arm around his shoulders, but she sensed he had more to say and probably needed to get it all out.

'I couldn't argue. She's got it all worked out, you see. Apparently, she doesn't think I'd have any trouble finding a bride.'

He sighed and turned back to Kenzie and Muriel.

'And much as I love my grandmother, and much as I realise this is emotional blackmail on her part, none of her suggestions for finding a bride seemed like a great idea.'

'I imagine it could get terribly complicated,' Kenzie said, trying to hide a smile at the image of a line of beautiful young women lining up at the palace.

'Oh, but—'

That was Muriel attempting to make a point, but Alex was already back in full flow.

'Then I remembered Kenzie saying that she wanted to get married, so I was going to ask her if she'd mind awfully marrying me. A purely business arrangement, of course.'

This to Muriel, not to the intended bride!

But it was Kenzie who picked up on his phrase.

'Marrying you?'

'Yes, I thought the idea might suit us both,' Alex said, as if this was a normal conversation between strangers. 'I need a bride and you want to get married—it's like a contract arrangement—a business decision.'

Kenzie closed her eyes, but it made no more sense when the world was dark so she opened them again.

'You mean marry you in some pseudo ceremony then call it quits later that day?'

He looked horrified.

'Oh, no! I couldn't cheat my grandmother like that! I mean really marry, at least for long enough—a year or two—to see if we suit. We'd have to try to make a go of it—to be fair to her. But, of course, it wouldn't have to be for ever.'

Kenzie bit back the *but she'll be dead* retort that jumped to her lips, and went for the last bit.

'Of course? Why *wouldn't* you want to be married to me for ever? Not that any of this was likely to happen but it was a bit rude to rule me out so flippantly.'

He looked a little stunned and she realised she'd reacted far too forcibly.

'No, no! I didn't mean it like that—just that it would be an arrangement to please my grandmother. She's been so good to me, and it would mean so much to her and—'

'Let's stop right there,' Kenzie said, realising she needed to slow down this avalanche of an idea before it swept them all away.

'*My* intention,' she reminded him, 'is to get married *and have kids*—two—and I can hardly do that if I'm tied up in some kind of pretend marriage with you, and that's if it's even possible for foreigners to marry here.'

'Oh, it is!' Alex said, latching onto the last bit— probably the easiest bit—with a beaming smile. 'My grandmother got Robert—he's her butler at home—but here he's more just someone who looks after her. Anyway, she got him to check and there's a priest on the island, and after we've done a bit of paperwork and presented it all to the *amphur*, the local registration office, the marriage would be legal anywhere.'

'There, you see!' Muriel put in, already, Kenzie guessed, planning a wedding in her head.

'But that's my point,' Kenzie protested. 'I want to get married to have children. Being tied up in a marriage could mean I can't get on with it for possibly years—who knows how long a divorce would take?'

She was aware she sounded slightly hysterical but to have this man—and Muriel—planning her future was like a crazy dream.

'I wouldn't mind about the children,' Alex said, all kind magnanimity. 'In fact, I think that's the whole idea of it. Gran wants me married so she knows the name will go on.'

'McLeod? But surely there are hundreds of thousands of McLeods all around the world.'

Alex grinned at her.

'Maybe tens of thousands, but it's not the McLeod that needs to be carried on but Monroe—her name. Different clan altogether.'

He paused, before adding, 'You wouldn't mind a Monroe thrown into the children's names, would you?'

Kenzie stared at the man. Perhaps she was dreaming. She looked around her—Muriel, Alex, beautiful tropical island—no, this was real.

Pull yourself together.

She straightened in her chair, and looked from Alex to Muriel—still making wedding arrangements in her head from the blank look in her eyes—then back to Alex.

'This is totally crazy,' she said firmly. 'You can't possibly be suggesting making this marriage real—having children with me just to please your grandmother.'

'It's her dying wish!' he said soberly, although she suspected he was finding her reaction to the whole situation enormously diverting. No doubt because she was becoming increasingly flustered by it!

'You're here on the island because it was her last wish to die in this place where she had her honeymoon. I don't think people are allowed to have more than one dying wish—or at least to call it that!'

Now he actually smiled.

'I imagine you can have as many as you like—after all, you're dying, so who's going to be petty enough to count?'

Floored by this logic, she glared at him.

'It still doesn't explain your apparent willingness to marry a woman you barely know, *and* have children with her, just to please your grandmother.'

'Well, the children aren't part of the deal with her, although I know that's why she wants me married. But I threw that in as a kind of bribe to get you to say yes.'

'Oh, I see!' Kenzie could feel anger rising inside her. Not good as she didn't think well when she was angry. 'And have you also sorted out where we'll live, as I believe cohabiting would be essential in order to produce my children?'

'Our children,' he said, sounding so smug that if Muriel hadn't been there she'd have slapped his face.

'They're *my* children—you don't have to have anything to do with them,' she snapped, aware somewhere in her brain that this was a nonsensical conversation.

He smiled and she had to sit on her hands to stop any violence.

'Oh, but aren't all children better off with two parents? Isn't that the prevailing view of the pundits of childhood.'

'I wouldn't know,' Kenzie spat at him through clenched teeth, 'but I do know I managed very well with just a father!'

At which stage she stood up and left the room. It was

that or having a full-blown tantrum, which, she suspected, would delight Alexander Monroe McLeod, but might upset Muriel.

Down to the foyer and out through the front door, long strides putting her further and further from the totally ridiculous conversation in Muriel's room.

Maybe she'd imagined it!

Sunstroke?

She gave a huff of laughter at the ridiculous idea—she who'd been born and bred in the tropics, spent long days moving cattle from one paddock to another under a blistering, midsummer sun—sunstroke was unlikely...

And much as she'd have liked to think she'd been dreaming, she knew full well she hadn't been. It had been that stupid talk of bucket lists that had started it, and she'd responded by denying the idea of a bucket list when her only plan was to get married and have two children.

Then Muriel had got caught up in the internet dating idea, and somehow Alexander Monroe McLeod had decided he only had to ask, she'd agree, and his grandmother would die happy.

Had he thought she was so desperate? Had she *sounded* desperate when she'd spoken of it?

True, she did want it, and would like to get settled sooner rather than later, so the children could grow up with their grandfather and absorb knowledge from him, as she had all her life.

And now she considered it a little more rationally, wouldn't this be better than picking up a virtual stranger on the internet?

Hadn't hundreds of women been cheated by people they'd met on the net?

And at least with Alex, she knew he wasn't after her money. He probably wasn't even aware she had money. Not many outsiders could translate cattle numbers and square kilometres of land into cold, hard cash...

Perhaps, just perhaps, it wasn't such a bad idea. And it wasn't as if a marriage of convenience was a new thing. Most of the larger properties in Australia had been built up through fortuitous marriages over many generations.

Heaven preserve me! Am I really thinking I might go ahead with this?

She felt a little flip deep inside her body and she didn't think it was dread.

It was definitely a physical reaction, and unlike anything she'd ever felt before.

But that could be because he was a stranger—practically—and meeting the man who'd invented Doc-Says was certainly special, so that could explain the flip.

Except it had felt like excitement.

Attraction?

That something she'd felt between them almost from the beginning?

Although while a little physical attraction might be okay—a definite plus from the children point of view—it wouldn't do to fall in love with the man.

This would be a purely business arrangement...

'What do you think?' Alex asked Muriel as he watched Kenzie storm out of the room as if all the furies in hell were after her.

'I think it's an excellent idea,' Muriel declared. 'At least you both know what you're getting—well, who you're getting—but what you're getting into as well. Alex, you need a wife, and Kenzie needs children—it's perfect!'

Stunned by this pronouncement, Alex decided silence was the best response, although now the children had been mentioned, his body had tightened at the thought of sex with Kenzie.

Muriel waited until she was sure she had his full attention, then said, 'Now the wedding! I know your grandmother doesn't need a great fuss, and I imagine that butler person you spoke of will support you, and, of course, I'll support Kenzie. But afterwards, when your grandmother retires to rest or sleep, we should have a nice dinner in the restaurant. And champagne—of course champagne. Possibly some at the wedding itself, if your grandmother is able to tolerate a small glass.'

Alex would have liked to protest. Since he'd begun to think about it, the idea of having Kenzie in his bed had sent tension spiralling through his body, and, in his mind, should they need food or champagne, there was always room service.

But he'd been around Muriel long enough to know that nothing short of a bulldozer would stop her once she was in planning mode. And maybe Kenzie would enjoy a small—short?—celebratory dinner.

As his mind drifted to the thought that maybe these marriages of convenience were a good idea—saved all that hassle of dating—Muriel brought him firmly back to the present.

'Have you something to wear?'

It took him a couple of minutes to process the question.

'I've a couple of suits.'

'You know there are tailors in the village who could run you up a dinner suit, or perhaps a morning suit, in a matter of days.'

She paused, frowning.

'Or a nicely tailored tropical suit. That would be good for meeting Kenzie's father as well.'

Alex eyed the woman who was arranging his life.

'I can't see myself in whatever a "tropical suit" might be and I don't think a morning suit would be a good idea, do you? It would just embarrass Kenzie—even a suit might be a bit much in the morning. I thought grey slacks and a white shirt, no tie—nice and casual.'

'Hmph!' Muriel said, her lips pursing in disapproval, but fortunately at that moment Kenzie walked in.

'All right, I'll do it,' she said, standing in front of him with just an edge of belligerence in her voice. 'I imagine you'll want it as soon as possible. What do I need? My passport, I presume? Anything else?'

'A statement that you're single,' Alex said, pushing down a new kind of excitement rising inside him and sticking to the purely practical. 'If your father could get someone official like a lawyer to fax that through, or scan it and send it by email, we can get it translated by an official here.'

She nodded before returning to the chair she'd occupied earlier, about as far from where he and Muriel, who'd settled on the settee, as she could get.

'And I'm assuming a priest doing his thing will be sufficient for your grandmother? She's not going to want full bridal regalia and wedding cakes and things?'

Alex hid a smile and glanced towards Muriel, seeing from the tightening of her lips and downcast face she'd already been planning a wedding cake.

'No, no! The priest and the ceremony will be quite sufficient.'

Kenzie frowned at him for a moment.

'Then couldn't we just fake it?' she asked. 'Not with the real priest, of course, but have someone dressed up as a priest do the ceremony?'

He sensed this was a last desperate effort on her part to restore some normality to the situation. She didn't have to agree, of course, but he guessed the idea had more appeal to her than the internet dating had. As far as he could tell, she was a sensible, practical woman.

And she *did* want children!

So he couldn't resist teasing her with his answer to the 'faking it' suggestion.

'And cheat a dying woman?' he said smoothly.

Kenzie hung her head, and he could see the beautiful colour flushing up her neck and into her cheeks.

She really was something special, this woman he was about to marry...

'You're right of course. I shouldn't have suggested it again, but this is all so bizarre I don't know—it's not so much *what* to think but *how* to think about it.'

'You're worrying too much, making too much of it,' Muriel said quite sharply. 'It's a splendid idea because you both get what you want.'

She paused, adding in a softer tone, 'You'll have to work at it—the pair of you. Most people don't realise it, but marriage isn't easy. And a successful one takes work, a lot of work, although plenty of people don't bother.'

Kenzie stared at the woman she'd known for less than three weeks, and wondered just how long it had taken Muriel to realise the truth of her statement. That it *was* true, Kenzie didn't doubt for a moment! From what she'd worked out through conversations, Muriel had been married at least four times—maybe more...

Glancing from Muriel to the man who had so disrupted her morning—if not her life—Kenzie saw that he, too, was watching Muriel, and she guessed he, too, was wondering how long it had taken her to work out the advice she'd just passed on.

He was a handsome devil, this man she was going to

marry—probably—and she took his distraction as an opportunity to really look at him. With his dark hair and tanned skin, his unusual grey eyes were quite startling, and, she feared, they saw far too much for all he often hooded them, so he seemed to be watching people with a slightly weary compassion.

Or was she just plain nuts? Had this marriage talk gone to her head and somehow turned rational thought to fancies?

Fancies of attraction?

No, that had been there from their first meeting—or some form of it.

But given that attraction, she had to be careful it didn't go too far—develop into something stronger. This was a purely practical arrangement so Alex would get a wife and she'd get the children she wanted. It would be stupid to mess it up with anything deeper.

Surely there'd be nothing worse than one-sided love…

Could she wear the sarong to the wedding?

The thought startled her.

Had she decided?

Had she actually said yes?

Of course she had! Mere minutes ago…

She closed her eyes and tried to clear her head, no longer certain where any of the nonsense stood.

'You'll need a dress.'

Muriel obviously had no doubts at all.

'*Not* a wedding dress,' Kenzie said, possibly just a little too loudly.

'Well, you don't want all your wedding pictures to have you standing there in a sarong, do you?'

'Wedding pictures?' Kenzie said faintly, then felt a firm hand on her shoulder.

Alex had crossed the room to stand beside her.

'Just relax,' he said, the pressure of his hand and the quiet words enormously reassuring. 'It's not as if we can get married today! There are a few papers and things to get organised, but...'

He paused and smiled down at her, which dismissed any idea of relaxing.

'I'm taking it from the discussion of clothes that you'll definitely go along with it?'

She felt her head move up and down. After all, she'd been considering marrying a man she met on the internet and had coffee with in a neighbouring town. At least she knew this man—well, had begun to know...

'Famous!' he said. 'It is such a favour to me I'll do everything I can to see you don't regret it! I'll get on with the arrangements and see you both at dinner.'

And with that, he was gone.

Aware he had, with unexpected help from Muriel, more or less bulldozed Kenzie into agreeing to marry him, he should probably be feeling at least a small amount of guilt, but no.

This woman he'd so fortuitously come across at the Palace of Peace and Contentment fascinated him, not only with her conversations about her home—an unimaginable place—but with her easy smiles and laughter, and the way she flushed so easily when he teased her.

In fact, if the sensation he was experiencing could be described in any way, he thought it might be excitement—together with a strangely satisfied warmth.

Setting aside the temptation of stirring warmth and excitement together in his mind, he returned to his grandmother's suite, where Robert, with his unflappable efficiency, had produced all the necessary documents, already translated into English, that the priest would require.

His grandmother was propped up on an array of pillows on the bed and sleeping, but a lighter sleep than the deep coma-like condition that had shadowed the previous weeks.

He smiled to himself.

She'd be relaxed—at ease—never for one moment doubting he'd do exactly as she'd requested, and never for a fraction of a moment considering such a request could have been difficult, or even impossible.

Thank heaven for Kenzie, a practical, sensible young woman with her own very definite reasons for wanting to get married. And he quite liked children and was ready to have his own—so that wasn't going to be a problem.

The wayward part of his mind that had been keen to connect warmth and excitement was now running off at a tangent about how soon they could be expected to begin—

No, think about the wedding.

What did he need to do?

Breeding told him he should speak to her father—maybe not to do the old 'asking for a hand in marriage' thing, but at least to introduce himself and explain why the hurry. She'd mentioned cattle in some staggering number so it would be a big place, and with the name Steele and the general idea it was in northern Australia, he began his search.

The extremely efficient internet provided him with more information than he'd ever considered possible. If it was the right Mr Steele, then he could understand why Kenzie wanted to have children. The property was vast and had been, as she'd said, in the same family for generations. The original Mr Steele, settling on what, from the pictures, looked like arid red desert, must have had his own doubts about it, to have named it 'Speculation'.

But from the parts Alex had read, it had turned out very well indeed, although he had no idea what this meant in terms of money, but they must be doing okay.

He checked the time difference, found it was four in the afternoon in northern Australia and phoned, reaching, after some switches from phone to phone, Mr Steele himself.

'Angus Steele,' the man said by way of introduction. 'Do I know you, Mr McLeod?'

'Not yet,' Alex told him, 'but I'm in Thailand, staying in the same hotel as your daughter. Everything is fine, there are no problems, but...'

He paused, totally lost as to where to go next.

'You want to marry her?'

The words were such a shock it took Alex a few moments to compute them.

'Well, yes,' he managed. 'She phoned you, sir?'

'I've just finished speaking to her,' the man said, 'and if she's happy with whatever arrangement you're making, then that's fine by me.'

There was a subtext to the words that even over the phone Alex could clearly hear. Something along the lines of *but if you hurt her I will kill you slowly and painfully and bury your body where it will never be found.*

Maybe not quite so murderous, but definitely a warning.

'I will take good care of her,' Alex said, and realised, as he said it that he wanted very much to take good care of the woman he was about to marry—this woman he barely knew!

He knew she'd been hurt by the bastard that had sent her fleeing here, and even thinking about that knotted his gut in a most uncomfortable way.

She was different—special—and he'd meant what he'd said, meant every word...

'See that you do,' Angus Steele said, confirming in

words the subtext Alex had heard. 'I look forward to meeting you. Goodbye.'

Steele by name and steel by nature?

Not a subtle man, anyway, so probably not in the slightest bit concerned about a marriage of convenience.

It wasn't the fact that she'd thought he should be the first to know that had Kenzie phoning her father. It was more their closeness and wanting to share the knowledge that something big and important was about to happen in her life.

Because for all she'd tried to be practical about the strange proposal and the discussion that had followed it, it *was* a big and important thing in her life!

Brought up in a man's world, she'd had no sentimental feelings about wanting her father to give her away in a grand wedding ceremony. As far as they were both concerned, she and her father, she wasn't his to give away, but her own woman, making her own decisions about her life.

If there was one thing growing up on an isolated property taught you, it was independence because often all you had to rely on was yourself. True, at mustering time especially, there could be up to two dozen people on the property, a dozen residents most of the time, but if your horse shied at a snake and threw you down by the far dam, you needed to know which fence to follow home.

Would children growing up in Scotland, even for five years, be able to learn that knowledge, or should they make their home on the property from birth?

She shook her head—there were no children yet— and never would be if she didn't get her act together and work out what she was going to wear. And there they were again—the children! At some stage of their lives they'd want to see their parents' wedding photos, and she didn't want to be in a sarong…

Fortunately, before the children thoughts could go further, Muriel knocked on her door and came in with an armful of clothes, which she draped carefully on the bed.

'See if there's anything there that would suit you,' she said, and Kenzie smiled at her. Trust Muriel to be getting on with practical matters. 'And then tomorrow we could go down to the tailor in the village for any alterations.'

Muriel!

'You were going to rest,' Kenzie said, remembering her plans for the day.

Muriel waved a languid hand.

'Oh, I've decided I don't need that and Gan from down at the stables is going to bring my horse up here, and I'll get on at the side entrance where you showed me, and we'll do a little trek.'

She paused before adding, 'And I'll probably be late back for lunch so I phoned Alex and told him it might be a good time to introduce you to his grandmother—over lunch if she's alert enough to want any.'

'You did what?' Kenzie demanded, far too loudly, as the reality of the situation hit her like a fist. She was supposed to be the practical one in this relationship—the organiser—and she'd been dithering as her mind wandered down dead-end alleys about where her children—which she didn't and might never have—should live and their wanting—or not wanting—to look at her wedding photos...

'Sorry, Muriel, you're right, I have to meet her sometime.'

Muriel patted her arm in a soothing manner.

'That's all right, dear, all brides get a little uptight. I did before all my marriages, although you'd have thought I'd have got used to it. But every time I was so sure he was the right man—just showed how much I knew!'

Muriel departed for her ride with Gan, and Kenzie collapsed beside the pile of garments on the bed—most of which, she now realised, were elaborate evening gowns. Maybe she'd better visit the tailor down in the village who could produce a garment in twenty-four hours…

CHAPTER FOUR

KENZIE HAD BEGGED off dinner, claiming a headache, which Muriel appeared to find quite normal.

'Bridal nerves, dear,' she said. 'You order whatever you want and ask them to send it up, then have an early night.'

Going to bed at eight was certainly obeying those words, but sleep? How could sleep come when images of Alex and bridal gowns and children chased each other through her head? Even when she did sleep, well after she'd heard Muriel come in, the same apparitions danced through her dreams.

So Muriel bouncing into Kenzie's bedroom at what seemed like dawn but was actually close to nine, came as a literally rude awakening.

'I'm off for my ride,' Muriel announced. 'You make sure you go down to see the tailor, and don't worry about the cost. Whatever you decide will be my wedding gift to you.'

'But, Muriel, I haven't even tried on the dresses you've already left for me. There's sure to be something there that fits and looks okay.'

'Okay?' Muriel shrieked, in what Kenzie hoped was *mock* horror. 'You want to look better than *okay*! It's your wedding, remember!'

Only too well, Kenzie thought but didn't say. She promised Muriel she'd visit the tailor and, yes, she'd remember

she was having lunch with Alex and his grandmother, although what she really felt like doing was pulling the sheet
over her head and going back to sleep. She dragged herself
out of bed, showered and dressed, slapped her hat on her
head and set off down to the village.

Where she not only found the miracle tailor, but the man
she was going to marry, standing very still in the middle
of a very small hut, having lethal-looking pins stuck into
whatever it was he was wearing.

Inside out!

'Wedding finery?' she teased, hoping the little tingle
along her nerves hadn't generated the blushes that came
too easily. But even in an inside-out garment stuck with
pins, the man was decidedly handsome—and, yes, it *had*
to be attraction she kept feeling, which, all things considered, was probably a good thing…

'Gran!' he said succinctly, and her smile widened as she
heard the name that had obviously clung on from childhood, on his lips.

'And you? Muriel?'

'Of course,' Kenzie said. 'Her argument was that I
needed to think about the wedding photos.'

'Wedding photos?' Alex echoed faintly, wincing as a
wayward pin struck skin.

'Exactly!' Kenzie said, 'but I could hardly tell Muriel
there wouldn't be any wedding photos, now, could I?'

He said nothing, though the hint of a smile quirked one
corner of his lips.

'Gran—who has apparently decided it's not time for her
to die after all—simply pointed out that you'd probably be
disappointed if I turned up in a white shirt and grey slacks.'

He paused, smile gone and eyes thoughtful.

'Although photos would be a good idea. You'll want to
send some to your father, surely.'

And for some unfathomable reason Kenzie felt tears welling in her eyes.

Had Alex seen them that he stepped forward, pins and all, to put his hand on her shoulder?

She rubbed the overflow off her cheeks, startled by her reaction.

'I'm not at all sentimental, you know,' she muttered.

'Of course you're not,' he said, getting as close as the danger of the pins permitted and sliding his arm around her shoulders. 'Would you like him to be here?' he asked. 'I could have him flown over—it's no distance.'

Kenzie shook her head. As if her father *wouldn't* have been here if they weren't in the middle of mustering. She looked up at the man being so kind.

'I'm all right,' she said. 'I don't know why I went weepy on you, but I promise I won't do it again.'

To his surprise, the statement disappointed Alex, who'd found himself enjoying even this most ordinary of physical contact with Kenzie.

Had he been looking for an excuse to touch her?

Hold her?

If only to comfort…

He shook his head and stepped back for the tailor to fit more pins.

Not consciously, he hadn't—he was fairly certain about that, but he had to admit that ever since the marriage idea had raised its head the part of his brain not overseen by reason had been playing with any manner of thoughts.

And images, if he was honest!

'Well, I should be nearly done,' he said, when he realised the silence between them was growing heavier by the minute. 'Then it will be your turn.'

She'd stepped back from him as well, so the distance

was now quite safe, but he sensed that the confusion he read in her eyes was nothing to do with an absent father but more along the lines of what he'd been thinking himself.

Well, as Muriel had said, they were both young—fairly young for him—healthy adults so why shouldn't there be an attraction between them?

He felt his body stirring and asked the tailor—a little too abruptly—if he was finished.

'Nearly,' the man told him, just as a woman appeared and led Kenzie into a tiny, curtained alcove in a corner of the shop.

He *would not* think about Kenzie stripping off her clothes behind that flimsy bit of cloth. He'd think about fish, or what to order for lunch—probably the latter because thinking about fish made no sense at all.

Not that anything was making much sense when Kenzie was around. It had to be the wedding business because generally sense—common sense—was one of his best attributes.

Or so he'd always thought...

He eased out of the pale cream, Thai-style shirt the tailor was making for him, called a cheery goodbye towards the curtain and left, glad to be out in the sunshine among the milling market crowd, glad to be heading back to the hotel and, he hoped, some sanity.

He was on the very edge of the crowd when he heard a shrill scream from somewhere behind him, and turned, thinking it was probably some over-excited child. But it was followed by another, and a lot of excited chatter.

Reluctantly he headed back into the market, the noise now persistent enough for him to know where he was going. The crowd had formed a circle around a heavily pregnant woman who lay writhing on the ground, her baby clearly on the way. Alex pushed his way through and knelt by the woman's side, wiping her hair out of her eyes, feeling the sweat on her face.

'Has someone called an ambulance?' he asked, aware that many of the locals would speak English and should understand the request.

No reply.

He knelt beside her, and gently asked her name.

'Malee,' someone from the crowd replied.

'I'm Alex,' he told her, 'and I'm a doctor,' thinking this might comfort her while at the same time wondering whether he could examine her more intimately in front of so many people.

Then another figure erupted from the crowd.

Kenzie!

'Get back, get back, give her some privacy!' she yelled as she ran towards the woman, dropping to kneel beside her. 'Find a sheet and some towels, get something to cover her and something clean for the baby.'

This directed to a woman who'd tentatively followed her onto centre stage.

And as if by magic, lengths of material appeared, and bath towels still wrapped in plastic.

'Get a couple of the women to hold those up. The poor woman doesn't want the whole village watching her give birth,' Kenzie said to him.

'Malee, her name's Malee,' he said but Kenzie was already lifting the woman's knees into a position where she could check the cervix for dilatation.

Thankful for her presence, Alex organised the privacy screens, and sent someone to get water, and ice if it was available.

As quickly as the towels had appeared, water and ice arrived, and he knelt by the woman and cradled her head and shoulders, so she could sip at the cold water between pains.

'You'll be all right, Malee,' he said gently. 'You and the baby!'

Her hands gripped his supporting arms, fingers digging into them like talons.

'Head's crowned,' Kenzie said, glancing up at him briefly. 'I don't suppose you know the Thai word for push?'

But words weren't necessary. The woman screamed again, her fingers gripped the muscles on his arms so tightly he wondered if he'd end up scarred for life by this pre-wedding experience.

The baby arrived to a shout of joy from Kenzie, a sigh from Malee, and two ambulance attendants who took in the scene at one glance and immediately began to get both woman and baby into the ambulance.

Alex smiled to himself as he saw the reluctance with which Kenzie handed over the tiny, towel-wrapped infant.

'You wanted to keep holding it, didn't you?' he teased, as he took her by the elbow and forced their way through the still chattering crowds.

'Him,' Kenzie said, 'and I did not!'

She smiled. 'But it's always like a miracle, delivering a baby. There's something so…precious somehow about the perfection of it all.'

'You've had midwifery training?'

They were free of the crowds now, heading up the hill towards the hotel.

'Of course! There's not much point working in a country hospital if you can't deliver a baby.'

He slid his arm around her shoulders and gave her a hug.

'You did well,' he said, and though she tried to shrug off the compliment, he saw faint colour in her cheeks and knew she'd liked it.

They met up with Muriel when they reached the stables. She took one look at Kenzie and rushed towards her.

'What happened? Are you all right? There's blood on you.'

Kenzie moved out of the shelter of his arm, leaving a coldness down his side.

She grinned at her excitable friend.

'It's not my blood, it's the baby's—or more probably Malee's, the mother's—but it's definitely not mine. We just delivered a baby, Alex and I, down by the markets. Oh, damn!'

'What's wrong?' Alex asked her, a spurt of worry in his gut.

'I left my hat and shoulder bag down there at the tailor's. I'll have to go back.'

He caught her hand as she turned.

'I'll go,' he said. 'You go in and get cleaned up.'

'So I don't shock your grandmother looking like this?' she teased, holding out her hands and gesturing to the murky stains.

'Just go,' he said firmly, hoping his voice was steadier than his heart, which had reacted most erratically to the sight of her more or less offering herself to him, though, of course, she wasn't doing that at all, It had been a quirk of his imagination and…

Well, he didn't know 'and what', but he'd better stop thinking about it and get her things as quickly as possible so he'd be back in time for lunch.

A pleasant buzz, the result of having helped deliver a healthy baby, stayed with Kenzie as she showered and dressed in a demure yellow sun frock that her father always loved to see her wearing.

Would Alex's gran approve?

She found herself hoping the old lady would, as if the sensible business arrangement of this marriage had turned into something else.

Not that it had.

True, Alex had taken her elbow to get her through the crowd, but once they'd been through and out on the road to the hotel, he'd dropped it.

There'd been no reason for him to keep holding it, or for her to have expected it of him, but that temporary closeness had suggested togetherness, and wasn't that what marriage was all about?

These rambling thoughts chased through her head as she swiped on some pale pink lipstick and smoothed down the wildness of her hair, braiding it into a neat French plait.

Well, most of it. Those shorter bits that curled close to her face always did their own thing, and she didn't want to meet Alex's grandmother smelling of hairspray, which never held them for long anyway.

Satisfied that she was done, she went into the living room and did a twirl for Muriel, who told her she looked beautiful, and she hoped Alex realised just what a gem he was getting.

'You're looking good yourself,' Kenzie replied. 'All this horse-riding out in the fresh air obviously suits you.'

'I just love it!' Muriel said, her face aglow with remembered delight. 'I'm going out again this afternoon. Gan knows a little beach that's very private. He says the horses like walking in the water. Imagine that, Kenzie, me on a horse in the water!'

Kenzie smiled at her.

'Wish me luck!' she said, as she gave the woman who'd become a friend a quick kiss on the cheek.

'As if you need luck!' Muriel said. 'It's that Alex getting the luck, with you agreeing to marry him. Gan says—'

But before Kenzie could learn what Gan had said, the sweet chime of the bell at the entrance to the suite told her

Alex was here, ready, as he'd promised, to escort her up to the penthouse.

She greeted him a little distractedly, brushed aside his compliment on how she looked, and frowned back at the door she'd just closed behind her.

'Are you worried about leaving Muriel on her own?' Alex asked. 'You must get some time to yourself, surely.'

Kenzie shook her head.

'No, no! She's the most generous of employers and we get on really well.'

'But?' he probed, and again she shook her head.

'It's nothing and even if it is, then it's not my business, and certainly not something I could discuss with a stranger.'

His lips quirked into a wry smile.

'Am I still a stranger?'

The question brushed away the niggle of concern she'd felt earlier, and she considered it for a moment.

'Well, we're not exactly old friends, are we?'

CHAPTER FIVE

MRS MONROE—GRAN—proved to be a formidable woman, for all she was withered by age and propped on pillows in the most luxurious bed Kenzie had ever seen.

In the most luxurious room ditto!

A golden room that seemed to glow with sunlight, although the effect, Kenzie was pretty sure, came from the fine silk of the golden curtains that hung at the windows and formed a canopy over the old four-poster bed.

Here and there, silver touches, like the material covering the sofa, seemed to enliven the gold, while bright pink and green cushions provided, surprisingly enough, a pleasing contrast.

It was impossible not to compare it to the—well, drab furnishings of her own home. 'Home' on a cattle property was a totally utilitarian place, brown and grey the predominant colouring in the furnishings—practical colours out in the red desert country.

Perhaps if her mother had lived…

She felt a sudden surge of emotion, as strong as it was unexpected, and for a moment she longed for the mother she'd never known. She shut her eyes against tears, and shook her head to clear it, determined to get with the conversation.

'Gran was asking how you're enjoying your stay.'

'I'm sorry, Mrs Monroe—this room just took my breath away.'

The old lady smiled, and Kenzie saw in the sweetness of that smile how beautiful Gran had once been. The high cheekbones beneath her grey, sagging skin still commanded attention, as did her deep blue eyes, for all they were clouded by age.

'Alexander's mother was conceived in this bed.'

Why hadn't Alex warned her that his gran was a woman who spoke her mind?

It had been a statement of fact, apparently, and not something Kenzie could easily answer.

But she was here to impress, so she did her best.

'That must make it extra-special that you've been able to return with him,' she said.

'Return to die!'

It was another conversation stopper, but fortunately Alex came to her rescue, suggesting they order lunch.

'Gran has hers in a tray in her bed, but Robert has set up a small table for us close by.'

He waved his hand towards a small, round table, a snowy white tablecloth forming a backdrop to a vase of pale pink roses. Silver cutlery was set out in front of two chairs, both angled so anyone sitting there could see and be seen by the old woman.

'Alexander tells me your mother died in childbirth. That must have been hard on you, growing up without her.'

The words were weak and slow, but Kenzie sensed her interest.

'I have never known anything different,' she answered quietly. 'It has always been me and my father, although other people were around. My mother's mother lived with us when I was a baby, and we had two couples living on the property, and the women were always there for me.'

'Cattle, I think Alexander said?'

'Yes, Brahmans. They do best in the tropical conditions, they're fairly drought resistant and don't attract ticks.'

The old lady did not respond and Kenzie was thankful when Robert appeared, carrying a silver tray. He unfolded small legs on either side of it and set it over Mrs Monroe. Robert then placed a plate in front of each of them and a platter of meats, salad vegetables and exotic fruits in the middle of the table.

Mrs Monroe—far better to think of her as that, rather than the way too intimate Gran—was sipping from a tall glass of some indeterminate concoction that had a look of one of the green health juices that had become so popular. Anything, Kenzie guessed, to get fluids into her without tethering her to the unsightly paraphernalia of a drip.

Kenzie helped herself to meat and salad, her selection making barely a dint in the mass of food in front of them.

But her nerves were tightening and too many doubts were flashing through her mind. Should she ask questions of Mrs Monroe while she was drinking her juice? Or not speak at all?

She could ask about the juice, but that might prove too personal if it turned out it was purely medicinal...

Moving her food around her plate and becoming increasingly distracted, she finally looked up and glared at Alex, who was watching her with that damn smile in his eyes.

She frowned at him, hoping he'd pick up the conversational ball, but he was obviously enjoying her discomfort far too much to end it.

Talk about a bedroom farce!

'Is it medicinal, your juice?' Kenzie finally asked, and Mrs Monroe placed the glass on the silver tray and said, 'No, but Robert tells me it's very healthy.'

She paused, and Kenzie waited, hoping she had more to say, or that Alex might join in, but that was not to be. Silence once more settled like a shroud in the room.

Well, here goes!

'My father drinks a weird concoction that has beetroot in it, making it a vivid purple. He had severe arthritis in his hands and fingers and made the decision years ago to give up all the nightshade vegetables—potatoes, tomatoes, eggplant and capsicum. He claims it cured him, and his hands really are proof of it. Sweet potatoes are okay, apparently, and he loves his beetroot. Our gardener grows them especially for him.'

A muffled snort from across the table told her just how much the man she'd thought she might marry was enjoying this, but the silence increased the tension of her nerves, so if she had to chatter on, she damn well would.

Another glare across the table produced nothing but a bland smile.

She eyed the plate in front of her. No way could she eat anything. Her stomach was in knots, so it was with huge relief she heard Mrs Monroe's weak, tired voice.

Relief until she heard exactly what was being said.

'I think she'll do very well indeed, Alexander,' the old woman said, then she waved her hand, apparently dismissing them both, for Robert came forward to lift her tray from the bed, and she lay back in her pillows and cushions and closed her eyes.

Aware she was probably scarlet with embarrassment, Kenzie scrambled to her feet, murmured something she hoped would be taken as a thank you and farewell, and prepared to depart.

Needing to be out of the room, out of the hotel, anywhere in the fresh air where she could work out exactly what she needed to say to Alexander Monroe McLeod.

But he caught her hand as she passed him, and held it while he stood up, murmuring, 'You've eaten nothing. Come on and I'll take you down to the village for something hot and spicy.'

'I would prefer to be alone!' she said with as much hauteur as she could muster.

'Because I laughed?' he teased.

Fortunately, they were outside the suite by now, so she could turn to him and tell him exactly what she thought of him.

'You did that on purpose—left all the conversation to me. You didn't help one bit, and I ended up rabbiting on about beetroot, of all things! You could have helped, asked questions even, done something rather than sitting there enjoying every minute of the torment!'

He grinned at her.

'It was far too good to interrupt. Besides which, you will have impressed Gran no end. She believes people should all contribute something to the conversation.'

'*You* didn't!' Kenzie snapped, then realised he was still holding her hand.

And, worse, she'd done nothing about removing hers from his grasp.

And neither did she particularly feel like doing it.

Weird!

She caught up with his conversation, something about his grandmother loving him anyway, so he hadn't had to talk.

She'd remove her hand when they reached the lift, she decided.

Definitely before they walked out of it into the foyer...

But somehow, here she was, halfway down the drive, the hat he'd rescued earlier pulled down on her head, her handbag slung across her shoulder, and her hand still in his.

Well, they *were* getting married so maybe it was okay to hold hands with him—even if he was a stranger…

Alex felt a sense of enormous satisfaction as he walked, hand in hand, with this attractive woman.

There'd been women in his life, some passing through it, others more serious, but none had held his heart for very long. In fact, few had ever *touched* his heart, not the way he imagined his parents' hearts had been touched by each other.

He knew his focus on work had destroyed many of his relationships, but he'd sometimes wondered if there was something lacking in him, or if, perhaps, their early deaths had coloured his world too much. Had raised his expectations too high…

His memories of them from before the light plane crash in the highlands had claimed their lives had been of two people who had somehow become one. He'd seen their eyes meeting across a formal dining table, drawing small, secretive smiles from both of them. Seen how the casual touch of his father's hand on his mother's shoulder could draw colour into her face and a special light into her eyes.

They'd worked and lived and laughed their way through life, making everything around them seem brighter—more alive, more vibrant somehow…

But maybe the judgement of a twelve-year-old boy wasn't all that reliable.

And maybe what they'd had had been special, and his own failure in the love department was because he was looking for that magic he'd once seen, and even felt—for their love had wrapped around him as well.

They'd been in the highlands with Gran for his holidays, and he'd been staying on.

Gran's recipe for heartbreak and grief, though he hadn't known at the time, was to keep busy all the time.

They'd collected butterflies and heartlessly pinned them into a collector's display case, learned their names from heavy books in her grand library, patiently typed them out on her ancient typewriter...

Gran's ghillie, McNab, had taught him to shoot, for all his father had once said he had to wait until he was fourteen. Targets first—great round things that he could hardly miss, then cans on fence posts, more the size of vermin!

And with McNab and Gran and a picnic basket stuffed with goodies, they'd drive the small pony cart to the open land beyond the forest to shoot at the rabbits that ate the local farmers' crops.

And every day, even if only for an hour, he rode the big black gelding that had been his grandfather's horse. Exercising him, Gran said, though looking back Alex wondered if she'd asked him to do it because riding Duke needed all your concentration, so even on these jaunts high up into the hills, he'd had little time to feel sad.

He'd felt loss—*that* lived with him—lived as a shadow he doubted would ever leave, but he was kept too busy to wallow in abject misery. Besides which, as Gran had said one day when she'd found him crying, 'Monroes don't do emotion! It's just not done...'

Lost in the past, he was surprised to find they'd reached the market, where excited voices greeted them, obviously regarding them—or at least Kenzie—as the heroes of the hour after the delivery of the baby. The crush of people pressed Kenzie closer to him, and he felt the softness of her body. He dropped the hand he'd somehow been holding to put his arm around her shoulders.

For protection from the crush, of course...

No, admit it, he liked touching her, had liked holding hands and even more feeling her body close to his.

And best of all, it was a sensible, business arrangement, so he didn't have to worry if that spark of magic he'd seen within his parents' marriage didn't happen to him.

'What do you fancy?' he asked, and was pleased when she responded promptly.

'The satay chicken on sticks,' she said without a moment's hesitation. 'The ones you get at the place with the yellow umbrellas at the edge of the market, right near the beach.'

Not that he'd expected quite that much precision, but at least she hadn't said, 'Oh, I don't know, what are you having?' which was the answer most women he had known would have given.

He eased them through the crowd to the stall she'd mentioned, ordered the same for both of them, added some sparkling mineral water to the order, then joined her at a table right on the sand.

She'd kicked off her sandals and was flicking at the sand with her toes. Small, pink toes, unadorned by any hue of nail polish, but perfect nonetheless.

Perfect toes?

Was he losing his mind?

Maybe it was just that he wasn't used to seeing naked toes that hers seemed so…right?

But sitting there, seeing those toes flicking sand into little arcs in the air, he felt a sense of well-being and knew it stemmed from the woman by his side.

Knew it stemmed from the attraction he felt—not just for her toes but for the whole, beautiful package, who laughed and joked and smiled a lot and quite simply made him feel good.

Although it was probably a good thing that he was

physically attracted to her—something he'd only just got around to admitting to himself—given that she wanted children.

'So,' she said, using a napkin to wipe a smear of satay sauce from the corner of her upper lip, 'when's the big day?'

'Big day?' he found himself echoing, as his attention was diverted away from that upper lip. He could have licked that sauce off it—that's what he'd *been* thinking.

'The wedding,' Kenzie said, an unspoken 'stupid' lingering at the end of the two words.

He studied her now, wondering if she was as laid-back about all this as she seemed.

If he gave himself a slap on the cheek to get his mind into gear, would she think he was demented and back away from the arrangement as fast as her pretty feet would allow?

He closed his eyes and breathed deeply instead, aware that the gap between her question and his reply was lengthening by the second.

'I think Robert said tomorrow,' he finally managed. 'Would that suit you?'

'Of course!' came the answer, far too cool and off-hand. Maybe she *was* as laid-back as she seemed. Maybe it was an Australian thing...

Tomorrow?

She was getting married *tomorrow*?

Good thing this was a business arrangement, because she wasn't feeling the slightest hint of excitement!

Shouldn't she be?

Feeling something, at least?

But, no, a quick mental scan of organs found nothing untoward.

Perhaps not surprising when it was a purely business arrangement, something that suited them both...

Although if she gave any thought to after the wedding—in fact, the wedding night—well, that was different.

Even this quick reminder of it had set her nerves jangling, her stomach tightening, and heat sweeping up through her body, about to betray her with a blush.

'Thank heavens for the hat!'

And it was only when Alex echoed her words—'Thank heavens for the hat?'—that she realised she'd spoken aloud.

'I'd be getting a sunburnt nose without it,' she said, pleased with herself for being so calm.

'You might have already caught a bit of the sun, even with the hat,' he said, smiling at her as if he knew full well that she was blushing.

'Then perhaps we should head back,' she said firmly, refusing to acknowledge his tease.

'Well, I have to call at the tailor,' he said. 'Will you walk that way with me or go up on your own?'

'The tailor—I'd forgotten all about her. Mine's a woman, I think the wife. I'll come with you, although they'll probably want me to try it on to see if it fits so I could be a while. You should go on ahead.'

He smiled at her, something she was beginning to wish he wouldn't do because it was very hard for her to maintain her cool composure when he did.

'Don't want me seeing you in your wedding dress before the big day,' he teased, totally destroying any cool at all.

'It's not a wedding dress and it's hardly that kind of wedding day,' she snapped.

And the infuriating man smiled again.

But they did visit the tailor together, Alex collecting his shirt in a plastic bag while Kenzie, as she'd supposed, was ushered behind the flimsy curtain.

'You go on ahead,' she said to Alex. 'I could be ages and your grandmother might need you.'

He hesitated, and for a moment she thought he was going to offer to wait, but in the end he gave her a nod and walked away—much to her relief.

It had to be the imminence of the wedding that had rattled her nerves on the beach.

Was she sure about this?

Of course not, because that was just a sensible arrangement.

No, it had been thinking of the after-wedding scenario that had sent blood thrumming through her veins.

She had to forget that and concentrate on practicalities!

Being married and having two kids was definitely the goal, and when Alex had suggested it, the idea had made sense. A nice, clean, business kind of arrangement that would suit them both.

Then why was she so uptight?

Had it been the hand-holding thing?

At first she'd welcomed his hand taking hers after the ordeal of lunch with Gran, but then to keep hold of it—for her to let him—well, it had seemed strange somehow—but nice strange…

Which was where her confusion lay…

Although wasn't it good that she'd felt comfortable holding his hand? Given the children idea, they were going to do much more intimate things than that.

And there it was again, the excited little flip in her chest, the beat of her heart sounding in her ears.

And here came that wretched blush again!

How had she never grown out of it, as all her friends had?

Her mother hadn't been a blusher—she'd checked that out with various people who'd known her.

So why her?

She sighed, and slid into the calf-length cream slip of a dress the tailor held over her head.

Studied the Kenzie in the mirror.

Could one dress really make that much difference?

She turned slowly, feeling the silk sliding over her skin—

'It's perfect,' she said to the beaming woman, although now her stomach was knotting in case it looked too much like a wedding dress.

Well, it *was* a wedding dress—not beaded with crystals or layered with appliqué—no train, no veil, just a simple cream Thai silk sheath.

And she felt beautiful in it.

'Thank you so much,' she said to the woman, taking her hands and pressing them softly to emphasise her delight.

'It was my pleasure,' the woman said, 'to dress so beautiful a bride.'

But when Kenzie went to pay, she was told Alex had already covered the cost, and the annoyance he could so easily arouse in her steamed to the surface.

How dared he?

Did he think she wouldn't be able to afford it?

That she was marrying him for his money?

Though dimly aware that she was building mountains out of molehills, she continued to feel aggravated by his behaviour.

Demanding to know how much he had paid, she thanked the woman once again and headed for the nearest cash machine, withdrawing not only enough to pay him back but enough to cover any other expenses that might arise.

With the dress in its plastic bag, folded carefully over her arm, she made her way through the market, pausing by a lingerie stall that seemed to sell nothing but very erotic nightwear in bright blue, purple or red.

But she'd lingered too long. A small girl who should surely have been at school had sidled up to her.

'Things for you are inside, lady,' she whispered, guiding Kenzie towards a small door and waving her hand towards a display of beautiful lingerie. Filmy silk now, not the slub silk of her wedding gown but beautifully embroidered nightdresses, some with matching negligées.

Well, why not have something special—something a bit more seductive than her short, almost threadbare cotton nightshirt with the kangaroo on the front of it?

She bought three of the lovely nightgowns but restricted herself to one negligée, then wondered if she'd ever wear any of them.

Of course she would, she assured herself, but with every passing moment the reality of what she was doing became less and less believable—kind of foggy and far off, not looming like the word 'tomorrow' had suggested.

CHAPTER SIX

THE SOFT CHIME of the doorbell wakened Kenzie, and she leapt up from the sofa where she'd fallen asleep, the book she'd been reading now lying on the floor.

Muriel was dining with some friends who'd just arrived, and having had the chicken on the beach, Kenzie had stayed in the suite, picking up the book to stop herself thinking about what lay ahead, especially with nerve endings tingling beneath her skin and her brain tossing what-ifs at her.

Tomorrow.

She opened the door to find the man she didn't want to think about standing there.

'I saw Muriel at dinner and thought this might be a good opportunity to talk about some practicalities.'

'Practicalities?' Kenzie echoed, still fuzzy from her short sleep.

He smiled at her.

'Business matters,' he said. 'Do you think I might come in?'

Suddenly aware they were still in the doorway, she stepped back to let him enter and shut the door behind him.

'Business matters?'

Damn and blast, she was behaving like a moron, repeating everything he said.

'It's a business arrangement,' he reminded her, but gently, touching her lightly on the shoulder and guiding her back to where she'd been sitting.

She still couldn't get her head around it, her mind now considering the warm patch on her shoulder where his hand had rested.

'Are you contracted to Muriel or the hotel? I need to speak to someone about that.'

Contract? Come on, Kenzie, get with it here! Of course you have a contract.

'I answered an ad for a nurse/companion the hotel put online, but it was specifically for Muriel. She'd arrived here and hadn't liked whoever was available for her, so the ad wanted someone who could start immediately, and immediately if not sooner was what I wanted.'

'So, I'll talk to the hotel about it.'

Was it that small sleep she'd had that made this sound confused?

And had she had confusion written clearly on her face that he took her hand and said, 'Kenzie, we'll be married. The big bonus for me, right now, is that I'll have some company. I've been bored out of my skull these last few weeks.'

'So you'll tell the hotel I'm working for you, not Muriel?'

He shook his head.

'You'll be *living* with me, not Muriel!'

And before she could make even a feeble protest—*or* allow herself to think about that statement, he added, 'How else can we get on with providing you with children.'

'But Muriel. I'll be letting her down. I thought we'd get married for your gran then go on as before. I can't just walk away from Muriel!'

He took her other hand and held them both captive in his.

And smiled, which was her undoing, for the meaning

of his words about the children finally dawned on her and she could feel that wretched heat searing her cheeks.

He touched a finger to her cheek.

'I love the way you blush. My mother used to—she hated it—but sometimes one look from my father was enough for the lovely rosiness to colour her cheeks.'

Hmph! There really wasn't anything she could say to that! Except...

'To get back to Muriel,' she said, 'I already know there's no one on staff she wanted for a companion, so I'd be letting her down. Couldn't we, you know—couldn't I—'

'Couldn't we sleep together in Gran's suite and you come bouncing down to play with Muriel during the day?'

Kenzie nodded.

'No!' he said, and just when she thought that was it— just no, he continued, 'It wouldn't be right. Besides which I've already spoken to Muriel about it—I'm the "friends" she had dinner with tonight. She's more than happy for you to move up to the penthouse with me. In fact, it was she who suggested I come and see you now, so you can pack your things to have sent up tomorrow. She's quite happily reading to Gran as we speak.'

Kenzie could only stare at him. Maybe it was the speed at which this was all happening that was boggling her mind, but, whatever it was, she found it impossible to frame a sensible sentence—let alone an objection to his high-handed ways.

Alex could almost read the thoughts flitting through her head. Who was he to be making all these arrangements? That was probably the foremost of them, for he already knew—or guessed—enough about her to know she was fiercely independent.

No doubt as a result of being brought up in an isolated area...

While the kindness he'd seen and sensed in her—who else would have ploughed on so valiantly in that conversation with Gran?—would have her worrying about Muriel.

'Muriel will be fine,' he said gently. 'In fact, I think Muriel has already made alternate arrangements, and while she'll miss having you at her beck and call all the time, you've more than done your duty, teaching her to ride.'

His bride-to-be looked up at this, and smiled.

'Can you imagine how empty her life must have been that she's embraced it so enthusiastically?'

He squeezed her fingers and admitted, 'Actually, I can. It wasn't until I came out here that I realised I'd filled my life with work—to the exclusion of everything else. And when I didn't have work I found I had nothing. It's made me realise a lot of things about myself—some of them not very positive,'

And still holding her hand in one of his, he slipped his arm around her shoulders and drew her closer.

'At least meeting you and Muriel put a stop to that,' he said, wondering if, with her lips so close, he should kiss her.

Or was intimacy, in a business marriage, something that should be discussed first?

Having no answer to that inner question, he kissed her cheek, and felt a shiver of reaction run through the body pressed to his.

She eased away, slowly enough to make it clear it wasn't a reaction to the chaste kiss, but apparently to study him, for she sat, still close, and looked at his face, her head tilted slightly as if that made it easier for her to take him in.

He half smiled, and she smiled back.

'It's just a bit weird, isn't it?' she said.

His own smile grew.

'More than a bit,' he said. 'Far more than a bit.'

She continued her survey for a few seconds more, then leaned over and kissed *his* cheek.

'Muriel's probably tired of reading now,' she said. 'And I need to pack.'

She stood up and he joined her, still holding her hand.

'Goodnight kiss?' he suggested, in part, at least, to see her cheeks colour up again.

Which they did, and seeing her so flushed and lovely, blue eyes wary but excitement there as well, how could he not kiss her?

A quick kiss on her lips—a butterfly kiss—because deep inside him he had become aware that once he kissed this woman properly, it was unlikely he'd want to stop.

The day finally dawned, Kenzie greeted by a huge bouquet of Australian native flowers, although how a local florist could have sourced such blooms, she had no idea.

She didn't have to look at the card to know they were from her father. 'For you, darling girl, from all of us on Spec,' the card read, and Kenzie closed her eyes against her tears and pictured everyone at home, gathering, as she was sure they would—mustering or not—to celebrate her wedding.

The maid who'd delivered them to Muriel's suite went off to find vases, while Kenzie selected three white flannel flowers and two fronds of pink Geraldton wax, to provide some colour, tying them into a simple bunch with a piece of the silk the tailor had given her, probably intending it for her hair.

But she'd inherited her hair from her mother and in photos of her parents' wedding day, her mother had worn her hair swept up, and unadorned, even by a veil.

Now Kenzie smiled through threatening tears as she pictured those photos, realising that the dress she'd had the tailor make for her was almost a replica of her mother's—a simple sheath!

Muriel bounced into the room at that stage, so excited Kenzie suggested she sit a while to calm down. Dressed in an elegant, fitted dress, almost the exact pink of the Geraldton wax flowers Kenzie had chosen, Muriel looked beautiful, and Kenzie could see why so many men had loved her.

'Love's not enough,' Muriel said, as if Kenzie had spoken the words aloud. 'I've given it a lot of thought, this marriage of yours, and I'm beginning to think it's probably a far more sensible way to go. A kind of business arrangement with sex as a bonus. People talk about falling in love, but the problem is so many of them, me especially, fall out of it as well. So love isn't nearly as good a basis for marriage as something that's practical and sensible.'

The conversation then turned to the flowers, which the maid was arranging in vases all around the room.

'But they are beautiful!' Muriel exclaimed. 'Now, tell me all their names!'

'Not now,' Kenzie said firmly. 'I've got to do my hair and then we both need to head up to the penthouse suite. I won't be long.'

She went back into her bedroom, Muriel's voice following her, complaining that Kenzie hadn't taken her boss up on a promise to pay for the hairdresser, as Alex had paid for the gown instead.

Feeling decidedly foolish in the soft, cream shirt that hung out over his trousers, Alex paced the balcony. Gran was as good as he'd seen her since they'd arrived, and was arrayed in a spectacular scarlet bed jacket.

The priest had arrived and was sitting by the bed, talking quietly to her, while Robert was fussing around the room, arranging, on every horizontal surface, masses of the local orchids that grew wild on the island.

Horizontal—now there was a word.

Damn his brain!

For some reason, it was beavering away with thoughts—and even some rather risqué images—of his wedding night.

Not a thought for the ceremony itself.

And for all he was getting married to please Gran, the fact that he'd been attracted to his bride from the moment they'd met was causing all manner of doubts in his head.

And for a man of thirty-five to be suffering teenage angst—what if she's not physically attracted to me?—was ridiculous.

He heard the soft chime of the doorbell and left his room to answer it, his breath catching in his throat as he saw the woman he was about to marry.

Her dark, dark hair swept up into a tumble of curls on the top of her head, a slim-fitting dress emphasising her curves, and little more than a dash of soft pink on her lips, and dark pencil enhancing her beautiful eyes, she was the loveliest thing he'd ever seen.

'Well,' Muriel said, bringing him back to earth with a thud. 'Are you going to ask us in?'

He held the door open, still wordless, and watched as she walked inside, going immediately to the bed set up in the huge lounge area where Gran was propped like a queen.

Now his wife-to-be was speaking softly to Gran, and he was still standing there holding the door.

'She does look beautiful, doesn't she?' Muriel said, linking her arm through his and drawing him away so she could close the door. 'And don't forget to tell her so—later, when you go to bed.'

Dear heaven, how was he going to get through this, especially now damn Muriel had put the 'bed' word back into his head. Okay, so it was five o'clock, the time when Gran was usually at her best, but even then there remained many hours to get through before—

He pulled himself together, and crossed the room, taking Kenzie's hand and telling her she looked beautiful. He would definitely tell her again later, but right now he needed to get with the programme.

The priest had left Gran's side, standing up, while Robert bustled about, positioning them behind a small table at the end of Gran's bed, the priest opposite them, Muriel by Kenzie's side, Robert himself finally taking his place beside the groom.

Him!

Kenzie's hand had turned so she clasped his as well, and somehow, with a pounding pulse and tingling nerves, words were said, promises exchanged, then Robert was popping the cork on an exorbitantly priced bottle of champagne, Kenzie was bent over Gran, explaining the flowers she was carrying were Australian natives, and Muriel had seated herself on one of the couches and was holding her champagne aloft in a toast to the newlyweds.

Not 'happy couple', Alex thought, and realised that he'd relaxed. All that stuff that had been going on in his head had been nothing more than nerves.

He took two fizzing glasses from Robert, and crossed to join Kenzie at Gran's side.

'Very sensible, my dear,' Gran was saying.

'And what has my wife—' he liked the sound of that '—been saying that's sensible?'

He handed one glass to Kenzie and raised his to toast her.

'Just that she's keeping her own name,' Gran replied. 'I suppose you were too carried away with the wedding to actually read the papers you were signing. I do wish your mother had kept Monroe—though she probably didn't think about it. People didn't, in those days.'

It took a moment for Alex to process this information. His brain *must* have been in a turmoil that he hadn't taken it in earlier.

But now he had processed it, he found he didn't like it.

'Because of your father?' he asked Kenzie. 'To keep the Steele name for this property you have?'

She grinned at him.

'No! There've been other names down through the generations, but I could hardly get around introducing myself as McKenzie McLeod, now could I?'

She paused, then said, 'Do you mind? I didn't think it would matter, given the kind of marriage we're going into. I should have talked to you about it but, really, you wouldn't want to be married to someone called McKenzie McLeod, now, would you?'

Those darned blue eyes were laughing at him now, and it was all he could do not to sweep her into his arms, champagne flutes and all, and kiss those pale pink lips.

Would she respond enthusiastically?

Would those eyes cloud over with desire?

He closed his own eyes momentarily and breathed deeply.

Fortunately, Muriel saved him any embarrassment by announcing food had arrived, and Robert had magicked the little table where they'd signed their certificates into a place where they could sit and eat.

'Your gran's tiring,' Kenzie whispered to him as they moved to the table.

And he turned to see she'd closed her eyes, and waved away the little silver table Robert was about to set up in front of her.

'I think we should go on down to my suite,' Muriel said quietly, and Robert nodded.

'I'll have the food sent down there,' he said.

'And I'll pop back to see Gran when we've eaten, in case she wakes again.'

Kenzie took his hand, and smiled at him.

'*We'll* come back and see her,' she said. 'I think she'd expect that.'

He gave the hand that held his a little squeeze, and accompanied the women out of the room.

Why this hand-holding thing was sending her heart into a flutter, Kenzie had no idea. This was a business arrangement, but the fluttering heart and the turmoil in her stomach seemed to think it was the real thing.

Well, it would be as far as—well, sex was concerned. They both wanted children so it was a given it would be part of the deal.

She followed Muriel and Alex out of the lift, and into Muriel's suite, pleased when Alex gave a gasp of astonishment at the array of flowers and insisted on learning what they all were.

And talking about the wildflowers eased her tension, so the three of them sat down to eat from the array of dishes Robert had ordered for them.

Not that Kenzie really wanted food, her mind too occupied with what lay ahead. It was all very well, getting married in a hurry, getting married for purely business reasons, but they'd only exchanged one kiss.

One very hesitant kiss—so hesitant it hardly counted.

She glanced sideways at the man she'd so recently married, and wondered what it would be like to kiss him properly. He had lovely lips, if you could say that about a man's lips—nicely shaped and full but not too full, and—

'Out of here, the pair of you,' Muriel said, so suddenly Kenzie almost fell off her chair. 'You've got better things to be doing than sitting around with an old woman. And, Kenzie, dear, I know you were concerned about me when Robert organised for all your things to be taken up to Alex's rooms in the suite, but I'll be just fine. In fact, Gan is going to shift into your room and be my companion. I've fixed it all with the hotel.'

Kenzie's mouth opened, but no sound came out, and she could only stare at her friend—well, employer really.

Then Alex was saying, 'That's grand! Thank you so much, Muriel, for all you've done for us both. We'll be off now.'

He caught Kenzie's hand in his, and all but dragged her to her feet before steering her inexorably towards the door.

Once in the lift, he pulled her closer to him, smiling down at her.

'That priest left out the "you may now kiss the bride" part of our wedding ceremony so I thought I'd do it now.'

Still trying to come to terms with Muriel and Gan, Kenzie could only stare at him, until his face was too close for focus, and his lips were on hers. It was a gentle hint of a kiss, but at the same time it was a promise.

More will come, it said.

More kisses and much, much more…

They had actually entered Alex's rooms—a small lounge room off his bedroom—before she realised they'd left the lift.

CHAPTER SEVEN

HE PUT HIS arms around her, and drew her to him, just holding her for a moment before kissing her again.

It was much more of a kiss than the earlier one, and it drew a response she couldn't remember ever feeling before. It heated blood not only in her silly cheeks but all through her body, so it seemed natural to press closer to his cool one.

And joined at the lips, they moved together, Kenzie unaware of the direction but, yes, it was into his bedroom.

Now his kiss became an exploration, his lips brushing the corners of her eyes, the small sensitive patch of skin beneath her ear, lips again, then trailing lower, always warm, but seeking, searching, learning her.

His ear was close, and she could kiss his jawline, slide her tongue along it, then up to touch his lips, bringing his lips back to give hers more attention.

Her lips parted to the gentle invasion of his tongue, then a few mumbled words—

Too many clothes?

Whatever!

Now he was sliding the zip down at the back of her dress, slipping it off her shoulders, while her own hands were clumsily undoing the buttons down his shirt.

Too slowly apparently, for he stripped it off over his head, baring his chest, a fuzz of dark hair across his breast.

She felt his skin against hers, as hot as hers, she rather thought, but thoughts were hard to come by as she lost herself in his pleasuring of her body.

'You are beautiful,' he said at some stage, the words muffled against her skin, tongue teasing at her nipples so she felt an ache between her thighs—an urgency for more.

All clothes gone now, he led her to the bed, but where she'd hoped for satisfaction, he was apparently far from finished with his exploration of her body.

Lips and fingers now, his mouth suckling gently at one breast, and then the other, making her hold his head more tightly to her.

His hands slipped between them, fingers finding her sensitive nub. Teasing it now as his arousal pressed against her body.

How could she not take him, hold him, make him groan in return. He slid one finger into her and she tensed at the invasion, liking it, needing it, needing more.

But Alex was obviously not a man to be hurried as he continued to tease her while her hands roved his body, until they somehow rolled together, her on top of him, her hands sliding his erection into her moist, throbbing body.

A brush of his hands across her breasts, and she gasped and bit back a moan as her body climaxed and she collapsed on top of him, moving to tempt him further into her, teasing him in turn by pulling away, but never right away until he, too, gave a soft cry and dropped back, bearing them both onto their sides, bodies still joined, faces close, his expression one of surprise. An expression she was fairly certain was mirrored on *her* face.

'It was as if our bodies already knew each other,' he

said at last, and Kenzie snuggled closer, knowing exactly what he'd meant.

Had they slept that she woke, his back spooned around her? Desire hardening him again, exciting her, so she pushed against him until, still half–asleep, she thought, he entered her again, but not asleep for his arm was around her, his fingers stroking as he moved until, together, they reached orgasms that drew cries from both of them.

Surely then they slept, though Kenzie dreamed she'd lain close to him, her hands on his body, his on hers…

A roaring noise woke Kenzie, confusing her with its unfamiliarity, but then the bed was also unfamiliar, and memory returned.

Memories, plural, most of which brought her ever-ready blush not just to her cheeks but to her entire body.

She was glad of the semi-darkness as she remembered the excitement and surprising delight of the previous night. That she could have found—quite by accident, really—someone who was so well matched to her in bed was unbelievable.

Unbelievably wonderful, really.

And for a moment she lay and revelled in it, until the noise she'd heard became louder, more terrifying somehow.

She reached out a tentative arm, but the other side of the bed was empty.

Had Alex heard the noise and gone to investigate?

She listened, heard different noises—like screams and wails of anguish—distinctive, although she was on the top floor of the palace.

Instinct had her slipping out of bed, heading for the large balcony outside, when she realised she was naked.

Back inside, rummaging through the clothes in the suitcase she hadn't had time—it had been the kiss that had done it—to unpack the previous night.

She pulled on shorts and a baggy top and made her way outside, finding Alex there—naked—staring down at a scene of devastation below them.

But not even the sight of his naked body, lean and firm, or memories of what she'd shared with that body during the night could distract her from what lay below them.

Water swirled through the village, dragging everything in its wake as it receded towards the sea.

'What is it?' she asked 'What's happened.'

He put his arm around her.

'Tsunami, I imagine, though I've only heard of them, not seen one. This water is from the second wave I've seen come in. They seem to be getting smaller.'

'A tsunami—but that won't only be affecting this island, it will be swilling around villages on all the islands and on the mainland coast. How do such terrible things happen?'

'They're usually the result of an underwater earthquake but there should have been warnings—sirens and things.'

'We have to go down there—people will need help.'

He turned, pulled her into his arms and kissed her hard and fast.

'We'll get dressed first.' He was guiding her back into the bedroom, all practicality now.

'Wear something solid like trainers on your feet. We should grab something to eat. Robert's probably seeing to that right now.'

Back in their rooms, she stripped off the clothes she'd pulled on. She definitely needed undies, and jeans. Jeans were tough. And that long-sleeved cotton shirt.

Ignoring the scent their lovemaking had left on her body—there was no time for a shower—she pulled on her clothes and met Alex in the small lounge room where he was already tucking into sandwiches while Robert packed a backpack with towels and a first-aid kit that looked large enough to belong in an ambulance.

'I've got a backpack,' she said as she grabbed a sandwich and hurried from the room as she bit into it. 'Bottled water, Robert,' she called back over her shoulder.

She emptied out her smaller backpack and carried it back to where Robert had produced a dozen bottles of water.

'We'll put the first-aid kit and a couple of bottles of water into yours and I'll take the rest of the water,' Alex said, and within minutes, still chomping on sandwiches, they left the room, having to run down the fire stairs as the lift wasn't working.

'This place has a generator so there'll be power before long,' Alex said, as they went down and down the twisting stairway. 'I wonder if the hospital was affected. It's further down the slope of the mountain.'

Kenzie closed her eyes momentarily and prayed things wouldn't be as bad as they had seemed from up high, but the lower they went, the clearer the anguished cries of torment and grief became.

Finally, on the ground floor, they found the manager already organising staff to clear the grand entrance foyer. He took one look at Alex and Kenzie and said, 'You can send people here. We have staff who can treat the injured or at least make them comfortable, and we can feed as many as we need to—water isn't a problem as we have our own spring.'

Alex nodded and turned to Kenzie.

'You should stay and help here,' he said.

'You think?' she replied, with a look that stopped further conversation.

They jogged down the drive, past the stables where

the stablehands were trying to calm terrified animals—but at least it was dry, which meant any houses this high up would be okay.

But around the next bend they reached the high-water mark of the deadly tide that had devastated the tropical paradise. It must have swept in in the darkness then roared out again, taking houses, people and animals with it. All that was left was debris—a fallen palm here, the frond roof of a house there, broken bits of furniture, overturned cars and smashed tuk-tuks.

They'd both stopped, unable to believe the scene in front of them, then a cry from the left had them both turn that way.

A man was slumped against a still standing palm, crying out from pain and terror.

'Just be careful where you put your feet,' Alex said, in such a commanding voice Kenzie would probably have saluted had the situation not been so grim.

Stumbling through the chaos, they reached the man, who seized Alex's hand and babbled something totally incomprehensible.

Which obviously didn't bother Alex at all. He was crouched by the man, soothing him with words his listener wouldn't have understood either.

The man's right arm hung at an ugly angle from his shoulder. As Alex continued to examine the man, Kenzie reached into his backpack and drew out a bottle of water, holding it to the man's lips.

'I think it's just that shoulder,' Alex said as she bent close to him. 'Let's see if we can get him up, and we'll support him back to the stables and get one of the lads to take him up the palace. They'll have some form of pain relief in their pharmaceutical products.'

They eased the man to his feet.

'If you put his left arm around my shoulder I can take him,' Kenzie said. 'There'll be so many more that need help.'

Alex shook his head.

'You and I will stick together. We won't be the only able bodies out helping the injured, and we can do more together than separately.'

They'd reached the road and turned towards the stables when they heard the high-pitched crying of a child.

'You take him,' Kenzie said. 'I won't go far—just over there.'

She pointed to the ruin that had obviously been a house at one stage.

'I'll wait for you there, or come this way and meet up with you again,' she said to cut off his objection.

The cry was desperate, and she didn't wait for Alex to agree, simply headed off towards the noise, calling out that she was coming, although the likelihood of the child understanding her was slim.

She reached the wrecked building, seeing where the front wall had been sucked away by the receding wave. A tiny child, maybe one or two, sat on the ground in the middle of what once had been a room, screaming in terror at his abandonment in this devastated environment.

Still talking to him, soothingly and quietly now, she reached the child and knelt, smiling in spite of her concern. Felt all over his small body but could find no broken or dislocated bones.

She lifted him then, and held him close.

He'd been sitting near a grubby piece of material, possibly a sarong, and after rubbing him with a towel to dry and warm him, she fashioned a sling around her neck so she could carry him in front of her, his wails growing quieter as he was held close to her warm body.

Alex joined her and smiled at her inventiveness.

'He seems unhurt, just so dreadfully alone.'

Alex rubbed his hand over the child's head and drew a smile from the tiny boy.

'I'd offer to carry him but there may be debris to move and we don't want him harmed,' he said. 'And we'll stay up here near this tide mark as I think I'm right in saying they come as a series, these waves—the big one then maybe five or six to follow. I've seen two, so they should be getting much smaller.'

They'd treated five more people, most for minor wounds, before they found a woman curled up on the ground, a deep wound on her right thigh.

Alex knelt beside her, while Kenzie pulled out a water bottle and flushed the wound as best she could, then took some disinfectant from the first-aid kit and dabbed that around it.

'It needs stitching, but I'll wrap it tightly to stop further bleeding,' Alex said, but he looked worried.

Kenzie turned and saw what he'd seen—a long line of people making their way to the palace.

'You think we'd do more good up there?' she asked, and he nodded.

'I'm sure we would,' he said. 'Look down below us, there are many people out searching, and if you see the number of people heading up the hill, even if they aren't all injured, we should be there, helping.'

He reached out and wiped some dirt off her sleeve— smiled—and her body shivered with the memories of the intense passion they'd shared.

'But first we need to get this woman up there. I've checked her out and her left ankle's very swollen—she won't even be able to limp along.'

He hesitated, looking around before turning to Kenzie.

'She's small. Do you think you're up to helping carry her, if we cross our arms and she sits between us? We need only get as far as the road, where someone else will surely help.'

'We have to get her to her feet first,' Kenzie pointed out.

Together they bent over the woman once more, Alex explaining what they needed to do, although it was doubtful she understood. But once they had her on her feet, Alex supporting her against his body, she seemed to understand what they were doing, and not only sat on their joined hands but put her arms around their necks to keep herself balanced there.

Alex had already taken Kenzie's backpack and had it slung over his free shoulder, so they turned towards the road and made their way unsteadily through the debris towards it.

'You okay?' he asked. 'We could put her down while you go ahead to get help.'

She grinned at him.

'I'm fine. We breed 'em tough in northern Australia!'

He flashed a smile in her direction then nodded to the now sleeping child.

'Breed 'em tough here, too, the way he's sleeping with your arm squashed against him.

'I'm trying *not* to squash him,' she retorted, 'although I realise now I should have moved him to my back before we set out. But if I stop now, we'll never make it.'

They plodded on, and were almost at the road when they were spotted, two apparently uninjured men coming towards them.

'We will take her,' one said, and Kenzie smiled at him, pleased he could speak English but even more pleased to be relieved of one of her burdens.

Alex organised the transfer, then took Kenzie's hand and they all walked together up the hill…

Chaos reigned at the Palace of Peace and Contentment.

Alex took one look, and told Kenzie to go and get cleaned up, then found the manager, who was staring around at his beautiful foyer with a look of dazed incredulity.

'Most of these people aren't hurt but all of them could be carrying any manner of germs, so could you stand up somewhere and tell all those who are not injured to go over to the swimming pool and shower in the cabana there?' He told the man. 'They can wash their clothes and put them back on, then stay outside in the sun, unless they have an injured child and need to return to him or her.'

The man nodded.

'I'll send some staff to keep them in order while they wait,' he said. 'We *have* tried to keep the badly injured away from the less injured, but it's hard with so many people.'

'You just get the uninjured out, and have staff down by the stables to stop more uninjured coming. I know they'll want to look for loved ones, but right now we need to help those who need help.'

He left the manager climbing a few steps to get above the crowd and went to where people lay on a line of beds.

They must have pulled every unused bed from the suites above him. The man with the injured shoulder was sitting on the end of one of them, talking quietly to a woman who lay on it.

Someone—one of the nursing staff presumably—had fashioned a sling for him, and given him pain relief for him to be speaking so clearly in what was probably his second language.

He'd make a handy interpreter, Alex decided, and asked his name.

'Lamon,' the man replied, smiling brightly.

He'd definitely been given pain medication.

'Have you spoken to this woman?' Alex asked.

'It is her back, she cannot move her toes,' Lamon said.

'The hospital?' Alex asked, and the man shook his head.

'Water all through it, though the building is still standing. But the helicopter, it is all right, up there on the top,' Lamon told him.

Which meant that they could get the badly injured to hospital on the mainland if they could find the pilot.

He'd moved to the next bed, where a man lay on his side in the recovery position, while an older woman, he presumed a nurse, was washing mud from his body.

'It's hard to tell if they're hurt, with all the mud,' she said, then her eyes filled with tears.

'My family, down in the village, all the people are saying the village is gone.'

Alex patted her shoulder, checked the man's pulse and wondered where, in the Palace of Peace and Contentment, he'd find a stethoscope, thermometer, and boxes of gloves.

At least!

'Here we are,' a bright voice said behind him, and, while his body thrilled to the voice, he turned to find Kenzie, not only clean, and with the small child now strapped to her back, but pushing a trolley with a goodly array of medical equipment on it.

'Do we need the baby? Could you not find anyone to take him?'

'I didn't try,' his new bride said. 'He knows me now, and what's more, if he's there on my back someone might recognise him and claim him.'

Alex nodded. She was obviously thinking more clearly than he was.

'Antiseptic will be the big problem,' she told him now. 'Their storeroom doesn't seem to keep it in gallon containers like we do at the hospital.'

He grinned at her, ignoring the very surprising memories of the night before—that they'd been so physically well suited was nothing short of a miracle—and reached out for a stethoscope.

'This is Lamon,' he said, gesturing towards his helper. 'And I've a horrible feeling that this man on the bed has inhaled some of the mud he must have been buried in.'

He'd adjusted the stethoscope and was leaning over to listen to the man's chest as he spoke.

'That's two who should be in hospital,' he said as he straightened.

They found the woman with the cut thigh in the next bed. Lamon talked quietly to the woman in her own language while Kenzie undid their rough bandage and he, Alex, checked her chest.

It sounded clear, but the wound Kenzie had now revealed was far uglier than he'd thought in the dim light of early dawn.

'Is there much local anaesthetic?' he asked, and Kenzie shook her head.

'Ten ampoules,' she told him, 'and I'd say that wound needs a couple.'

'We treat her!' he said, in a no-nonsense voice. 'Holding onto some and finding it's not needed would be worse than not having some for someone further down the line. Other help will come. Emergency response teams will be gathering all around the world and by tomorrow the first will arrive.'

Obscurely comforted by his optimistic words, she pulled

on clean gloves and picked up some tweezers, broke them out of their sealed bag, then leaned in to tweeze tiny pieces of grit from the wound.

Alex watched as he changed his gloves and found an ampoule of local anaesthetic, drawing it up into a syringe.

'Try squirting the debris out with a syringe filled with water,' he suggested. 'Leave it a few minutes for the anaesthetic to work. I'll give her two.'

And though he was concentrating on his patient, he was also aware of Kenzie by his side as she tidied the dirty bandages into the bin on the bottom shelf of the trolley, adjusted the precious bundle on her back, and filled a syringe with water.

Weird how just looking at her brought warmth to his body even in this emergency situation.

Ignoring thoughts he shouldn't be thinking, Alex sorted through the things Kenzie had scavenged for the trolley, finding plenty of sutures.

Were the usual guests at the palace so clumsy that sutures were often needed, or had they been ordered in bulk and not used?

'I think that's clean, I'll check ahead,' Kenzie said. 'There are two French nurses on staff here and they're working from the other end, but now someone's cleared away all the onlookers, it's much easier to see what's what.'

Practical woman! Alex thought with a sense of gratitude that by pure luck he'd found her.

Concentrate on the job!

He bent low over the patient, setting the sutures carefully into place, leaving the ends to trim off later. She'd need antibiotics—would the palace have a supply of them as well?

'Alex!'

Kenzie called to him from two beds down.

'Two minutes,' he told her and finished his job, smearing antibacterial cream over the wound before covering it with a padded dressing and bandaging it again.

The man two beds down was another who definitely should be in hospital, with his broken tibia poking through his skin.

'There's a note saying he's been given morphine for the pain, but we can't fix this, can we?' Kenzie said.

Alex knelt to study the wound, shaking his head at the severity of the break.

'There's some bleeding but no major vessel involvement. We can fashion a splint,' he told her. 'Did you see anything that looked like splint material when you raided the supply cupboard?'

Kenzie shook her head, frowned, then said, 'No, but when I was searching for the supply cupboard I noticed some wooden packing cases out the back of the building. I'm sure we could rip the slats off them to use. Pad them with something soft and they'll be fine. I'll go and get some. Three?'

But before he could speak, she was gone.

Time to move on—he'd return to the man when Kenzie came back, though he couldn't imagine what would come in wooden packing cases.

He was too busy to wonder what was taking her so long until she returned, holding up three padded and bandage-wrapped pieces of wood that he knew he could fashion into an open splint to protect the leg when the patient was transported.

When? That was the question, and, he supposed, how? He doubted boats would put to sea while the waves from the tsunami were still making the waters dangerous.

With Kenzie's help and a little ingenuity, he then

splinted the man's leg and bandaged it to protect the open wound and jagged edge of the bone.

'Time for a break, you two,' a voice said, and there was Muriel, with a middle-aged man, presumably Gan, smiling beside her. He was pushing a trolley with an urn on it, paper cups, milk and sugar, teabags and little sachets of coffee.

On the lower shelf were piles of sandwiches.

'It was all I could think of to do that might help,' Muriel said, in rather apologetic tones. 'The kitchen staff are all too busy making soup and rice for all the people outside. And, of course, meals for the guests, most of whom really want to leave,' she added. 'So Gan and I did this.'

But Alex, suddenly realising he was famished, practically hugged her.

'Now stop,' she said, in her usual commanding way, 'and have a proper break while you drink and eat. Just tell me what you want to drink and I'll fix it, then help yourself to sandwiches and go sit on the steps and eat them.'

Alex glanced over to the grand, sweeping stairway that was a feature of the palace's foyer and was relieved to see half a dozen people sitting there, all eating and drinking, no one talking much, except in occasional murmurs.

CHAPTER EIGHT

NIGHT HAD FALLEN before they had all the patients still on the premises as comfortable as they could make them. But more were still dribbling in and Alex was trying to persuade Kenzie to go up to the room and have a rest.

One of the local staff had recognised the baby, and was happy to care for him, no doubt because she, like so many others here, had lost family in the village.

They joined the manager on the stairs, and saw the pain on the man's face.

'So many of our household staff and nurses lived in the village. A few have been found and come to us here, but I fear the loss will be great.'

It was such a sobering thought there was silence for a moment.

'Can you carry on?' Alex eventually asked.

The manager nodded.

'We have enough live-in nurses to cover the guests here at the moment, if they accept extra shifts, which they all will. But after this, without the village, will people even want to come?'

Seeing a large man, his right arm swathed in bandages up to his shoulder, coming through the door, Kenzie left Alex talking to the manager and headed for the new victim.

He was tall, and solidly built, and liberally sprinkled

with mud. What she could see of the skin on his face was grey with pain and fatigue.

But before she could reach him, he planted both feet on the floor and in a voice that could probably have been heard on the mainland, called out, 'I don't suppose any of you can fly a chopper.'

'I can,' Kenzie responded, walking quickly towards him. 'We use them for mustering back home.'

'Good,' he said. 'The chopper's fine, I just can't fly it, but word is you have some people with bad injuries. We can take two on stretchers, and two seated. One of my boys is bringing the stretchers now.'

Bemused by the conversation—it had been a very long day—Kenzie said, 'You want me to fly your chopper. I'd have no idea where to go.'

'I'll be with you, mate,' he said, the last word convincing her that he was, as she'd thought from his accent, another Aussie.

'Are you mad?'

Alex was standing beside her, one hand on her shoulder. 'You're going to fly this man's helicopter?'

'Well, he can't,' Kenzie said, pointing at the man. 'He's barely made it here. If I get him over to a mainland hospital, there's sure to be another pilot who can fly it back with me, *and* whatever medical supplies I can scrounge because you know as well as I do there are still more people coming in.'

'Ah, here's my boy. Where are your patients?' the stranger said.

Kenzie turned to see a young Thai man holding two collapsible stretchers.

'Maybe the man with the leg wound can sit,' she said, turning to Alex who was looking slightly dazed.

'You can't go flying off in some strange helicopter,' he said, then smiled ruefully. 'That was a stupid thing to say, wasn't it? You wouldn't have offered if you couldn't do it. I really don't know why I'm surprised.'

And still shaking his head, he took the stretchers from the young man and carried them over to their two unconscious patients.

The French nurses who'd been enjoying a break on the stairs immediately went to help him, while Kenzie led the stranger—stranger? Angel of mercy, more like—over to the man with the badly broken leg.

'I'm Kenzie,' she said as they made their way across the foyer, 'and the man you were talking to is Alex, a Scottish doctor.

'Brad,' the man said, holding out his left hand. 'Nice to meet another Aussie.'

But that was going to be the limit of any conversation for the man was clearly exhausted and, of course, Muriel had appeared from nowhere with Gan and the food and drink trolley.

While she hurried Brad over to the stairs, and Alex and the two nurses were getting the wounded onto stretchers, she reached the man with the broken leg and was glad to find Lamon, who'd acted as interpreter for them all day, sitting on the floor by the man's bed.

'We want to take him over to the hospital on the mainland in the helicopter,' she told Lamon, 'but he will have to sit up. We'll make him as comfortable as possible. Could you ask him if he thinks he can manage that?'

Lamon spoke to the very drowsy patient, who nodded and proceeded to sit up on the bed.

'No, just wait,' Kenzie said, holding up her hand. 'We need to work out how we're going to get you to the helicopter.'

'I'll find you help,' Lamon said, and disappeared out the

door, returning only minutes later with five men, mostly young and all fit-looking.

'Some of my soccer team,' Lamon said proudly, and Kenzie nodded at them all.

'They were by the pool, safe, not like so many others, even my family,' Lamon said, and Kenzie could only wonder at how the survivors were going to cope when the shock of the tsunami was over and reality set in.

'Here's a chair.' Alex had appeared by her side, holding both a chair and a sheet. 'I feel I should come, but the woman with the head wound will need the other seat.'

The concern on his face was evident, and the fact that he wanted to travel with them all—and her especially?—warmed her heart.

'And you're far more useful here,' she said. 'Because wounded people are still being found and brought in.'

He nodded, but looked far from happy.

Because she could fly a helicopter and he couldn't?

Probably not, she told herself. Perhaps he cared?

She dismissed that thought as well, and listened to his explanation.

'If we tie our man with the broken leg into it, he can be carried to the chopper. The splint at the back of his leg comes up above his knee so it can't be bent. I'll take one side so I can be sure the injured leg doesn't crash into anything.'

Kenzie could only watch as he and Lamon set up the makeshift ambulance and settled the man on it. Soccer players were already lifting the stretchers, and Brad, revived no doubt by food and coffee, was giving orders about the best way to get along the side of the hill.

'There's a better track above the high-water mark,' Lamon said. 'All the boys know it. Just follow them.

'We don't know what's under the top layer of mud,' Lamon said to Alex, 'so it's best to stay on the track.'

Brad was plodding valiantly along, while Kenzie had Adele, one of the French nurses, help her with the woman with the heavily bandaged head.

They were soon plunged into darkness as they entered the thick jungle, and now only torches supplied by the hotel lit the way.

It seemed to take for ever—first to reach the helicopter, and then to get everyone settled and strapped in.

Alex helped Kenzie into the pilot's seat, held her hand for a moment, his eyes on hers, unreadable.

Finally, he gave her hand a squeeze, and said, 'Come back safe.' And something in those softly spoken words brought tears to her eyes.

Brad climbed into the seat next to her.

'I've done a ground inspection,' he said, as she began checking the controls. It was an unfamiliar aircraft, but having flown many different choppers she knew the set-up would be similar and easy to handle.

'It's only a twenty-minute flight to the city,' Brad said, 'but the chopper might not make it back tonight. The other side will be as bad as this and a spare pilot might be hard to find.'

He was speaking across her to Alex, who merely nodded, touched Kenzie's hand again and shut her door.

'I don't have a commercial licence,' Kenzie said, as she started the engine.

Brad smiled tiredly at her.

'Do you think those folk we've got back there will care?'

He strapped himself in, handed headphones to Kenzie and put his own on.

'Just take her up and head east,' he said. 'I'll alert the authorities we're airborne and give you directions. No good trying the hospital we usually use on the coast. That will be in chaos. We'll go to the regional hospital in town. We can land on the roof there.'

He was leaning back, his eyes closed as he spoke, and as Kenzie lifted them into the air and headed east, she hoped like hell he didn't pass out completely or she'd be flying around looking for a building with a big helicopter cross on a pad on its roof.

She could fly a *helicopter*?

Alex had headed back along the track, his eyes on the noisy aircraft until he plunged into the darkness of the forest and the sound of it slowly died away.

He wondered why he was surprised. This was a woman who'd agreed to marry him when she barely knew him, why wouldn't she have a helicopter licence?

Yet a knotted feeling deep in his gut, suggested he wasn't quite as relaxed about this as he'd have liked to be.

He arrived back at the hotel, and after checking on the other wounded went upstairs to shower and see his grandmother.

'She's been in a deep sleep all day,' Robert told him. 'Which is probably just as well. It would not be good for her to see what has happened.'

'You're right,' Alex replied, feeling heavy hearted himself over the destruction. 'I'll have a shower and come and sit with her.'

'You should sleep,' Robert said sternly, and Alex found a tired smile.

'I can sleep in the chair after I've read a little more of the story.'

He went through to his own rooms to peel off his dirty clothes and shower. And as he walked through the bedroom, how could he not help but look at the bed, pristinely made, yet all he saw was Kenzie, naked in the rumpled sheets.

He shook his head, thinking again of their night of lovemaking—thinking how unlikely it had been—two people who barely knew each other being so well matched in passion.

But the thought that followed was less pleasing—an image of Kenzie at the controls of the helicopter, imagining her flying over the devastation on both sides of the gulf—

With the shower on full blast, he washed away further thoughts of accidents, and of the devastation they'd both seen. She'd be over land again by now, and he was thankful for the darkness, as if it might prevent her seeing how bad things were on the mainland shore.

He knew from memories of the last huge tsunami in the Indian Ocean that over one hundred thousand people had lost their lives. And as he rubbed himself dry, he sent a silent prayer to any god who might be listening that the death toll from this one would not be as horrendous.

Kenzie, exhausted but pleased Brad had found someone to fly back to the island, made her way along the track. The new pilot had elected to stay with the aircraft, explaining he could be called back for some rescue work.

The young Thai who was Brad's offsider met them, and said he'd organise to get the medical supplies she'd picked up down to the palace in the morning.

So she walked alone, concentrating on putting one foot in front of the other, so she could make it back.

A shower, then sleep—sleep for ever, the way she felt.

Was Alex at least resting?

Would his ER conscience let him go up to his rooms and sleep, or keep him on the ground floor with the patients?

He wasn't there, she discovered, coming in to find

nurses she hadn't seen before cleaning and bandaging wounds, Housekeeping staff cleaning the floors—a full-time job, it seemed.

'We're night staff usually,' one of nurses told her, 'but others are doing our shift and some of our guests have said to help here rather than stay with them. The doctor has his pager. We call him if he's needed.'

Pleased that at least in this corner of the island things were peaceful at the moment, Kenzie made her way up to the penthouse, grateful the lift was now working. No way would she have made it up the fire-escape stairs.

No Alex in the room. The surge of disappointment surprised her as she'd believed she was too exhausted to feel any kind of unnecessary emotion.

But once she'd showered and pulled on her familiar old T-shirt that had been serving her as nightwear, she found she didn't want to get into the bed on her own.

She crept through the small sitting area, quietly opening the door into the larger room where his grandmother lay.

He was reading to her, something she didn't recognise, but the sound of his voice was so soothing she crept a little further in and lay down on the sofa, pulling a cushion beneath her head and falling asleep immediately.

Too exhausted to read for a moment longer, Alex closed the book and put it on the small side-table. He took his grandmother's hand, and held it as he eased the chair back into a comfortable position and closed his eyes.

He was on the edge of sleep when a muffled sound, more a small snort than a snore, had him sitting bolt upright. Thinking it must have been one of Gran's nurses, he looked around but there was no one moving in the room.

Another small sound, barely there, and he stood up.

Kenzie was on the sofa, sound asleep, her hands tucked

under her head, a T-shirt with an animal of some kind on it covering her slim and beautiful body.

He looked around the darkened room, subtly lit by a few low-set nightlights, and found a soft angora throw he'd bought for Gran many years ago.

Carefully, he tucked it around his sleeping wife—he liked the word—liked even thinking it in his head.

Probably the novelty of it?

He smiled to himself, suspecting it could be more than that…

No, more likely exhaustion creating fancies in his head…

Back in his chair, he closed his eyes, content to be where he was—and somehow pleased that Kenzie was so close to him.

Was it the movement of Gran's hand in his that woke him?

Whatever! He was awake, and in the slow dawning of the new day he could see she was, too.

Her fingers stroked the back of his hand, fleetingly, a touch barely there, her lips parted, and she breathed his name. 'Alexander Monroe…'

No, not his name at all but her husband's!

She smiled, her eyes closed, and as her breathing changed, he leant in and kissed her cheek.

'I love you, Gran,' he whispered, and as his stomach knotted and his heart clenched with sadness, he knew it was goodbye.

CHAPTER NINE

KENZIE WOKE NOT to wails of terror this time but the clatter-clacking noise of a helicopter.

She looked around, her head woolly with sleep, certain she hadn't gone to bed in Alex's bed when she had got back from the mainland.

And the chopper she could hear wasn't the one she'd flown last night.

Was Alex right? Was aid beginning to come in to the devastated village?

Alex?

Where was he?

His side of the bed certainly hadn't been slept in.

She eased out of bed, smiling when she saw her night attire—habit had taken her back to her comfy old T-shirt...

All but sleepwalking, she made her way into the shower, hoping a good drenching would wake her up, because there were sure to be things she could still be doing to help the stricken island.

She found herself wanting—almost needing—to see Alex. To be near him, not even talking to him, just, yes, needing to see him.

A workaholic from all accounts, he'd be downstairs where survivors would still be coming in. The aid coming in would organise large-scale rescues, all to plan, and set up temporary shelters, arrange food and water, but until they could complete their preparations people would still come here.

And she should be there, helping.

She dressed in knee-length shorts and a sensible shirt, and slipped her feet into trainers, realising as she did up the laces that she was hungry.

Very hungry!

Hopefully, Muriel and Gan would still be manning their food trolley.

As she opened the door leading out to the penthouse foyer, she was greeted by Robert.

'I have been listening for you to wake up,' he said, and she smelled coffee and Danish pastries, and could have hugged the man.

She followed him as he carried it into the small sitting room.

'Mrs Monroe?' she asked, and Robert shook his head.

'Still alive, but barely. Alex spent the night by her bed, and now has gone downstairs to help where he can. He has a pager, you know, and I can get him back here any time.'

Kenzie nodded, and sat down beside the tray, wondering why she'd never given a minute's thought to what would happen when Alex's grandmother did die.

Because too much had happened too soon?

Because she'd seen this marriage as an answer to her immediate desires and not thought much beyond that.

So think now.

Presumably he'd want to fly her body back to her beloved Scotland.

And he would accompany it, for there'd certainly be nothing to keep him here.

Drink your coffee and eat a pastry, she told herself, aware that she was still tired enough to get weepy over trifles.

Not that Gran's death would be a trifle.

It would be a blessed release both for her and for Alex, but that wouldn't stop Alex feeling a heavy load of grief.

Should she go with him?

Would he want her to?

Would he accept whatever concern and support she could offer?

Useless thinking! Eat your pastry, drink your coffee, and get downstairs to find something useful to do.

Alex's heart stopped for an instant, as his wife, lovely hair neatly plaited back behind her head, came into the foyer.

She's beautiful, was his first thought, then his heart stuttered momentarily, but before she could tell him Gran had died—the thought that had caused the stutter—she smiled at him and he knew all was well.

Although 'well' was hardly the current state of affairs in his life, what with his grandmother, the complete devastation of this beautiful island, and the grief and hopelessness of its gentle people.

But still smiling she came towards him.

'Robert says you're to go up and have what he calls a proper breakfast, including black pudding no doubt.' She grimaced as if she'd once tried that particular treat and hadn't been impressed. 'But I told him you probably wouldn't. Have you had any more serious casualties while I was skiving off—sound asleep in bed?'

'Two have gone up to the hospital helicopter, and will be going straight into hospital, but most of the others are patch up their wounds and wait. The pilot who flew you back came down this morning with the medical supplies you brought with you, and that's been a great help.'

He paused, unsure whether to tell her more.

Leave her smiling?

She had such an open, happy smile…

'But?' she said. 'And don't deny there is a but, I could hear it in your voice.'

He smiled and touched her lightly on the shoulder.

Wanting to touch her.

Needing to touch her?

'The pilot is reluctant to take any but the most serious of cases to the hospital as it's already been overrun from people affected on the mainland coast.'

He paused, thinking about what he'd experienced in emergency situations like these.

'He's right!' he added. 'Over here the rescue teams will have a field hospital set up in no time, including, even here on the island, a small but efficient operating theatre.'

'I'd read about that kind of response,' she said, frowning slightly as she considered the information. 'Fully staffed?'

'Not the first response team because they bring with them everything *they* need for a few days from food and water, to accommodation, showers, etcetera, and mostly first-aid equipment. They can assess the situation and advise what else is needed and when. Sanitation is usually the most important practical issue, then food and accommodation, although that will be further down the list here where it's not raining or snowing.'

'You've done this before?" she asked, surprise evident in both the question and her face.

'Earthquake in northern Italy,' he said briefly, 'and once in northern Greece after a massive forest fire.'

She shook her head.

'No wonder you've found being here so frustrating. It makes what you're doing for your grandmother even more impressive.'

'Even more?' he echoed, a smile tugging at his lips. 'You've been impressed?'

'Very,' she said firmly. 'Now, stop fishing for compliments and tell me what I can do. Who needs a nurse right now?'

I do was hardly an appropriate answer, so he took her along the line of beds, explaining each injury, pointing out those with fluid bags nearly empty, and other patients who needed new dressings on their wounds.

He'd reached the final patient, the woman whose leg they'd stitched—kept in because of the unsanitary conditions outside and needing to keep an eye on her wound.

'How's she doing?' Alex asked the nurse, but her reply was interrupted by his pager going off in his pocket.

'I'm sorry, I have to go, it's Gran, but I wanted to check the patients first.'

He was looking so worried Kenzie touched his arm and looked into his eyes.

'Go,' she said. 'She's the one who matters now—she and you!'

But as he left, she wondered what lay ahead.

Within minutes, the manager had appeared at the reception desk—kept in a clear, red-roped off space on the far side of the foyer.

Another man, the assistant manager, she thought, soon joined them, and some weighty discussion was obviously going on.

Then a maid appeared at Kenzie's shoulder.

'Mr Robert in the penthouse called. He asks for you to come.'

Gran's dead.

That was all it could be.

Had Alex been in time to say goodbye.

These thoughts chased her to the lift and, as she rose to

the top floor, they kept at bay all the uncertainty of what lay immediately ahead.

A pale but dry-eyed Alex met her at the door.

'Your gran has died?'

He nodded, and she hesitated, but for only an instant, before wrapping her arms around him and holding him against her.

Was it the wrong thing to do?

For all they were married and had definitely enjoyed their wedding night, they barely knew each other as people, but instinct told her bereaved people needed physical comfort.

Even Alex?

She was thinking of pulling back when he moved, his arms going around her, holding her close, his cheek resting against her head.

He eased her into the room and closed the door, still holding tightly to her.

'I'll have to take her home to Scotland,' he said, 'to be buried near the husband she so loved. There's been a plane on standby over on the mainland for weeks now. It's been free to do other local flights but always aware this was coming up.'

Barely understanding the logistics of this, she nodded, then leaned away enough to tip her head so she could see his face.

'Would you like me to come with you? It would be a long way home with only your memories for company.'

A slight smile tilted one corner of his lips.

'That would be a very wifely thing to do.'

It was a half-tease, and the tension in her body eased. He would have come to terms with his grandmother's death some time ago, so maybe his grief now would be easier to handle.

'I *am* your wife!' she reminded him, then paused before adding, 'But no black pudding!' so she could see a proper smile.

He released her, stepping back and running his hand through his hair—looking more distracted than she'd ever seen him.

'There's so much to think about, even though I made all the plans, step by step, before we came out here, but now...'

'Now you can't think about them, so do whatever needs to be done first—the plane presumably—and we'll think about the rest later.'

'You *will* come?'

He sounded so hopeful she felt a flutter of excitement, not exactly in her heart but definitely in the region of her chest.

'Of course,' she said, and he smiled and pulled her close again.

'Thank you,' he said. 'I'm back on track now.'

She eased away from him.

'That sounds more like the man I know. Can I help?'

He looked at her for a moment.

'Pack?' he said, and smiled. 'Though I imagine your island clothes won't be quite sufficient for our Edinburgh winter.'

'I'll get something when I get there,' she said. 'I'm sure they have shops in Edinburgh.'

'If you don't mind wearing my clothes until you get to the shops,' he said.

He bent and kissed her lightly on the lips.

'I must rush,' he said. 'We've got a helicopter coming for us at four. It'll land on the hospital pad in the city. Can you be ready by then?'

'Of course,' she said, and went over to the door that led to their two rooms.

Of course, she didn't have anything suitable for an Edinburgh winter, but there were online shops all over the world. If she got busy now, they could have some clothes waiting for her by the time she arrived.

She'd need an address—but Robert would have that. Save her bothering Alex.

Robert would know what she should buy—and where!

She had a feeling the where was important for the people who inhabited Alex's world.

Robert not only told her where but produced a list of what she'd need, assuring her she could find everything she'd need from a couple of online stores.

He advised some warm layers for under her clothes. Next came skirts and warm sweaters, coats, both weatherproof and woollen. Tweed was always good, and cashmere very nice.

Kenzie's mind boggled at the list but they were leaving at four and she needed to get online. She figured if she had enough clothes to last a couple of days, she'd find time to visit the shops herself.

It was a hurried choice, and given the circumstances, and having known Gran slightly, she went for mostly formal blacks and greys in choosing outer clothing, though she found an irresistible dark blue coat with a mock fur collar and a tight-fitting hat to match and added them to her purchases.

The total made her gasp, but she had to phone her father to tell him what was happening, and he'd soon transfer more money to her credit card.

Money! What should she do about that? She'd need some cash to carry around.

In what?

The backpack she'd been using here?

Back onto the online store, she went to handbags, chose one and added it to the list, though what she'd ever do with a cashmere coat and leather handbag back in Darwin, where she mainly shopped, she didn't know!

Though she did know the leather handbag was likely to go mouldy the first wet season...

Alex packed while Robert handled his grandmother's things. He knew the plane had cabin connectivity so he could make any necessary phone calls on the journey.

And he was thinking about this because?

Because he wanted to be busy, thinking of other things, not wanting to inspect the knotting of his gut that had happened when Kenzie had said she'd come.

He should have hugged, her, told her that was wonderful. After all, she'd hugged him when she'd heard the news.

But nothing in his upbringing had taught him how to express his feelings—his relief...

His delight?

He thought about the word and realised that's exactly what it was. Delight that she wanted to be with him at this time, delight that someone cared enough.

Really, just delight about the woman he'd married so precipitously!

He should have hugged her...

Monroes don't do emotion!

The flight to Scotland was uneventful. Kenzie had worn jeans and the only long-sleeved top she'd brought with her, with her now battered trainers on her feet.

Checking her across the aisle, sleeping soundly, Alex was again glad she'd wanted to come. She'd divert attention from him while he went through all the business that had to be done—the funeral, and all that entailed in organisation, the reading of the will, and seeing its provisions were set in motion, decisions about Gran's flat in Edinburgh, then her country estate, and a check that all was well there.

And much as he longed to get back to work, to lose himself once more in something that provided interest, and escape from emotion, he knew there was much to do before he could turn away from his duties.

Having Kenzie there would alleviate some of the aggravation all this would cause…

Poor thing, he thought as he looked across at her, she had no idea what lay ahead of her.

CHAPTER TEN

'I DON'T KNOW why I was concerned about how you'd manage in such an alien environment,' Alex said to Kenzie when, within minutes of their arrival at his flat, she'd had a shower and washed her hair, reappearing in a pair of warm navy slacks and a soft blue jumper, her wet hair pulled back from her face by a band he thought might be what's called an Alice band.

'And as those are certainly not my clothes you're wearing, how did you manage that transformation.'

She grinned at him, thinking of the journey from the airport with her wrapped in his warm camel coat.

'Internet shopping, and a list from Robert of what I might need to begin with.'

He shook his head and smiled at her.

'Ahead of me at every turn,' he said. 'But I can tell from the cut and quality of those clothes they'll have cost plenty. Just how did you pay? I should have been giving you money, shouldn't I?

Her turn to smile.

'I have plenty of my own, thank you,' she informed him. 'Let me worry about my personal finances. Get on and do what you have to do so you can get back to work, which is really what you want to do. Right now, we should eat and go to bed, so we're both fresh in the morning. Robert says he's ordered dinner for us both to be sent in, though where from I've no idea.'

At that moment, the front doorbell chimed, so she assumed she was about to find out where dinner appeared from, and what it might contain.

'Someone knows how to cook good beef,' she said between mouthfuls some time later. 'This is delicious.'

'Knowing Robert, he's ordered it from the best restaurant in Edinburgh. My grandmother always ate there until she became ill, and that's when he started having small amounts of food sent in for her.'

Kenzie studied him for a moment, looking vaguely puzzled.

'He's going to miss her as much as you do,' she said quietly. 'Has he somewhere he can go?'

Alex stopped eating, knife and fork both poised in mid-air.

'Damn, I hadn't thought of Robert, although now I *do* think about it, he has a small landholding up near Gran's home in Wester-Ross—that's in the northern Highlands. He might go back there, or he— I just don't know.'

'If he wants to keep working, could he work for you?'

Alex sighed.

'If he does want to keep working, he'd certainly be welcome. I know he must have organised cleaners to come into this flat so it would be clean and tidy when we returned. Although would you care to have him around?'

Kenzie had to smile.

'Are you asking if I'd prefer to do not only my own washing and ironing and cleaning and tidying, and yours too, for that matter, then no! I'm not made for doing nothing— well, nothing but housework—I'd want to work as well.'

'Surgical nursing, right?'

She nodded.

'I might be able arrange something. I certainly can talk to a few people, and find out exactly what's involved.'

They finished their meal with amiable chit-chat, eating slowly, or so Kenzie felt.

She was exhausted after the rush to leave the island and long flight, but felt lost about the protocol of going to bed with her business partner in this marriage, without the wedding excitement, and their tentative kisses that had led them inexorably into bed the first night.

Did she just get in and wait?

But what side? He'd have a particular side for sure, but both bedside tables were clear, apart from a small lamp on each. Whoever Robert had sent in had done the job thoroughly.

The wardrobes had been easier, one full of obviously male clothes, so she'd arranged her meagre belongings in the other one.

And what to wear to bed was another problem. That first night—and her colour rose thinking about it—clothes had not been needed, and though the rooms here were warm, centrally heated, she felt embarrassed about getting into one of the silky little numbers she'd bought on the island.

She took off her elegant new clothes, and in bra and panties—far too pretty to be called plain old undies—she went into the bathroom to have a wash and clean her teeth.

Should she have another shower?

But she'd had one earlier and as Alex had been on the phone since they'd hit the ground, he might be ready for one now...

Who'd have thought married life could be so difficult?

Back in the bedroom, she was standing at the bottom of the bed, struggling with these problems, when Alex walked in.

'Very fetching!' he said with a smile in his voice. 'I'll just have a quick shower and join you in bed.'

And with that, he disappeared into the bathroom.

Leaving Kenzie exactly where she'd been before his appearance with the dilemma of which side of the bed.

Damn it all, she wasn't dumb.

She marched to the door and pushed it open, taking a minute to enjoy the lean, flat-muscled length of his body.

'Which side do you sleep on?' she asked, above the splash of the water.

He opened the glass door and smiled at her.

'Whichever side you're on,' he said, then laughed as heat flooded her face.

'Surely a real marriage would have been easier,' she muttered to herself as she stomped back to the bed. The couple would have been intimate beforehand—in most cases at least—but this business thing was proving difficult.

She found one of the pretty Thai nightdresses, took off her underwear and pulled it on, then climbed into the massive bed, refusing to think of other women with whom he might have shared it.

This was a business arrangement.

But in spite of her angst, she was all but asleep when she felt the mattress move, and Alex's long arm reached out and drew her close so he could spoon around her.

'We're both far too tired tonight, but I'll make it up to you tomorrow,' he whispered into her ear, then he nestled in beside her and she fell asleep to the sound of his breathing growing deeper and slower as he, too, fell asleep.

She woke, confused at first, then remembered where she was, Alex now sprawled on his back beside her, sound asleep still.

She crept out of bed, went to the bathroom, then quietly

crossed the room to open the dark curtains just a crack so she could see what lay beyond the room.

It was eight o'clock local time, but the streetlights were still lit, and a faint fog made the buildings seem to float above the ground.

So this was Edinburgh!

Lovely old buildings stretching out along the opposite side of the street, no doubt matched by the one she was in. They were joined, and very stately, with painted front doors and small shrubs of some kind in painted pots on either side of the few steps that led up to the doors.

An urge to be out there, looking about, exploring, was almost enough to take her over to the wardrobe to start pulling on clothes, but Alex's arrival stopped her, his arms scooping her up.

'This is far too early for Edinburgh to wake up. You can go exploring all you want later in the day.'

He carried her across the room and she laughed as he all but dumped her on the bed, climbing on top of her to give her a hearty kiss on the lips.

'Welcome to Edinburgh,' he said, and proceeded to show her just how welcome she was.

For Edinburgh or for him? she wondered much later, when she'd regathered her senses after some tumultuous lovemaking and was enjoying a coffee and croissant that he'd brought in and placed by the bed.

Then he'd sat, bent and kissed her again, before becoming Mr Efficient, setting down some money, his address and two phone numbers, a map of the inner city—'I doubt you'll get much further in your explorations today'—and finally a credit card.

'The pin number is on the map so don't lose it,' he said. 'I'm sorry I can't show you around but there is still so much to do.'

She touched his face, and said, 'Go, do what you have to!'

She'd have liked to add, 'And I don't need your money or your credit card,' but she thought it might upset him, and he had enough on his plate at the moment.

Best she leave them both behind. She had the map Robert had given her, marked with the shops she might like to visit, her own credit card and money she could exchange for the local currency.

Once dressed, she checked her phone.

She had sent a long text to her father from the plane, and had tried to ring him the previous evening, but they would still be mustering and he was probably out at one of the camps.

She'd try again tonight.

It was four days later that she woke to the realisation that she had fallen in love with Alexander Monroe McLeod! Had probably loved him for some time.

It wasn't that she was seeing more of him, he was as busy as ever, and the conversations they did have over an occasional dinner or breakfast suggested that his gran's estate was large and convoluted.

The funeral was coming up—a trip to somewhere north, very far north and very cold, he'd told her, adding that the church was always freezing.

They'd drive, not fly, maybe take their time driving back if she'd like that, although at this time of year fog and the thin mist Alex called haar would probably spoil any view.

Forewarned, Kenzie pulled out her warmest underwear and the boots she'd found herself on one of her expeditions into the beautiful city. For the funeral she'd wear the grey cashmere dress and dark blue coat, thick black stockings and her boots.

Long underwear, slacks, jumpers and the thick tweed coat should do for the trip, as she'd need to be able to peel off layers when she was inside.

Alex's car was a sleek, black saloon, immeasurably comfortable. For what seemed like hours they drove through the city, suburbs, maybe small towns that had been consumed by the city—built-up areas with plenty of traffic.

Ring roads with numbers on them seemed to weave back and forth, the traffic still thick.

A fine, misty rain made conditions even more diffi-cult, so Kenzie could sit back and take in the view of the different style of buildings they were passing, enjoy the occasional patches of green, until, at last, they were on a narrower freeway, with less traffic and what seemed like endless fields rolling towards mist-shrouded mountains.

'It looks as if it would be beautiful if the mist cleared,' she said, and Alex turned with a quick smile.

'That's hardly ever,' he said, and she thought he might be joking, but wasn't sure.

They stopped for a break occasionally, each time, as she clambered out of the warm car, Kenzie was glad for Rob-ert's advice, for even through her layers, the chill pierced her skin.

'Here at last!' Alex eventually said, pulling the car off the rough country lane they'd been on through tall stone pillars and onto a gravel drive that seemed to stretch to infinity.

Or somewhere into the mist!

'You go on inside while I get the bags,' Alex told her, and Kenzie hurried up the stone steps and was pleased to find Robert there to welcome her into a vast space, hung with portraits of ancestors, whether Alex's or someone else's, and, yes, a suit of armour near the bottom of each of the wide stairways that clung to the side walls…

Thank heaven for Robert!

Did he have the ability to be in two places at once?

It was only with great effort she held back the hug she'd have liked to give him or his doppelganger, for the journey had turned into a seemingly endless odyssey with who knew what at the end.

Alex breezed in, wisps of mist clinging to his clothing.

'Staff in place, everything in order?' he asked Robert, who assured him all was well.

And as if to prove it, Robert beckoned to someone behind him, and a couple of young women appeared. Neatly dressed in slacks and black tops—fortunately for Kenzie's composure not in dinky maid uniforms—they smiled a welcome.

'Millie and Mairi,' Robert said. 'They'll take the bags up and see everything's ready in the rooms. You'd like a drink to take off the chill, sir?'

And although Kenzie was surprised by the 'sir', it was obvious Alex had barely noticed, if at all.

'Whisky would be great, Robert. Kenzie, what about you? Gin and tonic, or dare you try Scottish beer?'

'I do have some mulled wine. I thought Kenzie might find it warming,' Robert said, before Kenzie had to make a choice.

And at least Robert was still treating her as herself— she'd definitely be put out to be called madam, if that's what went with sir for females in posh houses.

For as Robert drew them from the entrance into a small drawing room—more portraits but hung this time on beautiful wallpapered walls, stripes of crimson, alternating with rose vines—she realised what this definitely was—a very posh house.

She thought of the big rambling old house she called home—always dusty, impossible to keep clean. It was considered something special as Outback houses went, but this?

Could it be a castle?

Alex took her arm and led her towards a chair by the big open fire, easing off her coat as they moved.

'Gran was up to date enough to have installed air-conditioning into a lot of this old pile, but somehow fires make things homely.'

'Homely?' Kenzie said with a grin, and he shrugged.

'We only use a few of the rooms. Most of them are closed off except in summer for a few open-house days.'

So even before DocSays, her husband hadn't been short of money. Though it wasn't his probable wealth that bothered Kenzie—she had plenty of her own—but the place itself, his position in it, his being at ease in it while to her it was totally alien.

She had no doubt that she could, in time, make herself fit into it, in her own way, of course, and maybe for parts of every year, but was it what she wanted?

Only if it came with love.

The thought came out of nowhere, *and* before she'd even sipped the mulled wine Robert had pressed into her hand.

She did sip now, and studied Alex as she enjoyed the warm, delicately spiced drink. He was talking to Robert about the funeral arrangements but she didn't want to listen, she wanted to look at him.

Look at him and try to work out when love had entered the arrangement between them—when she'd stupidly forgotten it was a business arrangement and fallen in love…

Although, if she thought seriously about it, it had probably started way back at the island, when she'd been attracted to him from the start. Then the talk of a convenient marriage—while it had excited her nerves and set the blood pounding through her veins, she'd damped down the feelings by reminding herself it wasn't that kind of marriage.

And given that he was so insistent that Monroes didn't do emotion, she'd shut those feelings away rather than embarrass them both!

CHAPTER ELEVEN

THOUGH THIS HOUSE appeared to be as isolated as her own property back home, the funeral was extremely well attended. Kenzie eventually gave up on any attempt to remember names, hoping that those who were important to Alex and the family would go back to the house for food and drinks.

They'd have to go somewhere or remain in a frozen tableau around the grave.

'You're cold, I'll get Robert to take you home,' Alex said, taking hold of her gloved but still frozen hand.

'But shouldn't I stay?' she asked half-heartedly, already regretting the purchase of the stylish boots when she should have bought something with warm lining.

'No, they'll think you need to see to the arrangements.'

He dropped a kiss on her cheek and steered her towards Robert, who stood, stiffly aloof at the head of the grave.

And one look at Robert's face was enough to tell Kenzie it was for Robert's sake as well as hers that Alex was sending them home, for the grief on his features made her want to cry for him.

Once at the car, she refused the back seat, and climbed into the front beside him, sliding across the acreage of seat, to rest her hand on his arm.

'This must be terribly hard for you,' she said, and saw the slightest of nods.

'You were with her a long time?' Kenzie asked gently.

'Man and boy,' Robert replied, and she could hear the pride in his voice. 'Were but a stable lad in the beginning, but learned the house from the bottom to the top.'

He paused before adding, 'And a finer woman you would never meet!'

Kenzie could hear the soft Scottish burr in his voice beneath the carefully cultivated language of the butler who would put aside his grief, check that all was in order for the funeral feast, and be there to greet the guests when they returned.

Heard grief, too, and hoped that somewhere there was someone to comfort *him*.

Back at the house he saw her to the door, sent someone to put away the car, and suggested she take off her coat and change into dry shoes.

She looked at the line of wellingtons, and outside boots neatly stored in a large cupboard off the entrance hall, and realised life wasn't all that different from back home.

Apart from the weather—and the butler, of course—but in her mind's eye she could see all the work boots lined up in the big hall at home, and for a moment felt very, very homesick…

Alex watched Kenzie and Robert drive away, and felt a sense of loss. She'd done no more than stand beside him, staunchly upright in this foreign setting, murmuring thanks for condolences when required, acknowledging introductions.

Yet now an unfamiliar ache in his chest suggested that he missed her.

He turned his attention resolutely back to the family

and friends coming forward to speak to him, assuring all they'd be welcome back at the hall, suggesting they all needed something to counter the chill of the day.

Gran's solicitor touched his arm, suggesting a meeting later in the week, and with a pang he realised he'd have to consider the future of this estate—the Monroe estate—where he'd spent every Christmas and school holiday in his youth.

He spoke to a few stragglers, villagers who'd hung back but who had loved Gran as much as he had, for she had been their champion in all things.

No, he probably couldn't sell the estate...

He hadn't realised how much Kenzie had helped until, with all the guests departed, and everything set to rights by the army of helpers Robert had produced, he saw her slumped in a big chair in front of the fire, her usually bright face white with fatigue.

'You didn't have to stay—you could have gone up to the bedroom much earlier,' he scolded.

'It didn't seem right,' she said. 'Besides, everyone was busy and I doubt I'd have found my way.'

'You ask someone,' he said firmly, upset that she'd stoically stayed on, upset he hadn't thought to look out for her and see her taken up to bed.

She was sleeping soundly when he finally got up to bed, and, as exhaustion claimed him, he climbed in beside her, reached out one hand to rest it against her shoulder, and fell asleep.

He slept until the sun, that rarely seen star in the northern sky in winter, was bright behind a fine crack in the curtains.

No Kenzie, and the stab of disappointment he'd felt was

probably because he'd have liked her to be there, to have held her, made love to her...

'She's out walking,' Robert informed him, 'but I told her you'd want to drive back today so she won't stay out long.'

'Far too cold for a tropical flower anyway,' he said to Robert, who surprisingly had his own comment to make.

'I doubt a little thing like the cold would daunt Miss Kenzie. I'll get your breakfast, sir.'

'Enough of the "sir", Robert,' Alex told him. 'We've lived without it for the past month or more, so surely we don't need it now.'

But Robert had glided off on silent feet before Alex had reached the end of his objection.

He sighed.

Robert had cared for his dying grandmother as gently as a nurse, but she'd always been madam to him, and probably always would be in his memories of her.

How strange Kenzie would have found it all, yet she'd never betrayed the slightest hint of discomfort or uncertainty.

He'd chosen well in this marriage of convenience, he decided, then laughed at the absurdity of the thought.

Had he had a choice?

She'd been right there, wanting the same thing he had—marriage!

It was the fact that they were well suited—in bed at least—that was the greatest discovery.

And again, for a moment, he wished she'd stayed in bed...

Walking in borrowed gumboots through the silent, misty morning had brought a sense of great peace to Kenzie.

The place had a feeling of vastness—nothing but moor and mountains as far as she could see.

Not that that was very far!

But she'd felt at home in the silence—it spoke of home—so she'd walked, always keeping the huge old house in sight, brighter now the sun was burning off the mists.

She'd go back to Edinburgh with Alex and talk to him there, tell him she was going home.

She'd been up at six, pulling on her coat and creeping from the dark bedroom to sit downstairs beside the dying embers of the fire in the small drawing room, computer in hand as she worked out how to fly from Edinburgh to Darwin with the shortest possible layover between flights.

It was a task that had seemed impossible at first, going from one international airline to another, until she'd gone to a site that compared flights and prices—not for the cost of the trip home but for the length of the journey.

Once she was away from here she wanted to be home as quickly as possible.

So she'd booked what she'd found—out of Edinburgh tomorrow and back in Darwin just over twenty-five hours later. She'd let her father know from Dubai, the first stop on the way, and he'd meet her so she'd be back on Spec a matter of hours later.

And you're glad—it will be wonderful, she told herself, but doubted herself would agree any time soon.

She made her way back to the house to find Alex up and apparently waiting for her.

'I'm sorry to be in a rush but there's so much to do and I really want to go back to work next week.'

He held her arm to steady her as she pulled off her gumboots, and she knew she shouldn't be excited by such a practical touch, but of course she was.

Excited and saddened.

'Did you enjoy your walk?' he asked, all politeness

when what she really wanted was for him to drag her up-stairs into the bedroom and—

Well, that wasn't going to happen.

'I've asked Robert to organise a flask of coffee and some sandwiches for the trip back. He said you had some tea and toast before you went out, do you want anything more substantial before we leave?'

She looked into the face she'd really just begun to know, and read his concern.

And something else?

Confusion?

Alex confused?

She scoffed at the thought, and hurried up to the bedroom to gather her things—*and* put on her boots!

She'd have to visit Melbourne in winter every year for the next ten years to get full value out of the clothes she'd bought, but as she packed them away she knew she was thinking flippant thoughts to keep her mind from what lay ahead.

Somehow—sleeping for a large part of it—she got through the journey back to Edinburgh.

Robert had been left behind to see to things on the estate—yes, she *had* listened to the conversations after the funeral, or some of them at least.

Dinner had once again been delivered magically to the door—not burgers and chips but chicken à la King in crispy pastry cases, cooked to perfection, with scalloped potatoes and carrots and peas. Bread and butter pudding to follow!

'It was my favourite on school holidays,' Alex said. 'Do you like it?'

He sounded anxious, so she assured him she did, but the look of anxiety lingered.

'I'm not going to be much fun to be with for a few days,' he said finally. 'The legal people want everything sorted as soon as possible, so it will be meetings, meetings and more meetings.'

Anxious again as he said, 'You won't mind exploring on your own?'

She set down her spoon, unable to eat any more, although it was the most delicious bread and butter pudding she'd ever tasted.

'Actually, Alex, I need to talk to you about that.'

He began to speak but she held up her hand, determined to get it all said.

'I hope you won't feel you cheated your grandmother, because it isn't you, it's me,' she began, then realised that didn't make much sense if you didn't know what came next.

She hurried on.

'You see, when I married you I was absolutely certain that this kind of business arrangement would suit me fine. That I could do it without any concerns, even enjoy it because you seemed like a nice guy.'

'Well, I'm glad you at least thought that.' Very stilted—very Alexander Monroe McLeod!

Best get it over with.

'Yes, well, the thing is I've discovered I can't do it—do a business marriage—and I'm sorry to let you down, and I'm happy to pay all the costs of a divorce, but I've realised I want a different kind of marriage.' She could feel the heat flooding her cheeks, but soldiered on. 'One where I can love and be loved.' She hesitated for a moment, then said, 'There—that's all. I've booked a flight home tomorrow, so I'll just go and pack.'

She fled—no other word for it—getting out of that room

so quickly she had to pause to catch her breath before tackling the stairs in front of her.

Gobsmacked didn't begin to cover Alex's reaction. He sat, staring at the door through which his wife had disappeared, battling to understand exactly what she'd said.

He'd been so pleased with his marriage—with his *wife*! So happy they were compatible in bed, so filled with admiration for her when she'd been thrown into a massive social occasion at the funeral—proud as Punch really!

And now she was gone.

Well, going, but with a flight booked and not a word to him!

He should feel angry or at the very least aggrieved but the tightness in his gut wasn't either of those emotions.

Not that he knew *what* it was…

And he had meetings with the lawyers all day tomorrow so wouldn't be able to take her to the airport.

And he was thinking this because…?

He shook his head, trying to clear it, trying to work out if there was something he could do.

But it *had* been a business arrangement—a marriage of convenience—so could he in all good faith complain that she wanted to leave?

Yet more than anything he wanted to hold her in his arms and make things right between them again.

In *bed*! A voice inside his head scoffed. Hasn't she just told you that's not enough…?

CHAPTER TWELVE

LEAVING WITHOUT SAYING goodbye to Robert had been harder than she'd realised, which was why, she told herself, she was sitting in the taxi, crying as quietly as she could, not wanting to attract the attention of the driver.

But it was the only way! she reminded herself.

To stay in the marriage, now she knew she loved Alex, would be agony.

She had no doubt he liked her well enough, and they were certainly good together in bed, but her heart would always want to hear words of love, and, as Alex had told her many times, Monroes didn't do emotion.

Yet he'd loved his grandmother, she knew that—knew from the way he'd looked at her, the gentle way he'd taken her fragile hand. Knew from the feeling in every word as he'd read to her—yes, he did feel emotion for all his denial.

Just not for her, and why should she expect it? She'd known what she was getting into.

Had even *thought* it a good idea!

Well, it *had* been, compared to the difficulty of internet dating when you lived in the middle of nowhere…

No, falling in love with him had been her own fault—well, partly his for being such a—a fine man, she decided was the only apt description.

How could she not have fallen for him?

Done what had seemed impossible—unthinkable—when she'd first agreed to his proposition.

And even though she'd married him with the idea of having children, she'd discovered she couldn't live with him without love—without being loved…

Edinburgh airport wasn't nearly as vast as London's Heathrow, but anything bigger than Darwin's international terminal seemed vast to her.

And confusing, although that was good as she had to think about finding her way to the right departure lounge and didn't have time to think about Alex.

Unfortunately, for the twenty-five hours and twenty minutes after boarding her first flight, she'd have plenty of time for that particular reflection.

Although, with stops in Dubai and Singapore, and perhaps a sleep on each flight, and food—they always fed you on international flights—

She stopped in the middle of the main concourse to pull herself together, to have a stern talk to herself about the practicalities of what she was doing, and the uselessness of regrets.

With renewed determination, she studied the departures board, joined a long queue to check in her luggage—one heavily packed backpack—found her way through security to where she had to be, and finally settled into a comfortable business-class seat in the giant aircraft.

She accepted the glass of champagne handed to her pre-take-off, drank it, and closed her eyes, not wanting to see the famous old city from the air, not wanting to think…

Alex hoped he was making all the correct responses to the lawyers' talk. They certainly didn't seem to sense there was anything wrong with him.

Well, there wasn't, was there?

He wasn't sick, he wasn't worried about work or money, or even what to have for his dinner. Wasn't worried about anything.

Except his wife had left him, which didn't, he realised, precisely *worry* him as cause him a strange kind of disconnectedness.

Not a good state to be in when talking—or more listening—to lawyers. But he knew how everything in Gran's estate would be bequeathed and to whom. He'd known for years, had read every change in her will, so really did he need to be here?

He'd have to sign things, of course, but they could be sent to him.

He'd decided the previous evening, when the fact of Kenzie's departure had sunk in, that he'd be able to handle this interminable meeting with Gran's—and his—lawyers. After all, Monroes didn't do emotion.

So why was his mind throwing up gruesome images of plane wrecks, intermingled with images of her beautiful body resting beside him, her sleepy smile as they drew apart after making love—

'Alex!'

The word was sharp enough for him to realise it wasn't the first time this person had spoken it.

'Sorry,' he said, 'it's been a hectic few days.'

'Hectic couple of weeks, from the sound of things,' William—he thought it was William—said. Lawyers all seemed to look the same to him—maybe it was the pin-striped suits and sober ties...

'Archie was asking about your will now you're married. You'll want to change it, won't you? If you give us just a rough idea of what you'd like, we can get on with it while we're doing the transfer of your grandmother's bequests into your name.'

Alex stared blankly at William—he was almost certain it *was* William—at a total loss as to a reply.

I'm not married any more, sounded stupid, besides which, saying it out loud would make it more real, and—

And what?

And he didn't want it to be real, he realised. He very much didn't want it to be real!

'Let's just get Gran's estate settled first,' he finally said, because his mind was in more turmoil than ever now he'd figured the 'real' thing out.

William, or maybe Archie, said something, but he knew he didn't want to be in that office a moment longer. He wanted to be at the airport, finding his wife, talking to her, trying to work out what the hell had gone wrong…

'Do you know if there are any direct flights from here to Darwin?'

'Darwin, Australia?' one of them asked, but, lawyer-like, he woke the laptop sitting on his desk and began to search.

'None direct,' he said. 'There are multiple ways to get there, all with at least two stopovers and flight changes as far as I can see. Is she from Darwin, your wife?'

He turned the laptop so Alex could see the list of flights that would eventually take Kenzie back to Australia.

And would she even fly into Darwin?

Would that be the closest to her home?

Archie was asking something, but Alex barely heard his voice, his mind grappling with the fact that he knew so little about his wife.

But he did know the phone number!

He looked back at the list of flights again, searching to see when she'd be expected to land in Darwin—

If she was going to Darwin.

He stood up.

'Sorry, but I need to go. You both know what to do, and anything that needs a signature can wait until I get back.'

'Get back?' they echoed in unison.

'From Australia,' he told them, and left the room.

Logistics—it was just a matter of logistics. He had no idea if one of the charter planes he used when travelling could fly that far without refuelling, or even with one pilot, but one phone call to the company and all that would be sorted.

It would be hot in Australia, possibly even hotter than Thailand, but he had lightweight clothes from his stay there, and jeans—he was pretty sure jeans would be the thing he'd need. He'd go back to the flat, organise a flight, pack and be ready to go whenever they had a plane available.

As he hurried down the corridor his mind was already on that plane, travelling out to a place with fifteen thousand head of cattle...

And one lithe and lovely dark-haired woman!

The interminable flight finally landed in Dubai, where Kenzie, totally lost as far as time was concerned, phoned her father.

'I'm coming home,' she said succinctly. 'ETA Darwin two-thirty tomorrow afternoon. That's if tomorrow is Thursday out there.'

'Are you okay?' her father asked, and she assured him she was before telling him they were calling her flight and she had to go. Any explanation—worse, any kindness from her father—and she'd have burst into tears in the middle of one of the world's busiest airports.

She'd left the lounge to find a quiet corner to phone her father, but now returned, working her way down the array of food choices but not tempted by any.

Maybe a cold beer. They had Coopers, which her father favoured, so it would give her a taste of home.

But a phone call and cold beer did little to repel the thought that maybe she'd made a mistake.

Just maybe, getting on a plane and flying home had been a stupid thing to do—irrational even, and she was not an irrational person.

They could have talked, but what was there to talk about in a business arrangement?

Besides which, Alex had already said he'd be tied up with lawyers all day, and possibly the next day too, and she knew he was hoping to get back to work the following week.

And from what she knew of emergency room doctors, there'd be little chance of talking after that.

No, it was the best thing to do—get out of there and begin to put her life back together again.

This she was confident of doing, though putting her heart back together…

An attendant came to tell her the flight to Singapore was boarding and she thanked her warmly, glad to have something definite to do—something to think about apart from Alex.

A pre-take-off champagne and she'd close her eyes and sleep. No turning back now.

But once in her seat, she did check her phone before turning it to flight mode.

No message from Alex, and why would there be?

Business arrangements broke down all the time and, given the extent of his own wealth and his gran's estate, he'd have to know a lot about business.

She drank her champagne, and closed her eyes. Once at Singapore she was almost home…

Apparently, it was relatively easy for a private jet to fly to Australia.

'No worries, mate,' the man he'd spoken to said. 'I'll come myself. Need a trip home.'

Further questioning told him they'd use three pilots and have a short stopover in Abu Dhabi.

'When do you want to leave?' the obliging man asked.

'Whenever you're organised,' Alex said, feeling what could only be excitement somersaulting in his stomach.

'Let's say six tomorrow morning. You've used us before, you know where to go?'

Half statement, half question.

'I'll be there,' Alex assured him, wondering at the same time whether his newfound Aussie pilot knew much about the place where they were headed.

'Up the gulf,' Kenzie had said, which hadn't meant much to Alex until he'd found a map of Australia online and seen the huge gulf at the top of it, and the vast amounts of land around said gulf.

A different excitement stirred inside him now. To be going somewhere new, somewhere entirely different.

How had his life become so proscribed, so work-focussed, that he'd never so much as considered seeing more of the world?

He'd never have got as far as a small island in the Gulf of Thailand had it not been for Gran.

Never met Kenzie.

Never—

What?

Fallen in love?

He wasn't entirely certain that's what it had been, just that being with her was unlike any other connection he'd ever had with a woman.

And being without her—the prospect of being without her for ever—unbearable…

CHAPTER THIRTEEN

'WHERE ARE YOU going after Darwin, mate?' the Aussie pilot, Tom, asked when he came back to sit with Alex on the last leg of the flight.

'A property called Speculation, somewhere up the gulf, I believe.'

'Wow!' the pilot said. 'That's some place! One of the biggest in Australia, I've heard.'

There was silence for a few minutes, no doubt while he considered Alex's destination, then he said, 'Why are you flying into Darwin? Someone meeting you there?'

'No, but I understood it was the closest major airport.'

'It is that,' Tom told him. 'But Spec's got a good airstrip. RFDS—that's the Flying Doctors—put down there for a regular clinic every couple of weeks. Same size plane as this. Actually, same model—well, some of the planes are the same model. It's a while since I flew for them.'

It took Alex a minute or two to make sense of this conversation in his head.

'You can land on the property?'

'Sure can. I'll have to get on to them to let them know we're coming, although they're such a big place they don't have to move stray cattle off the runway like some of the places do.'

Moving cattle off the runway?

Clinic runs?

Increasingly intrigued by this glimpse into what Kenzie's life must have been like, Alex had to ask.

'What are clinic runs?'

Tom smiled at him.

'Hard to get your head around our Outback,' he said. 'A clinic run is going out to do a few hours, maybe a day, at a specific place—very small settlements like some of the opal mining towns or a property somewhere. People come a hundred, two hundred k to see the doc. It's like your GP has moved into town for the day, and you make appointments, kids get vaccinated, pregnant mums checked, older people might have issues—diabetes is common.'

'So once a fortnight the service flies a doctor—'

'And nurses,' Tom put in. 'Sometimes a dentist.'

'A team, then, out to this property to see whoever needs a bit of medical care or treatment for ongoing issues. I knew of the service but thought they mainly attended accidents in rural locations—emergency stuff like an ambulance. It's unbelievable!'

'Not really, mate,' Tom said. 'They do the emergency stuff, all right, and risky that can be. But the regular clinic service has been going on for decades now. People out in the bush rely on it. You want a coffee? Something to eat?'

As Tom departed to fix a snack in the small kitchen, Alex battled to make sense of what he'd heard. He'd always known Australia was a vast land, but he'd somehow imagined all that space in the middle of it was empty, not dotted with properties as big as Scotland, or tiny opal mining settlements.

And the more he learned, the more he wanted to know. Somewhere in the mists of time, he'd seen Kenzie taking their children—why only two?—back to Australia from time to time, maybe staying a month or so, but he'd be busy at work. It had seemed a sensible arrangement.

Until, of course, he'd realised that he couldn't last twenty-four hours without Kenzie, let alone a month or two. And, given that life-shattering discovery, he now thought he'd probably miss his children too.

Children he didn't have—might never have…

No! That was plain impossible.

He'd see Kenzie, talk to her—she was the most pragmatic woman he'd ever met—and together they'd work things out.

Kenzie positively bounced out of the plane at Darwin, excited to be home. And if she was sick at heart, well, that was for her to know—her and only her.

Once through customs, the tall, rangy figure of her father in his daggy, wide-brimmed hat brought a few tears to her eyes, but she hid them against his shirt as they hugged each other.

He took her backpack from her, linked his arm through hers, and said, 'I've brought the chopper—we'll be home in no time.'

'Had you finished the muster or am I being a nuisance?' she asked, and he squeezed her hand.

'You could never be a nuisance but, yes, we've finished the muster, you'll see the road trains full of cattle heading for here as we fly home.'

They walked the kilometre to the private section of the airport, Kenzie asking questions to keep her father talking.

Talk about cattle numbers and expected sales figures was easier than enquiries about her marriage or what she was doing home.

Her dad wouldn't ask—he never had—apparently

firmly convinced that in her own sweet time Kenzie would tell him what was bothering her.

It's how they'd always worked, from the time when she had been little and had seen one of the manager's bigger boys teasing the dogs. She'd had to weigh up telling tales, which she knew wasn't right, and the dogs' welfare, and had eventually chosen the dogs, although that boy had called her a tittle-tat for months afterwards.

'So, given the drought and the floods, how bad or good were the numbers?' she asked, because now she'd remembered that she'd had quite a crush on that boy a few years later, and didn't really want to think about that either...

Her father talked her through the muster figures.

'We saved all the breeding stock from the floods—already had them in the hill paddock. Lost one of the good bulls, but the Ainsworths have a beauty they're wanting to sell.'

It was normal, everyday chat and Kenzie felt it like a soothing balm spread across her body. She was nearly home—everything would be fine.

As her father filed his flight plan, she bought some bottled water, then she was in the air again and, no, she wasn't going to cry, but as they grew closer to the cluster of buildings that was home, her father patted her knee and said, 'We'll be right, lass. We'll get through this.'

'What the hell?'

She'd been busy mopping up tears, so hadn't seen the strange aircraft on the runway until her father's exclamation.

She peered at it—no insignia...

'It's not RFDS,' she said.

'And not been here long—dust not settled yet,' her father said. 'That's one of the lads going out in the ute to meet it.'

The chopper slowed, then gracefully dropped down onto the pad close to the house, the strange plane now a distant glimmer.

'He must be taking off again that he's stopped down there, not taxied to the house,' her father said, but the sight of her so-familiar home, the big house, with the smaller buildings clustered around it like chicks around the mother hen, had brought fresh tears to her eyes.

Wayne, their foreman for many years, was there to help her down, giving her a hug to welcome her home.

'Pleased to see the old place, eh?" he said, one lean brown finger wiping a tear from her cheek.

'You bet!' she said, because that would be expected of her.

And being home *was* good.

It was home! A place to heal, with time and space to build her life again.

'Apparently, the bloke on that fancy jet's here to see you,' Wayne continued. 'Ute's on its way over now.'

He pointed to the dust trail behind the very dusty vehicle.

Bloke on a fancy jet?

It was the only way Alex ever travelled.

Her stomach turned over and her heart leapt, but she told herself it was more likely to be one of the lawyers.

Her father was standing beside her—Wayne on one side, Dad on the other—unknowingly giving her the strength to face whoever got out of the ute.

'Mr Steele?' Alex said, as, immaculately dressed in chinos and a short-sleeved blue shirt, he stepped out into the dust and held out his hand. 'I'm Alex McLeod.'

Her father shook hands, saying, 'You've come to check us out?'

Alex shook his head, then turned to Kenzie.

'I've come to see Kenzie,' he said, and reached out to take her two hands, which were hanging limply on the end of her arms as she tried to get over the shock of what was happening.

'What with my grandmother's funeral and all the travel, there's a lot of things we didn't get around to saying to each other.'

'Kenzie?' her father said, in a voice that asked if she was all right with this.

'I'm fine, Dad,' she managed, although she knew she really, really wasn't.

Why was he here?

Surely he hadn't come to discuss divorce!

All of that could be handled over the net.

'Why don't you take Alex up to the homestead, out on the side veranda is cool at this time of the day, and I'll send Maggie out with cold drinks,' her father said, apparently realising she'd been struck dumb *and* unable to move.

'You'd like a beer, Mr McLeod?'

Whoops!

Her father clearly thought Alex was up to no good, arriving like this. The iron in his voice suggested he'd guessed she was a mess, and he only had one person to blame.

'Call him Alex,' she managed, and felt those long slim fingers that had traced her body and brought her such pleasure in bed tighten on hers, just briefly.

'Side veranda,' her father repeated, and stalked away towards the house.

But Wayne was still there, and would remain, Kenzie knew, until she assured him she was okay.

'This way,' she said to Alex, detaching one hand so she could lead him through the gate into the garden, and around the shrubs to the side veranda.

Which got rid of Wayne, but left her with Alex…

'Some place,' he said, waving his arm in the general direction of the other houses and outbuildings.

She snatched her hand away.

'What are you doing here?' she demanded. 'Did you come to check out where I live? Some place, is it? Not what you expected? A tin shed maybe!'

'Kenzie!'

His voice was soft, and shaking slightly.

He put his hand on her shoulder and turned her towards him.

'I've come to tell you I love you,' he said, blurting out the words as if saying them slowly might be impossible.'

He touched her cheek.

'Love you and want to be loved by you,' he said, his voice rough now. 'I came to find out if I could be that man you wanted to be married to—the one you could love and be loved by.'

Kenzie stared at him in total disbelief.

This was Alex—Alex 'Monroes don't do emotion' Alex. Standing in the shrubbery, telling her he loved her.

Well, she thought that's what he was telling her.

'Where are you, Kenzie? I've brought drinks but first get yourself up here so I can give you a hug, girl. The old place is a mausoleum without you around.'

'That's Maggie, with drinks,' Kenzie said to Alex.

He smiled and answered, 'On the side veranda. We'd better go.'

And, Alex-like, he took control, steering her along the path, up the three steps and onto the side veranda, where she let go of his hand for long enough to give Maggie a hug, and introduce her to Alex.

'This the husband, then?' Maggie said. 'How come he comes on a fancy jet and you had to fly commercial?'

This really wasn't the best place to try to sort out why Alex was here. Too many protectively inquisitive people around—too many people who loved her and were loved by her.

So, rather than answer Maggie, she turned to the man in question.

'Did you mean what you said just then—about loving and being loved by?'

He half smiled.

'Of course!' he said. 'Have I ever said anything to you I didn't mean?'

Had he?

She couldn't think.

But if he had said that—

'You love me?' she asked, just to be sure.

'And why wouldn't he?' Maggie demanded huffily.

'I do,' Alex said, and drew her closer, to show her just how much in a kiss that stole her breath.

Kenzie broke away eventually, reasonably sure Maggie had stayed to witness most of it.

She'd be reporting back to the men in the kitchen that everything was all right with their girl, and any minute her father would join them on the veranda.

She led Alex to one of the low-slung, wood and canvas chairs, and sat in one beside him, reaching out for a cold stubby of beer, handing him a cooler to put it in.

'Aussie pub!' she said with a smile, and when he touched her fingers as he took the beer, she knew everything was going to be all right.

'Can you stay?' she asked, and he smiled at her.

'As long as you'd like me to,' he said.

She had to laugh.

'You'd be bored silly after a couple of days and I thought you were itching to get back to work.'

Weird conversation when her internal conversationalist kept shouting, *He loves me!*

But most of the words she wanted to say and hear were best left to the privacy of their bedroom, probably in the bed Maggie would be making up for them right now!

'It's a bit late now, but tomorrow, if you can stay on, Kenzie'll show you around the place,' her father said, appearing on the veranda with his beer in his hand.

'You've just missed the muster—it's been hectic, so right now we're all taking a few days' break.'

There was a slight pause before he added, 'But if you're out in the western paddock, Kenz, you can check the bore there. I was going to do that today.'

'Until you had an SOS for a lift home.' Kenzie smiled at the man she loved most in the world, in fact, at both the men she loved most in the world.

And now Alex had relaxed enough to be asking questions of her father. How many people lived on the property? How did the cattle get to market? Was that Darwin, the market?

They had dinner, just the three of them, in the dining room, rather than the kitchen, Maggie producing steak tartare as an entrée, Kenzie guessing it was a test for Alex as well as one of her favourite foods.

'There'll be other things if you don't like it,' Kenzie said to Alex, but he ate with every appearance of enjoyment, complimenting Maggie when she returned to get their plates.

Roast beef, followed, rare and pink inside, perfect Yorkshire puddings to go with it, crisply baked potatoes, a sweet yam of some kind, and fresh cut beans.

'This food is magnificent,' Alex said, when Maggie returned with horseradish and mustard for the table.

'It's our own beef,' Maggie told him, 'so it's not that hard to get it right.'

'She's hiding her light under a bushel,' Kenzie teased, as Maggie turned to leave the room. 'Cooking is her passion and we've dined like royalty ever since Maggie took over the kitchen from the previous cook my grandmother had trained.'

'He's the one taught me about Yorkshire puddings,' Maggie admitted. 'He was a good cook, just getting old and tired.'

'Well, just make sure you're passing on your skills to one of the next generation,' Angus told her, and she beamed at him.

'Not the next, but the next. Young Tracy's mad about it! Always under my feet in the kitchen.'

'Tracy's one of Maggie's grandchildren, growing up here on the property. Her father's in charge of the horses.'

'Horses?' Alex turned to Angus. 'I'd have thought those bikes would have taken over most of the stock work.'

Her father nodded.

'They did, for a while, and we still use them to go around the boundaries, checking fences, things like that, but—'

'Dad's going back to the old ways.' Kenzie finished for him. 'Using horses seems to keep the cattle calmer, mainly because calm cattle don't drop weight. We've even cut back on helicopter mustering, although we still use the choppers, flying higher, to find cattle that have wandered into the hills.'

'Hills?' Alex echoed weakly. 'From the air it looked as flat as this table.'

'That's more than enough for the poor chap to take in, Kenzie,' her father said quietly. 'Go for a drive tomorrow, show him the hills and the dams, give him more of an idea of the place.'

'I'd like that,' Alex said, 'but don't horses mean more—you call them stockmen?'

'They do and we like it that way. During the big muster we bring in extra horsemen, but here on Spec we have up to a dozen at any one time.'

'They come and go,' Kenzie explained. 'Even the ones who grew up here.'

'Grew up here?'

Alex was aware he was beginning to sound like an echo, but this place was so much more than he'd expected. The food was as good as anything he'd ever eaten at one of Edinburgh's top restaurants.

And now it appeared there were other children apart from Kenzie who grew up here.

Kenzie took pity on him.

'We've always had two or three couples living here, their kids growing up here. When I was born, Maggie's youngest was three, so she kind of took me on as well.'

'Maggie's husband is the station manager now.' Angus took up the explanations. 'But back then he was head stockman, a job one of his sons does now.'

'And another of her sons is the property mechanic, working with one of our old mechanic's daughters in the big shed,' Kenzie said.

'And now we're confusing you,' Angus put in. 'Simply put, and you'll see a lot of it tomorrow, we usually have at least two married couples living here—three at the moment. And they all have children and sometimes the children stay on, or go away to learn a trade, or study and come back.'

'Our bookkeeper is one of the old mechanic's children and the teacher, Belle, is the eldest of Maggie's children.'

He couldn't help it—had to echo, 'Teacher?'

'Well, there are always kids to educate and they mainly do School of the Air, but to have a trained teacher with them, helping out on all their lessons, is wonderful.'

Alex held up his hands in surrender.

'Don't tell me any more,' he said. 'My mind's already boggling at it all.'

Kenzie laughed—a sound he'd thought he'd never hear again. It warmed him all over.

'Think of it as a village in the country,' she said. 'Isolated but sufficient within itself. We even have a village shop.'

'Now you're teasing me,' he said, and she shook her head.

'We buy in bulk the staples like flour and sugar, butter and powdered milk, washing powder, soap—everything a shop might need. And everyone gets what they need when they need it. It only opens in the afternoon and usually one of the older kids works there.'

'Kenzie loved being in the shop, right from when she was little,' Angus told Alex.

And Kenzie added, 'We also get in treats like crisps and lollies. Soft drinks and beer, too.'

Astounded, Alex shook his head.

'I'll just have to wait and see,' he said, finishing his glass of the very acceptable burgundy Angus had produced to go with the beef.

'Come out and see the stars,' Kenzie said, getting to her feet. 'You'll excuse us, Dad.'

'Yes, go. You've both had a long day and should by rights be suffering terrible jet-lag.'

'Phooey to that—he needs to see the stars.'

And, Alex conceded, as he held Kenzie close to his side and looked up at the sky, he *had* needed to see the stars.

'There are more of them than I'd ever have believed possible,' he said quietly, so awed by the brilliant arc of starlit sky above him he could barely breathe.

'And they're here to give you their magic every night,' Kenzie said, turning to lead him back inside. 'Except in the wet, of course,' she added, and Alex dimly remembered her mentioning such a phenomenon once before.

There was so much for him to learn, it could take a lifetime.

And *that* thought planted a tiny seed somewhere deep inside him. He'd think about it later, but right now kissing Kenzie in the starlight seemed a better idea, kissing her in bed an even more exciting one.

He held her close, kissed her once, then turned back towards the house, the shadows of a few of what Kenzie had called house dogs trailing at their heels.

He had more questions later as they lay in bed, relaxed after making love, slowly and emotionally, saying with their bodies what their words had already said.

'Tell me about growing up here,' he said, and she leaned up on one elbow to kiss him on the lips.

'Tomorrow,' she said. 'You'll understand more when you've seen the place, but right now I need to sleep.'

He wrapped his arms around her and pulled her close, so she fell asleep to the sound of his voice, whispering about love.

CHAPTER FOURTEEN

THEY TOURED THE property the next day, taking a ute rather than horses for both the air-conditioning and speed. Kenzie kept the bore in the western paddock for last, because she knew they'd be hot and tired by then.

'It's a lake,' Alex said in amazement as she drew up by the bore that fed into the man-made dam.

'And great for swimming,' she told him, when she'd checked the bore and walked down to the water's edge to join Alex, who was still amazed to find this water in the arid land.

'Can we swim?'

Heat was pounding down on them, and Alex's pale, Scottish skin was flushed with it.

'That's why we're here,' she said, and began to strip off the worn cotton T-shirt and shorts she'd been wearing, having to tug off her boots first—boots and socks, shorts and shirt, bra and panties soon lay in a neat heap on a large rock by the edge.

'Last one in's a dirty rat,' Kenzie challenged.

'But I've got more clothes on than you,' Alex protested.

But Kenzie was already in, breaststroking across the water, diving down out of sight and emerging with her hair slicked back from her head.

'My beautiful mermaid,' Alex said, when he emerged from below the water beside her.

He took her in his arms and kissed her, not an easy feat as the water was deep and they both had to keep their legs moving to stay afloat.

'You've blown me away—you know that, don't you?' he said, when they'd crossed the dam and were sitting on a rock on the other side. 'This place, the people, the space, the cattle—the sky! Even in the daytime it's just vast.'

Kenzie kissed him.

'That's nearly as good to hear as when you said you loved and wanted to be loved by me,' she told him, her heart still tripping at the memory of his words.

'I do, and I do,' he said, returning her kiss. 'Love you more than I could ever believe possible. I was sitting in this lawyers' boardroom with William and Archie and I couldn't make sense of a word they said, because my head was filled with you and—although this sounds strange— with the emptiness of not having you in my life. I've known both those men since I was at school, but I couldn't tell which was which because all the time my mind was on you.

'I thought I might catch you at the airport, mentioned flights to Darwin, and, probably realising I'd lost my mind, one of them brought up all the possibilities, and I knew I couldn't begin to guess how you'd travelled. So I excused myself, told then to send the papers to me to sign, and left, phoning the executive jet company as I went down in the lift.'

He kissed her again.

'Did I mention I loved you?'

'Many times,' she assured him, kissing him back. 'And I love you, more than words can ever say.'

Then somehow, on the hard slab of rock by the side of

the dam, they were making love—urgently this time, needing affirmation of the words they'd spoken.

They swam again then drove back slowly, Kenzie showing him the machinery shed, the little school house—a school in miniature with computers on all the desks.

'It's how they talk to their teachers and the other kids,' Kenzie explained, but it was all too much to take in. He needed to think, to remember where they'd been and all that had been explained, then realised he'd need a lifetime to learn it all.

Well, he had a lifetime, didn't he?

Most of one…

Back at the homestead, Angus announced they were having a barbecue to welcome them both to Spec and celebrate their marriage.

It was held in a huge shed, hay bales for seats, a forty-four-gallon drum cut in half lengthwise to provide the base for a fire, an iron grill to throw the meat onto.

Other drums held ice with bottles of wine and 'stubbies'—small-sized bottles of beer—sticking out of it. Long tables were laid out with appetisers and salads, and kids scampered around in the dirt, swung from trees outside the shed, climbed the hay bales, and generally had a great time.

It was a totally foreign atmosphere, yet he felt relaxed. Happy?

Definitely—especially with Kenzie by his side…

But it felt more than that. The place intrigued him and the people surrounding them—so open in their delight to have Kenzie back amongst them—

It was special to her and he could understand why…

She introduced him to all the adults, explaining who they all were. An old, gnarled-looking aboriginal stockman gave her a big hug, and tears rolled down both their cheeks as he said gruffly, 'Your mum would have been so pleased.'

'Bahlu came here with Mum when she married, from her parents' property down south. He was her spirit guardian, he always said, and then mine,' Kenzie explained, as Alex produced a handkerchief to dry her eyes.

They ate, had a glass of wine—another fine red that complemented perfectly cooked steaks—and sat on scratchy hay bales while people came to talk to them, to wish them well, to kiss Kenzie and hug her, more often than not.

He was halfway through a piece of pavlova filled with cream and passionfruit when a loud voice blaring from a speaker silenced the entire crowd.

'You there, Spec? Over,' it said, and he saw Wayne move to take up a small device that was obviously connected to a radio system.

'Spec here, go ahead.'

'Single vehicle RTA about fifteen k south on the Riverbend Road,' the disembodied voice said. 'Motorcyclist called it in on a cellphone and he's waiting by the vehicle. Says you might need to cut the two people out. RFDS alerted, they'll land on your strip as the road there's chewed up with all the road trains on the move.'

'Got it, Rob. We'll attend. Over and out.'

Alex turned to ask Kenzie what it all meant, but she was gone, already heading towards the big mechanics shed where most of the vehicles were garaged.

He followed.

If she was going out to this accident, so was he—after all, he *was* a doctor.

Arc lights lit the cavernous space and he found her and

Wayne grabbing bags off a shelf and throwing them into the flat bed of a ute.

'I'll come,' he said, and she nodded, then ducked as Wayne went past him with what looked like the giant pincers of some prehistoric insect.

Aware he could only keep out of the way—these two obviously had their routine down pat—he began to look at what the ute already contained. Two large rectangular objects drew his attention and he turned his head to see what was written on the label on the side of the closest one.

Self-inflating airbed? On a rescue mission?

'In you get,' Kenzie said to him, apparently indifferent to road rules and safety regulations, Wayne climbed into the back of the vehicle and settled on top of one of the still-packed airbeds.

The engine was already running and the vehicle slowly moving off as Alex flung himself into the passenger seat, then they were off.

'You do this often?' he asked as the vehicle bumped over corrugations on a track he didn't know. Although it was dark beyond the headlights, so maybe he had been that way.

'You'll have to get the gates,' she said, and he realised she was so focussed on getting to where they were going she probably hadn't heard his question.

Twenty minutes later they pulled up beside the motorcyclist, whose battery was probably draining as he'd kept his headlight on so they could see him.

'I got the passenger out, and wrapped my jacket over her,' he said, 'but the driver's trapped. He's got a pulse.'

Kenzie thanked him, but Alex had already found the injured woman and was kneeling by her.

'Can't see much,' Alex said to Kenzie as she arrived by his side, bags slung over both shoulders.

Then suddenly the scene was lit by battery-operated arc lights Wayne had set up near the ute, and he could see not only the injured woman but the portable defibrillator that was one of the bags Kenzie had carried over.

'Do you want to check the driver?' she said to him. 'Wayne will be over there now with the cutters. I've got a fairly comprehensive medical kit in that other bag there. Take it in case you need it.'

The light was strong enough to reach the vehicle, and they could see the crumpled front end, and the engine block pushed back into the driver's side.

'If we can get the seat out with him in it, we can get a good look at him,' Wayne said. 'I've cut the seatbelt and moved it a couple of centimetres. Can you get that door open and look at what damage I might do if I move it more?'

Opening the door might have sounded easy but it took a great deal of physical levering with a short crowbar to actually detach it from the hinge end and pull it away.

But at least now he could examine the driver, who was unconscious but had a pulse, for all it was thin and thready.

'He's clear of the steering wheel,' he reported to Wayne, 'but the way the engine's come back has trapped his legs.'

He felt around with his hands, and found the wetness of blood. Lots of blood!

It seemed to be coming from his left thigh but there was no way he could tell for sure, and even if there had been, he was in no position to apply a bandage or tourniquet.

He shoved at the engine block, not intending to do the impossible and move it, but to see if it was likely to move if they attempted to get the man out.

Nothing.

'I think if we can get the seat out from under him, we'd be able to slide him out,' he told Wayne. 'Short of a crane arriving to lift the entire engine, I can't see any other option.'

Wayne looked around.

'Never a tree when you want one,' he muttered. 'We've got a winch and a good tow rope and could have tried it ourselves. But the seat's definitely moving and if we can both work at it we might get it looser. There's another small pinch bar—thing with a gooseneck—in the ute. If you grab that and get in the other side, we'll do this thing.'

Alex needed the pinch bar to get the other door open but once crouched inside he saw what Wayne was doing to release the seat from its anchors, and within minutes had it loose enough to cautiously lower it enough to slide it backwards.

'The girl's conscious. They'd had a fight! I've wrapped her in a blanket and left her with Steve—he's the motor-cycle guy. What can I do?'

Kenzie had come over and was standing beside the car.

'Get a pad ready to staunch bleeding and bandages, a stethoscope if your travelling medical chest carries one,' Alex told her as the seat they'd been working on dropped and they were able to gently move the trapped man out from under the front of the vehicle.

Blood spurted from his left thigh and Alex clamped his hand over it.

'Find something we can use as a tourniquet on his thigh,' Alex said to Wayne, who within seconds had magicked up a professional mechanical tourniquet, which he wrapped around the victim's upper thigh and tightened.

'That's eased the flow,' Alex said, taking the pad Kenzie held out, then binding it tightly to the wound on the leg.

'Time check?' Kenzie said, and Wayne gave her the exact time he'd tightened the ligature.

'You two have done this before?' he said, while his hands and eyes were checking out their patient for other injuries.

'Practised enough,' Wayne said laconically.

'Then do we splint his damaged ankle or leave that for the flying doctors when they arrive?

'Stabilise it,' Kenzie said. 'Even with the airbeds it's going to be a rough ride home for them.'

Alex was wondering just what they had available to do that when Wayne said, 'No pulse!'

And Kenzie whipped out the second pack she'd brought from the utility, and began to assemble a portable defibrillator.

'I'll shock him,' Alex said to her. 'Done it enough times in ER.'

'But not with a portable, I shouldn't think,' Kenzie said, not exactly pushing him away but making it very clear she was in charge.

'We've all trained on it—the senior staff,' Wayne explained, while doing chest compressions on the man. 'And once a year the RFDS have us do a simulation on their dummy during one of their clinic visits.'

Alex was only half listening, so he was surprised when Kenzie said, 'Clear,' and the man's body jolted as the shock went through it.

They all watched the screen, waiting for the miraculous wavy line that would tell them his heart was beating again.

Nothing.

'I'll do it again,' Kenzie said, and Alex, who'd taken over the chest compressions from Wayne, moved his hands.

And this time it worked, the heart lines appearing like magic on the screen.

'That's the plane,' Wayne said, apparently hearing a sound that was inaudible to Alex, although now he picked it up, and even saw the lights as the aircraft drew closer.

'We'll get them back to the strip. Wayne, you drive and Alex and I will stay in the back. Time check?'

For all that had happened it was surprising that it was only fifteen minutes since Wayne had applied the tourniquet. It would be safe to keep it there for an hour but it was essential for everyone concerned with the rescue to keep timing it.

Kenzie packed the defibrillator back in its small box with a feeling of relief that it had actually worked on a patient, but there was no time to gloat. The self-inflating mattresses were already filled with air, but they had to get both patients onto the lightweight stretchers and into the tray of the ute.

She glanced at Alex, now fitting a moon boot around the injured man's ankle, and wondered what he'd made of the whole adventure—well, hardly adventure, perhaps episode...

Now he and Wayne were slotting the two pieces of the stretcher together under their patient.

She returned to the young woman—Debbie—and with Steve's help got the other stretcher under her, for all she protested she could walk to the vehicle.

'No way,' Kenzie told her. 'There's every chance you've suffered a concussion. You were out to it when Steve found you.'

Once loaded up, they thanked Steve for his help and his call for assistance and, as he rode away to wherever he'd been going, Alex gave Kenzie a hand to scramble into the tray of the ute, where she settled beside the young man.

The plane had rolled to a stop and the steps were down by the time Wayne pulled up beside it. One of the nurses came down first, then Bill, one of their regular doctors, who helped Kenzie down from her perch and gave her a big hug.

'And you're the doctor chap who's married our Kenzie,' he said to Alex when Kenzie introduced them. 'I don't suppose you're looking for a job?'

Alex smiled at the suggestion, while Kenzie tried to imagine how different tonight's emergency situation had been, compared to the A and E department where he worked.

But all A and Es had their share of drama and excitement so maybe it had just been second nature to him...

Though he did go up into the plane.

Wanting to see his patients comfortably installed, or wanting to see the fit-out?

'Fantastic, isn't it?' he said, as he reached the ground again. 'I've flown in emergency evac aircraft in other places, but this is so streamlined.'

'Has to be,' Bill said. 'We never know what to expect from one minute to the next.'

The engines revved behind them and Bill held out his hand.

'Nice meeting you,' he said, and climbed back into the aircraft, bringing up the steps behind him.

The party at the big shed was winding down, although young people still danced and sang to the music now playing.

'Dad must have gone to bed,' Kenzie said to Alex, nodding towards the noise. 'They'd never play pop music with him around.'

'Not gone to bed but gone to get a vehicle to take you two back to the house. Wayne'll take the ute.'

Her father appeared out of the shadows, and they stood and watched the plane take off, before getting into one of the big four-wheel drives to head back to the house.

* * *

'It's like a big extended family,' Alex said, as he and Kenzie entered their bedroom. 'Even the flying doctor chap seemed to belong.'

'It *is* my family,' Kenzie said.

They showered and went to bed, reaching for each other, surer now of each other's bodies and how they fitted best. Slow, languorous lovemaking that left Kenzie all but asleep beside him.

But as she slept, he tried to consider the enormity of the place he'd seen only part of today, to consider the people—her family—any one of whom would skin him alive if he hurt her.

He smiled to himself. As if he could! The love he felt for her was unlike anything he'd ever experienced.

And it was *that* that had him lying awake by her side. Staring out through the French doors, glimpses of the magic sky visible through the shrubs.

Could he really take her away from this dry, red-brown land she loved? From the people who loved her?

And how could their children learn enough from their grandfather and the men and women around him, if they were only here a couple of months a year?

Could his children swing from trees or climb hay bales, or roar around on little dirt bikes—they'd been doing that as well—back in Edinburgh?

There was a freedom in this place, and magic too, and, yes, he knew an enormous amount of work and organisation must go into it to make it run smoothly, yet Kenzie knew she could take over from her father, and would expect her children—or one of them at least—to want to do the same from her.

And beyond that was the totally surreal experience of the accident they'd attended. Wayne and Kenzie heading out to help some strangers, so organised they'd even had a professional tourniquet. He wanted—needed, he rather thought—to learn more about their first-aid equipment, while seeing the Royal Flying Doctor Service in action had stirred something in his gut.

Was there a job there for the taking?

'It isn't all skinny-dipping and beer and barbecues,' Kenzie told him when he tried to broach something of what he felt the next morning.

He was already up when she awoke, and had walked around the buildings close to the house. He'd had a cup of tea in the kitchen with Maggie, and had brought a tray to Kenzie in their bedroom, sitting on the bed while she drank it.

'I do realise that,' he said, 'but, anyway, that will be your job. But I wonder, if we switched, lived here and went to Scotland for holidays? Could you teach me to fly?'

'A small plane like we have here or the chopper, yes. You'd need proper professional lessons before getting your licence. Why?'

'Because I think I still have to be a doctor, and Tom— one of the pilots who flew me here—was talking about the Flying Doctor service, then last night I saw it all in action—not just you and Wayne as professional as any paramedics, but the plane coming in—it's like a special kind of magic, the way things happen out here in the middle of nowhere, to use your words.'

He smiled and bent to kiss her on the lips, tasting honey from the hives they'd seen yesterday, and Kenzie, his beautiful, magical wife…

She kissed him back then returned to his question—the teach me to fly one.

'You don't need to be able to fly to be a flying doctor. They have pilots.'

'I do know that,' he said. 'But if I could fly, I could get back here from Darwin much faster than driving when I have my days off.'

He paused, then added, 'Do you think that would work? Maybe an apartment in Darwin where we could both live when I'm on duty. Some of the time, anyway.'

She moved the tray from her legs and sat up very straight.

'Are you saying we'd live here? You'd move here? Alex, it's stinking hot and dry and dusty except in the wet when it buckets down without stopping the heat, and everything grows mould. And there's nothing here—no theatre, no movies, no lovely restaurants to dine in. It's about as far from beautiful, civilised Edinburgh as you could get. And you'd want to *live* here?'

He smiled at her.

'You'd like to, so why wouldn't I?' he said. 'And think of the children—the freedom they'd have. Not having to put on wellingtons and raincoats every time they go outside— even in summer a lot of the time.'

He paused, trying to find the words.

'I saw those children last night, Kenzie, and thought every child deserved a taste of what they've got.'

'Oh, Alex, do you really mean it?'

Kenzie's doubt and disbelief was written on her face.

'It's barely been two days. How can you tell you'd like it? You'd be bored, and you hate boredom.'

'I won't be bored if I'm working, and I'm assuming after some years here I might have learned enough to be useful to either your father or you. I like the way your father's thinking about calm cattle and I think drones could probably do the work your helicopters do now in spotting cattle for muster. Drones are silent.'

Kenzie shook her head.

'He's got one drone, but is only just learning how to fly it. Maybe a drone licence before your pilot's. I can ferry you around until you get that!'

'So it sounds doable?' he asked, suddenly aware of the huge change to his life he was considering.

'More than doable, *and* wonderful!' she said, giving him a hug. 'But we need to do a fair bit of homework about it all. You've got responsibilities back in Scotland—your grandmother's estate for one.'

'That's been managed by the same family for almost as long as the Monroes have owned it. I can keep in touch via the internet, and if we visit once a year—maybe during your wet—I can check all is well.'

'You really think so?' She looked at him, doubt in her lovely eyes, as if fearing this might not be quite real.

And he heard the doubt when she said, 'We still need time to think it through. It has to work as smoothly as possible or you might resent making the decision.'

'Resent the decision to live with you in the place you love? I doubt that very much,' he said, and kissed her, glad she'd removed the tray from the bed when the kiss turned into something more intimate.

EPILOGUE

'I THOUGHT MONROES didn't do emotion,' Kenzie said softly as Alex, cradling his newborn son, kissed her, hands trembling and tears streaking his cheeks.

She wiped the tears away with the edge of the sheet, and kissed the dark-haired head of her infant.

'Only sometimes,' he said, reluctantly settling the baby back in her arms.

He was in the crisp white shirt that was the uniform of the RFDS doctors, and had flown in from a road accident just in time to be with Kenzie for the birth.

'So, Andrew Monroe Steele, are we happy to go with that?' he said to her, his hand on her shoulder, needing to touch her.

She smiled at him.

'Too much if we add McLeod?' she said, smiling at him.

'Getting to be a bit of a mouthful,' he said, but he *was* pleased.

'Then we drop the Steele,' she said. 'He doesn't need it, he'll know he's a Steele.'

'Andrew Monroe McLeod! I like it.'

She reached out her free hand to cup his cheek.

'So do I!' she said. 'Everything about it! Especially the Monroe because your grandmother brought us together, and the McLeod, because that is you.'

He leant in carefully so as not to disturb Andrew, and kissed her on the lips, seeing the colour rise in her cheeks and happiness shining in her beautiful blue eyes.

* * * * *

COMING SOON!

We really hope you enjoyed reading this book. If you're looking for more romance, be sure to head to the shops when new books are available on

Thursday 20th March

To see which titles are coming soon, please visit
millsandboon.co.uk/nextmonth

MILLS & BOON

Coming next month

HEART SURGEON'S SECOND CHANCE
Allie Kincheloe

Dread pooled low in Rhiann's stomach as the door to the exam room opened with a slow and ominous creak. Broad shoulders in a white coat filled the space and her eyes roamed the doctor's familiar form, taking in the subtle changes time had wrought. Three years ago, he hadn't had those deep lines etched into his face. His dark hair had a little more silver at the temple than she remembered, but he was as lean and handsome as ever.

Dr. Patrick Scott stepped into the room, his eyes looking down at the screen of the silver laptop in his hand. His movements carried the spicy aroma of his cologne into the small room, those pleasing notes covering the harsh antiseptic and teasing a part of her that had gone dormant since her divorce. But on top of the overtly masculine scent, he brought with him a wave of sadness that hinted at tragedy.

"Hello, Mrs. … Masters, um…"

His deep gravelly voice trailed off and his sky-blue eyes jerked up to meet hers when he recognized her name. The slight fake smile he'd had on his lips when he opened the door faded fast. From the ice that frosted over his gaze, the animosity he held for her hadn't eased since she'd last seen him.

The exam room door shut behind him with an audible click and the laptop clattered slightly as he set it roughly on the counter. "What are you doing here?" An uncharacteristic coldness in his tone sent a shiver coursing down her spine. Patrick's voice had always held such emotion, the rich timbre broadcasting his feelings with the simplest words. In all the years she'd known him, Rhiann had never heard this distant tone.

Rhiann hugged the baby in her arms close to her chest, tears filling her eyes as she fought to keep her emotions from overwhelming her. She'd wished the time since they'd last seen each other might have given Patrick clarity and soothed the raw edges of his anger, but clearly not enough time had passed. Now she could only hope that he was professional enough to put their personal grievances aside and focus on her child's best interests, and she needed to keep a clear head today, so she stuffed her feelings away as best she could. She had known coming here was a risk, but there was no other way or she'd have explored it already.

"I need your help. Well, he needs your help. This is my son, Levi. He has a heart defect and the cardiologist at St. Thomas wants to do surgery to fix it. But if anyone is cutting my baby open, I want it to be the best surgeon I can find." She paused to swallow down an oversized lump, "And that's you."

"You expect me to save someone you love. How ironic." A single dark eyebrow raised as he stared down at her, his expression unreadable and as cold as marble. His eyes searched hers, for what she didn't know. Just as she was sure he was about to tell her to leave, to scream at her like he had the last time she saw him, his gaze flicked down to the baby in her arms, and the ice in his eyes melted the tiniest bit.

Continue reading
HEART SURGEON'S SECOND CHANCE
Allie Kincheloe

Available next month
www.millsandboon.co.uk

MILLS & BOON
True Love
Romance from the Heart

Celebrate true love with tender stories of heartfelt romance, from the rush of falling in love to the joy a new baby can bring, and a focus on the emotional heart of a relationship.

MILLS & BOON

HEROES

At Your Service

Experience all the excitement of a gripping thriller, with an intense romance at its heart. Resourceful, true-to-life women and strong, fearless men face danger and desire - a killer combination!